Also by Aaron Dick

Where The Fields Grow Light Series
Book 1: Where The Fields Grow Light
Book 2: When Hidden Eyes Grow Dim

***

Rotten
There Is A Stranger Here
omens: A Collection

A Baker's Coven

Aaron Dick

Cover Art by Jono Dempsey
Cover Design by oliviaprodesign

This book is dedicated to my long-suffering editor Kat.
After a lot of creepy short stories and horror books,
I thought she deserved something a bit funnier.

Prologue

The thief snuck into the alley beside the Trivial Lampshade tavern, taking advantage of a burst of attention-grabbing laughter and song. He ducked under the orange light that spilled through the windows from the common room fire. With cautious steps, he slipped through the shadows towards the deeper darkness behind the tavern, as secret as a black cat on a moonless midnight.

To be clear, this is not a simile. The thief was covered in a deep, black fur beneath his clothes, which is quite typical for the catfolk, and no moon glowed over the city of Senoonheim that night. Though, to be fair, it was actually well past midnight.

The thief entered the alley and immediately planted face first into someone's back.

"Shhhh!" they hissed, flapping a hand at him without turning to see who he was.

The thief grunted and hopped backwards.

The back belonged to an elf in a long, black cloak, wearing a black neckerchief wrapped around the bottom of his face. The elf was accompanied by two broad dwarves with similar face coverings. Tufts of black hair from their beards stabbed out around the edges of the material.

The last member of their group was a red-eyed, snakefolk woman, and all four of them were peering around the next corner. The group's eyes moved as one, tracking the staggering footsteps of adventurers on the main street. Adventurers who had clearly drunk more than their fill in the Trivial Lampshade and now sought safe lodgings elsewhere; something the masked foursome were obviously keen to help with. Although finding a safe place to sleep didn't seem a high priority. The gutter was probably a top choice in their eyes. In any case, they were far too preoccupied with their search to notice the thief behind them, who turned and crept away in the opposite direction.

The thief paused by the back door to a building, waiting for movement further down the alley to cease. A wooden barrel full of food scraps reeked by the doorway and a cloud of flies launched themselves out of the barrel and into his face. His pink nose twitched and his whiskers danced as he tried to ignore the angry cloud of tiny insects. A whiff of old fish elbowed past the swarm and the thief licked his lips.

The movement he had noticed in the alley came from a human woman with long, red hair and long, dark robes covered in embroidered, yellow sigils. She was hunched over the lock of a door, shifting her arms and trying to cover small flashes of red, magical light with her body. Her companion whooped in victory when the light flared, before clapping their hand over their mouth. They stood barely higher than the woman's waist and had long, pointed ears and broad shoulders.

The woman turned to glare at the gnome before opening the door, and they both stepped inside.

With the alley clear, the catfolk thief swallowed his mouthful of rancid fish and darted forwards. He was already running late and the guards might return at any moment. He clambered up the wall of the building the two adventurers had just broken into, catching the windowsills and beams with his claws until he reached the roof.

At the top, the roof sloped slowly down to either side of him. At the far end, a facade rose, stretching two or three stories over the street below.

The building beneath the thief's paws was the temple of Rhebok, goddess of victory. From the street the facade looked like thick, marble columns holding up a triangular pediment carved with a relief sculpture of the holy animal of Rhebok: the shark. To either side of this intimidating design, square towers lifted even higher. To the casual pedestrian the front of the temple was a display of the power and glory of the goddess. From behind, it was just wooden planks and canvas and nails.

The thief's chest swelled as he strode forward. This was where catfolk truly felt at home, strolling the rooftops of the city, alone above the world and beneath the stars. He felt as though he was climbing a staircase of smoke, ready to join a crowd of other rooftop denizens in a whirling dance.

"Who's that?" snarled a voice from beside the thief.

He launched himself sideways and behind a chimney, crouching down with his breath panting, his panic rising, and his fur on end. He grabbed his tail and tried to smooth the fur down while he waited for the owner of the voice to reveal themself. His desire to dance had been summarily squashed.

A shape detached itself from the shadows at the foot of the facade and clanked forward to look around. It was a construct: an artificial person typically created by a contrivancer or wizard. Constructs were often built to complete tasks the creator felt were too menial to undertake themselves. Such chores might include cooking or cleaning or killing off the rabble who insisted on rebelling against one's tyrannical rule.

This one looked as though it fit into that latter category. It was a remarkably skinny suit of armour carrying a crossbow, and it moved with the lurching, clicking motion of gnomish clockwork.

After the construct had looked around, using a slit in its visor that must pass for eyes, it turned and clunked its way back to the facade, where it climbed to the top as quickly as it had walked across the roof. Once there, it clung to the side of a tower and aimed its crossbow out into the city.

The catfolk thief took his moment to dart away from the temple and its crossbow-wielding occupant, deeper into Senoonheim and the assignment still awaiting him. His ears twitched at a loud twang behind him, followed by splintering glass and a short shriek.

Once he was further into the city, the thief looked into the alley below. Another group of bandits were bunched at its mouth, looking for ripe pickings amongst the passersby in the street. Behind them, yet another group of bandits tiptoed closer, clubs held high as they readied themselves to ambush the ambushers. Deciding that perhaps this wasn't the alley that would suit his descent, the thief moved on.

The next alley looked perfect. It was quiet, small, and tight, and it led directly to the building he had been told held his target. He hopped from eave to sill to barrel to cobbles and prowled the narrow, grimy path between the buildings looming on either side.

A trio of the High Lord's soldiers rounded the corner ahead of him.

The thief straightened and pushed his dark hood back down around his neck. As the soldiers drew closer, the thief smiled, opened his eyes wider and tucked his hands behind his back. He wasn't actually holding anything incriminating that he had to hide, but knowing you are doing something that should get you into trouble makes most people want to hide their hands. Perhaps they think it will give them a chance to do something surprising to any accusers who notice them.

The man leading the trio looked the thief up and down and groaned.

"Oh come on, what normal person in their right mind is skulking around these bloody crevices at this time of night?" he asked as he rubbed a callused hand down his face.

The thief smiled harder and shrugged.

"It's alright Sarge, he's probably just out to do some star gazing, aren't you sunshine?" offered the satyr next to the first soldier. The satyr wore the same standard issue, dark-blue cloak that all of Lord Cornucervin's soldiers wore; but, as he stood only a little taller than four feet, he had it wrapped around himself in a makeshift toga.

The three soldiers and the thief all lifted their eyes to the top of the alley.

The buildings at either side had been built to make maximum use of all available space, which meant that they reached out towards each other like teenagers who had been separated for a lifetime. (Well, perhaps a few hours, anyway). The thief thought he saw a single star twinkling through the narrow gap between them. It might have been some grime in his eye.

He lowered his gaze to the soldiers again.

The satyr grimaced. "Or maybe not so much."

"Look," he went on, shuffling his hooves on the cobbles. "We've been at it all night already. Burglaries, kidnappings, demon summonings, you name it. Sarge is nearly at his wit's end, aren't you Sarge?"

"Please, don't get me involved," moaned the large man.

"All I'm saying is, we just need to make sure you're not up to any funny business," continued the satyr. "So, are you?"

The thief and the satyr stared at each other.

"Up to any funny business, I mean."

After a moment, the thief shook his head.

"See, that's what I thought! Come on Sarge, we've done our duty. I say we take the newbie and find some part of the city that's actually sleeping for a change. Give ourselves a bit of a breather for a minute."

"There's nowhere in Senoonheim that sleeps through the night," snorted the sergeant, but he waved the soldiers on and they walked past the thief without another word. The newbie did give the thief a second glance, but that was because the newbie was a skeleton; his skull was not attached firmly and it bounced around as he walked, spinning and grinning at everything around him.

The thief watched the soldiers leave. Then he studied his surroundings. He opened a leather pouch at his side and pulled out a piece of parchment, unfolding it to reveal a sketch that he held up at arm's length, comparing the drawing to one of the buildings halfway down the alley. The thief smiled.

Chapter One

Mira's dreams were pushed aside by the noise of Senoonheim at night. This city that she had made her home for the last year was always restless, like a puppy that had been told not to move while a treat was left on its nose. The city shivered and whined constantly with the coming and going of adventurers from the Unlit Hills beyond it, always a moment away from pouncing on their fortune. Even in the middle of the night, the streets were filled with masked and furtive figures.

Someone banged into a pile of crates in the alley behind Mira's bakery and swore as the racket echoed in the narrow space. Mira sighed and pressed her face deeper into her pillow, trying to ignore it.

The clatter in the alley rose until it became a scrabbling on her wall. Mira groaned, then rolled out of bed and sat on the edge of her thin mattress. Memories of home had risen in her mind all night, making her toss and turn as she tried to deflate each one, only for another to rise in its place.

She drew a deep breath as the last wisps of the memories faded. "Alright, alright," she muttered to herself. "I'll get up."

Mira stood and stumbled over to her single, small window. She pulled aside the threadbare curtain and found herself staring into the black-furred face of a catfolk man who flinched at the sight of her.

The man was hanging onto the windowsill with his claws. Mira imagined it must be an awkward spot to sit. She unlatched the window and pushed it open. The man's eyes widened as he ducked underneath.

"Uh, hello," he purred with a smooth voice. He smiled guiltily.

"Is there something I can help you with?" asked Mira with a raised eyebrow.

"Maybe?" The man's tone rose. His shining, green eyes glanced over her shoulder and his ears flattened on top of his head. "Is, uh... Is this the residence of the Merchant Bophades?"

Mira snorted and crossed her arms, stepping slightly away from the window so that the man could see her room in all its spartan glory.

"What do you think?" She rolled her eyes.

It was not a large room, nor was it filled with comfortable furniture or meaningful knick-knacks. Mira had arrived in Senoonheim with nothing, and she had spent the last year trying to make her bakery successful, which had used up all of her time. The room had bare wooden walls and a plain rug spread beneath her bed. When she stood in the middle of the room, there was just enough space to spin around with her arms outstretched, so long as she didn't mind knocking things off her dresser or hitting the thin metal pipe that carried smoke away from her small iron woodburner. Sleeping in this room was like sleeping inside one of the crates that had just been knocked over in the alley.

The man shrank away from the windowsill.

"Look, I'm sorry, I must have had the instructions upside down," he jabbered as he began to climb back down the wall.

"I should think so," snapped Mira as she swung the window closed. She saw him drop to the cobbles of the alley, and a dog started barking from a building nearby. He spun in circles, hissing, his fur standing out in spikes, and then bolted away down the alley and out of sight.

Mira sighed and shut the curtain. *I may as well get down to the bakery anyway,* she told herself.

She fetched her candlestick and concentrated on the faint reflection in its metal. A tiny flame sputtered into life at the wick, and Mira smiled. The candle was barely bright enough to outline the edges of the room in dull orange, but it was just enough to allow her to get dressed. She did so efficiently, pulling on her long skirts and tight-sleeved shirt, tying the cords firmly.

She examined herself in the mirror over her dresser. She turned her face from one side to the other, then pulled her thick, black hair back and tied it behind her head with another short cord. She smoothed her pale dress over her curves and then grinned into the mirror. "You look bloody stunning!" she told herself.

Mira's reflection grinned back at her. "See? You're gorgeous and outgoing. There's no reason for you to still be lonely at the end of today!"

Her smile faltered, but she straightened her shoulders and put her hands on her hips.

"Not that you need anyone to be happy! You got out of Whinnia and all the way here by yourself. You're going to be fine!"

The crack in her voice proved that she still hadn't tricked herself into believing that.

She had lived in Senoonheim for nearly a year, and she still hadn't met anyone.

There was Wimus, who delivered her flour. He was nice, although not especially quick-witted. To be honest, trying to speak with him during deliveries made them take twice as long because he had to pause, set down his sacks of flour, and then marshall his thoughts in order to respond to anything Mira said to him. She didn't think he would be the most gregarious of friends.

But Mira had been so wrapped up in getting her bakery established that she hadn't really met anyone else. She had barely explored the town itself more than a few streets to either side of the bakery. She felt pulled thin, like dough that was stretched too far. She just wanted to be able to share her thoughts with someone, to make a connection so that she didn't feel so isolated.

"I am going to be fine," she told herself. "It's all going to change. Today, I'm getting out into the city and I'm going to meet some new people!"

In the shop below her rooms, Mira pulled a pale apron from its peg behind the door to the bakehouse. She stoked the fires in the ovens and began filling them with loaves as they reached temperature. While those baked, she was mixing more dough, kneading and rolling and twisting it into the shapes she needed, seasoning some with herbs and seeds, and setting them aside for later. It was hot work, and sweat began to build up on her forehead.

Mira enjoyed this time of day. Pushing the dough into shape was satisfying, and it felt as though she had control over something in her life. After the upheaval of the last year and the losses that had come along with them, it was all she could do to take control of the bread in her bakery.

She dipped her fingers into a small ceramic jar on the bench and winced. The supply of panicgrass dew she had gathered with her coven sisters in Whinnia was nearly empty. Drops of the thin liquid gave a magical boost to the flavour of whatever she added them to, making sweets sweeter and savouries savourier. Unfortunately, she hadn't been in that coven long enough to learn how to collect and prepare panicgrass dew by herself.

The dew running out was a reminder that she had no one else to rely on in Senoonheim. She had to be self-sufficient, just as she had been before she had met the witches of Wallis.

By the time she noticed dawn leaking across the sky through the broad window at the front of her shop, Mira was filling the shelves with loaves and twists and rolls in all shapes and sizes. She slid another tray into an oven and then heard the tinkle of the bell over her front door. The first customer of the day.

He was tall and wore the sturdy clothes of a labourer. They hung strangely over the bright yellow feathers that covered his skin, and his eyes were much larger than human eyes. Mira hadn't met any birdfolk before moving to Senoonheim.

"Do you have anything with a strong aroma, luv?" he asked in a gravelly voice much too deep for the small and delicate shell-like cone of his beak.

"I suppose the garlic and rosemary scrolls are pretty noticeable," suggested Mira, picking one up and passing it over. The man plucked it from her fingers and held it to the nostrils at the top of his beak. He sniffed and then blew out a large, satisfied breath.

"Ooo yeah, that's good, that is. Strong but tasty. I'll have four of 'em, ta."

Mira smiled and nodded and gathered the rolls for the man, bundling them into some cheap cloth from beneath the counter.

"Where are you headed today, then?" she asked as she handed the package over.

"Mining on the north face." The birdman blinked slowly. "Gotta keep these nostrils clear so I don't miss anything. But I imagine I'll be ready to lay myself down before lunchtime!" he finished with a chuckle.

"That sounds like a tough day. I hope that the rolls keep you going." Mira told him the price and he handed over a few small coins.

"They will. A smell like that will help keep my passages clear and my senses keen. Thanks muchly."

Although it was a pleasant chat, the birdfolk man left as quickly as he had come. This was how it usually was for her. Her customers left before she could find out more about them, to try and build a friendship. No wonder she had struggled to meet people in Senoonheim.

She caught a glimpse of her reflection in the broad shop window and shrugged at herself. A pair of young men swung the door wide as they came in. Mira's day had begun.

Chapter Two

Mira's day became the usual endless round of serving, bread and ovens, pulling fresh loaves out for sale, talking to her customers, and tidying up. Just after dawn, there was a rush of workers heading out into the city: soldiers and guards, messengers and merchants, builders and miners. Then came a steady stream of families, children, mothers and fathers and grandparents, all grabbing a little something for lunch or to prepare for dinner later. By lunchtime the tide of customers ebbed and Mira was able to tidy up. She prepared the store for the next day and then stood behind the counter, waiting to see if more customers would come in before she finally decided to lock the door and swing the sign in the window to 'Closed'.

True to the promise she had made herself that morning, Mira had tried to engage with as many customers as she could. She asked about them, trying to uncover something about their personalities, hoping one of them might be open to talking in the afternoon, or showing her around the city. But no one had time to spare. Most didn't even slow down long enough to acknowledge her greetings when they entered the bakery.

This was the part of the day that Mira hated the most. She would stand behind the counter in her bakery, alone, and watch as the people of the city walked past right outside her window. She would prepare dough and leave it to rise, set up ingredients for the morning, refill barrels and tins with spices and flour from the sacks in the coolroom, all in the silence of her empty shop.

Back in Whinnia she had at least been able to see the other witches in her coven. She would spend afternoons laughing at Bovo's stories, trying to learn as much as she could about witchcraft from the halfling woman. But she had no one to laugh with in this new city.

Finally, she locked the door, the same as she always did, looking out into the streets, willing herself to step out into them, to become a part of the ever-moving crowd that filled Senoonheim. But her exhaustion rose and her head felt as though it was stuffed with old rags and she thought about how early she had to wake in order to get the bread baked in the morning and she told herself "maybe tomorrow" before heading upstairs to her apartment and bed. As she always did.

***

Mira pulled a large, round loaf off the shelf and tucked it into the cloth bag the middle-aged woman with long gray hair had handed to her. Mira smiled and passed the package back to the woman.

"Thank you so much! My husband just loves to get home and cut some slices of your bread to go with the butter and cheese and chutney," said the woman.

"You're very welcome. It's a pleasure to know that my baking is being appreciated."

"It certainly is! We're so glad that you moved here and opened this bakery."

"I am too." It was nice to hear someone say it. And if this family thought her baking was good, maybe they'd be kind enough to go a step further.

Mira drew a breath and set her shoulders. "You know, I haven't seen much of the city yet. Would you consider taking me on a bit of a tour?"

The woman blinked and smiled, but her forehead creased. It was a tiny fold of skin, almost imperceptible, but to Mira it may have well been a gaping chasm with regular donkey tours down to the winding river in its depths. It was the minute split in the stone floor where one slate had settled a breath lower than the next, just enough that it would set a cart wobbling and spill its cargo to the cobbles.

Mira quickly raised a hand and waved it in the air between them, brushing aside the woman's excuses before they had even emerged from her throat.

"No, no, forget I asked. You're probably very busy anyway!"

"I – Yes, I am quite busy." The woman grimaced and handed over a few small coins then left the shop in a hurry. The bell over the door tinkled softly and Mira watched the woman walking away down the main street, nervously glancing back at the bakery as she went. A ratfolk soldier wearing full-body plate armour covered in massive, curved spikes walked the other way and waved to the lady genially.

Mira's reflection made a sympathetic head bob from the window, shifting the long black ponytail that sat on her shoulders. She closed her eyes and squeezed her hands into fists and then released her tension. She shook her head. Getting out of the isolated routine she had established in this city was proving to be harder than she had thought.

The bell over the door tinkled and a young girl walked in. She wore a soft, green hat that melted down her head and a very pale red tunic. She had a wide smile and, when she saw all the loaves of bread on Mira's shelves, she put her hands to her mouth and gasped.

"Widgeon! Come in! This is such a lovely place!"

Before Mira could react, a large duck had waddled up to the door that the girl was holding open and strolled into the shop. This was not one of the birdfolk, this was a regular duck, with a green head and dark brown wings. It was a *very* large duck, its head nearly level with the girl's shoulders. It deliberately looked over at Mira and nodded before proceeding to quack once and then walk alongside the shelves, investigating the bread on display.

"Um, I don't usually allow wildlife into my shop," Mira began, but the girl only giggled.

"That's alright. Widgeon is very placid, not wild at all."

Mira was going to argue her point, but the animal seemed to be behaving itself, so she just shrugged and waited behind the counter as they explored.

The girl picked up some different breads and carried them in a pile in her arms, while the duck walked alongside her, supervising with a very mat-ter-of-fact quack. She tottered over to the counter and spilled her pile forward. Small rolls, a tank loaf, some rye and a baguette rolled over the counter.

"You want all of these?" asked Mira doubtfully.

"Yes!" The girl said the word emphatically, as though it was a punctuation of its own. The duck elaborated with an accompanying quack.

"Are you sure you'll be alright to carry it all?" asked Mira. "I have some cloth that you could wrap around it, but they are all so differently shaped that it might not help much."

"That's okay, we are going to eat it all now."

The duck started quacking excitedly.

"Shhh Widgeon, we'll be there soon."

The girl paid and scooped up the bread loosely in her arms, crusty shapes sticking out in all directions like a wheaty, crumbly bouquet. Mira opened the door for her and watched as the odd pair set off down the street before returning to the counter to await her next customer.

***

"By any chance, do you have some goblin bread in this bakery?" asked the dwarf peeking over the top of the counter in front of her.

"Not at the moment I'm afraid," Mira answered. "I do have some dwarven bread. Good, hearty stuff. I got the recipe from a mining family. Plenty of pumpkin and sunflower seeds."

The dwarf wrinkled his nose over a well-manicured beard with three small braids in it.

"Thank you for the suggestion, but no thank you all the same, lassie," he said with a small shake of his head. "I've eaten my share of my people's bread through the years, and I must admit that I've come to be tired of it. It's the goblin loaf that has fired my tastebuds in recent times." He grinned as he spoke, his eyes twinkling like diamonds.

"That's interesting," said Mira, trying not to lose herself staring into the dwarf's clear eyes. "I grow tired of certain foods every now and then as well. I'm sick of apples at the moment," admitted Mira. She blushed and cleared her throat, wondering why in the world she thought that would make good conversation.

The dwarf smiled, and the movement made his whole face glow. His light eyes sparkled as though Mira was the sun reflecting from his irises.

"I still have a fondness for an apple myself, but I'm glad you see what I mean!"

"Why goblin bread?" asked Mira, trying to get the conversation back on course. "I've made elven bread and dwarven bread before, but goblin bread recipes always seem a little... chaotic."

"I think it is that variability that entices me." The dwarf leaned one arm up on the counter and raised an eyebrow. "I've never been one to be content with what satisfies everyone else."

Mira coughed again and avoided his gaze.

"Goblin bread is certainly variable," she stammered. The recipes that Mira had seen for goblin bread usually involved very personal measuring methods. One recipe might explain that it required three handfuls of flour, while another mentioned a mouthful of water. When Mira had experimented with the recipes, she had used educated guesses and a range of measuring cups instead of body parts. The first recipe had called for 'a decent whack of every spice you have', while the second had said 'poppy seeds are acceptable but under no circumstances can you ever use sesame'. All in all, goblin bread seemed to be whatever a goblin said it was.

"I'm sorry to disappoint you," she said to the dwarf.

"Oh, I couldn't be disappointed conversing with a fine woman such as yourself," grinned the dwarf. "My name is d'Earthy. Master Ulvilhelm d'Earthy." He wielded his dazzling smile at her again. "As you unfortunately do not have the bread I seek, perhaps you could be convinced to come and spend some personal time with me? Perhaps we could discuss something less dough related in our own time?"

Mira was quite overwhelmed by Ulvilhelm's flirtatious presence. After a year without proper personal interactions, all of her conversational skills seemed to have atrophied and she felt like a teenager again. Despite her blustering declarations that she wanted to get out into the city and meet people, suddenly she was not sure if she was ready.

He was good-looking though, and she was excited by the idea of talking to someone who wasn't a customer. Even if his romantic suggestions didn't work out, at least she would be getting out of the routine that kept her in this single building.

She breathed in deeply, trying to still the quiver in her chest as she prepared to answer him.

"You know what?" she said. "I think that I would really like that. My name is Mira. Did you have anything specifically in mind?"

Ulvilhelm's smile shone from beneath his beard.

"I am going to the games on Friday night. Would you join me? I could come by and meet you right here at six in the evening?"

She smiled. "I'll see you here then."

Chapter Three

M ira stood outside the bakery door and pulled her pocket-dial from her pocket. She twisted the brass with practised ease before dropping it from her fingers and holding it out in the sun's light. She squinted at the shadows that criss-crossed its metal arcs.

"Pretty late," she murmured to herself. She glanced up and down Siltrap Street. The passersby wore the determined faces of people who had important places to be; perhaps a discreet rendezvous, the evening meal that had been prepared for them and was now growing cold on the table, or whichever tavern would serve them more beer even though they had thrown up on the bouncer. Regardless of the destination, they were not going to allow themselves to be distracted along the way. Certainly, they didn't look like the sort of crowd that would be breaking down her door in search of delicately sugared biscuits or a particularly fine sesame loaf.

Mira drew a curtain across the window. She caught the eyes of her reflection as she did and paused.

"Come on. You can do it," she whispered to herself. She gritted her teeth and nodded. With her confidence swelling after her encounter with Master d'Earthy, Mira was going to explore Senoonheim for herself.

Mira covered the shelves with a long, light cloth, and then walked out the door and turned to lock it. Just as the bolt clunked into place, shouts from behind caught her attention. She turned and saw a team of goblins sprinting along the street.

At the front of the group ran what she had to assume was the goblin leader. He wore a fur-trimmed tunic with padded shoulders that jutted out a foot further than his actual shoulders on either side. His conical, metal helmet had two large horns that poked from both sides of his head straight up into the air, adding an extra foot or two to his height. All in all, he gave the impression of a giant caltrop running along the street.

Everyone else moved to the sides of the road and stopped, turning to watch whatever was going on and ensuring that they weren't drawn into it.

Mira stepped out without thinking and held up a hand. The goblin leader pounding his way down the street went cross-eyed as he tried to keep watching her hand, but he did manage to stop in front of her. He had just enough time to say, "Oh now what you bloody–" before his companions ran into the back of him, plunging him into Mira, and sending the lot of them tumbling to the dust. A chorus of laughter rippled from the people watching.

The leader lifted himself off Mira and glared down at her.

"What's your problem, lady?" he growled.

"What's *my* problem?" Mira replied to the goblin leader incredulously. "What's *your* problem! Where I come from, a team of goblins racing down the street warrants investigation!" Her conscience had forced her into action before she had even realised that her body was moving. She began twisting and struggling to extricate herself from the pile and get to her feet.

The leader's eyes narrowed as he leaned down closer to her. She turned her head away from his breath.

"You're not trying to say goblins are always causing trouble, are you?" he snarled.

"Is she accusing us of something!" The other goblins, who were all trying to disentangle themselves from each other like a sentient ball of wool, commented in chorus. "Oo, the nerve of some people!"

Footsteps pounded down the main street towards them and Mira turned her head to see a tall figure wearing a suit of armour that enclosed them completely. Not a single gap was left to expose any hint of who was beneath the metal plates, not a fingernail or a glimpse of the back of a hand. The metal shone like the surface of a mill pond on a still winter's morning, and golden flowers were engraved around its edges. The figure's helmet was even shaped into a face mask that wore the bland, emotionless, human visage of most highly regarded statuary. Wisps of golden hair peeked from below the helmet, the only clue as to who this person was.

"Stop thieves!" bellowed a deep voice from somewhere behind that still face.

"Cheese it," shrieked one of the goblins still tangled beside Mira. "He's onto us!"

"You stole something?" Mira yelled at the lead goblin, who was now standing directly on top of her, pulling at the arm of one of his companions to help them upright.

"And? You didn't know that when you stopped us!" he said self-righteously. "You heard what Trug said lads," he continued. "There's no point hanging around to try and explain things, especially when he's got the right end of the stick. Move those feet!"

"Hey!" she yelled and reached out, trying to grab one of the goblins by the scruff of their neck. Her fingers tore through a ratty edge of cloth and then the gang were racing away from her down Siltrap Street. The armoured figure thundered up to her.

"Thank you for trying, ma'am!" it yelled.

"Of course," muttered Mira with a hand on her head. "I love being run over by goblins. Any time."

She held out a hand to the armoured man, who dutifully took it and hauled her to her feet. He stood beside her, bouncing gently on his feet, his helmet turning to look at the goblins and then back to her.

"Keep chasing them, by all means," she said, and the man launched himself away in a heartbeat.

"Thank you!" he called over his shoulder. His metal boots crashed with the cacophony of a shelf of cookware falling to the floor as he left in pursuit of the goblins.

A low humming noise rose in the air over her head, and Mira looked up to see a huge bee bobbing lazily through the air. It was as big as a puppy, and its multi-faceted eyes glistened as it buzzed past, following the commotion into the distance.

Mira dusted off her skirts. She looked around and met the eyes of the pedestrians that were still watching from the sides of the street.

"Well?" she asked, glaring at them. "No support from any of you?"

A woman standing under an awning shrugged.

"If I chased every goblin running down the street, I'd never stop running," she said.

As if to emphasise her point, a pair of goblins rushed up the street in the other direction. They were rolling a small barrel between them, kicking it from one to the other. A kobold chased after them, yelling, "Hey I need that!"

Mira sighed. Clearly just running into interesting people on the street was no way for her to make new friends. The Sprog and Sparrow, a nearby tavern, should be a much better location to try, so she set off towards it.

Chapter Four

P eople were drifting into The Sprog and Sparrow the same way birds edged closer and closer to a picnic. They never quite met the eyes of anyone already there and spent a lot of time squawking at each other, but every movement somehow seemed to accidentally bring them a little closer.

Mira looked around curiously as she walked inside. She had come to this tavern a few times over the last year, when she had managed to force herself out of her room. It was one of several along Siltrap Street, and it had provided her with a good, hot supper when she needed it, but she had always eaten quickly and then headed back to her apartment. Being able to eat a hot meal that she didn't have to prepare was enough of a relief that she was completely wiped out by the experience. She never stayed long enough to see who came in at the end of the day.

The bar itself was being occupied by tall, broad figures, as though someone was erecting a barrier using men and women who resembled the stone slabs sometimes used to make large circles on grassy plains in order to confuse later inhabitants. The monolithic people formed a wall between the drinks on one side and the common room on the other. These farmers, guards, and builders were going to ensure that not a single measure of liquor broke the line. Most of them stood stoically, ordering one tankard after another of dark ale, though occasionally some would break off and move into the corners to drink silently with one another. It was like watching a cliff slowly eroded by a river of beer.

Mira asked the young woman behind the bar for some white wine and then turned around to lean on the bar and examine the patrons. By the looks of them, this was a worker's place. It was either that, or a body builder convention had descended on Senoonheim. Every second person walking in the front doors had to turn sideways so that their ridiculously broad shoulders were able to fit through the door. More than one arrival looked as though they had been inflated, all bulges and curved, shining surfaces. Beside these gigantic, muscular patrons walked groups of skinny but hard individuals, the sort of people whose skin had been leathered by the sun and wind and whose muscles were only as taut as strictly necessary. Mira had worked alongside a few of that type back in Wallis, the capital of Whinnia, and she knew that they were as wiry and strong as steel wire.

There was a lot of camaraderie on display as the crowd ordered their drinks, laughter and slapping of backs, but there didn't seem to be any actual conversation happening. Despite the smiles and laughs, most of the people in The Sprog and Sparrow were getting down to the serious business of drinking the pub dry.

Four figures hunched in a booth to one side of the common room, wearing the dark blue cloaks of High Lord Cornucervin's soldiers. The High Lord ruled the city from his Porcelain Throne, and his soldiers made sure everyone who lived there knew it. Mira caught a glimpse of the metal badges of authority on their chests. From past experience, she knew it bore the deer's head crest of the High Lord.

A new group trudged in through the door, muttering to each other as they entered. They wore sturdy clothes, mud speckling their legs and boots. One by one, they stood to the side of the door and pulled off the boots, revealing feet so hardened and encrusted with calluses that they reminded Mira of tortoises. Though most of these workers were human, there was a minotaur amongst them, his bovine face blank and bored as he waited for space to pull off his filthy footwear, and an orc who was scratching his chin with a clawed finger.

"Oi, Darid," said one of the others. The minotaur blinked and pulled his attention to the man standing next to him.

"What?"

"You're so out of it at the moment. I was wondering if one of the girls in the field passed along some illicit cud?"

The others all burst into laughter while Darid's brows creased in annoyance. He snorted and clapped the man on the shoulder.

"No, the cows didn't pass along anything. I guess my mind is elsewhere because it's just so boring being surrounded all the time by monkeys who fling their own filth at each other." He gestured at the man's mud-soaked clothes, and Mira noticed that Darid was cleaner than his companions.

There was a round of "oooooohhhh" from the others in their group and the man who had made the first insult blushed and grinned.

"Come on, I'll get you a cider," he said as he wrapped one solid arm around Darid's broad shoulders. They smiled at each other and the group of cowherds tromped to the bar.

Next through the door was a trio of people wearing tight clothing that was entirely black, as dark and pristine as if they had dyed the clothes outside the door before coming in. Their torsos were criss-crossed with leather straps, and thin belts wrapped their thighs, the hilts of small blades sticking up from the belts and straps in regular rows. The lining under their short cloaks was a deep, blood red. They were laughing together as they came in but the laughter stopped the instant they saw the High Lord's soldiers.

The soldiers in the booth got to their feet and stared at the newcomers. Silence spread through the room with the pop of ice thawing on a lake. Mira shifted on her stool and glanced around the tavern to check if she should be getting ready to dive over the bar for safety.

On the other side of the common room, a thin woman wearing a red blouse and a long purple skirt stood up slowly. Her ginger hair was bound in a long braid that reached all the way down her back, contrasting with the sickly, green colour of her face, and her large nose bore an impressive wart near the tip. A fluffy, orange cat sat on the table next to her, licking its paw and cleaning its ears. The woman saw Mira watching her and winked.

Then she bent over a little and held out both hands at waist height. She began clicking her fingers, shaking her hands up and down as she did, keeping a short repetitive rhythm. Others in the tavern quickly jumped up and joined her, mimicking her rhythm with wide grins on their faces, filling the space with synchronised clicking.

Within moments, one of the High Lord's soldiers turned to face the woman and yelled, "Oh stuff off, Elschefla!"

The tavern burst into laughter, including the black-clad newcomers, who walked forward to greet the soldiers with smiles and hugs. Together, the two groups went to the bar to order drinks.

Chapter Five

"What were you trying with that backflip, Khazar?" said one of the soldiers, a large orc woman with short, brunette hair and broad, round shoulders. She grabbed one of the black-clad figures by the wrist and hauled him into a hug. The skinny man's eyes bulged as he was wrapped in her heavily-tattooed arms.

Then they stood back from one another. He put a hand on the small of his back and stretched, twisting to recover from the hug.

"I was trying to get out of the way of the bloody crossbow bolts you lot were loosing," he laughed. The corners of his eyes creased over the cloth wrap he wore to cover his mouth and chin. The large woman grinned, which was an intimidating sight given the large tusks that protruded from her lower jaw, and slapped him on the shoulder. He yelped and grabbed his shoulder.

"You didn't have to worry about that. Renada's a terrible shot."

"Hey!" A soldier with a scraggly, brown beard and heavy, black gloves glared at the back of the orc woman's head, but she showed no sign that she was aware of him at all.

Mira looked back down at the wine in her glass. She could see a wobbling reflection of her dark hair and round face in the pale, yellow surface. The reflection wrinkled its forehead and she pressed her lips together.

"Come on Mira," she whispered. Then she sat up and set her shoulders. She blew out a nervous breath, took a sip of her wine, then stood up from her seat and marched over to join the noisy crowd of bandits and soldiers.

"Good evening!" she said loudly as she approached. The orc woman with the tattooed arms turned and looked down to greet her with a wide smile.

"Hello!" She extended a massive hand. Mira reached out to shake it and found her hand wrapped by the woman's fingers like snakes coiling around a mouse. Mira winced as the snakes squeezed, crunching the bones in her hand into new alignments.

"Who do I have the pleasure of greeting?" said the large woman.

"My name's Mira. I've not really been out in Senoonheim before and I've decided to try and meet some new people."

"Then welcome to the greatest, newest city in the Unlit Hills! My name's Troo!" She stepped back and spread an arm wide, as though she was responsible for the landscape around the city. "I've lived here for ages! Almost three years now!"

"Three years? That's not a long time, is it?" Mira was surprised at how comfortable Troo was if she had only been in the city for three years. She held herself like someone who had grown up in the streets of the city, learning all its secrets through exposure. "Surely it takes longer than that to really settle into a place?"

"Only if that place is old and established! If we had found ourselves in Coobal's Passage or Noakontautoom then maybe it would take some time to really learn our way around the alleys. But Senoonheim grew up at the explicit instruction of Lord Antlers on his Porcelain Throne, and he only began giving those instructions fifteen years ago!"

Mira hadn't learned much about the lands outside of Whinnia in her youth. She had grown up in a very small village, and left that for the town of Wallis as soon as she could. She had never heard of Senoonheim before the day she had been forced to leave her homeland entirely.

On that day, she had joined whatever merchant caravan she could and then jumped off the wagons once they rolled through this city. It looked nice enough to stay, and she had managed to hire rooms to start a new bakery. She had assumed that she had never heard of it before because of her own insularity, not because the town hadn't even existed.

"I can't believe that this city is only fifteen years old! Look at the streets out there," she declared as she waved a hand towards the tavern windows, indicating all the things that lay outside. "Those buildings have vines all over them and heaps of walls are crumbling! These streets must be ancient!"

Troo leaned in closer and spoke to Mira out of the corner of her mouth in a conspiratorial thunder, acting for all the world as though no one else could hear her, although Mira was sure that most dogs would have howled quieter. Out of respect, the soldiers and bandits conversing next to them deliberately raised their voices in a vain attempt to drown her out.

"You're right, Senoonheim looks like a good, old-fashioned, ancient city. There's a reason it looks that way." Troo glanced around the room, as though worried who might hear what she said next. Mira leaned in closer and looked around as well, but the room was filled with the same solid workers as before so she had no idea how to tell if any of them were spies. She also wondered what Troo could be about to say that any spies might want to discover.

"Artisans," finished Troo right beside Mira's head, the syllables blasting into Mira's eardrums and shaking her skull.

"Artisans?" repeated Mira, blinking and shaking her head to try and reduce the ringing echo that lingered in her ears.

"Aye, and only the best of them!"

"What do you mean, 'Artisans'?"

"I mean that Lord Cornucervin only brings in the best artisans to make sure his city attracts the right sort of people! He figured out pretty quickly that the best way to get people into Senoonheim, make money for himself and the people here, was to encourage adventurers to come by."

"Adventurers." Mira's voice was flat. Adventurers had travelled through Whinnia from time to time and she hadn't been impressed by the ones that she had met. Grumpy old men who refused to be separated from their walking sticks and who sat around smoking their pipes all day. Elves and dwarves who glowered over the stockades, watching the wind catch at pennants. As far as Mira was concerned, adventurers just made everything moody and depressing.

"You're saying that this whole city is an adventurer trap?"

"Yup! The walls might as well be made of cardboard and the streets paved with glue," agreed Troo happily. "The best paper town in all the Misplaced Kingdoms!"

"Why would Lord Cornucervin want to do that?"

"Have you ever known an adventurer not to gather up every coin of treasure they encounter like a magpie that was granted dozens of claws? And do you know any adventurers that can actually keep track of that loot once they have it?"

Mira was unable to reply. Even if she had had much experience of adventurers, Troo conversed in the same manner as an avalanche, with statements rumbling from her mouth like boulders bouncing through a valley. All that you could do if you were caught in the way was to hope you kept your balance while scrabbling to find a way out the side.

"Of course not!" said Troo. "Adventurers are worse than squirrels for tucking things away and then forgetting them completely! And Lord Antlers just provides a good place for them to tuck those coins."

"I see." Mira was finding herself dazed and scrambling for a mental footing. "And how do you fit into this picture?"

"I've been one of the Lord's loyal soldiers for ten months. He pays me well to keep the streets safe and to guard whatever he needs guarded."

"So you all are paid to keep the streets safe?" Mira inclined her head to one side, indicating the others in the dark blue cloaks of the Lord's soldiers.

"Correct."

"Then what's all this about?" Mira tilted her head the other way, now indicating the chumminess between the soldiers and the darkly-clad bandits who had recently joined them.

The small crowd laughed.

"It's one thing for the streets to be safe enough that people can get to work and go home at night. It's quite another to have streets where adventurers pass through like foxes through a hedge!"

"I don't understand."

"If there's nothing threatening the adventurers, then there's nothing to stop them passing by. These guys are like the thorns in the hedge that slow the fox." Troo slammed a hand onto the shoulder of the nearest bandit, who staggered.

"And we want the fox stuck in the hedge?"

"You bet we do!" The soldiers and bandits around them raised a small cheer. Troo lifted her pewter tankard and held it towards Mira, who shrugged and lifted her wine glass to tap against the side of it. The glass rang like a crystal bell.

Chapter Six

The door to the Sprog and Sparrow opened. It was a young man with tightly-curled, black hair wearing a loose, yellow robe. He had the nervous expression of someone who has done something wrong and a preemptive flinch covered his face. His staff was taller than he was and he rested on it as he looked inside the tavern. The end of the staff was shaped into four, tight loops of wood that held a glowing, green gem.

Mira found herself surrounded by a grumbling tension. Troo and her soldiers all narrowed their eyes, but they didn't direct their suspicions towards the newcomer. Instead, they scowled into the suddenly-re-masked faces of the darkly-clad bandits. The bandits met them glare for glare, their hands emptied of glasses and tankards and now hovering by the hilts of weapons. Muttered insults crackled around the room, a barely audible background of trouble, creeping through the air like the yowls of distant alley cats. Mira's neck hairs stood to attention and she wondered if she could use her wine glass to stab someone in the face if she had to.

The young man in the doorway paused and scanned the room with widening eyes. The farmers on the other side of the tavern stared back with blank expressions. The minotaur chewed his cud slowly. Then he leaned to one side and spat, a glob of dark cud clanging into a spittoon near his feet.

"Uh, good evening," said the young man. His voice managed to crack five times in four syllables, and Mira had to stifle her grin.

A heavy silence greeted him.

"So, I was just... I was just looking for the rest of my party..." He tried to smile, but the shine on his forehead belied his nerves.

"I guess they aren't here then," he squeaked, as though he believed that his sullen audience might appreciate a running commentary. "I might just try calling them anyway." He coughed to clear his throat and then called, "Sparowl? Hetagor?" His voice was too loud, yet it was immediately absorbed by the crowd of staring figures instead of echoing in the room. "Right. Yes. They aren't here then, clearly. So I'll just. I'll just. Yes."

The young man turned around, trying to strike a balance between fleeing as soon as he could and maintaining the level of dignity that he must have felt befitted him. All that actually meant was that his yellow robe swirled around his legs and tangled between his ankles, nearly tripping him on the doorstep. He caught himself on the doorframe and paused, then dusted himself off and stepped back out into the street, closing the door behind him with a thud.

Laughter erupted from the patrons of the tavern and Troo collapsed onto the shoulders of a nearby bandit, whose own cackles stopped as the small thief bore the solid weight of Troo, buckling like a wooden stool beneath a stockhorse. She slapped him on the back and made his eyes bulge.

"Adventurers!" Troo declared loudly as she stood up again. She wiped a tear from the corner of her eye. "You have to love the silly buggers!"

She turned back to Mira and took a gulp from her tankard.

"So, you were going to tell me what brought you out to the newest city in the Unlit Hills?"

"There's not a lot to tell, really," Mira said as she took a sip from her wine. "I couldn't stay in Whinnia, so I had to find somewhere new. Senoonheim was on everyone's lips when I was escaping, so it seemed like a good place to get set up."

Troo's eyes narrowed.

"You want me to ask about what it's been like for you getting set up somewhere new, but I'm far more interested in why you couldn't stay in Whinnia. I hear that it's very flat out there, is that right?"

"It's flat where it isn't steep," Mira recited the old saying from home. Whinnia was a land of plains, but large, rocky hills jabbed up from the grass sporadically. These hills were where the horse-lords built the forts that they ruled their households from, keeping watch over their horse-herds and flocks, sending their soldiers to and fro. The lands around these hill-forts were known as the Far-Grasso Sea, as they swept in rolling, green waves from one horizon to the other. Mira described the landscape to Troo, who nodded.

"Makes sense. Not too different from around here then."

"Here? The Unlit Hills?" Mira snorted. "The key word that strikes my attention in that name is 'Hills,' Troo." Mira waved a hand towards the wall of the tavern, trying to indicate the landscape that lay beyond and further than the edges of the city.

Troo grimaced good naturedly and shrugged.

"There's the hills to the south of the city, yeah, but there's plenty of grassy plains out to the north!"

Mira thought of the farms and roads and rivers and copses and, yes, occasional grassy meadows that spread out like a patchwork quilt to the north, bounded by the Unlit Hills to the south, and with slow rolling hills throughout. The land around the city was divided into squares based on the whims of the people who lived in it. She had travelled through that patchwork on her journey to Senoonheim and the idea that someone might see the manicured and tended landscape that surrounded the city as in any way similar to the Far-Grasso Sea made her grin.

"Alright Troo. It's kind of the same," she laughed.

"I knew it! But this is all more prevarication. Let's get back to the juicy stuff. Why did you have to leave?"

"Do you know anything about the First Seat of Whinnia?" Mira asked.

"I am now aware that there is something called the First Seat of Whinnia."

Mira chuckled. "The First Seat is the leader of the leaders of the houses. He's in charge."

"Okay. And he told you to leave, did he?"

"Yes."

"Why exactly would the leader of a country tell some woman that she needed to leave his lands? What on earth could you have done to upset someone so important?"

"I got into trouble with an important man who was close to the First Seat. I'm sure that my complaints about the way he was managing trade in Whinnia didn't help either. I didn't like how he was dealing with bandits in the plains."

"Ah, I've heard this sort of thing before. Usually there's some damp fellow wearing all black involved. Did your First Seat have some gross second-in-command type?"

"Yes, the leader of the Froge, a frogfolk tribe from the west. Loam has the ear of the Seat and is just awful. He's an unctuous worm."

Troo swallowed a mouthful of beer and thought about what Mira had said. She sniffed then asked, "Literally?"

"What?"

"Is this Loam fellow a man-sized worm, or perhaps descended from draconic wyrms, or something like that?"

"Oh I see, no! No, he's frogfolk too, but astoundingly unpleasant. He tried to get me to share dinner with him a few times, and eventually I had to turn him down forcefully. That was the final straw and I was summoned to the First Seat's Great Hall."

"He convinced the boss to kick you out because you wouldn't court him?"

"No," began Mira, before pausing. "Well, yes, I think so. But that wasn't the excuse they gave. The Seat claimed it was because of all my complaining about the bandits. Undermining his authority."

"They didn't want to spend treasury money on guards for the merchants, I imagine? Not when they could keep it for themselves? I've seen that sort of thing before."

"Actually, the thing I really had a problem with was the way he kept inviting bandit leaders to his hall to discuss the issue."

Troo's eyes widened.

"Maybe he was trying to convince them to leave–"

"And none of the merchants," finished Mira.

Troo nodded slowly and then lifted her tankard towards Mira.

"Yup, seems like a good place not to be. Welcome to Senoonheim, I suppose!" She took a large gulp from her drink and then scrubbed her mouth with the back of her arm. "Not that our advisor is much better."

"Oh? What do you mean?"

"Lord Antlers has his Court Wizard, Satonak. A few months ago, the old fool took it on himself to start watching the city much closer than the High Lord ever did."

One of the bandits rolled her eyes dramatically. "The old hairball has been getting into everyone's business recently," said the bandit. "Nothing good ever comes of advisors who start poking their nose in, let me tell you."

"Loam didn't have a nose," said Mira, but she understood.

Mira kept talking with Troo and her companions for as long as she could, but had to excuse herself when she realised that the sun was setting.

"I have to get a full night's sleep and get up before dawn to open the bakery," she explained apologetically.

"Totally understandable," declared Troo, who reached out and gathered the smaller woman in for a hug. "But we're here most nights! Hopefully we'll see you again soon!"

Chapter Seven

Mira left the tavern and strolled through the city back towards her bakery, her mind crowded with memories of her former life in Whinnia and the way Loam had driven her out. She remembered standing outside her bakery there, looking down the muddy street at the tall, peaked buildings of Wallis, the capital. Wallis was built on the top of one of the highest peaks rising from the plains and its cold wooden houses covered the vertiginous sides of the hill. Grey clouds swept overhead so close that Mira might reach out and pull down some of the delicate threads inside.

Through that dismal scene, she remembered Loam loping his way through the mud towards her bakery. Stumbling along next to him were a pair of smaller frogfolk men. One carried a large bouquet of bright flowers, small, circular puffs of petals in pink and yellow and orange that were called Wide-Eyes. The other was lugging a broad wicker picnic basket on his side. The weight of the basket pulled him nearly horizontal as he walked. Both of the smaller men tripped over their own feet as they rushed to keep up with their leader, who didn't act as though he was aware of their presence at all.

Loam stopped in front of Mira and smiled, a skill he hadn't perfected. His mouth stretched uncomfortably and then he clicked his fingers at the servant panting next to him. The man flinched and then shoved the bouquet forward, spilling loose petals into the puddles at their feet.

"These are for you," said Loam in a voice that sounded as though he had swallowed oil.

Mira took the bouquet and thanked the servant, who stared at her. Loam waved him away, and the shorter man scarpered down the street as though he had just been released from a prison cell. Perhaps, in a way, he had.

"Thank you," said Mira politely. "These are very pretty." The flowers would have required some poor members of Loam's Froge society to spend far too much time seeking blooms on the plains. Flowers like this were hard to find. Not to mention, Mira could already feel an itch in the corners of her eyes and was fighting a desire to sniff.

"Of course they are," said Loam. "Right. Are you ready to go?"

Mira looked at the servant carrying the basket. His eyes bulged and she wondered if it was because he was struggling with the weight of the picnic that Loam had devised, or whether that was just how some frogfolk's eyes looked. Her mind turned to the advice she had received from her coven, Bovo and Amella.

Mira had left the tiny village she grew up in when she was very young, eager to see the world, or at least to see more of it than anyone else in her family ever had, and finally ended up starting a bakery in Wallis. Of the few people she had grown close to in her new home, Bovo and Amella were the ones she spent the most time with. Bovo was always ready to convince Mira to come along and have some fun, while Amella brought years of experience to any conversation. When she discovered they were witches, she had been excited to learn more.

Mira had complained to the two of them about the way Loam was ordering her to join him for a picnic and both of them, despite their varied personalities, had said that she should go with him.

Mira considered all this as she snuffled from pollen and watched the frogfolk man struggling with his basket while Loam stood unencumbered. Loam was an awful person, presumptuous and uncaring. He worked closely with the First Seat of Whinnia, who was one of the worst leaders that the horse-lands had ever seen.

She shook her head. "No. I'm not ready."

Loam blinked slowly, an impressive sight on a frogfolk of his size. It was like watching a storm spread across the dome of the sky, if the sky was a glistening frog eye and the storm was a blubbery eyelid.

"What?" he said.

"Loam, I tried to say this when you suggested it the first time," said Mira. The fear in her stomach grew with every word. At the time, she hadn't known what refusing such a powerful person would mean for her. But, alongside her growing fear, her confidence grew as well. She knew that every word was the right word, that this was what she had to say. She might be scared of what would happen next, but it would be whatever it had to be. "I am not interested in you romantically. I don't want to court you."

Loam's face scrunched up. He looked as though a chicken had just spoken to him. He was being confronted with something that he found amusing, but it was doing something that he couldn't comprehend.

"But I have everything you could ever want."

"Like what?" asked Mira.

Loam spread his arms, indicating the large bouquet and the picnic basket.

"Pretty dates aren't everything I could ever want Loam."

"What are you talking about? I can buy anything you want, I can order anyone to take us wherever you want to go. Every whim would be fulfilled if you were with me." Anger bubbled up in red blotches on Loam's cheeks, like gas in a mire.

"I understand that, but I also need to be interested in you. I need to enjoy spending time with the person I court. I need them to encourage me to be my best self."

"I make everyone into better people," growled Loam.

Mira pursed her lips. "I'm sorry, it's still no."

Loam narrowed his eyes and snatched the bouquet from her hands. The flowers erupted in a shower of petals, leaving him holding a bunch of long, green stalks. The servant beside him shrank away, still clutching the massive basket.

"You aren't going to tell anyone that you refused me," Loam snapped.

"Loam—"

"I'll get you a good horse, from the First Seat's stables." He nodded, as though agreeing with himself, sending a ripple across his pale flesh. "In return, you have to say nothing about this at all."

"Loam, I don't want a horse from you."

"You just want to ruin my reputation!" Now Loam became frantic. Spittle formed on the edges of his lips, and he shook. "But you won't get away with it! No mere baker will tear me down!" He leaned closer and stabbed one finger towards her. "You are going to be a no one in this town, do you understand me? A nothing and a no one, and no one will listen to any of your lies anyway! You always were a no one, despite your attempts to pretend that you were more than that!"

Loam spun around, and his feet slapped angrily down the street. The Froge servant shrugged at Mira and then turned to trail after his furious master. Mira's shoulders sagged as the tension ran out of her body. Why did he say that she had attempted to be someone important? She only ever tried to be herself. How could someone think she was pretending otherwise? Nevertheless, she had managed to stand up to him, and she was proud of herself. But what would come of it, she had no idea.

Chapter Eight

Within a week of Mira's rejection of Loam, the people of Whinnia had stopped looking her in the eye as they trudged through the streets with shawls and cloaks pulled tight against the cold. They might simply have been busy, focused on where they were going in the uncomfortable weather, but Mira knew the people here. Even when drenched by the rain, they would normally smile and wave as they passed. Something had changed.

"Hey, do you need some bread for your evening meal?" she asked a frazzled woman who was trying to chase down a young boy with long brown hair. The woman stared at her, looked at Mira's shop, flinched as though the building had jumped at her, shook her head slightly then rushed after her boy.

"What is going on?" Mira muttered as she went inside out of the wind.

She had barely set herself behind the counter when the door banged open to admit a round figure with a single, sharp tooth poking up from her lower lip. Her tiny, black eyes sought out Mira, and thin strands of black hair fell over her forehead.

"Hello! How are you doing, young Mira?"

"Hello Amella." Amella was one of those women everyone thought of as an aunt. Somehow she could bustle into anyone's home, cup of tea in hand, before they could stop her. Inevitably, she would lean forward and inquire into the health of some obscure relative that the family themselves might not even remember.

In Mira's case, Amella was also a witch, and Mira had been learning witchcraft from her.

"Things are slow at the moment. No one seems to be coming in. I don't think I've sold a single roll for three days."

Amella nodded. "Yes, I had a suspicion that something like that might be happening." The older woman cocked her head slightly, looking sideways at Mira. "I have a question to ask you about all that actually. Has anything happened recently to change how the townsfolk see you? Perhaps you said something to the wrong person and word has spread?"

"Said something?" Mira frowned. "I don't think so. Why would you ask that?"

"I've heard some things." Amella shuffled closer. She lifted her hands up to shield her mouth and leaned in closer, as though someone might be listening. "People are saying that you turned down Loam," she confided in a conspiratorial whisper.

Mira sighed. She had been hoping that the man's threats were hot air, but this sounded like he was doing exactly what he had warned her he would do.

"Yes, I suppose I did."

Amella sighed and her shoulders drooped.

"I don't mean to criticize you dear, but that would do it."

Mira drew a slow breath. She felt confused and angry, and that anger heated the breath in her lungs.

"I can't believe this. That cruel man told everyone in Wallis not to buy from me, because I wouldn't agree to court him?"

"Yes." Amella was blunt, taking no care to soften the word. Her tiny eyes were bright.

"And they all went along with it! They just followed his instructions! None of them decided to support me in having a say in my own life!"

"Yes."

Mira leaned on the counter, tensing her shoulders and gripping onto the wood. She looked up at Amella with narrowed eyes.

"You and Bovo both thought that I should do it. Do you really think I should have agreed to spend time with him? To string him along? Just to avoid him lashing out at my business?"

"Yes."

Mira staggered as if struck.

"I can't believe you'd say that. What if he had thought it was going well? What if he had asked me to marry him!"

The round face of the older witch looked back at her with a calm, still expression.

"No. You can't be serious," said Mira.

"I didn't say anything!" protested Amella gently.

"You didn't have to! You might as well have been shouting!"

"It's not the end of the world," said Amella. "There are much worse ways to live your life than with a man that you don't much care for."

"I don't understand how you can say that." Mira stepped back from the counter. She felt as though she was seeing Amella for the first time, through fresh eyes. "You told me that being a witch is all about creating authentic relationships. You and Bovo have been trying to teach me to fully understand myself so that I can create a connection to an entity that will empower my witchcraft further, my bravura honda. You said that that relationship needs to be honest and open so that I can truly learn from them. But now you're saying that I should marry some awful person just because he could make my life difficult if I don't? Doesn't that mean betraying who I am entirely?"

Amella shifted her head very slightly sideways, tilting it to look at Mira. She wore the same expression people wear when a child begins speaking about something only proper grown ups usually know about, such as bewilderingly precise details of military history, the exact dimensions of ancient animal skeletons, or why it's okay to let poor people catch easily preventable diseases if it would require money to avoid.

"I'm not saying that Loam would be your bravura. But courting him would not just be to avoid pain. He's wealthy enough that it might bring pleasure too," said the round-faced woman.

Mira pressed her lips together firmly.

"No. I won't do things that way."

"Suit yourself," replied Amella. "But just don't complain when the chickens come to roost." She smoothed her dress and then swirled around to walk out of the shop and back into the streets of Wallis. "Stubborn little wretch," she muttered as the door closed behind her.

Mira stood with her mouth hanging open. She couldn't believe what had just happened. For the first time in years, she wished that she was back in her village with her family. Then she might have someone she could talk to.

She kept repeating what Amella had said over and over in her mind, trying to figure out if she had misunderstood something. But the people she confided in the most in Wallis were her coven.

Her throat grew tight, and the heat of tears built up behind her eyes. She sniffed and rubbed at her face with the heel of one hand. How could someone who had been teaching her about something so personal suddenly say something so awful? Had she completely misunderstood what Bovo and Amella had been saying about what it took to become a witch? Mira was sure that what Amella was suggesting was antithetical to everything that she had learned so far about witchcraft.

As she swam through rolling waves of disappointment and shock and anger, Mira looked at the empty streets and the averted eyes of the people walking by. Only one made eye contact with her: a very young man with a nervously wobbling throat who wore the livery of the First Seat.

"Uh, you are Mira of Far Rocks, right?"

Mira shrugged and shook her head slowly in surrender.

"Yes, that's me. What now?"

"The First Seat has asked that you attend him in his hall as soon as you can."

Mira looked at the boy, who swallowed elaborately and shuffled his feet.

"When you say as soon as I can, I assume that means now, and not after I've gone home to get over how awful this day has been for me. Am I right?"

The boy's eyes bounced around and he nodded.

"Alright, lead the way," Mira sighed. As the boy began walking up the hill, she took a deep breath, clenched her fists open and closed, and followed him.

Despite her trepidation, she knew there was only one way that she was going to deal with this. She was going to tell the First Seat the truth.

Chapter Nine

Mira entered the Great Hall of the First Seat of Whinnia. The room was long, and low at the sides, though the ridge of the ceiling overhead rose nearly five horses high, depending on how well fed the horses were. Thin tapestries hung at regular intervals along the sides, creating a hallway that led past the huge fire in the center of the room to the dais where the First Seat sat. It was a quirk of Whinnian design that circular fire pits were built in the middle of most of their buildings. Perhaps it said something about the people of Whinnia that for hundreds of years they hadn't thought to change anything about the situation. To be fair, they spent a lot more time outside than inside. Mira coughed some of the smoke out of her lungs.

She wished that Bovo and Amella had taught her more already. If she knew some sort of charm to keep her safe while she confronted these men she would have been much more confident. Instead, she had learned how to make muffins extra tasty and little else. Maybe she should have brought some muffins, to get on First Seat Bower's good side.

No, she thought to herself, he doesn't have a good side.

Mira paused at the entrance to examine the nearest tapestries on either side. One was dyed in a vaguely vomit-coloured yellow, and embroidered with the outline of a winged lion. The banner facing it on the other side was dyed a deep green, with the pale outline of a coiled serpent. Each was the symbol of a household that supported First Seat Bower.

Mira shook her head. Why was it that so many people were happy to ignore some very worrying signs of what was going on around them? The heads of these houses should have challenged Bower by now, in Mira's opinion. Being the First Seat relied upon the support of the houses of Whinnia, and surely one of those houses must want to be in charge over Bower?

Mira considered the idea and realised that she was wrong. There were a great many people who found it much more useful to be close to the person in charge, but not to be that person themselves. After all, who got the blame when things went wrong? The person in charge. How often would that person have any control over what went wrong? Almost never. But, contrary-wise, who got to benefit when things went right? The households close to the top. Maybe they were simply riding the coattails of the First Seat, waiting to dive clear before he rode off a cliff. She supposed they even had a replacement ready and waiting.

"Welcome Mira, what brings your lovely self here?" The voice slid like oil spilled on ice, streaking across the room into her ears. Mira shuddered. Loam had been beneath the green serpent banner, talking to someone, but he sped over to stand beside her, moving his feet in tiny steps. The movement left Mira with the impression of a centipede scuttling through the dirt.

"I was summoned here, Loam."

"Really? You were? Oh my, I wonder why that might have happened?" Loam's massive eyes shone in the firelight and Mira was impressed that he didn't snigger at her directly. She was sure he would normally relish demonstrating his petty power play, making it absolutely clear that his actions had brought her into this situation. Mira wondered if he was holding back because there was worse to come.

She blinked as she examined him and then smiled. "I've never noticed it before, but your face looks like a broad, full moon. Pale as a fish's belly and for exactly the same reason. Neither a fish's belly nor your face ever get close to the sun."

A crease folded in the middle of Loam's face where a human would have a nose. Ridges bunched over his eyes and he opened his mouth to say something back to Mira, but no words came out. She reached up and patted his cheek, pausing as a layer of slime stuck to her fingers.

"That's alright, Loam. I'm sure your toadies can figure out how to play this game for you. You come and see me once they give you a retort, alright?"

His pasty face flushed with red patches, and Mira spun away. Why had she done that? She knew his anger at her was already causing trouble, why would she make it worse? Of all the gross men that flocked to the Great Hall, who flattered and pandered to their infantile leader, why had she decided to antagonise the one who the Seat most often seemed to listen to?

She tried to stifle a grin as she walked away from him. It had felt bloody good.

Mira hurried to the dais beyond the fire. Sitting on top of the raised area, the First Seat's chair was a plain, wooden bench with a saddle set on top, the sort of simple structure that got called a sawhorse. It was probably as close as First Seat Bower got to anything called a horse any more, given the bone injuries in his ankles that he claimed kept him from leading his cavalry around the distant bounds of Whinnia and the Far-Grasso Sea.

The First Seat itself was originally an admired symbol of the occupant's leadership, a position deriving from their actions on horseback across the plains of Whinnia, with their demonstrated experience and ability causing the heads of the households to uphold the Seat as a first among equals. But, over the years, the saddle had been made more cushioned so that its occupant could sit easier in the hall for longer periods of time. Various First Seats had grown older in the saddle, so they had instructed that back support be added. The sawhorse had been rebuilt, with extra bracing incorporated so that there was no embarrassing sag when the First Seat sat, and so that the back could now be levered into a more comfortable reclining position. The First Seat was now more like a sun lounger than a throne.

First Seat Bower lay in his saddle and watched Mira advance through his tiny, squinting eyes. Mira felt as though she was being watched by a near-sighted molerat. Wrinkles bunched and shifted on his face, never pausing, which meant it was impossible to tell exactly what thoughts and feelings were bouncing around in the large cuboid block of his head.

Gossip in the market was that the heads of the houses spent their time worrying about the flittering thoughts in Bower's mind and whether they could be anticipated in a way that would profit one household or another.

Mira knew they were kidding themselves. She had met a few men like the First Seat after leaving her village, and she had helped women get away from them in more ways than one. She was sure that Bower didn't have any more clue about what he was thinking from one second to the next than anyone else.

He wore the traditional clothing of the First Seat: a thick, fur loincloth and a heavy crown. Massive boots covered his feet, with pale fur pouring out of the top. Tradition held that the First Seat also be bare-chested, although straps of studded leather were often considered acceptable accessories. It was a uniform designed for the sort of young, bold, and generally triangular leaders that Whinnia had experienced in its past. However Bower also wore a heavy red cloak that was pulled tightly around him, covering most of his round body. A sword was stabbed into the wooden planks of the floor beside him and he held the haft in one hand as though he was about to pull on the sword like a lever.

"Mira of Far Rocks," said the Seat in his slow, arrhythmic style, as though he had been reminded of what he was saying halfway through saying it.

"Bower," she replied with a small nod of the head. There was a rush of air as dozens of onlookers sucked in a breath. She hadn't used his title. The First Seat's face screwed up like an old washcloth. He released the sword's hilt and jabbed a sweaty finger at her. The sword remained exactly where it was, the no longer functional symbol of authority having been built into the dais floor generations ago.

"That's rude, you are a rude woman." Spit flew from his mouth as he spoke.

Mira knew better than to say anything to a man like this.

"I've heard that you are complaining about me. Spready nasty nasty lies about the way Whinnia works. Who are you to say anything about me? You're nobody, you're filth."

Mira had heard it all before. The First Seat was the sort of thin-skinned person who was proud of their strength, and took every opportunity to tell everyone how strong they were and what feats they had accomplished. Like all such bullies, they acted as though they were huge and strong, but the facade of their strength was as thin as the painted cloth backdrop of a travelling actor's troupe. The slightest breath of criticism sent the whole thing fluttering and revealed there was nothing beyond it. Their accomplishments were always figments of their own imaginations.

At this point, she might as well just tell the old fool what she really thought.

Chapter Ten

"I just thought that perhaps the First Seat should be sending soldiers out to drive off the bandits that are hunting in the Far-Grasso Sea. Maybe then merchants would feel confident to trade through Whinnia again?" Mira said to the First Seat.

"How dare you! Whinnia is the safest place in the world! And all the best merchants come here all the time! The only problems here are caused by the non-humans, and humans who support them!"

A chorus of voices around Mira echoed the First Seat. Loam looked shocked. Clearly he had expected her to defend herself against the poison he had whispered into Bower's ears, not to attack the Seat instead. Mira felt a warm glow as she let rip with all the thoughts she had kept hidden about the loathsome leader.

"That's an odd claim to make when one of your top advisors is non-human," she began, pointing at the frogfolk man standing beside the First Seat. "The markets here in the capital are smaller than ever, and I'm having to pay more and more for less and less sugar," she snapped. Her stomach clenched as the room went silent. Loam stepped up next to the First Seat and leaned down to whisper in his ear. The Seat's face twitched as he listened.

"I won't put up with such treasonous discussions. You will stop spreading such awful awful lies or–" The Seat pulled himself higher in his chair and narrowed his already small and squinting eyes. "Or you will stop everything."

Mira felt the threat enter her ears and slice down her spine like a cold blade.

Mira felt a stab of relief when the First Seat yelled for her to get out of his sight. He didn't order any of his soldiers to grab her, and she hoped that he wouldn't think of it at all. She left the Great Hall in a cloud of shock and fear, unsure of what else was happening behind her as she rushed to get home.

She had expected such a threat as soon as she was summoned to the Great Hall, but she wondered whether she would have heard it if she had held her tongue? Maybe she would have been fined or put in the stocks instead? Surely that would have been enough to assuage Loam's bruised ego? But she hadn't been able to stop herself from insulting the leader of the Froge further or from loudly opposing the First Seat's delusions. It was one thing to commiserate with others in the marketplace where his cold-armoured soldiers might not hear them, but to say it directly to his face?

Mira stumbled through the streets of Wallis, panicked thoughts spiralling in her head. She was sure that she didn't have long before the First Seat would figure out exactly how he wanted her to suffer and send his soldiers after her. She needed help.

She rushed down the hillside to Bovo's house.

Bovo's home was small and rough-hewn, and the door was closed. Mira knocked. She called. She tried to open the door, but nothing happened.

"Hello?" she shouted. A gaping silence answered her. It was the empty, waiting sort of silence that is heard particularly when someone is trying very, very hard to be quiet. Mira cupped a hand to the door, pressing her ear in close. Not a sound came from inside.

"Bovo?" She tried one more time. Perhaps Bovo was out. After all, the halfling witch was a sociable woman who enjoyed getting out around town more than sitting around her house. As Mira left, she wondered if that really was a faint thud somewhere inside the building.

Next, she tried Amella's home, a tiny rundown building that better suited the word 'hovel'. The door barely hung on to its hinges and creaked as it shifted in the breeze. Smoke curled up from a hole in the roof.

"Amella, thank goodness you're home," said Mira as she pushed at the door, then pulled on it, then lifted it over a protruding knot of wood, then shifted it back and forth until it finally whined open. She stepped into a gloomy, empty house. The fire pit in the middle of the room was dark, holding only a few orange embers that quickly faded as she watched. The last curls of smoke drifted through the hole in the roof.

"Amella?" Mira asked the empty house. Nothing answered her.

She fought to keep her tears from escaping. Right when she needed them, the women who had become her closest friends and had been teaching her about witchcraft had vanished.

She scrubbed at her face and exhaled sharply. There was no time to feel sorry for herself. Bower might send soldiers after her at any moment. She had to get out of Wallis at least, and maybe out of Whinnia entirely.

Mira sped back home, her mind racing ahead of her body, already planning how to leave town and what she would need to pack. By the time she was actually scooping up her possessions, it was simply a matter of letting her hands catch up to her thoughts. She had just stuffed some clothes into a large pack when she heard unusual noises outside. Footsteps, and the distant thunder of voices, a grumbling storm rolling closer. Mira snuck over to peek through the gap around the door.

A group of the First Seat's soldiers were gathered in the middle of the street. Bands of red cloth were wrapped around their arms and they carried both spears and scowls. In front of them stood the wobble-throated boy who had brought her the summons to the Great Hall. As she watched, that lanky boy gestured at the door and two of the others marched forward with the inevitability of an avalanche.

Mira's reflection was a pale ghost in the window. She blew out a long, deep breath and watched as the approaching soldiers blinked and started coughing on the path to her door. They hunched forward and dropped their spears. She might have just enough time to get out if she hurried.

She checked that the bar locking the door was secure then ran back to her pack. She didn't have time now to finish gathering anything, she would have to make do with what she already had.

As the door began to rattle beneath the blows of the soldiers, Mira crept out a small back door. She told herself that she would have to stop judging people based on the way that they presented themselves to her. Just because the messenger had looked like a silly young boy who was out of his depth and who should never have been entrusted with ordering those soldiers around, that didn't actually mean that he wouldn't follow his orders out completely. He might worry about the effect he would have on her, maybe he would feel guilty about his role in years to come, but she'd still be the one suffering.

Mira snuck through the streets until she made it to the market. Night was falling, so most of the stalls were empty, though a few enthusiastic or desperate sellers were still shoving their wares at passersby.

"Would the pretty lady like some pretty gemstones?" asked one, holding up a necklace of aqua-coloured spheres. Mira frowned.

"Oh, come on Robi, you and I both know that those are barely more valuable than glass."

"Mira? Sorry, I wasn't looking closely."

"It's fine." Mira glanced over her shoulder, but saw no sign of any soldiers. Perhaps she had outwitted them through the cunning manoeuvre of leaving via the only other door. "Is Malcomb still around?"

"I think he was helping Dulamo pack down," replied Robi, pointing over his shoulder with a thumb.

"Thanks."

Mira rushed through the street and was relieved to see that Robi was right. Malcomb was helping a middle-aged woman take lamps and candlesticks off a small table and tuck them into a small wagon.

"Malcomb!" she called. Relief snatched at her throat and she thought she might cry.

"Mira?" Malcomb's eyes widened and he barely managed to open his arms before she crashed into the hug. "What's going on?"

"I need to get out of Whinnia," she said into his shoulder. She looked up at him. "Loam has convinced the First Seat to punish me."

"For not going on a picnic with him? Surely it can't be that–"

"I said, where did she go!" yelled an angry voice from the other end of the market, accompanied by the crash of a crate falling. Malcomb pushed Mira behind him as he looked down the street.

"It's some of his SNOW soldiers," he said. She shrank lower.

"I told you," she hissed. "Men with egos as fragile as Loam and Bower, they lash out all the harder when they feel rejected!"

"Alright, alright." Malcomb turned to face her. "Dulamo was heading out of Wallis anyway, I'm sure she can hide you in her wagon." He shifted his gaze to the other woman. "Right? I'll owe you."

Mira turned to look at the metal-worker. The older woman shrugged and nodded.

"Once you're out of Wallis, you can send me a letter and I'll let you know when things have calmed down." Malcomb lowered his face and looked deeply into Mira's eyes. "It's going to be okay."

There was another crash from the marketplace.

"We have to go now," stammered Mira.

"Yes, you two go. I'll try to slow them down." Malcomb smiled. He gave Mira one last squeeze of a hug, and then headed towards the soldiers who were searching the market.

"Come on luvvie, let's go," said Dulamo, and Mira followed her. She watched Malcomb spread his hands as he approached the soldiers, before one stepped forward with a raised fist. She flinched away and never looked back.

Chapter Eleven

M ira shook off the memories of Whinnia that clung to her like ticks. They were unpleasant, and she had been having such a good time in the Sprog and Sparrow, conversing with Troo. She had to get to bed if she was going to be up in time to bake the bread in the morning, but she wished she could have kept talking to the orc woman. She would have loved chatting with more of the bandits and soldiers that Troo knew as well. She finally began to believe that she could build connections with some new people in this city, and she felt as though she had let herself down by cutting it short. She hoped that she had made a good impression.

The soldiers had been pleasant enough, but it was Troo who Mira really felt she could build a friendship with. Troo was up front and direct. She wasn't the sort of person who hid what she thought and made it a struggle for others to figure out.

Mira had had enough of people who made themselves into puzzleboxes and painted smiles on the outside.

It was probably something to do with the way Troo looked so strong. Troo was built like someone who had grown up lifting heavy objects out of the way and had never been told to stop. Mira imagined that such a person would be similarly strong with their emotions, moving bad emotions and reservations aside, hoisting themselves up with confidence.

In contrast, Mira always felt as though she had to be careful when she spoke. So often in her life her tongue had been the cause of her troubles. Even before she managed to make enemies of the most powerful men in Whinnia, she had lost valuable business contracts because she had told visiting merchants exactly what she thought of their dealings with others. When she was young, her aunt had even stopped visiting after Mira made one too many comments about her aunt's treatment of her uncle. Now, Mira tried to catch herself before she let her thoughts tumble out of her mouth untested, like a herd of fluff-tailed deer startled by wolves.

The last pale orange streaks of sunset were still hanging about to the west as she strolled home. A chill flowed down from the Unlit Hills to the south, seeping under doors and down spines. The streets were still full of people, making their way to their own favourite taverns or heading home after working late. She pulled her shawl closer around her shoulders as she stepped along Siltrap Street, lost in her thoughts.

She didn't notice the dark figure who leaked out of one of the many alleys she passed. The figure glided after her. They were not dressed in black, as they would have looked like a person-shaped hole in the world whenever they moved in front of lit windows. Instead, they wore deep browns and greens, almost black but not quite, so gave the impression of a shadow that had become detached from its owner and was now carefully avoiding the soap and needle and thread that might entrap them once more.

The figure gained on Mira as they both moved down the street. By the time she turned to her door, stepping close and reaching into her pocket for the key, the shadow was an arm's length from her. This was an entirely accurate and specific measurement at that moment, because the figure had reached out one arm and was about to loop it around Mira's neck, when an entirely unconnected arm with a wide, outstretched hand at the end erupted from the darkness and pulled the shadow backwards by the scruff of the neck. The shadow squealed.

Mira turned with a start.

"What the–"

Behind her stood a tall, wide-shouldered figure in gleaming metal armour. Golden filigree decorated the edges of each metal plate, and wisps of golden hair peeked from beneath the face-concealing helm he wore. He was holding a darkly-dressed, skinny woman up by the collar of her top. The woman twisted and screeched, her body bent and curled like a mouse with its tail in a trap, and she clawed at the metal gauntlet that held her. When she realised Mira had turned around, the woman froze mid-wail. Her eyes swivelled to focus on Mira and then the woman's face relaxed out of its panic. Her tongue licked across her lips slowly, and then she smiled nervously.

"Good evening," she said with a demure nod, as if she wasn't being held up so high that her feet couldn't touch the ground and was now slowly rotating away from Mira. "How are you?" she asked, and her face conveyed every sign that this was a genuine question, sincerely seeking an answer.

"Good evening, thank you, I'm quite well," Mira began, before she shook her head slightly and interrupted herself. "What? No. Who are you? Both of you?"

"Good evening ma'am," declared the armoured figure in a loud, clear, carrying voice. More than one passerby on the street flinched at the noise and paused before deciding to move on quickly. It was the sort of voice used by someone who did not concern themselves with other people's perception of them. "I should have introduced myself when we met earlier, I do apologise! My name is Prevos."

With his spare hand, the figure reached up to lift the helmet off his head and then held it against his hip. His face revealed him to be catfolk, with a shaggy mane of reddish hair that tumbled around his face and down to his shoulders. His muzzle was softly rounded and covered in a thin layer of tan fur, and golden eyes watched her from above a dark nose. Mira wanted to reach out and run a finger through the fur on his forehead. When she realised that her hand was actually moving forward, she grabbed it with the other. The man gave no indication that he noticed.

"I would shake your hand, but I am afraid I must keep hold of this miscreant," he said. He hoisted the skinny woman a couple of inches higher as he spoke, shaking her a little. The woman rattled.

"That's fine," Mira replied. With effort, she dragged her attention away from his silken mane to the woman. The woman stopped trying to tug her clothes out of Prevos' grip and smiled even wider at Mira. The effect was spoiled as her collar slowly stretched and tore in the armoured man's gauntleted grip.

"Good evening! Uh. I'm Nerishma. Can I interest you in learning about Varivixes the Mosquito Goddess?"

Before Mira could respond, Prevos had lifted Nerishma higher and twisted his hand so that she spun to face him.

"A follower of Varivixes? Praise Trankwill and her still waters! Is there a shrine of Varivixes in this city?"

Nerishma's eyes were so wide that Mira grew concerned that they might pop out.

"Uh. Uh. Yes, probably. I mean, surely. Yes?" Nerishma babbled. Her legs were drawn up beneath her as though she was a roosting bird. Mira had never seen someone whose bluff had been called harder than this, and she had watched people gamble against Loam, whose main strategy when playing cards was to remind his opponents that he was a close friend of the First Seat.

"I seek communion with the mother of the biters. I will have to ask you to lead me there," said Prevos.

Nerishma began nodding furiously.

"Of course I can do that, obviously, and I'd be very happy to do so! But I will need to put my feet on the ground you see, in order to walk, and–"

"Not at all, I will carry you. But before we can go on such errands, I want to know what you intended to do to this young woman?"

Mira started. She had become drawn into the conversation, as though she were watching a performance from an acting troupe. If Prevos had not reminded her that they were not on stage, she would have begun digging in her pockets for a pouch of roasted nuts or applauding.

"Wait a second. Intending to do to what young woman? Are you talking about me?" Mira asked.

"I grabbed this mosquito follower as she walked up behind you and reached out towards your neck," explained Prevos.

Mira turned her gaze slowly to the woman spinning beneath Prevos' fist, and her eyebrows climbed so far up her head that they needed trained experts to guide them to the summit. The woman chuckled nervously and shrugged.

"The large man raises a good point. What were you intending to do exactly?"

The woman winced.

"Offer you a religious pamphlet?" she suggested in a voice that was as certain of the outcome as a coin spinning in midair.

The three stood in silence. Mira's gaze shifted along Nerishma's body, down her arms, to her hands, which held nothing. Mira's eyes drifted down to the ground, which was bare. Then she lifted her gaze slowly back up to meet the other woman's eyes.

"That sounds good. I'm always interested in finding out about a new religion." Mira held out a hand expectantly. "Where are they?"

Nerishma smiled tightly and patted at her sides with both hands.

"Oh bite me, I must have left them behind! Such a silly one I am. Maybe I could just go and get them for you?"

Mira shook her head and groaned.

"Oh just let her go would you?" she said to Prevos. His face was calm and didn't shift at her statement. For a second she wondered if he had not heard her. Then his fingers released their grip and Nerishma dropped onto the dirt and cobbles. The woman squawked and scrambled to run as quickly as she could into the deepening shadows of night that slowly filled the street.

Chapter Twelve

"Are you sure it was the best idea to let that mosquito worshipper go?" The tall man in his gleaming armour turned his head to watch the woman disappear into the shadows further down the street. His breastplate was so wide and clean that Mira felt as though she was looking into a gilt-framed mirror.

"What else should I have done?" she sighed.

"I was under the belief that the woman may have been a thief, and if I am correct then she would have intended to harm you and to take your possessions." He turned his head to look at her again. His eyes were huge and shone with golden light, even in the darkness of the night. "That would not have been acceptable."

Mira laughed.

"I agree! But you caught her, and she hadn't actually done anything to me yet so I can't imagine that the High Lord's soldiers would be bothered to do much with her."

"Perhaps she could have been encouraged to undertake service in her community as a way to atone for her intended misdeeds. She could have been a mentor to other wayward youth." His eyes widened further and he gasped. Mira saw thin sharp teeth at either side of his mouth, behind the furry muzzle. "By Trankwill! I forgot to get her to tell me the way to Varivixes' shrine!"

Mira laughed again, her smile pressing hard into her cheeks.

"I don't think she was actually very religious at all," she chuckled.

"Do you think not?" Prevos looked genuinely concerned.

"I really don't."

The two stood at the doorway outside Mira's bakery in silence for a moment longer. Mira coughed.

"Were you just passing by here? Is that why you saw her trying to mug me and stopped her?"

"Not at all. I have been waiting for you. I was standing in the next doorway."

"Sorry. You were waiting for me?" Mira's stomach tightened. She had bad experiences with men who were unexpectedly outside her home in Whinnia. Suddenly, the largeness of Prevos was a much more real aspect of his presence. The calmness that covered his face began to seem more like an implacable threat.

"Indeed, just here!" He pointed helpfully to a small alcove not far from her front door. It was shallow and well lit. She looked up and down his figure again, tall and broad and muscular and completely covered in armour.

"How on earth did you hide all of this," she waved her hands around at him, "in there?" she finished, pointing at the alcove.

He looked down at himself and then over at the alcove. After a second he turned back to her.

"I can be very sneaky."

"Apparently you can! Nerishma certainly didn't see you either!

"I just wanted to make sure you were not upset by what happened on the street this afternoon!"

"This afternoon?"

"Yes. The incident with the goblins."

"Oh. Oh!" Suddenly Mira realised where she had seen him man and his gleaming armour before. He was the one who had bowled past in pursuit of the goblins that had knocked her over earlier. "Right, you were chasing the goblins!"

He nodded with a very earnest face.

"No, I'm not too upset," said Mira as she relaxed a little.

"Oh good, I wouldn't want you to blame yourself."

"No, that's fine, don't even worr–I'm sorry? Blame myself for what?"

"For getting in the way." Prevos's face remained infuriatingly passive. Mira's own face screwed up in anger.

"Excuse me? Getting in the way? I was just walking on the street! They ran into me!"

"Yes, but you slowed down my pursuit. By helping you I was held up enough that the goblins escaped. Of course, you weren't to know that you would have such an impact by carelessly wandering through the street."

"Carelessly?" Mira wondered if her eyes were as wide as his looked.

"I just thought that maybe it would be good to remind you to be more careful of what's going on around you." He motioned in the direction the skinny thief had run off. "And I was right! Look at what nearly happened here because you don't pay attention. You didn't realise I was waiting for you, and you missed that skinny woman following you." He smiled at her. "She was behind you all the way up the street, you know."

He actually smiled! As though what he was saying was simply a friendly bit of advice, like suggesting that you might want to cut through the floral market to get to the castle faster! How could he not see how patronising he was being?

"Yes." Mira spat the lie as though she could taste its bitterness. For a moment she was going to elaborate on the untruth, but then she decided to hold her tongue and dare Prevos to challenge her.

His golden eyes looked around the street and he cleared his throat. The sound was a deep gravelly rumble.

"Well, perhaps that is all then," he said.

"Perhaps it is."

"Goodnight Mira. I hope that you take care." He bowed his head towards her, shifting the waves of hair that surrounded his face, and then lifted his helmet and slid it over the top of his head. Mira waited for him to walk down the street before unlocking her door and slipping inside.

Mira leaned back against the doorway and briefly considered grabbing some of the older bread off her shelves, swinging the door back open, and sending a stale roll flying at the head of the infuriating man. She wondered if his silly helmet would ring like a bell if she managed to hit it dead on.

Then she took a deep breath and pressed her hands onto her thighs. Why had she let this man set her off so easily? It was so insulting of him to think that she was unaware of her surroundings. As if she was little more than some self-obsessed teenager! She stalked through the store and out a small doorway at the back, heading up the stairs to her room. She slammed the door behind her and stood face to face with herself in her bedroom mirror.

Her hair had come undone and wisps were sticking up from her head in all directions. Her cheeks were flushed red and her eyes were wide. She raised an eyebrow at herself.

"Yes, I know, I'm being ridiculous," she told herself, waving the self-critique aside. She turned and got dressed for bed, avoiding her own eyes in the mirror.

"I just don't appreciate being judged so poorly," she tried to explain as she found some hot embers and started building a fresh fire to warm the room through the night and provide her with a few final embers in the morning to start the ovens.

"You have made a very good run of ignoring people who underestimate you in the past," she argued as she climbed into her bed and pulled her sheets up to her shoulders.

"This is different," she protested as she snuggled deeper into the warmth of her bed.

And why might that be? came her final comment to herself in her head, but she decided to pretend that she didn't hear it.

Chapter Thirteen

Mira woke up with fresh determination running through her veins. She had been out and she had met new people and she was going to do it again!

Without a group of friends who could remind her of her value she had begun to lose her confidence and doubt herself. That was why she had been so upset by a stranger claiming she didn't pay attention to the world around her last night. It had nothing to do with the way his deep rumbling voice shivered its way down her spine. *So, if I build up more friendships,* she thought, *then I'll restore my self confidence at the same time.*

Mira looked her reflection in the eye as she got dressed, pulling her jacket on roughly and tying it tight around her waist.

"You just need to start another coven," she told herself. "That's a great way to meet new people. Find some other women ready to become witches and continue the journey you started in Wallis."

She smiled, trying to outwardly show the confidence that she was trying to achieve, while ignoring the feeling that her stomach had just plummeted off a cliff at the thought of starting a new coven. After all, she had had a coven in Wallis and in the end those witches hadn't shown her the support that she was now looking for. She breathed in deeply and nodded. It was worth a try.

Today, she would find a scribe to make some posters that she could put up, to let people know she was gathering a coven. With that goal in mind, Mira headed down to her bakery and started her day.

***

The ratfolk man on the other side of the counter sniffed suspiciously at the dwarven bread in his hand. When one of the ratfolk sniffed suspiciously, it was a sight to behold. The usual folds along his snout grew secondary ridges of their own.

"You sure this'll last?" he asked, squinting his dark eyes up at Mira. "I've no desire for it to fall apart in my pack today. I'm squeezing into a few small places later on and if it gets all crumbly then I'll be out a much needed meal."

"Absolutely," Mira assured him. "You'll fit through the tunnels with it no problem, and it won't fall apart." Dwarven bread was designed to withstand being battered into the rock walls of narrow mines. It was one of the densest breads she made. She practically had to haul each fist-sized roll onto the shelves with two hands, and she had ensured the shelves themselves were reinforced underneath. It was like stocking cannonballs. She was confident that the bread would survive whatever the man was going to put it through.

"Tunnels?" The man's fur stood on end, and his eyebrows met in an angry V shape. "I didn't say anything about tunnels! I'm finishing the final joists and beams beneath the new tavern being built at North End!" His eyes narrowed. "Did you think that just because I'm ratfolk I spend my days crawling around through holes in the ground?"

"Oh." Mira sucked in air between her teeth. "I'm sorry? I might have assumed something like that, but there's plenty of miners who shop here." She hoped that the explanation would mollify the man.

"I'm one of the most qualified carpenters in Senoonheim!" he snapped, drawing himself up to his full height, a little over Mira's waist. "And you know what happens when you assume something, don't you?"

They both nodded.

"You make an–" she began, but he spoke over the top of her.

"You reveal your prejudices and expose yourself to justified critique." The man looked into her eyes, clearly judging whether or not she meant what she said. Finally, he snorted and nodded sharply. "Thanks for apologising."

He passed over a couple of coins and then left with his dwarven bread.

Whoops. I don't have enough regulars to be offending people that easily! I'll need to think more carefully about what I say in future.

The shop was quiet. Mira drummed her fingers on the counter and stared out the window. After a short time with no further customers, she decided to close up the bakery. Closing a little early would mean she could set out into the city to find a scribe. If she had them make up posters to stick around the streets, then she might be able to find some other women who were interested in helping her form a coven.

Soon, she had set out with determined steps along Siltrap Street, as if she had any idea of where to look for such people.

Within seconds, Mira realised someone was walking next to her. Their footsteps clanked regularly. She turned her head and saw the shining, armour-covered figure of Prevos striding along beside her.

"Hello?"

"Good afternoon!" he declared, tilting his head to acknowledge her.

They walked on together in silence.

At the next intersection, Mira pursed her lips and stopped walking.

Prevos stopped as well. He turned his helmeted head to look at her, and then looked forward into the crossroads. Other pedestrians wandered around them, parting like a stream around an upturned dinghy.

Mira tapped her foot and sighed. Then she started walking again. Prevos strode along with her, keeping pace perfectly.

"Alright," she said, stopping and turning to put a hand on his chest. The metal felt cool to the touch. Her hand was so small on its wide expanse. She pulled her hand away and cleared her throat. "What's going on here? Are you following me?"

"I am not following you!" he protested.

"Oh." For a moment she felt a bit embarrassed for assuming such a thing.

"No, I ensured that I never fell behind! I am walking *with* you!"

Mira pressed into her eyes with the heels of her hands and then rubbed both hands down her face. She tried a more specific question. "Were you waiting outside my shop for me to come out?"

"Of course!"

"And why did you do that?" she asked in the slow voice of a parent talking to a toddler holding a hammer who was standing next to a pile of broken glass.

"I wanted to ask you a question." Prevos's helmet bobbed from side to side and his shoulders hunched a little. He brought his heavy metal gauntlets together and tucked one set of fingers into the other. "Um."

Mira couldn't believe this. The big dope seemed to be nervous.

"Go ahead and spit it out then." She couldn't wait to hear how he was going to disparage her now. Was he going to ask her how she managed to run her own bakery when he had decided that she was clearly incompetent at any sort of planning?

"Well you see, it's just that I was wondering if you would like to accompany me to the shrine of Varivixes?"

Chapter Fourteen

M ira stared at the huge armoured man standing in front of her. Prevos shrunk a little under her gaze, while still towering over her.

"The mosquito shrine is not actually very far away," he stammered in explanation. "I tried to find the little thief and ask her to take me but I could not. So I made enquiries around the city all morning until I found someone who knew of the shrine."

Mira continued to not speak. She didn't know what would fall out of her mouth if she opened it in the face of this.

"It's just that I really did want to seek communion with the Biter Goddess, and it's not very far from here, and then I thought that you looked a little interested when she mentioned it last night so I wondered if maybe you might like to come along."

His voice faded as he spoke, losing the thread of confidence that held him up, a puppet whose strings dangled lower and lower. Mira pressed her lips together and made a short humming noise.

"Nevermind," he babbled into the face of her silence. "It was a silly idea. Of course you don't want to go to the shrine of Varivixes! No one wants to see a mosquito goddess, what was I thinking?" Prevos shook his head and turned away.

Mira groaned. "Look, it's very, uh, nice of you to think of asking me to come with you," she acknowledged. "But I don't have time for something like that right now. I need to find a scribe who can quickly and cheaply make some posters for me."

Prevos froze in place, half turned away from her. His back straightened.

"That's perfect! The contrivancers' quarter is right next to the shrine!"

His description of the quarter did sound like the sort of place that Mira was looking for. She was surprised that the mosquito goddess would keep a shrine near such a place.

Although he wore a heavy, metal mask that covered his entire face, Mira could just imagine the childish light in Prevos's eyes as he watched her, waiting for a decision.

"Oh alright," she finally allowed, letting go of the tense refusal she had been holding onto. "Seeing as I'll probably find my scribe there anyway, I may as well walk with you."

The large man's back stiffened and his shoulders straightened, the only outward sign that he was pleased by her decision. However, happiness rolled off him in waves. It was like standing next to a puppy who had been certified the goodest boy and was now vibrating in joy. Mira thought it was ridiculous.

When they resumed their walk through the city streets it became clear that Prevos had lost his ability to walk in silence. Instead, he punctuated their journey with self-evident directions and an explanation of why he wanted to visit the shrine.

"You see, I don't follow Varivixes personally, but she has a connection to Trankwill, the goddess I do follow. It's just down here on the left. She is the goddess of still waters, have you heard of her? Around this corner, I think it's at the end of this street. Nevermind, you don't need to know who she is, really. Mind your step there, that cobble's missing. Anyway, obviously seeing as her holy places are still waters and pools, the mosquito goddess shares some space with her because her children grow in such places, so I thought that she might look kindly on me."

Mira wasn't sure whether she should respond to his endless chatter or not. On one hand, he hadn't been directly insulting towards her for a change, and he was clearly trying to be friendly, in his peculiar way. On the other hand, if she made even the smallest positive grunt then he might take that as encouragement to keep talking and the prospect of him continuing this monologue made her panic a little. Eventually, she decided that she would have to say something, if only to allow the large man enough time to breathe.

"Is there something that you are looking for from Varivixes in particular? Why not just pray to Trankwill if she is your patron goddess?"

"Trankwill sends peace to those who settle the world into calming stability. I bring her peace to this city by resolving as much conflict as I can, such as catching those goblin thieves the other day. But I have a problem that is not related to smoothing troubled waters across the city."

Now, finally, Prevos walked in silence. Mira chuckled at the extreme change.

"Go on," she encouraged him. "You can tell me more."

"It's just that... You may not have realised this, but people often find me annoying."

Mira stumbled and grabbed onto one of his arms for balance. He pulled her upright and looked down at the ground below her feet.

"I'm so sorry, I missed that cobblestone!" he said with concern. "I should have pointed it out to you."

"No no." Mira waved his concern aside. He knew he was annoying? She was shocked to find that he had such self-awareness. "And you think Varivixes can do something about people finding you... like that?"

They turned a corner and walked on. Prevos said nothing for so long that Mira worried he hadn't heard her, when he finally responded.

"Varivixes is the queen of biters, those most infuriating of insects, disliked by everybody. She must have some advice for someone who lives that way but wants to change."

They walked the rest of the way through Senoonheim in silence.

Chapter Fifteen

The Mosquito Queen's shrine turned out to be a small affair built onto the side of a building. Mira nearly walked right past it. When Prevos pointed it out, she initially thought he was directing her attention to yet another interesting architectural structure. She wondered whether it was a small fountain that no longer worked, or a bird feeder, or perhaps a sort of miniature wall garden.

The stone shrine pushed out of the unused side of a building that looked as though it was probably a stable. A breeze picked up as they stood in the street and let Mira's nose know that the building was most certainly a stable.

The shrine's small roof was almost as far off the ground as Prevos's head. Someone had made a crude attempt to carve its walls into the sort of vine and leaf patterns that might be expected on a really fancy temple. The effect was endearing, but not realistic. It reminded Mira of a pottery cup made by a small child for their parents: while the intent was admirable and the product itself would probably be treasured by those it was made for, there was no chance that it would ever actually function in quite the way a properly made one would.

The bottom of the shrine butted out from the wall at Mira's shoulder height. A bowl was set into it, covered by the pointed roof overhead. The bowl was deep and the still water inside it was quite green. The water's surface was dimpled by the presence of small insects and water creatures underneath.

"Varivixes is lucky no one has taken this down," said Mira, looking around the busy street. It was easy to imagine a blacksmith or carpenter, working nearby and surrounded by the incessant humming of mosquitos, storming out with their heaviest hammer and knocking this shrine to the ground.

"They may find her children frustrating, but most people respect the gods more than that," said Prevos. Mira raised an eyebrow at his obvious naivety but didn't argue with him.

"Do you need some privacy for this, or..." She let her voice trail off. She wasn't sure exactly what the golden-eyed catfolk man intended to do in order to seek communion with Varivixes, or how he was going to ask his questions of the goddess. The shrine was on an unused side of the building, but the street here was certainly well-trod. Traders and servants and merchants and customers flowed through it like ants in the dirt.

Prevos stood still as he considered. After a minute's contemplation, he nodded slowly.

"You may stay if you wish, but I will have my attention on the shrine. Thank you for joining me on this walk." He turned to face her and Mira wondered if he was smiling. It was hard to know what he was feeling when his expressions were hidden behind the serious human face of his helmet. "I would be pleased to walk you back to your bakery once you have spoken to a scribe, if you would like. I will wait here for you as long as I can."

Mira murmured in response. She wasn't actually sure herself what the noise meant. It certainly wasn't an actual word. On the one hand it might have meant "That's alright you don't have to wait for me, I wouldn't want you to waste your day if I end up somewhere else." But there were also undertones of something else in the noise, something a bit more like "Oh that's very kind of you, I'll see you later then."

She turned and walked back to Trace Road, the main street of the contrivancers' quarter, with a strange tingle in her stomach. At the corner, she looked back at Prevos. He was still watching her. Mira jerked in surprise and felt her cheeks heat as she spun away from Prevos. She hurried around the edge of the building so that he couldn't see her.

Focus Mira, she told herself. *You need to find a scribe so you can start a coven.*

Finding a scribe wasn't hard in the contrivancers' quarter. The more difficult thing was deciding which one to use. All sorts of writer, scribe, and calligrapher shops were set up along the streets. Some even sat outside the buildings on rugs or at small tables. Their wares were displayed in rows on improvised stalls, and Mira was interested to see how identical they all looked. The same small parchments with a variety of names written in careful lettering, and usually the same names on those parchments. The same fancy invitations with spaces left to insert the hosts' names once they were purchased.

"Hey, why does your writing look the same as her stuff?" Mira finally asked one of the scribes on the side of the street, a lanky human who had folded his stick-like legs beneath him in the manner of a praying mantis. His head twisted in response to her question, still mimicking a mantis as he examined the wares of the woman next to him. He blinked slowly as he studied a message on her rug that had the same elaborate border and heading as one that lay on his.

He slowly twisted back to meet Mira's eyes.

"She probably uses the same spell as me."

"What?"

"Yeah. All you need to do is get a Twinstone Gremlin binder and transcribe some Aether Instruction to it."

"I don't know what any of those words mean," Mira admitted.

The man shifted his position, a process that took a long time. His legs rose ponderously, spun into a new configuration, then lay back down.

"I have a 3G binder at home. It's a metal plate with runes inscribed on it that binds gremlins to it. Mine binds three gremlins, which makes it pretty quick. Then I just transcribe some AI from the scroll that came with it onto the plate, and the gremlins complete the task for me!"

Mira looked back over at the objects lined up on his rug, and then at the identical ones on the low table beside them.

"So she must have the same 3G binder and use the same AI?"

"I guess," smiled the man.

"Why should I buy these off you when I could just get my own binder?"

The man's smile froze.

"In fact, getting a 3G binder at all sounds like it's complicated. Why don't I just write my own letters and invitations?"

His tongue ran nervously along his lips.

"Sore hands?"

"Thank you, but no thank you. I'm going to find a professional."

Mira headed into the next scribe's shopfront.

This shop was filled with rows of tables. Small animals sat beside each table. The animals looked a bit like humans, but much smaller and skinnier. They were covered in dark fur, in a range of colours from deep, earthy brown to soft grey, and some had speckles of each. A man with sharp facial hair stabbing from his lower lip and each nostril walked quickly forward from the back of the room, hands clasped in front of him and a broad smile on his face.

"Hello my dear woman! My name is Wallium. How can I help you today?" His smile was as thick and shining as the layer of grease on a slow cooked pig. His hair hung in solid wings to either side of his face that shined wetly, the ends curling in under his chin.

"Good afternoon," replied Mira. "I just need some posters made up."

"Absolutely, that is well within our capabilities! Please, step this way."

Wallium wound a path between the busy tables to an empty bench at the back of the room. Mira tried to peer over the strange animals' shoulders as she followed him. Some of them clutched pens in their fists and stabbed inky blotches across the paper on the table in front of them. Others had eyeglasses tucked over their small ears and their tongues protruded from the sides of their mouths as they laboriously scratched letters into order on their sheets.

One of the creatures was leaning back from its table, a mug ensconced in its hands. The creature saw Mira looking at it and met her eyes calmly. It lifted the mug to its lips and sipped, never once pulling its eyes away from her. As it lowered the mug, it shifted its hands and Mira could see words painted onto the side of the mug. They said "Crappy Diem".

Chapter Sixteen

Mira followed the slick man to the bench at the back of his shop. Shelves full of paper and parchments stood next to it, with a box of glass ink bottles set to one side. Wallium arranged himself on the bench facing Mira, placed a sheet of paper down, and picked up a pencil.

"So what does your poster need to say?"

"Obviously I'll leave the fancy attention-grabbing designs up to you, but basically I want to let people know that I am going to start up a witches' coven and that I am looking for people to be part of it."

"Looking for people to join up, yes I can do that. Do they need experience?" asked Walliam with a raised eyebrow.

"No, total beginners are fine."

"Any costs of membership? Economic or metaphysical?" asked the scribe as he made some notes.

"Not initially, but if they are keen then they may have to make some sacrifices later on."

"No upfront fees, that's always a good thing to put out there. Alright, how soon do you need this done by?"

"I was hoping to get about ten copies before I left today. Is that possible?" asked Mira.

Walliam sucked air through his teeth.

"Rush job, huh? Look, it can be done, but there'll be a bit of a cost to it, that's all. Do you have time to take a seat while I draft up a first version for you?"

Mira negotiated the price with Wallium quickly and then made her way past the tables of animals towards a row of chairs at the front of the shop. A few of the animals started screeching, lifting their hands over their heads and waving them towards each other.

"Oi," called Wallium from his bench. He picked up a metal syringe and used it to squirt water at the noisy animals. They yelped and shivered under the short spray but then returned to the strange job they were working on.

"What's going on with all these creatures anyway?" Mira asked as she sat down.

"The monkeys?" Wallium barely looked up from where he was passing his pencil over the paper. "What about them?"

"These are monkeys, are they?" Mira was intrigued. She had heard of monkeys before, but had never seen any. She understood they were wild trouble-makers, and couldn't be trusted. They got their hands into everything, stealing food and anything shiny. But she had also heard that they had some differences from humans too.

These ones were much calmer than any of the stories she could remember, even accounting for the squealing she had just seen.

"What are they doing?" she asked.

"I'm running an experiment." Now Wallium did raise his head. "You see, I've been training them for years to help me run off copies of my work quicker than other scribes. I'll show you how they do that once you're happy with your poster. But when they aren't being used for that, I encourage them to practice their letters. My theory is that if they all churn out as much writing as possible, then eventually, even if only by accident, they will create some poetry that will be incredibly popular."

"Do you really think they could accidentally create something worthwhile?" asked Mira.

"Absolutely! They are going to make me a fortune or my name's not Shax-peer!"

Mira didn't have to wait long before Wallium finished his first draft of the poster and brought it over. She asked to make the heading bigger, to attract more attention. She also realised that she needed to tell prospective witches to meet her at the Sprog and Sparrow on Saturday nights. There were two days until the next Saturday, so if she could get the posters up soon she wouldn't have to wait long before meeting some new friends!

Wallium made the adjustments and then beckoned her over.

"Watch this!"

He handed the inked final version of the poster he had made to a monkey at the end of a table. All the monkeys at this table were moving more deliberately than the others, and some wore shirts and pants. One had a pair of suspenders to hold its pants up, though one of the bands had fallen off its shoulder.

As soon as the first monkey had the poster, it leaned forward and began scribbling. It passed the original to the next animal almost immediately, and then the paper it had been working on followed. Once the papers were passed it grabbed a new sheet of blank paper and continued, working furiously. The second monkey added to the copy of the poster it had received. Moments later they both passed these along, until ten monkeys were working on different stages of the poster. The tenth monkey handed the original to Wallium, quickly followed by the first of the copies. The scribe shook a little sand over the ink to set it, just as the first monkey passed a final sheet to the second monkey and then leaned back in its chair.

Within moments, Wallium was standing with ten full copies of his poster in his hands, each looking exactly the same as the others.

"That's amazing," said Mira with wide eyes.

"Thank you!"

Mira paid the agreed price, tucked her posters under her arm, and left, ready to advertise her coven.

The streets of Senoonheim were as packed as the yard of a theatre, with all the accompanying insults and calls that would be expected there. The sun was still a long way from the horizon, as though it too, wished to wait and see what other excitement the city might offer. Mira pulled her portable sundial out of a pocket and held it up.

"Yeah, I have time," she muttered before heading towards the corner where she had last seen Prevos and the Mosquito Queen's shrine. It would be pretty uncharitable to simply leave Prevos here by himself, she told herself as she dodged a path through the crowd in the street, especially when it wouldn't do her any harm to walk back to her shop with him.

As soon as she stepped away from the scribe's shop the stone wall opposite her exploded, shattering outwards in a cloud of dust and wooden splinters. As broken planks rained down around them, Mira stared at the pieces. She would have sworn the wall was stone, but the pieces covering the ground were clearly wood. She remembered what Troo had told her about the whole city being an adventurer trap, and that it may as well be made of cardboard and glue. Was this one way the city had been built to meet the expectations of the adventurers that drove its economy?

They expected to come to a city that was huge and old and full of secrets, and such a city should be made of stone and brick. But building in stone and brick must have been too slow or expensive for Lord Cornucervin, and would have required skilled builders who already lived in the area. Lacking time and expertise, it looked as though the High Lord had built a fake city over wooden scaffolding.

The faux-stone wall had been torn apart from the inside by a heavy body, one that had smashed through and then crumpled to the road. The dark grey, furry figure was now lying in a ball, curled up amongst the debris. As the people on the street dusted themselves off and turned to see what was happening, the figure pushed themselves up on shaky arms. They lifted their head and Mira realised that they were a werewolf. The werewolf growled and their mouth pulled open in a terrifying snarl that exposed rows of long white teeth glistening wetly under a thick layer of saliva.

"Which way did he go?" the werewolf yelled to the world at large.

Mira met the eyes of some of the others who were still standing in the street. Everyone who had been walking past had stopped when the werewolf ripped through the fake stone wall, and a few of those nearest to the eruption had even been knocked down. Those people were now glaring at the werewolf. But none of them had seen anyone else that might have been who the werewolf was talking about.

"I know he's here somewhere," called the werewolf, as though any of the crowd around him knew what was going on. He finally pulled himself to his feet and stretched, causing the large muscles of his chest and shoulders to shift like a blacksmith's logic puzzle. He lifted one hand and tucked it behind the back of his head, and then pointed down the street with the other. The position caused his muscles to flex enticingly, even though it wasn't a very effective way to point. Mira was sure that the werewolf was trying to look as impressive as possible for his audience. A woman near the back of the crowd whistled, and a few people clapped.

Chapter Seventeen

"Who are you talking about then?" asked an older man standing close to the werewolf. "I don't think any of us seen anybody unusual." He took his hat off, scratched the top of his head between two, small, conical horns hiding in his hair like shellfish in seagrass and then slipped the hat back on.

"You would know him if you had seen him," the werewolf growled, his eyes narrowing. He swept a hand across the crowd, warming to his story. His voice deepened and slowed as he spoke to fill the street. "He is cunning, like a–"

"Wolf," offered the man in the hat.

"No!" snapped the werewolf in a normal tone. "Cunning like a fox, nothing like a wolf at all! There's nothing duplicitous or untrustworthy about wolves! That would be a terrible analogy!"

"Not from the stories I've heard," muttered the old man with the horns.

"Oh really?" snapped the werewolf. "And what stories have you heard?"

"There's a group of pigfolk brothers I've met who certainly thought that–"

"Were they specialised zoologists, then?"

The old man's forehead wrinkled.

"No, I don't think so. They appeared to be farm labourers–"

"Then they can hardly be trusted to have properly researched their claims about wildlife, can they! I bet they didn't present any findings that had been thoroughly analysed to any reputable bodies for verification!" finished the werewolf. The old man shrugged and walked away.

"Anyway," said the werewolf, returning to the crowd and his storyteller's voice. "This evil soul has found sanctuary in your wonderful city, hiding himself among you so that he might escape the justice that I bring. I have been sent by the Guildmasters of Acmay, to return the delinquent for trial!"

The crowd murmured at this proclamation. It was certainly dramatic, but it also sounded tediously officious. It seemed unlikely that there was further entertainment to be had here and so they returned to their errands. The werewolf had provided an interesting distraction, but it turned out that he was just another adventurer fulfilling his quest. He would soon either be beaten by whoever it was he was chasing, or capture them and leave Senoonheim. In the meantime, deliveries still had to be delivered. A woman next to Mira sighed with a shudder and turned away from the strapping werewolf.

But before the last members of the crowd returned to their normal business, a strange sound reverberated between the buildings. It sounded like someone pretending to laugh, closing their mouth between each annoying discharge.

"Maa Maa Maa!"

The crowd turned to see who the newcomer was, and whether it would be worth missing their next appointment.

Further down the road was a lanky birdfolk man. A large, red crest topped his head like a rooster's, and he was wearing a deep blue shirt and tight green leggings. His thick orange toes had black claws poking from the end, and he was scratching at the road with one.

"You fell for my ruse," he crowed, resuming his strange artificial laughter and clutching at his sides. "How could you believe that black paint on the wall was truly a tunnel!?"

Mira had never seen a werewolf blush, but that was the only word she could think of to describe the way the fur on his shoulders and cheeks stood out in little spikes before slowly smoothing back down. He waved a hand towards the hole that he had just made in the wall.

"It was dark in there. Anyone would have struggled to tell what lay before them, you dodger."

"Then why proceed at pace, you foolish dog!"

The werewolf snarled again, lowered himself slightly, and then launched towards the birdfolk man, racing in an unusual mix of four and two legged gaits.

His arms dipped to the ground occasionally, keeping him upright and pulling him quickly down the road.

But the laughing man was faster, pushing himself away down the street in a heartbeat and disappearing like the wind. Within moments, both of them were out of sight. As quiet fell across the street now that the loud adventurers had left, Mira heard a humming sound overhead. She glanced up and saw a giant bee float over the rooftops and then head off after them.

"What is that?" she asked a gnarled dryad walking past with a huge bundle of twigs on her back. "I've seen them flying around before." The woman glanced at the bee and then shrugged.

"Looks like one of Satonak's drones. He sends them out to fly around the city and keep an eye on everything."

Mira recognised the name of the Court Wizard.

"What do you suppose the drones are looking for?" she asked.

"If Satonak's behind it? Trouble." The dryad shook her head, and an acorn fell to the ground. "Ever since he's been keeping an eye on the city, people can't do as they please."

"Is it so different from the way Lord Cornucervin ran things?" asked Mira.

The woman shrugged.

"Lord Antlers never minded what you did, so long as he got a cut. This bloody wizard though..." She snorted, hefted the twigs on her shoulders back into place, and continued down the street.

The rest of the crowd lingered a little longer, in case there was another surprise contribution to the scene. Then a small team of builders arrived to fix the wall, making it clear that there wouldn't be any further excitement, so the audience dispersed.

Builders were always busy in Senoonheim. These ones were a squad of five ratfolk, working together to support long planks of lumber that lay across all of their shoulders at once. They wore workbelts hung with chisels and hammers and pouches full of nails, and they got to work repairing the hole in the fake stone wall without fuss. Mira stayed to watch, impressed by how quickly they repaired the scaffolding holding up the wall from inside. Then they filled the gap with a fresh wooden surface, carving the shape of the stones into it.

One of them unslung a backpack while the others tidied up small bits of offcut wood and sawdust they had left on the street, cleaning up the damage the werewolf had caused at the same time. The backpack builder pulled out a selection of paint jars and brushes.

By the time the others had finished cleaning, the wall looked exactly like an old crumbling pile of stones, with lichen growing through the gaps between them. The painter stepped back and nodded happily, her whiskers twitching, and then stepped forward to hang a 'wet paint' sign on the wall. One of the other ratfolk slapped the painter on the back warmly and then they all hurried away again. The whole process had barely taken two minutes.

Mira shook her head and kept walking, impressed by the work she had seen. She turned the corner and froze.

Prevos was on his knees in the dust beside the shrine, with his arms stretched out and palms faced up towards it. He had taken his helmet off, and his long mane hung over his downturned face like a rushing waterfall of molten gold. A small crowd had gathered around him, and the whole scene made it difficult for others to pass, which meant that they stopped to investigate as well. The resulting jam was gathering more and more attention.

"What on earth is he doing?" a man in front of her asked the air.

"You know what I think it is," answered a short woman with a sack over her shoulder. "I think he's a fanatic."

The first man turned, satisfaction oozing from his face as he relished the success of his vocal lure, and he lifted his broad-brimmed hat to scratch his head as he engaged with her.

"A fanatic? Aren't they usually dressed in rags, and covered in holy signs and whatnot? Call themselves pigeons or something of the like?"

The woman shrugged, an impressive feat considering the size of the sack she carried.

"They can look that way, as you say. But they call themselves that because they're like birds, right? Some of them are pretty bloody things, all colours and giant feathers curling all over the place, but others are dingy little brown speckled things."

The man nodded.

"Which one's he then?"

"A sparkly one! Look at the shine on that armour!"

"No, I understand the question," said an older man leaning against the wall, pressing tobacco into his pipe. He used the stem to gesture at Prevos, a movement that drew in the other two, who stepped closer to him. The trio looked at Prevos together.

"A shiny bird is doing what it's supposed to do, right? Making a big show of dancing and singing so that every other bird around knows that the shiny bird is the best at being a bird. So with a fanatic that would be the equivalent of being dressed in rags and covered in sigils, surely? Standing on a box outside the castle, yelling about the end of the world, so every other fanatic in the city knows that they're looking at the best fanatic."

He drew a small pack of matches from a pocket and lit one, sucking on his pipe until it caught.

"On the other hand, a drab little bird isn't doing anything impressive, and same with this guy. If he's meant to be a fanatic, he's got the mood wrong."

"That's my point!" replied the hat man happily.

The woman with the sack scowled.

"I dunno about that." She stepped forward, walking up beside Prevos. She reached out and rapped on one of his upstretched arms, making a sound like a dish that had been dropped and was rolling in a tight circle on the ground.

"Hey? Are you one of these fanatics then?" she asked.

Chapter Eighteen

P revos lifted his head and brought his arms down. He used one hand to push his mane back and hook it behind his ears. He blinked as though he was just waking up and turned to look at the woman who had spoken to him.

"Ma'am?" he asked. His whiskers shivered in confusion.

"Me and these lads think you might be some sort of fanatic, but we're not sure about this outfit of yours." The woman waved a hand towards his armour. "It doesn't really match," she added.

"Outfit?" Prevos looked down at the plate armour covering him and then back at the woman with wide eyes. "This is my holy armour. I received it when I was commissioned into the Order of Trankwill."

"He *is* a fanatic," the woman yelled back to the men standing near Mira, turning away from Prevos. "But he's a special one that gets armour."

"Fancy that," murmured the man with the hat. Appreciative muttering spread throughout the audience that blocked the street.

"Look, that's all very interesting, but are you done here or what?" yelled a voice from the far side of Prevos, where the crowd coming up the street was thicker.

"Excuse me?" Prevos's ears twitched.

"You'll need that armour if you don't get out of the bloody way, that's all I'm saying," yelled a different voice from the crowd.

"Alright, I think that's enough!" Mira called out. She hurried forward, scooped an arm under one of Prevos's and lifted him to his feet. Or at least that was what she intended to do. Instead, she felt herself pushing her own feet deeper into the ground. Trying to lift Prevos and his armour was like trying to lift an entire house by herself. "Come on, up you come," she said loudly, smiling at the crowd.

"Mira, you returned!" Prevos smiled broadly and stood up with the clatter of a cutlery drawer being slammed shut. The crowd shuddered back into motion with a noise like a waking cat's yawn.

Mira pulled Prevos to the side of the street to be sure no one would claim he was still in the way. Then she realised she had his hands in hers and let go quickly.

"Of course I came back. It would have been weird to leave without you." She looked up into his happy face. "Did you do what you wanted to? Did you commune with Varivexes?"

His smile turned into a frown.

"I tried, but it was hard to tell if she was listening."

"You wanted her to help you avoid annoying people, right?" asked Mira.

"Yes."

Mira considered the way he had set himself in the middle of a narrow street full of traders.

"Yes, I don't think she really taught you anything worthwhile yet," Mira said.

"I fear as much," he sighed. "Still, sometimes Trankwill speaks to me in my dreams or introspective moments. Perhaps I may yet hear from Varivexes!"

"Yes, maybe," Mira agreed, to let him keep his optimism. "Come on, I need to put these posters up. I was going to start at the Sprog and Sparrow." She patted the roll of papers under her arm.

"Very well," agreed Prevos. "On the way, I would be pleased to hear about your life before you came to Senoonheim."

***

Before she had ever met Loam, Mira stood at the edge of the market in Wallis with her arms crossed, leaning against the rough wood of someone's home. She looked out on rows of tables and stalls, piled with food and leather and metal and crowded with morning customers intent on finding a bargain before some scoundrel snatched it away. Early morning browsers in the market seemed to feel that they accrued a moral authority when they spotted a bargain first, although apparently the same authority didn't apply to any one else who might get in before them.

The travelling merchant Malcomb mimicked her position against the wall and pulled out a small, leather-bound flask from a hidden pocket in the small of his back. He unscrewed the cap and offered it to her. She smiled and held up a hand to show that she didn't need any, especially not as the sun was still yawning its way over the horizon. Malcomb took a slow sip and then replaced the cap and tucked the flask away again.

"That's good after a long night," he said.

"What was so long about it?" asked Mira.

"I've been setting up all night. We arrived after sunset. Travel through Whinnia has become pretty dangerous," he replied, scrubbing his fingers through his hair. His eyes were wide and the skin beneath them was dark.

"The roads are getting overgrown?" Whinnia was a broad and flat land, covered in waving fields of grass and some grains, occupied by little other than the nomadic herds of stock animals that the Whinnians shepherded from one area of the realm to another. That meant that there were few permanent roads built across Whinnia, but many common roads instead.

Common roads existed where travellers and herders trampled down the grass, pressing the soil into packed dirt through the sheer number of creatures travelling over it. If you were going where many had gone before in Whinnia, then your way would be easy. However if you decided to take a path more grassy and in want of wear, you could, but you would contend with overgrown plants that fought your progress, and soft soils that would rise up about your feet and try to pull you into the dark mud.

"If it were only that," grumbled Malcomb. "No, it was the bandits."

"Bandits?" Mira was surprised. She knew that bandits existed, but she had been chatting with Malcomb when he came to trade in Wallis for five years and he had never suggested that they were an impediment to him and his wagon train before. "Have they grown brave or stupid enough to attack a merchant train with armed guards?"

"They try and, honestly, it's hard to fight them off! There's something co-ordinated happening out there in the Far-Grasso." Malcomb turned to look away from the market and down the hill beneath the buildings of Wallis. It was as though he were staring out across the grass, picking out memories of the roads he had travelled and the dangers he had encountered. Unfortunately, the buildings of the town completely filled his vision, so, instead, he was treated to the sight of a woman emptying a chamber pot into the ditch.

Malcomb's face twisted and he turned away, then refocused his attention on Mira.

"They knew when to strike. They knew when my teams would be tired. And they stopped before they bled me completely dry."

"That might just be awful luck?" suggested Mira, half question and half hopeful wish.

Malcomb shook his head.

"No chance. They all wore red bandanas tied around their upper arms. It was like a uniform or something. They were part of a group."

"Red bandanas?" A shiver ran down the back of Mira's neck and she clasped her fingers together to stop them from shaking. "Tied about here, with a long piece hanging down the side?" She touched her left bicep.

"Exactly," said Malcomb with surprise. His eyes grew wider. "Have you seen someone dressed like that?"

"It's worse than you think," she said. She nodded her head a little to one side and Malcomb turned to see what she was indicating.

Walking through the aisles between the market stalls were two large men with long hair tied into tight ponytails. They wore functional leather armour with metal plates affixed to it and they were chatting cheerfully to each other. The two men strolled forward without paying any attention to whether or not something was in their way. Neither of them seemed to notice the way the market-goers ducked away from them with the swirling movements of limbo dancers. Both wore a red bandana around their left arms.

Malcomb made a quiet choking noise, as though he had swallowed a mouthful of water the wrong way during a funeral. He fought his own body to avoid being noticed, and Mira watched his neck twist as he tried to keep the noise to himself. She put a hand on his elbow.

The two men walked by and headed further down the aisles. Mira waited until she was sure that they wouldn't overhear her, and then another minute just in case, before she lifted her hand from Malcomb's elbow.

"They've been showing up all season. The First Seat brought them into Wallis."

"Bower brought them in?" Malcomb's brow creased. "On one hand, I'm not surprised by the ridiculous decisions that old fool makes. On the other hand, why would he bring grass-pirates into the city?"

"He even invited some of their leaders to join him in the Great Hall."

Malcomb shook his head.

"I suppose if they spend all the money they stole from us merchants, then that's one way to get our money back?" He smiled weakly. "Seems a poor substitute instead of just keeping the Far-Grasso Sea safe for merchants travelling through it in the first place though," he added with a scowl.

"I agree. I knew there was something strange going on with them. I mean, you always see travellers passing through Wallis who like to act tough, but these ones have even more unearned confidence than most." Adventurers that came through Wallis were usually travelling from one mighty warlord's tower to some lost and haunted mine. They always claimed they were do-gooders, but they spent more time slamming huge doors open and striding through them than actually helping anyone.

"If they are connected to any of the bandits who stopped us out there, then be careful. I truly don't think they would have any qualms about stubbing out our little lives like candles at the end of the day," Malcomb muttered. He kept his eyes on the bandits as they walked away through the market.

Mira nodded.

Chapter Nineteen

"**C**ome on," said Malcomb, shaking off the encounter with the red-armed bandits as though they were fleas on his sides. "There's a performance going on this morning and I think it would be a great way to get our minds off all of that trouble!"

"What sort of performance?" asked Mira. She thought about the sort of entertainers that came through Wallis, trying to earn a bit of coin in the market square before continuing their travels. "Fire dancers? Maybe a falconer?"

"No, this is theatre! I saw them setting up overnight!"

"Theatre? Like, actors?"

"Exactly!"

Mira was impressed. Wallis had no actors of its own, and she had heard descriptions of plays before but never seen one. The people of Whinnia entertained themselves with long, repetitive songs about the exploits of the great heads of the houses, sung by old men sitting in the warmest spot by the fire and accompanied by slow, mournful plucking on simple stringed harps. Listening to their assonant stories of men drinking loud enough to wake monsters and then dying on a dragon's pile of gold had never been Mira's idea of a fun night. But plays sounded different.

"Alright, you're on," she grinned.

Malcomb led the way through the market to the square at the far end. There were a few performers plying their trades already at work. One was a man covered in grey paint and standing on a box. Mira assumed he was meant to look like a stone statue, but he rather spoiled the effect by constantly waving his arms to shoo away the birds landing on his shoulders. Judging by the streak of droppings down his back, he wasn't having much luck keeping them away.

Behind the performers a broad wooden platform had been erected. It stood two feet above the muddy ground, and looked as though the builders had scrupulously avoided buying any planks the same length as each other. At the back of the stage hung a wide curtain of canvas, painted with blue sky and grey clouds. Sitting on the stage in front of the curtain were some pieces of scenery. To the right, Mira saw a strange triangular shape, about as tall as her shoulder, with dark smears painted on it. She couldn't tell if it was built of wood, or cloth, or something else.

"What is that?" she asked, pointing at the triangle.

Malcomb glanced over.

"Looks like Wallis to me."

"Really?" Mira took another look, surprised. She didn't spend much time out on the plains, so she had never been reminded of what the steep hill Wallis was built on would look like from afar. *I suppose it was something like that,* she thought, remembering when she had arrived as a teenager. If you squinted your eyes and already wanted to think that it was Wallis. "So my next question would be, why is there a mini construction of the town on the stage?"

"I'm not sure," said Malcomb. "Look, here they come! Let's find out!"

Mira was surprised to see an elf man walk through a gap in the curtain at the back of the stage and stride to the front. He wore incredibly tight pants. If she hadn't seen the seam running up the side of his legs, Mira would have sworn that the material was actually just a layer of paint. Strange, puffy shorts bulged like a ball around the top of his legs, and he wore a tightly buttoned doublet. He looked around the market and bowed as though he was accepting a welcoming applause, although Mira and Malcomb were the only ones paying attention. An old woman by the statue man leaned over and spat in the mud before wandering away.

"Welcome my lords and ladies," bellowed the elf with a smile. "It is my pleasure to bring you the story of the last king of Whinnia! Attend the tale!"

He bowed again and swirled away behind the curtain.

"Do you know much about the last king of Whinnia?" Mira whispered at Malcomb's shoulder. He shrugged.

The actors came out and a story unfolded before her eyes. It was like nothing Mira had ever seen before. The people on stage wore poor-quality clothing. Their make-up was painted on so heavily that she could see the thick moustache of one man beneath the pale colour that was meant to be his skin and the darkness of his grinning lips.

But, despite the glaringly fake construction of everything on the stage, she fell into the story completely. She believed that an old man was the young prince, son of the previous king. She believed that the small construction on the side of the stage really was Wallis, and that these events were happening there. She wasn't the only one entranced, as more and more people walking through the market stopped to watch.

The prince was spoiled and greedy, indulged with treasures from his father. But then his father died and the prince was crowned. The new king travelled across Whinnia with his soldiers and returned in triumph, declaring the land to be free from fear. But a ghost followed him into his hall, a ghost that consisted of a broad, white cloth draped over the head of some actor, with their hands poking out from underneath and dusted with powder. The ghost lifted their hands over their head and gave out the kind of wobbly "whoooooo!" that could only be forced from the throat of someone extremely aware of how ridiculous they look but who is being paid to do it anyway. The ghost warned the king that peace cannot be declared by the whim of a ruler, especially not one who manages their lands through the secret observations of hidden supporters instead of by their just authority.

At this point in the play a snakefolk man walked onto the stage, wearing a long, dark headdress that fell over his shoulders. At least, Mira assumed that the green scales painted onto the human actor's face were meant to make him look like a snakefolk man, but she had never met one of the snakefolk so she had no real idea. He stood beside the king and called out: "There was a time when I searched for steel, but then I found that secrets are stronger!" Other snakefolk peeked around the edges of the scenery, representing the spies that the king's accomplice had sent throughout the kingdom.

"Just like Loam's Froge society, am I right?" whispered Malcomb, with a good-natured poke of an elbow.

Mira giggled.

"Shhh, one of them might hear you." She smiled and pushed him back.

"Our eyes will blaze a path to paradise!" said the snakefolk man in the headdress with a horrible smile. Then a feast was brought for him and the king to share.

As they ate, the snakefolk characters slipped away, and new actors snuck on stage. They moved with exaggerated tip-toe steps, which Mira supposed was meant to show that they were sneaking and the king would not notice them. The new actors wore rags with patches that were similar to the banners of the Whinnian Houses.

"As always, poor leaders invoke the anger of the common people," said Malcomb.

They watched as the horselords and commoners rose up around the king. He sneered and said, "I spurn thee like curs in my way", then tried to kick some of the nearest ones back down to the ground. But there were too many of them and they surrounded him like a wall, hiding him completely from view. A gleaming knife rose above the pack of actors and then plunged down. A scream shook the market and then the crowd of actors dispersed, revealing the king lying on the floor in a pool of red rags that were laid out around a knife hilt sticking up from his back.

There was a celebratory scene after the death of the bad king, and a quick scene that showed the horselords choosing the first First Seat to rule Whinnia, but then the play was over, the actors were bowing, and a handful of crew were walking around the audience with bowls, seeking contributions from those who had watched. Mira gladly threw some coins in the bowl, and then moved to the stage so that she could have a closer look.

She ran her fingers across the miniature hill. It had a rough texture, the stiff scratch of canvas covered in paint. Up close she could see previous layers of colours that had been painted over.

"This has been other things before," she said over her shoulder to Malcomb.

"Indeed it has! That small, misshapen lump has been a stalagmite in the Mines of the Black Chasm and a coral reef beneath the ocean, suitable for a crab to sing upon," said a new voice.

Mira looked up and saw the actor who had played the last king of Whinnia crouching on the stage beside her. She could see his wrinkles were filled with makeup in an attempt to make him look younger than he was. The stitches in his clothes were so loose that they looked like a ladder between his sleeves and shirt.

"It's amazing how convincing something can be, even when we know it isn't real," said Mira.

"Just like the real world," nodded the actor. "All around us are people trying to convince us that they are kind or friendly, or strong and intimidating, or" —the actor glanced over Mira's head before finishing softly— "or trying to convince us that they are competent rulers."

He stood up and waved to Mira and Malcomb.

"Thank you for watching the play," he grinned. "And watch out for the actors in your lives," he added with a wink.

"I don't know any actors," said Mira.

"Oh, you do!" he said. "Everyone you know is playing a part, and one day that mask might slip. We performers are just honest enough to let you know what our part is when you meet us."

Chapter Twenty

Mira remembered another walk through the market in Wallis, months after she saw the play. The market stretched along the main street of Wallis, which wound back and forth up the hill to the First Seat's Great Hall at the summit. She looked over piles of pale and dirty root vegetables in their baskets: turnips, carrots, potatoes. Mira picked up one carrot in particular. The woman behind the stall raised an eyebrow and said, "I noticed that one too. Make sure your husband isn't the easily intimidated type if you buy that one." Mira laughed along with the woman and didn't bother to explain that she wasn't married. That she had never even been tempted.

One of the next stalls was lined with small apples of such a pale red that they were almost yellow.

"Not the best crop at the moment, is it, Joni?" she said to the woman behind the stall.

The thin woman shrugged. She wore a long, dark blue dress with two thick straps over her shoulders, and a thickly woven cream-coloured tunic underneath.

"No, they aren't the best. More sour than I would like. But still, they're apples and they're edible. Do you want one?"

"I've got to save my money for flour and seed," explained Mira regretfully.

Joni smiled.

"Go on Mira, have one anyway. If I know you, you've been up and rushing around without remembering to stop for any sort of breakfast for yourself."

The woman made a good point. Mira was very aware of the tight grumbling coming from her stomach. She accepted an apple.

Mira bit into the fruit as she walked away, and then held the morsel in her mouth while she looked over the next stalls. With Joni only a couple of tables away, Mira couldn't spit the sour flesh of the apple out without looking ungrateful. And she knew it would be ungrateful, even if the taste was making her tongue curl backwards. An apple was an apple, and this one was free as well. Mira crunched slowly, trying to ignore the foul juice that ran down her throat, until only a thin core was left.

She was looking for a good place to dispose of the core when she bumped into someone.

"Oh, I'm sorry!" she exclaimed and turned to see who it was.

The man she had bumped into looked small due to the way he hunched forward. When she thought back on the moment, Mira was amazed that he gave this impression, as he was a tall figure when uncurled. In fact, he could be quite an imposing presence when he wanted to be. But he stood bent forward as though he had grown up in tunnels that were much too small for him and never overcame the habit. He held his arms curled in front of his chest, like a mole.

Some people exude the natural smallness of their soul, no matter how they try to puff themselves up.

He looked her over, eyes travelling up and down in the most direct evaluation she had ever experienced. He valued her out in exactly the same way she had seen cattle hands give a visual inspection to a cow they wanted to buy, and he did it with just as much disregard of the animal being measured. Mira was about to slap the man when he smiled and spoke.

"No trouble at all, from a, uh, lovely specimen such as yourself." His face was broad and pale and covered with a thin film of dampness, like the underbelly of a fish. He was one of the frogfolk. Mira had met a few others of his kind before. His dark eyes and limp smile made her feel sullied, as though his words alone were making her dirty.

"My name is Loam," he said, extending a hand towards her.

"Oh, you're Loam Ratsweat?" Mira couldn't help replying. She had heard of him. Of course she had heard of Loam. Everyone in the whole of Whinnia knew exactly who Loam was, although she imagined that most of them wouldn't have been able to identify him if they saw him. Loam Ratsweat was the leader of the Froge, a tribe of aggressive frogfolk who were seeking to build their influence in Whinnia. He had been very successful in his efforts, rising to become a personal advisor to the First Seat of Whinnia. He was probably the most powerful person in the realm, given that rumours said the First Seat was losing his marbles to old age.

Loam grimaced, although he kept his hand out. Mira reached out and took it, intending to shake it, but he pulled her hand closer and twisted his, so that her palm was facing the ground. He pulled her hand up to his thick lips and kissed the back of it before releasing. She pulled it back as quickly as she could without being insulting. When she thought she could get away with it, she wiped her hand on the back of her skirts.

"It so frustrates me when people pronounce my name that way," complained Loam. "It sounds like something... unsanitary."

"I'm sorry," said Mira. He waved her apology aside, no more concerned with her apologies and feelings than he would be concerned about a fly.

"It's actually Rats-Weat. From Rats-Wheat. Wheat from the town of Rats. It's a very distinguished name, steeped in history."

"Oh." Mira didn't know how distinguished his name could be. She had absolutely never heard of his name before he had gained prominence in the politics of Whinnia. Surely that meant any renown attached to the name came from his own political manoeuvring in support of the current, terrible First Seat? She didn't think such behaviour was distinguished, but then again some people kept ferrets as pets and loved them despite their slippery, evasive nature and the way they bit the fingers that fed them. Perhaps the same could be true of politicians.

"Where is Rats?"

"It hasn't been called that in a long time," said Loam dismissively.

"Is it part of Whinnia? It sounds a bit like it could be a village in the west?"

Loam frowned, and looked around as though he was searching for something else to talk about instead of answering her question. Suddenly his eyes brightened as a thought bubbled up to the surface of the mire that was his mind and he focused his attention on Mira.

"What are you here in the market for?"

Hardly the sort of deft segue that Mira might have expected from someone with a commanding political reputation.

"Buying some stock for my bakery," she explained.

"Oh, you have a bakery! How fascinating!"

Mira immediately regretted her admission. He was exactly the sort of person who would now be spending far too much time lingering around outside the shop, waiting for the chance to come in and keep her talking when she had work to do.

"I have a sweet tooth," Loam said with a smile. The smile revealed how gummy his mouth was, belying the idea of a sweet tooth or, indeed, of any teeth. Mira felt a shudder building in the base of her spine and fought to hold it off.

"Perhaps I will see you there sometime," she said weakly, hoping that the conversation would end.

"You can be sure of it," he said. "I will seek out your shop in search of something tasty." His eyes roamed across her. "I am sure that I will have my appetites met by your talents."

Mira couldn't hold back the shudder any longer and it rolled up her back and then out through her limbs. The movement made her snort sharply.

"I can see the idea excites you as much as it excites me," said Loam. "Try not to get carried away before I see you again." He nodded his head in a half-bow and then walked away through the market.

Mira wiped her hands on the front of her skirts. She didn't know how someone could make another person feel so unclean by just the way they spoke and the movement of their eyes, but Loam had perfected the skill.

Chapter Twenty-One

Memories pressed forward but Mira only gave a brief explanation of her life in Whinnia to Prevos as they walked back through the streets of Senoonheim. He looked glad to hear her story, but when she lapsed into silence he kept both sides of the conversation going by himself. He even managed to prompt himself into explaining further details; ("Why was I on my knees by the shrine you ask? Well, the reason for that was..."), a skill that Mira found remarkable. She was happy to let him talk as she wasn't sure what else to say. She felt uncomfortable giving him more details about Whinnia. The idea felt like it would leave her vulnerable, though she couldn't pinpoint why.

The reason Prevos was on the street was that he had assumed a pose associated with prayer in Trankwill's temples and was meditating in an attempt to make contact with Varivexes. He had hoped that the connection between the goddesses would allow him to reach the mosquito queen. He was disappointed to not have felt any clear response, but his hopes remained high that communication was coming.

"Here's the tavern," interrupted Mira when they arrived at the Sprog and Sparrow. Prevos paused and looked up at the sign. Painted on the broad, wooden board was an image of a baby wrapped in white cloth. The corners of the cloth were brought together and held up in the beak of a small, round, brown bird. The artist had gone so far as to add drops of desperate perspiration leaping from the bird's face, to indicate the effort needed to carry such a relatively gigantic package.

Prevos frowned. Laughter came bubbling out of the tavern. He shook his head.

"Thank you for the invitation, but I will not enter such premises. They promise distraction from my holy vows."

"Really? What vows have you taken?" asked Mira.

"I must abstain from gambling and drink and lesser vices, so that I may remain focused on Trankwill's wishes for the world." His voice changed when he spoke like this. It was flatter, and deeper, as though he was reciting something that he had read out loud over and over before, but his eyes lost their focus and she could see that even he wasn't really listening to himself.

"That's very interesting," said Mira. "Sometimes I wish I had the self-discipline to do something like that."

"Yes, because you are surrounded by temptation all day," agreed Prevos.

Mira snorted. "I'm sorry? What do you mean?"

"You bake sweet treats and cakes." Prevos banged a fist to his stomach, making the armour clang. "Such things are a burden on a person's body and cause them to struggle when they should not. It must be difficult to be part of such a trade."

Mira gritted her teeth. They had been having such a good afternoon so far.

"Perhaps it is not so big a deal as all that," she said. "You should try one sometime, perhaps you will see that your vows are too strict."

"My vows are not too strict," replied Prevos, his eyes widening in surprise. "They are simply what is required for me to uphold Trankwill's desire for peace throughout the world. She brings peace to my soul."

"Didn't you say you wanted people to find you less annoying?"

"Yes, but I don't understand why you would mention that."

"Surely telling people that their lives are temptations and the things people enjoy doing will lead to trouble isn't very peaceful?"

"Why must you vex me?" He frowned. "In any case, I will not enter this tavern."

"Okay. I will be back soon, I need to put these up all around."

Inside the Sprog and Sparrow, an early evening crowd had already begun to gather. A few workers who had already knocked off were sitting among the tables, but the tavern was being propped up mostly by weathered, older folk who always appeared in such places. Mira was sure that these people didn't actually have homes but existed only within the walls of the tavern. Sometimes she wondered whether they were actually wood spirits, following the planks that had been made from their trees. Perhaps their tough, wrinkled skin was a manifestation of the bark that would otherwise cover them. The inevitable look in their eyes suggested that over the course of their lives they had seen everything and could no longer be surprised.

Mira walked to the bar and leaned on it. There was no one behind the bar. She turned to look around the tavern in case one of the staff was tidying the tables or serving one of the grown-in regulars. Nothing. She turned back around.

A large woman with a fleshy jawline stood behind the bar, looking at her. The woman's hair was black and thick and rolled off her head like a landslide. Eyebrows like black fences dominated her face. A small toothpick stabbed forward from the corner of her mouth.

"Greetings," she said in a long, slow, deep voice.

"Uh, were you there the whole time?" asked Mira. She leaned forward to peer behind the bar, wondering if the woman had enough space to hide there if she crouched.

"Yes," she said warmly. Something about her accent meant that she managed to use roughly five syllables to pronounce the single E in the word. Mira was fairly sure she even heard an extra E at the beginning before the Y.

"Do you know the owner of this tavern?" Mira asked.

"Yes! Me! My name is Jacqui Nytona, and I am a regular human bartender." The woman smiled and her teeth glinted sharply.

"I see. Well, it's you I need to talk to then. I was wondering if it would be alright to put up one of these posters in the tavern?" Mira unrolled her bundle and laid one out across the bar. At the last second, she lifted them away from a bubbling puddle of what she could only hope was spilled beer.

Jacqui peered at the posters and smiled.

"These look like very positive community building posters that would encourage lots of new people to visit the bar, people who might not have anyone who worries about where they have come from or whether they return. What a lovely idea this is!"

"You don't mind? Oh great! I'm hoping that I can meet the coven here, at least to start. You might even make some money from it."

"Outstanding!" replied Jacqui. The tavern owner graciously provided some simple tacks for Mira which she used to stick the poster up on the wall near the door. The attention of the bark-skinned regulars shifted in her direction, so she stepped aside to let them see the poster more clearly. She turned and addressed them all.

"There's going to be a coven meeting here, from Saturday night onwards. We'll welcome everyone!"

No one applauded this brief speech, which was a bit of a let down in Mira's estimation.

After she left the tavern, Mira and Prevos moved in an expanding spiral through the nearby streets, leaving posters in every tavern willing to let her put them up, and on the walls outside those that objected. Mira convinced most of the barkeeps by insinuating that she might bring future meetings of the coven to them. By the time the sky was beginning to darken, Mira had run out of posters.

She and Prevos stood facing each other as the streets slowly drained of passersby.

"Thank you for coming with me today," she said.

"You are welcome, I have enjoyed myself."

"That's hard to believe. You spent most of the time just standing outside, waiting for me."

The catfolk man nodded seriously. "Walking and talking with you was pleasant."

"I hope so." Mira smiled. "In any case, I try to get to bed early, so..."

"That is good practice. Trankwill blesses those who take care of their bodies."

"Good. Thank her for me. See you later I guess."

"Good evening, Mira."

Prevos put his hands at his sides and bowed slightly before walking away down the street. Mira watched him go, thinking carefully. *Is he really who he seems to be? The people I left in Whinnia turned out to be someone different on the inside, and this city itself seems to be just the same! Will the people here be any different?* She caught the eye of her reflection in the window of a shop. Her eyebrow raised and she smirked at herself.

"Are you pleased by the idea that he is who he seems to be?" she asked herself. "Are you wondering whether Master Ulvilhelm d'Earthy is who he seems to be too?" Her cheeks grew warm. She tore her eyes away from her reflection and hurried home.

Chapter Twenty-Two

M ira dreamed about life back in Whinnia and woke up with sheets binding her tighter than a kidnapper's ropes. She disentangled herself and reminded herself that she wasn't in Whinnia anymore. She didn't have to deal with any of their nonsense.

"You didn't think it was nonsense while you were there," she said to herself as she tied up her hair in front of her mirror.

"Well, maybe there was more nonsense at the end," she admitted, before turning to the door and heading down to her shop. "Loam and the First Seat brought a lot of problems with them, but my friends back home were good."

She began preparing her bread for the day and remembered how quickly Bovo and Amella had vanished as soon as she got into trouble with the First Seat. She thought of the advice they had given her to deal with Loam. "Maybe they weren't that good, really," she murmured. "But I haven't done any better here."

She had never thought of herself as the sort of person who struggled to make friends. But here she was, alone.

Mira straightened her back and reminded herself that her new coven was in progress. Gathering a few witches would be just the thing she needed to build up a community around her once again.

Then she rolled forward, stretching and kneading the dough on the bench in front of her. She smiled as she pressed into the dough. As always, she felt better when she took control of things, whether it be the bread beneath her hands, or the coven that she was building. She wasn't going to be alone anymore.

Mira sweated and puffed while she moved bread in and out of her ovens, setting the crunchy loaves on their shelves and then bustling to get more. Rolls and bread, biscuits and small cakes, all laid out with care. She sighed sadly as she used the last of her panicgrass dew from Whinnia and set the empty jar back on the shelf. She dashed between the shop and kitchen as customers trickled in alongside the first glimpses of early morning sunlight. Eventually, she finished the day's baking and was able to settle into the regular routine of serving customers.

The bell over the door would ring, she would smile at the person who came in, exchange pleasantries with them as they bought something from her, and then take a deep breath before doing it all again with the next customer.

She was just taking a moment to roll her shoulders and loosen her muscles when she heard the hollow dong of someone knocking on the front window.

"Hello?" she called, peering out the window. Standing outside and ducking his head under the "open" sign hanging in the window was a narrow man with pale skin and small eyes. His light brown hair swirled in a thin tuft from the top of his head, like the tail of a bird.

The man was opening and closing his mouth, twisting his lips into exaggerated positions.

"I'm sorry, what do you need?" called Mira, hoping he would clarify what was going on. The man seemed to realise that he had been seen, because he smiled and shook his arms in excitement. He then leaned a little lower under the "open" sign and repeated his strange mouth movements, now adding elaborate hand gestures to his face shapes. He looked as though he was playing an invisible musical instrument.

Mira sighed.

She walked around the counter and over to the door, pulling it open and leaning out to talk directly to the man.

"Are you alright?" she asked.

"Oh!" The man acted surprised to see her, as though he hadn't been exchanging ever more fervent but opaque communications with her through the window only moments earlier. "Hello. I was just wondering if you were still open?"

Mira turned her head slightly and looked at the "open" sign next to his face, an oval of pale wood with black letters on it.

The man followed Mira's gaze, turning his head and facing the sign mere inches away from him. Then he turned back to her and smiled again. He didn't say anything.

"So..." Mira began, motioning for him to finish the sentence.

He mimicked her hand circling and his forehead creased.

"So... are you open?" he asked again.

Mira tried to restrain her moan but it wriggled free of her grasp before she could stop it.

"Yes. I am," she told him, before waving for him to follow her inside.

Once inside the shop she placed herself behind the counter again. He walked around the walls, inspecting the bread that lined the shelves. He made small, confused noises as he moved, like a dog being confronted with a vegetable dinner.

"Do you need any help?" Mira asked.

"No no, thank you, no I'm fine," he replied with a happy smile that immediately melted off his face as he leaned closer to the loaves, squinting at them as though they had been decorated with holy writing that he could not translate.

Mira watched him drift around the store. He barely noticed two other customers come in, buy their rolls, and leave. Suddenly, he pointed to the pile of scones at the end of the counter.

"What are these?" he asked.

Mira followed his finger to the small handwritten sign she had placed in front of the pile, then back up his arm to the completely unaware face that was watching her.

"Those are scones." She paused, trying to anticipate what it was that had given him trouble. "Do you know what a scone is?"

"Of course!" he laughed. He looked down at the pile. His eyes slowly crept sideways to look at her again.

"They're a bit like a cross between a roll and a cake," she explained. "These are cheesy and have a bit of paprika in them. They're very tasty and filling."

He smiled again and straightened up.

"That sounds perfect! How much are they?"

Mira closed her eyes. She knew that the price was written on the same sign that he hadn't been able to read.

"They cost twenty-five each."

"Excellent, I'll take one!"

Mira opened her eyes again and picked one of the scones off the pile. The man dug a hand into his pocket and left a handful of coins on the table. Mira passed him his scone and then began flicking the coins towards herself along the counter, counting as she did.

"Five, and ten is fifteen, and one is sixteen, and two, and two and two..." She paused.

"This is twenty-two," she told the man.

He smiled again.

"Twenty-two is less than twenty-five," she continued.

He did not respond.

"You still owe me another three for the scone please," she added, nearly in tears.

"Oh!"

He dug in his pocket again and pulled out another coin, reaching over to place it directly on her palm. She looked down and saw the outstretched wings of a penguin in flight impressed onto the coin beside a large number two.

Mira felt as though she was going to explode. All her energy was draining out of her feet, and leaving a pure ball of frustration in its place. She didn't know whether she was going to collapse in hysterics or scream in the pale man's face. Instead of either, she drew in a deep breath and then said, in a voice so calm that deer would graze happily in it, "This is only worth two. You need one more."

The man continued his search. I'm just going to give it to him anyway, Mira had just thought in despair, when he triumphantly removed a larger coin from his pocket and thunked it down onto the counter.

They both leaned in to investigate the coin. In the center of its octagonal shape, the number twenty-five was clearly visible.

"I have a twenty-five!" declared the man.

"Enjoy your scone," answered Mira, picking up the coin and shoving the others back towards him. He scooped them up and poured them into his pocket once more then took a bite from his scone as he left the shop.

Mira bones washed away in the flood of relief that poured through her as the door closed behind him and she collapsed onto the counter.

That's probably enough customers for today then. Thank goodness the guild inspector is coming soon.

Chapter Twenty-Three

T he representative of the Reverential Ensemble of Bakers walked around Mira's bakery with a face that suggested he had just unwillingly licked a lemon. He made a great display of leaning in over the heavy wooden shelves and running his white-gloved finger along the surface, before holding it up to peer at his fingertip. After he repeated this process on the seventh shelf he spun around to face Mira, one finger held accusingly aloft. His eyes were wide and shining with triumph, and his lips twisted in a victorious smile. It made him look like a ferret who had caught a bird. Mira leaned in to inspect his finger herself and, when she squinted, was just able to make out a slightly darker discolouration on the tip of his finger.

She lifted her eyes to meet his eyes. His face was frozen in his expression of smug pleasure. Mira wasn't sure if he was even aware of her presence. She sighed, leaned back against the wall and crossed her arms.

"Yes, I see. You have found some dust," she said.

"Found some dust?" he spluttered. "You belittle this as just 'some dust'? What does it say to the reputation of the Reverential Ensemble when our customers find their daily bread absolutely coated with filth?" He waggled the finger at her, and his face darkened.

Mira rolled her eyes and didn't answer. The representative sent by the guild in Whinnia had been like this as well. In her first year there she had received a list of complaints that sent her barely-twenty-year-old self into a panic. In response, she'd sought out the actual rules required by the guild. She had gone to the guildhouse ready to argue her case, only to have an older woman listen to her concerns briefly in the front room, then chuckle and send her on her way. The woman had reassured her that she wouldn't be stricken from the guild-roll over anything so minor.

After that experience, Mira had familiarised herself with the full guild rules. It hadn't taken her long to memorise them, and they weren't remotely as strict as the inspectors wanted them to be.

In her time in Senoonheim, she had worked to eliminate any problems the inspector might find, only for him to make up new offences whenever he thought he could get away with it. One time he had triumphantly scooped a spoonful of flour out of a small barrel in her kitchen before calling her over.

"And what do you call this!?" he had asked, shoving the spoonful of white powder towards her, spilling a pale cloud on the floor as he did.

"Flour?" she had replied slowly, unsure of his point.

"Ah, but what is in the flour!?" he snapped back. He stuck his little finger into the spoon and then licked some of the white dust off the end.

Mira watched him, wondering if he was going to offer any more explanation than that, but when he didn't she answered: "… More flour?"

"This flour has been diluted with sawdust, hasn't it!" The man's eyebrows were quivering violently.

"Sawdust?" Mira looked closer. "I don't think so," she said.

"I can taste it! It's earthy and bitter. That's oak!" The man smacked his lips as though trying to get the taste out of his mouth. Mira glanced at the barrel he had been inspecting.

"Do you think that, maybe, you can taste oak in this flour because this flour has been sitting in an oak storage barrel?" she asked.

The man glared at her for several seconds and then jammed the spoon back into the barrel and left it there. He had signed her off for the guild after that visit, but Mira knew that he wasn't happy about it.

The current inspection went much better. Apart from the faint concept of dust on a single shelf, the guild representative was unable to come up with any other potential infraction. Mira thought he would shake himself apart in frustration.

After the guild inspector left, Mira grinned to herself. She had managed to send him on his way with his vindictive punishing nature entirely unfulfilled. It was a petty victory, but after the last few inspections it felt good.

Sometimes Mira wondered whether it was even worth putting up with all this petty frustration in order to remain part of the Reverential Ensemble of Bakers. Of course, trying to leave the guild was frowned upon quite seriously. Seriously enough that the representative that they would send to discuss the situation would be made of more muscle than a horse, and would probably express no emotion at all while they destroyed her shop or her face, depending on how apologetic she was.

But Mira had to admit that the guild didn't really need to use the stick that they kept in reserve for such situations. They had plenty of carrots to share with other guild members. When she had first started her bakery, the guild had provided ingredients and training for her to get started. They asked for a cut of her profits, but they also made sure there weren't too many bakers in her quarter of the city. There was a lot of benefit in working together with others.

Chapter Twenty-Four

F riday night arrived. Mira sat in front of her mirror, staring at the few pots of makeup she had scraped together during her time in Senoonheim. She had never known which makeup suited her best and generally just painted a black point against the outer corner of her eye. She didn't want d'Earthy to think that she was as desperate for company as she actually was, so she wasn't going to try too hard to impress him, but she figured it was a good opportunity to see what effect she could achieve. She reached out tentatively for a ceramic jar and lifted the lid.

Once she was done, she moved downstairs to wait in her shop. She stood at the door, wondering if she should step out and wait under the darkening night sky for d'Earthy. She liked the idea of waiting inside. That way, if he didn't arrive, she could save some face and simply return upstairs to her bed. On the other hand, it meant that if he did arrive and she chickened out, she could simply claim that she forgot or had something else come up.

In the end, she decided to stop letting her fears allow her to hide from her own life. Between spending an evening with this man and starting up a new coven, she was going to make it happen.

Just as she made this decision and placed her hand on the door handle, ready to open it and step outside, she saw d'Earthy walking along the street, heading straight for the door to the bakery, as though he was actually going to pick her up and take her out for the evening. Her breath froze in her throat.

For possibly the first time since she had arrived in Senoonheim, she heard the faint ringing of bells somewhere, tolling the sixth hour.

"Oh come on," she muttered to herself. "He's punctual *and* keeping up his end of things? That's not real, he's not real."

But the unreal dwarf had already reached the door and knocked firmly, as though he expected her to be ready and waiting for him, as if she believed that he would keep his word. This was the worst. Mira closed her eyes and started counting in her head. It would be far too embarrassing to open the door as soon as he knocked. That would look like she really was desperate. The fact that she had indeed been waiting just inside the door only made the situation worse. She wished that she had decided to wait outside even thirty seconds earlier.

She reached a count of thirty in her mind and opened her eyes again, ready to open the door. But that was when she saw that d'Earthy had pressed his face up to the bakery window, his hands cupped over the top of his eyes, shading them so it was easier for him to see inside. He made eye contact with her and waved.

Mira wanted to throw up. Instead, she opened the door and stepped outside.

"Oh, you're here already?" she said, wondering if he would believe that she had just reached the door herself, without hearing his knocking.

"Aye, but I saw you waiting there for a minute, so you heard me surely," he said, unabashed, smiling cheerfully.

Mira was glad for the fading twilight. There was a chance it was hiding the fiery blush that had reached her cheeks.

"Do you attend the games often?" she asked, trying to change the subject.

"Every now and then," he replied with a wink. He reached up and put his hand in the crook of her elbow. It was too far down for her to put her hand in his. But he didn't just rest it on her arm. His fingers pressed into her arm, with just enough pressure to show that he would direct her as they walked. It was a nice feeling. They walked off into the darkening streets of Senoonheim.

The Xenoxanthian Amphitheatre took up a whole district deep in the city, far from the East Gates, which most newcomers arrived through. It was a tall, round structure set amongst the ramshackle and jammed-together buildings of the poorer inhabitants of Senoonheim. By the time Mira and d'Earthy reached its arched entrances, the sun had completely set.

However, the contrivancers of the city had created a solution for this. The walls of the arena were pocked with sconces, and torches burned brightly in them all. An agitated swarm of workers scurried around the walls all night, replacing burnt out torches with fresh ones before moving on to the next. But torches alone weren't enough to truly illuminate the crowd that had come to the Barbarian's House of Dreams for entertainment.

One contrivance for lighting up the arena looked like a massive bowl, made of smooth, white ceramic, mounted on a strange set of curved and toothed scaffolding. The structure holding up the bowl reminded Mira of her pocket sundial. A set of heavy glass jars were mounted on the sides of the scaffoldings, and coils of twisted copper wire wound from the jars to the bowl. The bowl itself glowed with a strong, white light that lit up the streets around the arena more effectively than torches ever could.

The contrivancers were a strange group of magic-users. Bovo and Amella had taught her that most practitioners of magic used recipes and rituals to direct the magical energies of the world to their own purposes. Contrivancers, however, were convinced that they could become smithies for magic. They hammered and smelted magic and bound it into tools that could be used by anyone, in the same way a blacksmith forged a sword for anyone to use.

Wizards tended to look down upon them for this reason, explaining that if magic was meant to be used by everyone then why was it so hard to learn the proper spells? Obviously a person would need to be as intelligent and as focused and as provided with free time through the labour of others as a Wizard in order to learn magic. Groups of people who have something that would be good for everyone often use this logic to explain why they don't share it. They assume that the reasons that they have access to it are unshakeable laws of the universe, and not simply a reflection of the way their society is created.

Both the contrivancers and wizards were mostly correct in their assumptions about magic, as it turned out. Contrivancers were indeed able to create tools that shaped magic to a particular function and then pass the tool on to someone who had need of it (or at least had enough money to pay for it). Of course, there was no way to ensure that the new owner would respect the magic that had been bound into their fresh toy. A blacksmith who made an effective sword and sold it to an enthusiastic youth might not technically be to blame when the idiot child chopped off their own fingers, but it was no surprise when the community looked sideways at them. So it was with contrivancers. Magical accidents involving their devices were far too common, so no one really trusted the designers or their tools.

Which was also why Mira ducked away from the bowl that clicked in its scaffolding over their heads as they queued up and entered the arena.

"Come on, I know exactly where to find the best seats," grinned d'Earthy.

"Do you come to the arena often?"

"Oh yes!" d'Earthy's eyes flashed with enthusiasm. He slapped his chest with an open hand. "I have even competed!"

Chapter Twenty-Five

The seating in the arena was stone steps arranged so that spectators sat in front of the feet of those behind them. More of the strange ceramic bowls overlooked the arena so that the audience could see what was going on below them, which was nothing yet. The seats rose steeply so that even those at the highest seats were close to the sandy floor filling the oval space below. Mira rubbed her seat. It felt cold and coarse, exactly as she would expect stone to feel.

"Is this really stone?" she asked d'Earthy.

He raised an eyebrow at her.

"Yes. Why would you ask that?"

Mira didn't answer. If he didn't know why she would ask such a question in Senoonheim, perhaps he wasn't the right person to be asking about it anyway.

D'Earthy shuffled a little closer, placing one of his arms behind Mira as he leaned back a little. She became very aware of how close he was sitting to her. It wasn't unpleasant.

"Would you like something to eat?" he asked.

"Yes, thanks."

"Oi! Chuck us a pair of your roast birds!" d'Earthy bellowed down to a passing vendor. Given his mouth was less than a foot from Mira's ears when he did this, it made her entire skull rattle like a drum. She widened her eyes and then closed and opened them slowly, as if her eyelids were wiping clear the impact of his yell.

The vendor threw a small, roasted bird at him. D'Earthy caught it handily, and grease splattered across his arm and chest. Then he caught the second, with the same result. He threw coins one at a time to the vendor until the vendor waved and moved off to find other hungry spectators.

D'Earthy held out one of the birds to Mira.

"There you are!"

He looked so pleased with himself that Mira decided not to berate him for screaming in her ear and then splattering her with hot oil. Instead, she tried to find the least grease-covered part of the bird so she could take it from him. She eventually decided on the tip of one charred wing. She held the bird away from her clothing as thick drops of grease slid down its sides before sploshing onto the stone-that-was-probably-stone below her feet.

D'Earthy tore into his bird one chomping bite at a time. Mira watched him with wide eyes, and then began her own. She tried to pull away small pieces to eat without smearing her cheeks, but it was difficult, especially as d'Earthy elbowed her solidly halfway through and said "It's good, right?" She nodded and tried not to grimace as more of the liquid fat spotted her dress.

Mira finished nibbling the last pieces of bird and was just looking around to decide what to do with the bones when d'Earthy slapped a filthy hand onto her back and yelled "Here they come! Hurrah!"

A line of people was jogging out from a door at one end of the arena. They wore an assortment of different armour styles and carried some of the most exotic weaponry Mira had ever seen. There were twelve in all, and they sorted themselves into a rough circle, facing out into the audience. They all crossed their chests with their right forearm and shouted: "Hell has gone and heaven is here! Let us entertain you!"

The arena erupted with massed cheers.

D'Earthy was whooping next to Mira. He leaned forward now, and the excitement of being close to him had faded.

Mira had never come to the arena before, but she had heard about it. Regular displays of combat were held here, and the people of Senoonheim loved coming to watch. She knew that it could be dangerous, even for the audience, but that risk only seemed to make it more popular. Fighters came from distant lands to show their skills on this sandy floor, all for the chance of winning a share of the huge profits the arena pulled in. There was a reason one of its many names was the Barbarian House of Dreams.

The twelve warriors who had saluted the crowd marched out of the arena, leaving it empty. Whichever contrivancer was responsible for the lighting bowls around the walls made some adjustment and they dimmed, allowing Mira to see a low wall in front of the seating. Flaming torches ran along its top, separating the audience from a drop onto the sand of the arena. Drums began to pound, a galloping rhythm that wound the crowd to a higher degree of anticipation. With little more than the torchlight illuminating the arena, Mira couldn't see exactly what was happening.

The light-devices flared back into full force, shining on a tiny figure running alone across the arena to its centre. It was hard to judge their size with no one else around them, but Mira was sure that the figure was half as tall as the other warriors had been. She could just make out the large, round ears and long, thin tail of one of the ratfolk.

"It's Spartus!" yelled d'Earthy, practically bouncing on his seat. "It's The Devious Knife!"

As if on cue, Spartus reached the middle of the arena and turned with his arms outstretched, as though he was directing the sound of the cheers from the audience into his ears. Then he leapt into the air, flipping backwards and landing comfortably on his feet. The cheers redoubled. Spartus reached over his shoulders with both hands and drew a shining short sword in each.

"This'll be a great first match!" grinned d'Earthy.

"Who will he fight?" asked Mira.

"A paragon like him? Usually they'll get a good, strong renegade who can really get the crowd riled up. Either he'll win and be even more beloved, or the renegade will take it and that will make them even more hated."

"Why would someone want to win a fight and be more hated?"

"So they get hired again! The crowd wants to see a renegade get beaten as they deserve, so it's a great way to convince the organisers to bring you back. That's also why the organisers don't let the paragon beat them too often. Give people what they want too easily and they only want more."

D'Earthy was interrupted by a burst of boos and jeering from the crowd. A new figure had walked to the edge of the sand. They lifted something like a simplified trumpet to their mouth and began talking. Their voice echoed remarkably well across the arena.

"It's fitting that I find trash like you in a dump like Senoonheim, Spartus!" called the new figure. A fresh wave of boos greeted this statement. The figure raised an arm, as if waving to the crowd. Once the yelling had settled enough that he was sure he could be heard, he lifted the trumpet and spoke again.

"I told you last time we fought that I wouldn't let you rest. But I am here to say that I, Foiblem, have changed my mind. I have decided that I will let you rest." He paused and looked around the audience as their jeers slowly faded. Then he raised his fist again and yelled, "I have decided to bring you to your eternal rest!" He hefted a spiked mace into the air and the crowd booed yet again as he marched towards Spartus.

"What did you mean that the organisers don't let paragons beat the renegades too often?" Mira asked d'Earthy.

He tried to answer her while keeping his eyes on the two gladiators in the arena.

"They arrange who is going to win beforehand. It's all so that they can figure out the best way to keep the crowd coming back for more. It's a show."

"And people know that?" Mira was confused. "What's the point of watching something so dramatic happen if the ending has been planned out? Isn't the point that we are watching a fight and we are going to be surprised by the talents of the fighters, and the ending will come without us knowing."

"Yes, of course! And that's exactly what is happening! After all, do you know who will win this fight?" d'Earthy gestured down at the sand.

"No."

"And neither do I, and neither do most of the people here." He spread a hand at the seats around them. "The fight will still take skill and talent and luck. The fighters just know how to wrap things up the way that they want it to end, that's all."

Beneath them, the fight began. Despite being confused by d'Earthy saying that the outcome was already known, Mira found herself getting more into the action than she had expected.

Chapter Twenty-Six

T he ratfolk gladiator Spartus moved faster than anyone Mira had ever seen. Watching him race around his opponent was like watching someone swirl a skipping rope around themselves, looping and diving in a blur. He leaped through the air so quickly Mira wondered if there was magic being used on his behalf. Whenever Foiblem swung his mace, Spartus was no longer there. The little gladiator slashed and stabbed with his short swords, but didn't seem to be cutting through the thick, black armour that covered Foiblem.

When a hit did finally land on the renegade, Mira cheered with the rest of the crowd and pumped her fist. When Spartus took a glancing blow and spun aside, she groaned and felt her pulse quicken.

Soon blood began to show on each of the fighters, streaking over their arms and legs, visible even from the distant seats that Mira and d'Earthy occupied. She leaned over to him.

"They look like they are really getting hurt. I thought you said this was fake?"

"No, I said that they know who is going to win." The dwarf's eyes shone. "It's a real fight in a lot of ways. I have a friend who works as a healer for the arena, he says that some of the less skilled fighters can get dangerously close to unhealable."

Mira believed it. Healing magic was difficult and unreliable. The ingredients were so often incredibly rare, and could be extremely expensive, meaning that the correct ones might not be available. Mira suspected that healing spells used such ingredients as a type of sacrifice. If someone willingly gave up that much money to ensure healing was done, perhaps it demonstrated some level of devotion that was required for the spell to work. It was the sort of thought that a wizard would spend years experimenting with to see if it was true.

The fight was slowing down. The Devious Knife stood his ground more often now, as though gravity was pulling on him more powerfully. He used his two swords to guide the spiked mace in Foiblem's hands away from his body, instead of dodging away from the renegade's blows. One such swing caused the mace to slam into the arena floor over the top of Spartus's tail, the long spikes thudding deep into the sand. The entire arena groaned. Mira clutched at d'Earthy's shoulder, her fingertips curling against the edge of his thick, dark leathers.

He reached up and stroked the back of her fingers.

"It's a good move," he nodded. "It always gets the crowd worked up and on side with Spartus. Look at his tail."

D'Earthy was right. It was hard to see clearly from so far away, but the ratfolk's tail was twitching just as it had before, and Mira could make out no blood spilling from it.

"They're very good at what they do," emphasised d'Earthy. "The spikes from the mace go either side of the tail, and he pulls the blow just enough to avoid actually crushing it. A good renegade is worth a lot in ticket sales."

It seemed like this had been the signal for Spartus to redouble his efforts. He began to move faster, his blades spinning like an aggressive windmill as he drove Foiblem back, back, back towards the arena wall. Finally, he swung and slashed across the renegade's chest, causing blood to flow as the renegade collapsed to the ground. The crowd roared its appreciation as attendants rushed in and carried Foiblem from the arena. Spartus staggered back to the middle of the sandy space and lifted both arms, swords still clutched in his hands, before bowing deeply. He turned and bowed to four sides of the arena, and then attendants appeared beneath his arms, supporting him as he staggered out of sight.

"That was a big fight!" said d'Earthy. His face was as flushed as if he had been the one in combat. "Pretty unusual to start with a bout that big! Fixing up Foiblem will be pretty expensive."

Mira nodded.

"I see what you mean about it being planned but not fake. There was real danger there."

"Absolutely. Sometimes things can get really real."

Mira considered the idea: just because something was fake, that didn't mean it couldn't contain something real. The witches in Whinnia had turned out to be fake. But surely there had been something real in those friendships at first? And Troo had told her that lots of Senoonheim was fake, but people really lived here.

"And you used to do this?" Mira asked.

"Not at this level," sighed d'Earthy. "I was never a name in a one-on-one bout like this! I was just part of group melees from time to time. I used to do it more," he said, stroking the small braids in his beard. He had a wistful look in his eyes. "I still sign up for the open pike nights once in a while."

He went on to explain that the arena would often allow volunteers onto the arena floor to try their skills in a few bouts. If they did well, then they might earn a decent pouch of coin for their efforts. If they did poorly, then the arena would heal them, issue them with an invoice for that healing, and kick them back out into the streets.

"I can hold my own," said d'Earthy, leaning meaningfully on his arm so that his bicep bulged.

The next round was one of these open pike events. Four new figures wearing various types of armour entered the arena. One carried a long spear, while two others bore swords and shields. The final figure was a minotaur, tall and with sickly sharp curved horns. The minotaur carried no weapon.

"Will they fight each other?" asked Mira.

"Sometimes. It can all depend on what skills they bring."

A new door rattled open on the far side of the arena, and three massive spiders chittered out onto the sand. Mira had seen a lot of spiders in her life, though the ones she had seen before were usually smaller than the palm of her hand rather than the size of a small chariot. But these creatures shared very few characteristics with the spiders that built their webs in the beams of homes or the eaves beneath roofs. Regular respectable spiders would never be caught dead drooling slime like these large creatures did, and household spiders didn't go for eyes that glowed so redly. They would be spotted far too easily at night. Mira would be prepared to swear beneath the auspices of any god that most spiders she had seen before didn't have a row of sharp tooth-like spines running down the backs of their abdomens either. As soon as the spiders appeared, the minotaur with no weapon held her arms wide, and swirling balls of green fire burst into life around her fists. The crowd in the seats *oohed* appreciatively.

The volunteer fighters managed to work together to kill the giant spiders, though they were pretty badly cut up in the process. D'Earthy explained that a fight against monstrous creatures was probably "real", without a prearranged winner or plot, it being so difficult to train the animals to let a fighter win.

"More people are protesting against such displays than they used to," he said with a frown. "It's a shame. A proud tradition might be lost if the monster fights stop entirely."

Mira looked down on the ichor-soaked sand as it was cleaned in preparation for the next event and wondered if she might not agree with the protestors somewhat.

The rest of the evening flowed together in Mira's mind. There were at least two more monster fights, with groups taking on a Kestrelion in one fight, and a Corroder-Beast in another. There were three more gladiator fights, and d'Earthy was excited by each, squeezing Mira's fingers as the fighters yelled their little challenges and insults to each other before the fights began, and whooping when one fighter landed a particularly good blow on the other.

D'Earthy continued to explain a little about what was happening when Mira was confused, but there wasn't much for him to say that he hadn't said already. Before she knew it, the fights were done and the audience was getting to their feet so that they could proceed to not move while they waited for those in front of them to make their way out of the arena.

It is a peculiarity of people leaving a place all at the same time, that they will all gather their belongings, get to their feet, and then simply stand in place holding their things for achingly long and boring minutes at a time. If someone decides to remain seated instead of joining this display, they will be pointed out as 'weird' and frowned upon by their companions. Likewise, should someone decide that avoiding this tedious crush by leaving before the event is actually over is preferable, they too will be faced with judgmental cries. So instead every one stands and waits and wears out their knees. D'Earthy and Mira stood in the lines that clogged the amphitheatre, slowly creeping out into the streets and heading home.

Chapter Twenty-Seven

D'Earthy walked Mira home through the quiet streets of Senoonheim. At the door she turned to face him. He stepped closer, took her hands in his, and looked up at her. The moonlight reflected from his eyes, making them shine as they beheld her.

"I had a wonderful evening," he said.

"Yes, thank you for taking me," smiled Mira. "I'd never been to the arena, and I'd heard so much about it."

"Wasn't it amazing?" enthused d'Earthy. "I could tell that you were really getting into it."

Mira's smile twitched. The spectacle of the fights was exhilarating, but by the end of the night she definitely thought that if you've seen someone hit someone else with a sword once, you've seen someone do it a hundred times.

"I'll let you know when the next big event is on and we can go again!" d'Earthy added quickly, taking a small step closer to her. Mira was very aware of the space between them shrinking.

"That could be good," said Mira. She hated herself as soon as she said it. She had no aching desire to go back to the arena and see more of the same thing. She wasn't even sure if she wanted to get to know d'Earthy better, now that she knew how much he enjoyed these violent delights. But, before she could explain that a different destination might be a good idea, a chance for her to see another side of him, d'Earthy's face was moving towards hers.

His lips began to purse and his eyes slowly closed. Mira had a heartbeat to decide if she was going to lower her head to meet him, or whether she was going to leave him straining upwards and unanswered. It had been a pretty good night, she told herself.

Mira lowered her face to his and met his kiss.

The touch of his lips to hers was pleasant. His hands still held hers, and he squeezed her fingers again. The connection through her body, from her mouth to his fingers, tingled at the feel of him. Then they broke contact and leaned away from each other again.

"Good night," she said, and she stepped inside, swiftly locking the door behind her and racing upstairs to her room.

She pushed the door closed and leaned back against it, panting as though she had just fled from a wild animal. Her reflection caught her eye from the mirror over her dresser and she rolled her eyes at the sight of herself, panicked by a man's kiss.

"What did you say that for?" she asked herself. "You could have just told him that you didn't want to return to the arena. Now you're going to have to go back there."

She shrugged and stepped away from the door.

"It wouldn't be the end of the world, I suppose. It was kind of fun."

She refused to meet her own gaze as she changed into her nightclothes.

"Besides," she added as she climbed under her blankets, "kissing him was nice."

She rolled over and went to sleep, her own reply soft in her ears.

"Surely you want something more than nice from his kisses?"

***

Mira's dreams wound back to her days in Whinnia. She remembered that she was kneading a huge pile of dough in her kitchen when Loam walked straight in. As chief of the Froge, Loam always assumed he had the right to go wherever he wanted. Mira wanted to snap at him to get out, to tell him that he had to at least knock before he entered someone else's workplace, but she knew better than to say anything. Criticising someone with Loam's influence was as clever and safe as jabbing a sleeping dog with a pointy stick.

"Hello, my sweet," he said. His face wobbled and stretched as his lips spread like a receding tide, damply revealing a dead fish or a stranded squid. Mira realised with a start that he was attempting to smile. She would have expected the frogfolk to have lovely smiles, with their broad mouths and flexible skin. However, Loam looked as though someone had propped up the corners of his mouth with a coat hanger.

Maybe he's trying to be sincere, thought Mira, attempting to extend him the benefit of the doubt, but it only made things worse. Some people use facial expressions as though they learned about them from an informative brochure given to them by a well-meaning professional after too many incidents with their co-workers. Loam was certainly that sort of person. Instead of a friendly reassuring expression, he split his lips into something more like a hungry exposure of teeth.

"Hello Loam," said Mira with a shudder. "Why are you here?" She hoped her light tone would mean he didn't take offence. She pressed down on the dough with her whole forearm, causing a cloud of flour to lift and settle across her.

"Why, I am here to find out when we are going out for dinner!" He laughed, a series of moist barks that Mira enjoyed just as much as she had enjoyed his smile.

"I don't think we ever agreed to have dinner together?" Mira spoke as carefully as she could, trying to walk the line between appeasing the man's ego and ensuring that he actually understood that they weren't going to share a meal. She was concerned that there may not be such a line she could walk.

"This is true, I have been wondering where your reply to my note was. But that doesn't matter, because I'm here now! I decided to take matters into my own hands. If you need something done right, you have to step in and get involved." He crossed his arms on the edge of her workbench and leaned towards her. Mira desperately pulled her dough away from him, so that he wouldn't accidentally taint the flavour of her bread. "I can ask the First Seat to prepare some roast pig, just for us to share. However, I did think that perhaps someone as lowly as yourself might find that overwhelming." His grin showed just how much he enjoyed overwhelming other people. "And so I thought you might prefer to take in a simpler meal in one of the local taverns, or perhaps a picnic on the hillside overlooking the Far-Grasso Sea?"

Mira looked down into the dough that she was working on the bench. Hopefully the movement disguised the fact that she was thinking furiously, trying to find a way to turn him down safely.

"I don't think that I would enjoy a meal that the First Seat had arranged," she began to say, and Loam nodded before talking over the rest of her sentence.

"Say no more. I'll get some servants to prepare us a picnic tomorrow afternoon and then I will come past and get you an hour before sunset." He reached over and scooped his finger through the dough, picking up a gloopy chunk of it and slurping it into his mouth. "Urgh, I don't think that will be very nice."

You aren't meant to eat it before it's been baked, you ridiculous person, yelled Mira in the safety of her own head. Out loud, she just said, "Oh."

"We'll enjoy the sun setting from the hillside," he finished as he wiped his finger on the bench, leaving a thick, slimy trail of dough and frogfolk saliva. "Excellent, see you then."

Before Mira could open her mouth to say that she didn't want to go on a picnic with him, he straightened up and strode out of her kitchen. Mira stared at the door after he was gone, trying to put her thoughts in order. Then she slowly turned her gaze down to the tainted dough he had left behind. Finally she sighed deeply and pushed the dough into a bucket near the bench, ready to pass on to a farmer for feeding the pigs.

Chapter Twenty-Eight

"Was that Loam I just saw marching out of here?" asked a voice behind Mira. Mira turned and saw Bovo leaning against the kitchen door frame. The diminutive halfling woman had her arms crossed, her eyebrow raised and her lips smirked.

"Yes," groaned Mira. She slumped over the bench and began cleaning it so she could start again. "He came in to inform me that we are going on a picnic tomorrow."

"You don't look very pleased about that idea."

Mira snorted. "Who would be?"

"So what are you going to do about it?" Bovo asked.

"What can I do?" said Mira. "Loam isn't really someone I can just ignore."

"You really aren't interested in him at all, huh?"

"Of course I'm not interested in him. He's such a gross person, and he buddies up with the First Seat all the time." Mira shook her head in surprise. "Why would anyone like him?"

"You don't like the First Seat either?" asked Bovo with raised eyebrows.

"Bovo." Mira turned from her ovens and used her upper arm to brush some hair out of her face. "The First Seat is a buffoon and everyone knows it. Anyone who is friends with him is either just as stupid as that vainglorious donkey, or they are trying to use him to their own advantage. Loam might even be both."

Bovo nodded, but she peered over her shoulder and out the kitchen window before answering.

"You're right, he is definitely both of those; but he's also very temperamental. I would have thought that you would be tempted to go along, just to stay on his good side."

"By stringing Loam along? You think that would be a good way to avoid problems with the First Seat of Whinnia?"

Bovo shrugged.

"Maybe? It depends what you want out of life, I suppose."

Mira shook her head.

"I can't imagine how bad things would have to be for me to go out for dinner with someone as dismissive of other people as Loam Ratsweat."

"I can think of a few reasons why someone might put up with him," said Bovo, holding out a hand and rubbing her fingers and thumb together. She grinned.

"That's not me," said Mira.

Bovo just shrugged again, but her eyes still twinkled.

"The world takes all sorts. Listen, I actually came along here to make your day better. Join me tomorrow morning to gather dew and mushrooms."

"What for?"

"All the better to teach you magic potions with my dear," chuckled Bovo. She had been introducing Mira to the skills and spells that would turn her into a fully-fledged witch. There weren't many witches in Wallis and Mira jumped at the chance to learn from Bovo when she suggested the idea. Bovo specifically said that she could teach Mira ways to mix baking with magic. The idea of making love potion cupcakes for sweethearts to give each other made Mira feel like she was doing something good in the world.

"Alright, I'll see you then," she told Bovo.

***

People said Wallis sat on a hill because there weren't many other words to describe a massive outcrop of rock looming up from an otherwise wide and level grassy plain. Mesas and buttes were both more sheer than this hill, and tors were more fragmented. So the fingers of earth and stone that stuck up irregularly through the green blanket of the Far-Grasso Sea were known as hills.

The hill beneath Wallis was tall and thin, as they all were, which led to the strange architecture of the main city in Whinnia. In many places houses further up the hill used the roofs of lower buildings as foundations. Roads wound in serpentine loops through the streets, seeking the Great Hall of the First Seat at the very summit. The people of Wallis developed some of the most powerful calf muscles in the Misplaced Kingdoms, as their bodies constantly leaned so far forwards that an onlooker might suspect strings were involved.

Mira walked down to the town gates to meet Bovo before dawn, although hobbling might better describe the one-bent-leg sideways crawl that she used to navigate the hillside. Together, they walked, with feet practically en pointe, through the gate and down to the grass sea.

The gates of Wallis were constructed halfway up the hillside, a distance far enough from the plain that no one watched over Mira and Bovo when they were finally able to bring their ankles to right angles. Mira stumbled for a while until she managed to get her sea legs under her. Her muscles were slowly convinced to release their hold on her knees and she was able to enjoy the walk.

She stepped along the soft earth and ran a hand through the waving grass stalks that reached up to her waist, breathing in the freshly chilled air of morning before the sun had risen. A voice coughed from behind her and she turned around.

The top of Bovo's head, chestnut hair tied up in a small bun on top of her head, was barely visible above the grass.

"Sorry," said Mira. She hurried back over to the smaller witch. "Um. What shall we do about that?"

"Normally I'd either flatten the grass or find a horse," said Bovo. She scratched the back of her head. "But we don't want anyone coming after us and tromping all over the mushrooms, and I didn't see any horses down here."

She was right. The nearest horses would be tied up inside the gates of Wallis, where they were left by newcomers to the city.

"Ugh," Bovo groaned and her shoulders slumped while her head flopped sideways. She looked like a teenage girl whose parents were being gently encouraging and supportive. "Fine, I guess I have to do it this way." She pulled some objects out of the pack strapped to her back. Bovo quickly twisted the short lengths of what looked like bamboo together and then lashed some odd triangular pieces of wood to their sides. Then she planted one pole at an angle on the ground in front of her, placed a foot on the triangle, and hopped forward. She dragged the second pole into position and then stood eye to eye with Mira. Bovo smiled as she stepped back and forwards on her stilts.

"Alright, now I can see where I'm going! Come on!" she called to Mira as she strode off through the grass.

They were moving quickly, but when Mira glanced back she saw that Wallis was outlined by the rising sun.

"Bovo, didn't you say we had to collect the dew and mushrooms before dawn for them to work in your spells?"

"Yes, I did," said the halfling as she pounded along on her stilts.

"I think the sun would be shining on us if it wasn't for the hill."

"Probabaly."

"Doesn't that mean it's after dawn already now?"

"No." Bovo didn't stop walking. "There's so many ways to cast a spell. What you are doing is following a recipe that someone has found to achieve a certain result. Sometimes the recipe involves magic words, or special ingredients. Witches share those recipes, so that we can all find the best way to do what we need to. But like all recipes, sometimes people do things in different ways and they all work. Have you ever made scones?"

"Of course." Mira was confused. What did scones have to do with this mission to gather water and fungi?

"Did you use sugar and buttermilk and eggs?"

"What? No!" Mira had made simple scones with a healthy dollop of cream on many occasions, and yet she had never thought of making them with those ingredients.

"Some people do. And do you know what they pull out of the oven?"

Mira thought carefully as they stepped through the grass. What did people pull out of the oven if they used a different recipe for scones?

"Scones?" she said eventually.

"Of course!" Bovo managed to turn around on the stilts and then stood facing Mira. She had to step from side to side to maintain her balance in one spot, making her look like a child that desperately needed to relieve themselves but had been told that they had to wait.

"Its just like that with our spells. We are going to gather dew from the grass before any morning sun has struck it. That's before dawn, and if it isn't, it is close enough that my recipe still works."

"Why not collect some here?" Mira was very aware of the dew running down the blades of grass she was pushing through. Her shoes were already full of water that gushed up the sides of her feet with every step, and her skirts were sticking to her shins and thighs.

"Its not the right spot," replied Bovo, as though that were a reasonable answer that should assuage any curiosity, and not a cryptic bit of nonsense.

Mira put those thoughts aside and asked a different question.

"And the mushrooms?"

"We've got to have something for breakfast when we get back."

Bovo spun around to keep walking but before she took a step a large round dark shape rose from the grass before them, the hunchback of a whale breaching the surface of the Far-Grasso Sea.

The figure lifted out of the grass and turned towards the newcomers, their round back rotating like a model globe. The face that appeared around the edge of the bulbous shoulders was almost equally spherical, with bright button-sized eyes over a tiny nose and an incredibly wide mouth. A single, sharp tooth stuck up from the person's lower jaw.

"Oh, Amella, it's you!" said Bovo happily.

Chapter Twenty-Nine

"Hello little Bovo, my delicious slice of pie," said the woman rising from the grass. "And Mira, how lovely to see you following along into the damp morning grass when called."

Mira blinked.

"Bovo told me that we were gathering ingredients for some spells," she explained.

The woman nodded.

"Of course she did. Still training you up, I see. If there's one thing Wallis needs, it's more witches."

Mira was confused. Was this woman being genuine? Did she really think that the town needed more witches in it? Her tone sounded bright and cheerful, but there was an edge to it. It was the spoken equivalent of a dark fin swimming through calm seas. Perhaps she actually thought that there were too many witches in Wallis already. But Mira hadn't heard of any witches in Wallis other than the three of them, and it seemed like such a big place.

"That was my thought!" replied Bovo chirpily. She always took Amella at face value, which allowed her to keep her bubbly attitude bubbling as steady as a kettle over a fire.

"I brought her along to uncover the secrets that can be wrung from nature like the final drips of moisture from a cleaning rag," continued the halfling. "You're down here to get some good panicgrass dew as well I imagine?"

Amella nodded, watching the other two with placid eyes. Mira tried not to meet her gaze, as it always ended with her own eyes watering. The other woman never seemed to blink.

"Nothing better than panicgrass dew in my opinion," said Amella.

Bovo motioned Mira forward with her chin, as she was still wobbling around on her stilts, and instructed her on how to hold a small glass jar at the end of the thin blades that branched off the tall grass stalks, wiping traces of morning dew off the tip and into the glass container. Slowly, dribble by dribble, Mira filled and capped her jars.

Amella was doing the same, secreting the small jars somewhere in her dark dress and then always producing yet another empty one.

"Why did we have to come all the way out here?" asked Mira. "Surely we could have gathered dew closer to Wallis."

"There's no panicgrass back by the town," said Bovo. "Panicgrass is much better dew."

"And even if there was, we wouldn't like anyone else to see where we found our dew," said Amella, turning to look at Mira. "What a problem it could be if someone else took all of this before... us."

Mira nodded and tucked her jars away. She could feel her face flushing. *Why am I so flustered by this woman. She's including me in what she's talking about. Why do I feel as though she thinks I am an intruder?*

***

Mira woke up with a head stuffed with wool after her evening at the arena with d'Earthy, and a night caught up in her memories of Whinnia. She stumbled through her morning routine and it wasn't until after noon that she began to feel awake enough to really notice what was happening around her. Before long, she was turning the wooden sign in the shop window from "open" to "closed" and rubbing her exhausted forehead with the back of her hand.

Despite the best attempts of her customers, she had made it through the day without losing her mind and now it was time to head down to the Sprog and Sparrow and see if there were any other women interested in starting a coven.

She wondered how many witches there might already be in Senoonheim. Her heart beat faster and faster as she rushed through the streets to the tavern. She threw open the door and charged inside.

"Yargh!"

A hideous screech filled the room as light flooded in, refracting and bouncing from the glasses on the tables and the metal holding the furniture together. A wave of clear light washed through the room.

"Shut the bloody door!" hissed the same voice, from somewhere deep inside the room.

Mira kicked the door shut behind her, confused. She waited as her eyes adjusted to the gloom and then saw Jacqui behind the bar, her arms raised as a shield against the light. Someone else stood at the bar, his black hair brushed firmly back and down his skull. He wore a long, pointed beard, a flowing, floor-length black cape, and a sour expression. His face was flushed. He held a thin glass filled with a thick, red liquid. There was a stick of something green and leafy in it.

"Sorry?" said Mira. Their faces suggested she had done something wrong, but she wasn't exactly sure what. In such situations she generally erred on the side of apology, unless the other person was being a dick about it. In those cases, she erred on the side of doubling down.

"That's alright, I suppose, you weren't to know," said Jacqui in her booming voice. "Are you alright Makt?" she said, directing the question to the tall figure.

The man lifted his glass and took a delicate sip of the red drink. The liquid clung to the sides like shipwreck victims about to be washed away in a storm. He turned his gaze on Mira; she could see that the other side of his face was extremely pale, in contrast to the red glow she had already seen.

"I'll be okay," he said grimly. "It's only a little sunburn." Mira could see the man was restraining himself. A muscle in his cheek twitched.

"Sorry," she said again. Was he implying that simply opening a door had given him sunburn? Surely he meant he had been burnt earlier and the heat from the sunlight when she came in had made him uncomfortable. In any case, he grunted in annoyance but turned back to the bar, ignoring her now.

"I'd like a cider please, Jacqui," said Mira as she walked over to join them.

The tavern owner nodded. She gathered up a glass and filled it with a thick, purple liquid.

"It's made of plums. You'll like it dear." The woman smiled as she pushed it over the bar.

Mira took a sip. Jacqui was right, she did like it. The drink was crisp and tart.

"Has anyone come in asking about my poster?" she asked.

"A few people actually. But I haven't seen anyone come about it yet today."

Mira sipped her cider.

"That's good to hear that people were talking about it. Maybe some witches will come along soon. It's still early."

Jacqui shrugged and began wiping a glass clean with a thick rag.

The door banged open again and Makt yowled. Jacqui flung the glass in her hands to the floor, where it shattered, and spread the rag out in front of her like a greasy curtain. The light dimmed again as the newcomer shut the door.

"It's that flaming candle-makers shop across the road," explained Jacqui soothingly, or as soothingly as someone with the voice of a hippo can achieve. She reached out and patted Makt's arm.

"The sunset is reflecting off the windows and coming straight in the door."

"Why am I standing around here then?" snarled Makt. He snatched up his drink and stalked off to a booth far away from the front door.

Mira looked to see who had come in and found the entrance was now blocked by the broad round shoulders of Troo, the High Lord's soldier. The orc woman hoisted an arm into the air to greet Mira. It was like watching a tree trunk being chopped down in reverse.

"Mira! What a delight it is to see you here again!"

"Hello Troo." Mira smiled. She walked up for a hug and found herself enveloped in a rib-crushing embrace. She coughed as she was released.

"Come here to join the coven too, have you?" asked Troo as they both walked back to the bar. Troo ordered a large glass of the thickest, blackest beer Mira had ever seen. It looked like the sort of substance that could be used to waterproof a ship, and Troo began glugging it back by the mouthful as soon as it was served to her.

"Sort of. I'm actually the one who put up the posters."

Chapter Thirty

"The coven is all your idea? Oh, fantastic!" Troo clinked her glass of tar against Mira's cider. "I'm impressed! Knowing it's your coven makes me even more keen to join! Have you got anyone else in yet?"

"Not yet." There was another flash of light as someone entered the tavern. This time, the glare faded to reveal a short woman with a plain but friendly face, and a long braid of red hair running down her back. Her pale skirts swished as she strode into the bar, heavy, black boots peeking out from below the skirts with every step.

"Hello, is this where the coven is meeting?" she asked with a bright smile. Her lips were red and glossy and her teeth sparkled in tandem with her eyes.

"It is!" said Troo. She leaned forward to clap the new woman on the shoulder. The newcomer staggered and was nearly thrown to the floor. But she held her ground and kept her smile and brushed a hand over her head to tuck a few strands of hair back into place.

"Great! I was excited to see someone wanting to start a coven. I've always been fascinated by witchcraft. I have a feeling that I'll have a knack for it," said the new arrival.

"What do you do?" asked Mira.

"I'm a butcher." She smiled again, with light blue eyes in a face of pure innocence. "My name's Kirka."

Mira welcomed Kirka to the bar and encouraged her to buy a drink. Before long, the doorway filled with more women, all seeking a coven to join. Although most of them had no experience of witchcraft, they all shared the strange, subconscious attraction that draws people to new occupations.

Some people seek such things out of a desire to spend their time doing something that they enjoy, while for others it follows the discovery that there is a job that pays well and requires no actual accountability or regular working hours, like being a CEO. However, a few of the women were already witches in their own right, including Troo, which surprised Mira; women who were simply seeking the companionship of their fellow sistren.

The women who had come for the coven spread along the bar, blocking the regulars from making their orders. The line of confused and sweaty people behind them awkwardly walked back and forward, turning around and rubbing their hands at each other the way a stream of ants whose pheromone trail had been covered do. The room was filled with the manic energy of an attempt to solve a problem without actually engaging with it. Mira led her tentative coven away from all that nonsense and settled them around a long table at one side of the common room.

Mira and Troo sat at one end, with Kirka to their side. Two younger women sat to Mira's left, along the side of the table. One of them wore wispy clothing that gusted in the slightest breeze. A dark-furred rat dangled over her shoulder, nibbling the silver pendant hanging at her throat. The other had short fiery hair and wore a similarly diaphanous dress but her strong shoulders stretched the delicate fabric at the seams.

"When did you see the poster, Delorous?" Mira asked the woman with the rat. A cloud of black makeup obscured her eyes and ran down her cheeks.

"Just this morning. It had nearly fallen off the wall. I assumed someone had tried to tear it down to make sure that I wouldn't find out about it, but they were too late." She lifted a nut from the dish on the table and fed it to the rat. "People usually try to avoid me."

"I'm sure nothing like that happened," Mira protested. Delorous shrugged, and the rat turned to nip at her chin.

"How about you, Othniel?" Mira shifted her attention, hoping for a brighter response.

Othniel's face was covered in thick, white makeup, painted into the circle and vertical lines of a simple skull. Her eyes blinked in the middle of the painted visage.

"I don't know anything about a poster," she said with a wide smile. The sight of her actual teeth shining out from between the painted ones was unsettling. "I just saw a mob of women cackling in the bar and I knew that was where I was meant to be!" She lifted her beer to toast the fledging coven at the table.

At the far end of the table, a pair of older women lifted their glasses to join Othniel's toast.

"Ti," Othniel acknowledged the one dripping with gold and silver jewellery over her tight green dress and head scarf.

"Junka," she said to the older woman wearing a deep blue headscarf and whose clothing bulged ominously.

The other two women swallowed their drinks in huge gulps and then Ti whispered to Junka, who pulled a metal flask from somewhere under the thick folds in her clothes. Junka poured a clear liquid from it into their glasses and then they both leaned back, cackling.

To Mira's right, an antfolk woman sat quietly opposite the young women in their gossamer gowns. Her bulbous, insect eyes watched the others from over mandible jaws. She wore a long red dress, with black, chitinous arms poking from its loose sleeves. She was stroking the scaly back of a reptile no bigger than Mira's fist.

"Where did you get that lizard, Leena?" Mira asked.

"Yes, tell us about the gecko," added Othniel, her muscular arms propped on the table as she leaned forward.

"I don't think that he is a gecko," clicked the antfolk woman happily. "I call him Tiny." She lifted the little creature to her face and nuzzled him, her antennae dipping to rub across his back at the same time. "I found an egg and hatched it. I've been hand-rearing him ever since."

Mira studied the lizard warily. The pointy scales that ran down his spine looked sharp.

"And you're sure he's not going to get bigger than that?"

"It'll be fine," said Leena, motioning Mira's questions aside as though they were flies buzzing over her drink.

Next to Leena sat a woman with ginger hair tied back in a thick braid. She had greenish skin and a frog of a similar hue sat on her shoulder, looking at nothing.

Finally there was the tiny witch sitting on the tabletop itself. She stood no more than a handspan tall, and wore overalls the leafy green colour of forest undergrowth. She and the green woman were the only two who had brought along a traditional broad-brimmed pointy black hat. It was hard to interpret the expression on such a small face, but Mira was pretty sure it shifted from scowl to grimace to frown in a loop. She had heard Troo call the tiny witch Hattie.

"When have I seen you before?" the green woman asked Mira with a smile.

"I don't think you have," answered Mira. She wanted to ask if the woman felt sick, but thought it would probably be rude. She was chatting happily enough at the moment.

"No, I'm sure that I've seen you before! Do you get pulled before the judges often? Are you known by every n'er-do'well in town?"

"What? No!"

"No, I should have known that couldn't be why I recognised you, really. I see all those people a lot, I would have been able to place you in a second if that was how I knew you." She touched her chin as she kept thinking, and then snapped her fingers. "I know! You were my brother-in-law's new co-worker, the one who came up with a new system for categorising root vegetables, completely revitalising his warehouse!"

"No, I have nothing to do with organising vegetables."

"Oh that's a pity, I was so sure. And it's a lucrative field to be in."

"A potato field?"

"Yes, nothing beats a field of vegetables, sorted correctly on your sheets."

Mira stared at her. Something about the words she was using made her think that the woman was a few vegetables short of a field herself. The woman put her hand around her chin as she pondered Mira.

"But seriously, I'm sure I know you."

The frog on her shoulder stood up on its hind legs and leaned over to whisper in the woman's ear.

"That's it! Phranki knows! We saw you here a couple of days ago! You were having a drink with some of the High Lord's soldiers."

A faint memory of someone who was dressed like this woman tickled the back of Mira's head.

"You started clicking your fingers…"

"That was me!"

"I think someone called you Elschefla?"

"Yes! Wonderful! Oh, I am so glad to be able to place your face. Don't you hate it when you don't know whether your mind is playing tricks on you? What's your name?"

"Mira. I'm pleased to meet a real witch."

"Oh well, you're too kind." Elschefla blushed and twisted one of her feet back and forth on her toes. "With that finally nailed down, I have to thank you for getting all of this started. I've been missing being a part of a coven myself!"

The door to the tavern swung open again. The sun had set further now, meaning that there was no blinding flash. Instead, a skinny shadow slunk around the doorframe and insinuated itself into the room, for all the world like a cat that had leapt between fences and missed and was now prowling away, daring the world to notice its misfortune.

The shadowy woman looked around and then slid towards the coven's table. She inserted herself between Othniel and Ti, smiled around the table, and spoke in a voice like silk.

"Good evening ladies, is this–"

"Nerishma?" asked Mira before the new woman could finish her sentence.

The skinny thief who had been caught by Prevos before bolting away through the streets froze. She looked at Mira and her lips stretched into a morbid grin as her eyes flared.

"It is you, isn't it? Didn't you try to mug me the other evening?" asked Mira.

The thief's skin paled as blood drained out of her head. Mira worried that the woman might faint. As if called by an offstage cue, Nerishma's eyes rolled back in her head and she rolled down out of sight under the table.

The women squealed and leapt aside, ducking under the table to see what had happened. Mira stepped away to look down as well.

Under the table, Nerishma's face was low to the floor and she was attempting to creep away. She kept her hands and legs close to the sides of her body, looking like a centipede as she crawled slowly away while making only the tiniest movements.

"Nerishma." Mira spoke in her calmest tone, although a grin fought to escape the serious grip of her cheeks.

The woman on the floor froze again and screwed her eyes shut. There is a belief among children that if they cannot see someone then they cannot be seen in return, which leads to games of hide and seek which look more like games of mask and ignore. In moments of panic, plenty of adults desperately hope that this childhood memory holds true. Apparently Nerishma was one of them.

"Nerishma, you didn't end up stealing anything, and it looks to me like you've come to join the coven. I'm willing to let bygones be bygones, so long as you promise not to steal anything from any of us."

Nerishma sprang to her feet and leaned on the table between the other women.

"As I was saying, is this the coven I've been seeing advertised on the walls?" she asked with a smile.

The others laughed and Junka leaned in to hug her shoulders and then produced a mug from somewhere within her dress and handed it over. The older woman found her flask again, and poured a generous measure for Nerishma.

"We're glad to have you," said Mira. "I can't believe you used your real name the other night." She allowed the grin that had been fighting its way onto her face to have its big moment, and it launched itself into freedom with gusto.

Chapter Thirty-One

M ira's fledgling coven chatted about their backgrounds and jobs and families, the tiny angry witch sitting on the table punctuating the conversation with complaints about her husband and family. Their laughter spread through the Sprog and Sparrow like an infection. The room felt brighter and cheerier than any other time Mira had been inside it. Even Jacqui's laugh bellowed from behind the bar, although Makt hunched lower and lower in his booth.

Mira wondered if it was just the presence of friends brightening the room for her. Maybe their joy allowed her to really notice all the warmth the tavern had to offer. She had felt very lonely in this tavern when she visited before. Hopefully this would be a turning point in her time in Senoonheim.

After a second round had been ordered, Delorous steeled herself. Black makeup dripped from around her eyes, and her dark hair fell in a curtain in front of her face. She pushed it to one side, tucking it behind the rat on her shoulder, and said, "Not that it matters, nothing really does, but what happens now? Is there some sort of test to see if we can become witches? If I'm going to fail, it would be helpful to fail soon, so I can go home and be by myself. Again."

Troo chuckled into her drink as Mira blinked at the woman in her tissuey dress. The rat on Delorous's shoulder wriggled into a more comfortable position. Ten pairs of eyes, eleven if she including the rat's, turned to stare at Mira and she nearly choked on her mouthful of cider.

"Uh, right, well..." she began, summoning up everything she could remember learning back in Whinnia. "Basically, there's no tests, we are all witches–"

"Not all of us yet!" interrupted Junka, as she topped up her glass with whatever it was she had in that flask.

"–Or if we aren't, then we are going to help one another learn about what it involves. And then we just meet regularly to give each other some support and advice and encouragement! Tradition says we're supposed to meet under a full moon, but I'm not really worried about that."

The others at the table nodded. Hattie hefted a cup almost as tall as she was and tipped it very carefully towards her, gulping down huge mouthfuls of lager.

"Does that mean you will give us witchcraft lessons?" asked Delorous. "I've been told that I'm a terrible student." She absent-mindedly stroked the fur on her rat's head.

Mira pressed her lips together tightly. She had been afraid that this question might be coming.

"I will if I have to, but I have to warn you: I'm not really an expert. It would be better if we could find someone else."

"A terrible teacher for a terrible student," Delorous smiled. "How perfect."

"I'm sure you're a wonderful witch," Troo said to Mira.

"That's kind of you to say, but you don't know me that well yet." Tension bubbled awkwardly in her stomach. She didn't like this direction of conversation. "You haven't seen me try any magic or anything."

Troo shrugged in a way that suggested that she didn't need anything as nebulous as 'evidence' to assess Mira. All eyes were still on Mira, so she kept talking.

"The woman who taught me most of what I know said that witchcraft is about relationships," Mira began in the manner of someone hoping that someone else will take over. "You need to build a relationship with some magical spirit that can share their power and knowledge with you. We call them bravura honda. My teacher had made an agreement with a small god called Stomikaek, who had taught her certain rituals and recipes, so long as she provided him with what he needed."

"What was it that he needed?" asked Kirka. She was still smiling happily, but there was a certain glow in her eyes. Where some people's eyes began to glaze over when they drank too much wine, Kirka's eyes looked more focused than they had before, and her smile wider. Mira watched as the corner of the other woman's eye twitched.

"Ongoing blood sacrifice?" Kirka suggested.

"Oooo," moaned Delorous. Mira couldn't tell if the noise was an indication of disgust and trepidation, or of excitement. She laughed.

"No! Stomikaek only wanted her to spread the word about him to new places, which she was happy to do. But certainly some beings would ask such things of you, so whether you want to strengthen that relationship depends on what they are offering you in return and what you are happy to give."

"And what relationship have you developed?" Nerishma asked Mira.

"Me? I–"

Before Mira could finish, the door to the tavern slammed open. A gust of wind swirled into the room, bringing the night's chill with it. The walls of the room felt as though they were closing in and everyone in the tavern turned to see who was making such an entrance.

First came two young men in floor length, red robes. They were both attempting to grow out their beards, but neither had much to show for it yet. One's beard grew thicker and thinner in patches, so that he looked like a mangy puppy. The other's was so wispy that he looked as though he had walked through a cobweb and left the threads covering his lower face instead of wiping them away.

After them strode in a man who exuded waves of self-confidence. His eyes were large and fierce and burst from beneath gigantic, shaggy white eyebrows. His own beard was lush and thick and pale, exactly the sort of beard that a man could stroke thoughtfully while pronouncing upon the nature of the universe. He wore robes very like the ones the two younger men wore, though his were embroidered in small and fine golden sigils that glittered when they caught the light.

Two more young people followed him in, one man and one woman. The man was an orc, with the jutting lower tusks and green-hued skin that came with it. It appeared as though he was trying to follow the others' in an attempt to grow a beard, but orcs weren't renowned for their facial hair. From this distance Mira couldn't tell if he had actually managed to cultivate a thin goatee on his solid jaw or had just painted it on instead.

In any case, his face was more natural than the woman's beside him. She wore the same robes as the others, but on her they looked fantastic. Where the cloth on the men bunched and looked thick and scratchy, on her the fabric flowed, revealing the sort of long curves more often reserved for diagrams of the movement of the stars than living things. However, in contrast to the shapely figure she cut, she was wearing a fake beard. It appeared to have been knitted from grey wool and the black wires holding it onto her face could be seen from across the room.

"What wickedness this way comes!" exploded the old man in the middle of this entourage. He held out his hands and spread his fingers wide, stretching the skin between them taut. The final gust of wind curling through the door made his robes flutter dramatically, and banged the door closed again behind him.

"How wicked are you?" asked a farmer standing by the dartboard near the door.

"What?" The man turned in bewildered fury to face the farmer. The farmer was an older man with a thick neck and the sort of placid comfortable expression more commonly seen on the animals occupying the farm than its owner.

"You asked what wicked this way comes, right? But the only one coming in is you." The farmer lifted his dart and aimed carefully at the board on the wall. "Stands to reason that you are the wickedness coming then, aren't you?" He launched his dart towards the board.

The dart stopped as though it had already wedged its needle nose into the cork board, but it hung in midair halfway to its destination. The placid man blinked. He turned to face the old man in the robes, who held a hand out in a crooked gesture.

"Are you messing with me?" snarled the old man.

The darts player shook his head in tiny back and forth motions.

"I am here to protect the city of Senoonheim, and I will not be mocked!" His curled fingers twisted further and the dart crunched in on itself, falling apart and crumpling like a handful of flower petals. Voices muttered around the tavern.

Chapter Thirty-Two

"Hey, what's going on here?" cried Jacqui. The tavern-keeper materialised all at once within reach of the bearded man. The two semi-facial-haired youths looked as though they had been slapped, their mouths hanging open and their eyes bulging. For her part, Jacqui laid a hand on the angry man's shoulder and leaned in close.

"Surely a simple glass of your favourite human beverage would settle your nerves? We don't need all of this commotion, do we?" She smiled at the man and began to guide him towards her bar.

"Are you the person in charge of this untenable situation?" he asked in a rough voice.

Jacqui paused as they walked. The smile on her face didn't shift one speck, but Mira could see that the expression had changed. Moments earlier the smile had conveyed a sense of good-willing and calm, and a desire to keep the peace. All of a sudden, that same facial expression was a way to expose her bared and shining white teeth.

"This is my bar, if that is what you are asking me, sir."

"I demand that you round up whoever is involved with this coven." As he spoke, the old man pulled one of Mira's posters from a small leather pouch hanging from his belt. He had taken no care to fold it small enough into the pouch in the first place, and so the poster was scrunched into a fist-sized ball.

"Whoever made this poster," he continued as he struggled to unfold the ball enough for it to be recognisable to everyone else, "and tell them to leave the premises. In fact, you should ban them entirely!"

"I should kick out some customers, and bar their return?"

"Absolutely!"

"On whose authority do you make such a request?"

The man scowled but then snorted and answered her.

"I speak here for Lord Cornucervin. I am Satonak, the Court Wizard, and these are but some of my acolytes!"

The four accomplices ringing him waved sheepishly at the other patrons of the tavern. The orc man was shrinking under the attention directed towards him. He had tangled his fingers together in front of his waist and was struggling to pull them apart.

"I suppose I might have to consider any *advice*," and Jacqui glared at the man as she emphasised the word 'advice', "that came from the Porcelain Throne via the court wizard. Do you have any actual evidence that you are that person?"

"You need more evidence?" The man lifted his arms, bent as though bearing a great weight, and his fingers curled like the gnarled branches of a tree. The lights in the tavern dimmed and balls of coloured light appeared floating in the air between the tables. They bobbed around the man, flickering when they got too close to anything else. With a flourish, the coloured balls disappeared and the man straightened his shoulders and smiled with a raised eyebrow.

"That's very impressive, but it's not actually a form of identification," said Jacqui.

The man glared.

Before Satonak could attempt to be more intimidating, a voice from the other end of the room piped up.

"I sent away and learned the coloured balls trick when I was a lad actually, though I have to say the skinny wire things are bloody hard to see on your balls." The man who spoke was tall and slim and bald, and his skin looked as though he exfoliated with a cheesegrater.

"Aye, that's right, I seen 'em." This corroboration came from a short woman with her hair coiled up into buns on the sides of her head. "Max here showed me his balls once, and they danced about, all pretty colours, just like that."

There was an uncomfortable clearing of throats throughout the tavern at this revelation.

The woman pointed at Max, the self-proclaimed ball expert.

"He showed me the stiff metal threads that he used, it was all very clever."

The man put an appreciative and familiar hand on the back of the woman's neck and they admired each other with the sort of gaze that makes other people turn away in embarrassment.

"I did not use any metal threads, my dear lady," began Satonak, but Junka spoke up before he could finish his sentence.

"I make coins appear from my grandsons' ears all the time, it's hardly impressive. What have you got against this coven anyway?"

The man swivelled on his heels and focused on the table. A smile leaked across his face and he slipped across the floor towards them. He stood next to Mira, leaning forward with both hands on the table, so close that Mira could smell him. He smelt like dust and leather.

"Hello ladies," he purred, as though they had not just seen him yelling and ranting in the middle of the tavern. His beardy accomplices dashed up behind him and stood a step away from the table with their arms crossed, trying to look intimidating and not like they were catching their breath. "Fancy finding a whole table of lovely women such as yourselves, all sitting in one place. What brought all of you together this evening I wonder?"

His eyes were half-lidded and his cheeks bunched above his smile, the self-satisfied expression of a cat whose owner was scratching the little spot at the base of its tail. It was exactly the sort of expression that antagonised Mira. An outburst of anger rose up her spine like the bubbling steam of a kettle.

"What's it to you, bigface?" snapped Hattie from the middle of the table, in a voice as high and dangerous as glass snapping.

One of the robed youths behind the man stepped forward, but Satonak waved them back.

"I'm just going to give you ladies a few words of advice. Just some suggestions, as a friend."

"Some friend," muttered Othniel.

"Don't start a coven." He stabbed a finger into the tabletop to emphasise each word. "If I find any witches setting up formal groups in Senoonheim, I will be coming down on them very hard."

"What sort of response would you consider to be 'coming down hard'?" asked Troo casually. She shifted in her seat, which caused her shoulders to ripple like a landslide. The robed youth closest to her stepped away, and the woman with the fake beard adjusted it nervously.

"Lord Stanley Cornucervin owes much of Senoonheim's property to my counsel," answered Satonak. "He would allow me plenty of latitude to deal with a coven. I might have them imprisoned in the dungeons. I might confiscate their belongings so that they may not continue their evil gatherings. If necessary, I may employ my own personal skills in the chastising of any participants! And some of you don't look well to start with." He sneered these final words at Elschefla. The wizard flexed his fingers and orange sparks flashed around his hands, gathering into a ball of coruscating fire the size of a fist before flaring brightly and vanishing with a pop.

The women around the table said nothing else. Satonak nodded.

"I thought that might get your attention," he said. He spun around and beckoned his youths to follow him. Together, they stalked out of the tavern, though the patch-faced man did tug at Satonak's robes and jab a thumb towards the bar before they left.

"No, you may not get one for the road," snapped the wizard before the door slammed shut and cut off any further conversation.

Chapter Thirty-Three

M ira examined the faces of her erstwhile coven around the table, looking down at their drinks. Silence pressed on them like a weight.

"No," she said firmly.

"No what?" asked Troo.

"No, we're not going to listen to that pompous old fool," said Mira. She lifted her drink and held it forward, a torch held aloft to show the way in dark places. "I'm going to come back here every night, to help any of you who can make it. I'm going to be here to exchange recipes and rituals. And the Saturday after the next full moon, I'm going to meet my whole coven here, and the Saturday following every full moon after that!"

Troo reached out with her tankard and bashed it against Mira's, slopping alcohol over the sides.

"I'll be here too!" she agreed.

Hattie hoisted her drink as though she were lifting a barrel and staggered it down the table to join them.

"Me too!" she scowled.

The rest of the women voiced their support, all ready to join Mira in her unsanctioned coven. The sight of them, frowning at the memory of Satonak and his minions before letting the joy and delight they brought one another blossom on their faces, filled Mira with power.

"It's so strange," protested Elschefla. "I've been in Senoonheim nearly since it was founded, and I'm a witch, and he's never threatened me! What's got his beard in a knot over us all meeting?"

"He's been throwing his weight around more and more recently," Troo disclosed to them. "All the soldiers in Lord Antler's castle are talking about it. Ever since he managed to get the job watching over the city, he's been trying to make the decisions."

"He sounded frustrated that Lord Cornucervin is still the one who's actually in charge," said Kirka. "Did you see how he scowled when he said he was giving us orders by the High Lord's authority? He wanted to say it was his own authority that we had to obey."

"What is it about being a ruler's advisor that makes people think they should take over," muttered Mira. "I've seen men like this before."

"I just have to say one thing though," said Delorous. Concern lines wrinkled her otherwise smooth forehead.

"What's that?" asked Mira.

"The next full moon is only a few days away."

Everyone looked at Mira, who didn't react.

"But I'm just wasting my breath because you already knew that," said Delorous.

"Sure. Sure. I knew that!" blustered Mira.

Troo laughed.

"It's fine! We'll see the coven next Saturday!" said Mira. "For now, let's get another round!"

***

"Hello darlin', how's your evening going?" said a voice behind Mira while she waited at the bar for another glass of wine.

Mira turned and was surprised to find an orc man behind her.

His dark hair was held back from his face in a low ponytail, a wave that he pulled forward to flow over a shoulder. Mira could tell his shoulders were well-muscled because his tunic looked as though it had originally been designed for a child; the material stretched smoothly over his figure, outlining the shape of his torso, and nearly pulling apart along the seams. For a moment, Mira assumed he was topless and someone had simply painted a shirt onto him. Glimpses of green skin peeked out between the desperately-clinging threads.

The sleeves were just as tight, and he had shoved the cuffs up his forearms so they bunched above his elbows. Just as Mira noticed them, he gestured to the barkeep for a drink, and she watched the way the muscles in his forearms shifted and danced as closely as a hunter watches the bushes for a hint of their prey.

His tusks were polished to a shining white and framed the winning smile that he had deployed against her. Above the smile, his eyes were a strikingly clear autumnal-sky blue.

"It's going good," she breathed as she tried to accommodate the idea that such a pretty man could be standing in the room with her. Over his shoulders, she could see that she wasn't the only person in the tavern who had been struck by the epitome of desire that had appeared amongst them. Most of the women in the tavern had paused with their drinks halfway to their mouths, and more than one of the men was staring too.

"That is good to find out. From the frown on your face, I thought you were having a terrible time," said the orc as he stepped up closer to her. He picked up the bubbling purple drink he had ordered. She hadn't even noticed the barkeep put it down.

"I looked grumpy?" she asked. She was confused. He was so pretty, but that wasn't a very pleasant way to begin a conversation.

The pretty man leaned closer to her now. She felt the heat from his body, she smelt the earthy musk of him. She watched as he glanced down to his arm. Something was written on his wrist in small, black, scratchy letters.

"You do look grumpy. It's all those wrinkles in the corners of your eyes. Perhaps you need more sleep. I'll help you get a good night for a change." He bobbed his eyebrows up and down. "Let's go."

"Hang on, hang on," spluttered Mira. The mental fog that had been brought on by his appearance was lifting rapidly, as though someone was waving huge fans up and down inside her head. "You think I'll just fall for that? You're insulting me!"

"Better to have me talking to you than to be ignored by everyone else," the orc chuckled.

"What made you think that this would work," Mira growled.

"I went to pick up lessons," explained the orc with a grin. "Turns out that it wasn't about safely handling heavy weights." He leaned forward. "And you love it."

Mira picked up her wine and began to lift it towards the orc, but felt a hand catch her wrist.

Jacqui had stopped her. The barkeep pulled the wine glass out of Mira's hand and placed it back on the bar, then picked up a large jug of water and gave it to Mira.

"There you are love, much less wasteful," she grinned.

"Thank you," said Mira, before she upended the jug over the orc, who howled in shock. Mira returned the jug and then carried her wine back to the table where her coven were screaming in delight.

Chapter Thirty-Four

O range light flickered from torches, and candles and lamps around the common room. Mira sipped at her current glass of wine and then turned bleary eyes around the room. There were a lot more people around her than she was used to after a year of solitude in her shop, and her head felt heavy. Jacqui cleaned the large mirror that hung behind one end of the bar. The barkeep hunched in a peculiar way as she cleaned it, reaching out with her rag from beside the mirror instead of standing in front of it.

You need to go home, said a faraway voice in the back of Mira's head. She wanted to shush the voice, but was still sober enough to admit that it was right. She drank the final mouthful of her wine. The liquid crowded at the back of her throat, terrified of diving down into the alcoholic soup that filled her stomach. With an effort, she made herself swallow and then pushed her glass towards the middle of the table, almost hitting Hattie who was drinking from a glass large enough for the little witch to bathe in.

"I've got to go," Mira slurred. The women around the table all moaned sadly and began to protest.

"No, no, 'simportan'. I've gotta be up before dawn to get the baking going."

"It's before dawn now!" crowed Junka.

"'Sright, means you can start a fire and then come back for more wine," said Othniel. She tried to sit straighter in her dress made of spiderwebs, but slipped off her stool instead.

Mira considered this and then shook her head. She had to catch herself against the table, having been completely unbalanced by the movement and nearly fallen onto her face. She paused until she was sure that her head would stay in the right place before she said anything else. She had uncovered an obvious flaw with Othniel's plan.

"No, I'll be too tired tomorrow," she explained.

Othniel nodded in understanding as she clambered back onto her stool.

"I'll walk you out!" declared Troo, elbowing Mira in a friendly way.

Once Mira had climbed back up off the floor, the pair of them zig-zagged their way across the common room and out the doors. The night air was surprisingly chilly after the warmth of the tavern, and Mira sucked in a sharp breath.

"I think that went pretty well," said Troo.

"Yes, I think so too!" The icy night air stabbed into her brain and tore quickly through the warm blanket of wine that had wrapped itself around her. "Plenty of interest, and some people with some real experience, which is good because I am certainly not an expert."

"Maybe not, but you're a born leader." Troo grinned. "The way you just shrugged off Satonak's threat was pretty inspiring!" She stomped her feet to keep warm, sending ripples along the cobbles.

"Do you think he was serious?" asked Mira.

"Who, Satonak? The pompous and vain court wizard to Lord Antlers of Senoonheim?" Troo raised an eyebrow. "Who knows, maybe you're right. All those titles and airs were thrust on him unwillingly and he just wants to be left alone. I imagine he just comes down to random taverns to threaten groups of women because it's expected of all court wizards."

"Yeah, alright, I suppose he was serious," admitted Mira. "Do you know much about him?"

"Unfortunately, yeah. Satonak has been getting between everyone and Lord Cornucervin recently, and I work at the gentle whim of our lord on the Porcelain Throne." Troo shrugged. "Nobody in court likes him as far as I can tell, but what can you do when Lord Antlers isn't saying anything otherwise? I haven't been in this job for very long really. Means I haven't got the full view of everyone in the castle yet."

"So you'd say he is serious about the threats he made, but we don't know if he is cruel enough to follow through on them. Or is he more likely to send your colleagues around to arrest us, do you think?"

Troo shrugged.

"It's hard to be sure. I wouldn't be surprised if he did something pretty nasty when he was riled up. What I don't understand is why our little group got his underwear in a twist."

"Okay. Then we are all going to make sure everyone finds themselves a bravura honda as quickly as they can. They'll need support and protection against any little tricks he tries to pull." Mira tucked her hands under her armpits.

Troo grinned.

"I'm way ahead of you." She held up something between her thumb and forefinger. Mira squinted to try and see what it was.

"It's one of his hairs," Troo explained. "My bravura Alexol taught me a protective charm ages ago, and this is going to take pride of place in my next one. I'll show you the finished thing next time we catch up." Troo stood up. "Are you going to be alright getting home? You look a little wobbly."

"Yeah, I'm fine! See you later."

"See ya."

Mira wove through the street in the direction that she hoped was home. For some reason the road kept trying to roll over her, as though it was a wave in the sea. Every time the street tipped she slid sideways until she was able to regain her verticality, at which point it inevitably tilted the other way. Step by step, she staggered her way home.

After she banged into a water barrel outside one building, giving herself a knock on the shin that would surely develop into an impressive bruise, Mira stopped and hunched against the buildings around her. She needed a moment to nurse her injury.

Footsteps slapped on the cobbles behind her and then suddenly stopped. Mira squeezed her leg and tried to think straight. Why would someone else be out this late? She stumbled further along the street, holding onto the wall to help herself stay upright. She stopped, and heard the footsteps behind her stop again as well.

Like a shooting star, the answer came to her. It was obvious in the end. Who else would be out in these dark streets in the middle of the night, following her, and yet unwilling to actually speak to her? He'd been acting like that already.

"Prevos, stop following me," she hissed. "We had a nice walk, but this isn't appropriate!"

She turned around to confront the man but looked up into empty air, with only a sky full of stars occupying her vision. She blinked and lowered her gaze. *Ah, there he is*, she thought.

Standing a handful of feet behind her was a short figure dressed in dark clothes that blended perfectly with the shadowed streets of Senooonheim at night. With the starlight behind them, Mira couldn't make out more than their outline, which was shorter than her, and with an oddly arched back and shoulders.

"You're not Prevos," she said in surprise. Prevos was much bigger than this person. She put out a hand palm down in front of herself, holding it level with the top of the figure's head. Then she lifted her hand up until it was a good foot above her own head. "He's taller than you."

"No, I'm not Prevos," purred the figure in a voice that was as unyielding as a velvet rope; though the thing itself was soft and possibly even pleasurable to encounter, there was a promise of possible violence hidden behind it. The figure produced a knife from somewhere on its person and, for such an opaque shadow that revealed no features, the knife shone shockingly bright and clear.

"Now," said the figure calmly. "What do you have in your pockets that I might like?"

A bird called from somewhere nearby, the short warble bouncing off the walls so Mira couldn't quite pinpoint where it came from. The shining blade disappeared as quickly as it had appeared, and the shadowy figure turned their head, revealing a long, pointed muzzle. The figure stood statue-still until the bird called again and then they turned back to Mira.

"Sorry to bother you," they said in a completely normal voice before melting away down the street. Within three steps, Mira could not see them at all.

"Hello?" she called into the night, wondering what had driven the thief away.

"Prevos?" she asked.

Chapter Thirty-Five

Morning arrived like an unexpected mother-in-law. Sunlight burst into Mira's room with the same loud presumption of belonging, swishing the curtains aside and cheerily shouting into her sleeping ears that it was time to get up and start the day. Mira moaned and buried her head under her pillow, where the cool fabric soothed her burning head for a moment, before her hangover warmed up the pillow too much and sweat began to ooze from her head. Her temples were throbbing and pounding and her mouth felt both too full of thick, gross saliva *and* as dry as sand.

It was the second of these problems that finally forced her to get out of bed, which she immediately decided was a mistake. The change in altitude seemed to send all the blood rushing out of her head, after which it must have regrouped in her stomach if the pressure building there was any evidence.

After she had filled her chamber pot and wiped her mouth clean, Mira found her water pitcher and tipped some into a cup. She sipped at the lukewarm water as though it was the finest ambrosia, the drink of the gods, fighting to restrain herself from gulping great mouthfuls of the stuff down. She had to wait while the sips settled in her stomach, but they showed no signs of wanting to escape back up her throat and so she decided that she was doing well. She climbed back into bed and pulled her blankets over her head.

Mira heard a knock at the bakery door downstairs that pierced the little tent of self-pity that she had made for herself. She groaned and dressed slowly and carefully. Each piece of clothing sent shockwaves running along the surface of her skin, like a drum being struck, and when the ripples shook up her neck to the back of her head she felt her eyes cross. Eventually she felt capable of stepping one foot at a time down the stairs to her bakery.

The ovens sat cold and black in the kitchen. The shop itself was brighter than she was comfortable with. The day's sunlight was already streaming cheerfully through the window, a sign that she had slept far later than she should have. She stepped in, shielding her eyes, and saw that someone was leaning on the window, peering in.

Mira hobbled across the floor with her eyes squinting so far shut in fear of the light that she had to navigate the room by memory. She unlocked the door and swung it open, wincing at the deafening toll of the tiny silver bell above the door.

"Hello!" The simple greeting burst from the figure outside. They were a thin and pale-skinned elf man, whose ears pointed towards the top of his head through a fall of long and brilliantly blonde hair. Mira took in the dark green leather clothing, the serviceable boots, the bow and quiver of arrows slung about their person and groaned. The last thing she needed to be dealing with in her current state was an adventurer.

"Shop's closed," she creaked in a voice like a tomb door being shoved open. Her vocal chords complained at the gall of being asked to perform at all after an evening spent drowning in wine.

"Closed? What?" His face fell at her words. "You can't be closed, I need more of that thin bread!"

"Thin bread?"

"Yes!"

Mira held up a hand to slow the man down. His voice was already rising into the sort of shrill sound that summoned dogs, which put her skull at risk of exploding if it continued.

"Hang on. What's your name?"

"Leshgolos," he answered with huge doleful eyes and a protruding lower lip.

"For goodness sake," she waved the man's pathetic attempts to drum up sympathy aside. "I have a couple of yesterday's loaves on the shelves, but nothing freshly baked." She pinched the brow of her nose, trying to recall his words.

"What do you mean thin bread?" she asked as she stepped aside and held the door open, beckoning him to follow.

"Thank you so much!" The man practically skipped inside and rushed over to the few loaves left on Mira's shelves. Most of them were tougher loaves than she would usually be happy to sell. None of them seemed like anything she would describe as thin bread.

"It was here last time I came through," the man murmured as he ran his eyes over the shelves. "You sold me a stack of wafer bread, shaped like broad leaves. It snapped delightfully, and had just a slight sweetness to it."

His description sparked a memory somewhere deep inside the murky waters of Mira's memories.

"Did you buy it from me a season ago?" she asked.

"Yes!" he cried. Mira winced.

"I think that might have been an elven bread recipe I was trying out."

"That will be it, yes!" The man spun around with his hands clutched together under his chin.

"I'm truly sorry," she explained. "But that was an experiment. It kept well, which meant I could leave it on the shelves, but people usually only bought a single leaf or two, and then they didn't come back for any more for ages. The recipe called for a few unique ingredients that were tough to order in, so I decided it wasn't worth continuing."

"Noooo," the man groaned, sagging inwards at his knees. "The pile I bought last time got me through the Mines of Fanexcavat and the Sepulchre of Obliteration! I haven't eaten anything else for months!"

Mira's eyebrows rose.

"Wow, really? You've spent literal months eating my elven bread and nothing else?" She scrubbed a hand through her hair and squeezed the bridge of her nose, trying to clear her mind so that she could think more clearly. "I don't suppose you would be willing to put that in writing? I mean, I could get a little sign made for the window, and if you would leave your signature I could get a carver to put that on it too. Maybe a rating even? Say, how would you rate-"

But Leshgolos had rushed up to her and grabbed the collar of her shirt in both hands. Now that he was this close to her she could see how peculiar his skin was. He was covered in the usual smudges of an adventurer, the dirt and grime of someone who had been travelling hard and bedding down where they could. But his skin itself was as gleaming and smooth as porcelain. His breath smelt sickly sweet and she wrinkled her nose.

"I need more of the thin bread," he said in a low voice. His eyes pressed out of his head and his throat bulged like a bird that had swallowed a frog. Mira's blood froze.

Abruptly, he seemed to realise what he was doing and his hands jumped away from Mira as though she was made of fire. He stepped a pace back and brushed down her shoulders, as though he could straighten her collar and that would make his actions alright. "I'm sorry. I'm sorry," he stammered over and over. He stepped further away and began pacing around her bakery in a tight little circle.

"You just don't seem to understand," he complained as he walked, gripping his hands together tightly in front of him. "I haven't eaten anything else in so long. It's the only thing I can eat now! It's the only thing that fuels me through my victories! All three of my fellows passed in our attempts to seek out the Shadow Scorpion and to finally bring an end to the Never-Ending Atreus!" He was trying to act calmer, but his voice was growing shrill again.

Mira stepped closer to him and snarled.

"Listen my lad, I've already told you that I don't have it. I was kind enough to let you in when I wasn't sure what you needed, just in case it happened to be on the shelves, but now you have abused my generous hospitality and you need to leave." She spoke in tones that made it clear that she knew where the rolling pins were kept.

Leshgolos was caught unprepared and he spluttered as he looked around the room. Mira followed him step for step as he backed across the floor, clearly trying to think of something to do or say that might get her to change her mind. She threw a hand towards the door and stabbed a finger at it.

"Get out!"

There was a flicker of light on the silvery surface of the bell over the door and something heaved the door open.

"No, I need the bread!" babbled Leshgolos. His face had lost any hint of the possible threat and anger that it had momentarily held before, and now his cheeks were dragged low in desperation. He reached out towards Mira, as a drowning person reaches towards their rescuer, ready to pull them all down together. "Please!"

A familiar fear and anger clutched at Mira's throat. The elf's insistent behaviour reminded her of the way Loam had spoken to her. Both of them thought that their desires were more important than what she wanted. Mira wasn't going to stand for it. She was just frustrated that the elf only wore leather armour and no metal. And the sun was at the wrong angle this early in the day.

Mira unrolled her hand and glanced towards the front window. Though the light was strong, she was able to see a faint glimpse of both her reflection and Leshgolos's. She lifted her hand and lowered it over his reflection, taking his head between her thumb and forefinger. She squeezed a little, and smiled when he yelped. Then she flicked the image towards the door, and spun around to watch as the corporeal form of the elf was carried off his feet and flung outside.

Mira stepped up to the door and watched as Leshgolos rolled into the middle of the street and then scrambled to his feet. A fresh layer of brown dust settled across his smooth face and rumpled leathers.

"How dare you!" he yelled.

"How dare you!" she replied, stepping out onto the road as emphasis. Leshgolos ducked as though she had thrown something at him and then bolted away like a frightened rabbit.

A few passersby paused to look back at her after watching him race around a corner. She shrugged.

"Adventurers, what can I say?" she said. They snorted, nodded, and kept walking.

Chapter Thirty-Six

M ira retreated to a chair in her kitchen. Dealing with the elven adventurer had proved that she was in no condition to cope with any other customers, even if they were less obsessive than he had been. She lay back in her chair with a cold flannel across her forehead. Dealing with the annoying elf had drawn on reserves of energy that she did not actually have available after her night out.

It took half an hour before she managed to brew a hot pot of tea and pour the heavenly liquid into a mug. She tipped a double helping of sugar in and picked it up in both hands. The boiling mug warmed her hands and each piping mouthful fought with the cool moisture tracing down the sides of her head from the flannel. The contrast was glorious.

There was a quiet knock at the door and Mira ducked instinctively to hide. Then she peeked around the edge of the doorway and was surprised to see two of the women from the night before standing outside the window. She got up and smiled as she walked to the door.

"It's just you," she said as she let them in. "I didn't need to panic."

"Of course not dearie!" Junka smiled. When she smiled it made her face separate into a million thin lines, like heavy layers of oil paint depicting a steeple surrounded by huge whorling stars on the waving blanket of a night sky. She clutched a heavy blue shawl around her shoulders. "We wanted to come and see your little bakery. Aren't you so clever to do this! You must be very proud of yourself."

"I am, it takes a lot of work," Mira replied. "How did you find it? I didn't think I mentioned where my bakery was." Mira wondered if she had described her address to one of the women but then forgotten about it. She worried that she might have made a fool of herself last night if she was doing things and then forgetting about them.

"No, I asked Nerishma here to show me where to go."

The skinny, black-clad woman stepped forward from behind Junka and lifted one hand to acknowledge Mira. Nerishma didn't even move the hand from side to side, so it would be hard to call the gesture a wave. It was more like Nerishma was showing Mira her palm, as if that made for an interesting salutation.

"How are you feeling this morning, dearie?" continued Junka. "I imagine your head must be absolutely killing you today, you poor dear." Junka smiled sympathetically and stepped closer. She took one of Mira's hands in both of her own. "I did think ahead actually, and I brought one of my personal favourite remedies with me. Here." She pulled a small, flat bottle made from very thick green glass from somewhere in the folds of skirts and blouses that were bundled around her. There was a cork wedged in it, and a dark liquid sloshed slowly inside, moving with the patient glorp of yogurt.

"Thank you," said Mira.

Junka raised her hands in protest. "No need for that, no need, I just knew that it would be appreciated! When I saw you staggering off, I told myself: that's a woman who is borrowing far too much happiness from tomorrow! Just take a sip when you need it, and not too much. I was wondering if you'd like to come with Nerishma and I into the woods. We thought we might gather some mushrooms."

Mira was surprised. Neither of the women in front of her looked like the sort she would have expected to collect mushrooms in the woods. They weren't wearing floaty pants or dripping with dozens of bulky beaded bracelets. And what woods were there near Senoonheim anyway?

But, despite her surprise, she said, "Sure."

The three women set off towards the city gates. The main streets of the city were wide, like rivers, and stuffed with people. It was clear that they were designed to allow a lot of people to move through the city at once. The buildings on either side looked solid, with stone work on the ground floor and timber frames around pale, daubed upper stories. Tiled roofs angled steeply above them. The streets themselves were unpaved, which meant they were heavily rutted by the wagons trundling through the crowd, and filled with puddles that Mira hoped were from rain and morning dew but suspected were the result of cart animals relieving themselves. Some enterprising store-owners had laid out paving stones near the doors to their shops, enticing more customers by providing them with a way out of the mud.

Branching off the streets were dozens of alleys, the tributaries of the river, and these seemed much less well designed. Where the main street was broad, with clear windows for the shops, and shutters from the living spaces overhead, the alleys were narrow and cramped and often turned into tunnels due to the overhanging upper stories that leaned out so far that the buildings touched.

Mira and the others walked behind a single cart pulled by two large oxen. Its width forced everyone walking in the other direction to squeeze closer to the buildings, but the merchant on the driver's seat was singing a pleasant tune, and one of his assistants was selling stock from the back of the cart, so no one was complaining. The witches followed the cart through the gates and into the surrounding city.

When Mira had arrived in Senoonheim, she hadn't been used to the idea that a city might have walls inside the expanse of its buildings. Senoonheim was such a place, with walls deep inside its streets, and buildings sprawling around outside them.

In theory, as far as she knew, walls were supposed to be on the outside of the things that they were protecting. She wasn't an expert in the matter and so maybe it was naive of her, but she thought that it would be difficult to protect something if parts of it were outside the protective layer. It would be like a turtle with a shell that was only a little bit thicker than the rest of its skin, and really small so that it only covered a little spot in the middle of the turtle's back. Such a shell would barely be able to protect its organs from attack. What would be the point?

Mira would have been surprised to hear that such a creature did exist, hiding itself in the mud of the Emerald Mires to the west of Whinnia. Many frogfolk had lost their toes to the aggressive beaks of these turtles. This is because the turtles lacked a reliable physical defence and so had developed an effective psychological defence instead, generally described by herpetologically inclined scholars as "being violent little bastards". And yet, Mira wasn't wrong in her analysis of how useful shells and walls were for defending things. Perhaps if the turtles had developed proper shells, they wouldn't be considered a delicacy that the frogfolk were willing to lose a few toes over.

The towns of Whinnia would certainly never countenance protecting themselves in such a strange way. The tall, wooden stockades that surrounded their hill forts were always built at the extremity of the town. Given that Whinnian towns occupied steep hills, this meant their buildings were higher than the stockades, allowing the people an unobstructed view across the surrounding fields of the Far-Grasso Sea. No one had ever even tried to build any houses outside the stockades, but Mira imagined that if someone did then they would quickly be surrounded by some very confused and judgemental representatives of the HHA: the HouseHold Association, who would let them know exactly what they needed to stop doing immediately.

The HHA was a particularly Whinnian group. Each town was run by an important family who maintained a network of control through the favours they would grant on those they liked and punishment for those who did not follow their particular rules. This was the HouseHold of the town, and the Head of each House would have some connection to the First Seat of Whinnia.

Mira had wondered about the situation of Senoonheim's walls but had never had any friends to ask about it. With her fledgling coven under way, she finally had someone to ask!

Chapter Thirty-Seven

"Hey Junka," Mira said. "What's with the walls?"

Junka looked over her shoulder. The women had just come out of a long tunnel between the wooden gates at one end of the stone walls and the heavy iron grille that was raised at the other. Already they had walked far enough that the walls were half-hidden behind an inn and a tall house with a grocer's shop at the bottom.

"What about them?" asked the older woman.

"Why are there buildings outside the walls?"

Junka barked a laugh.

"The space inside the walls is full. Where else would people live?"

"But surely that's not safe?" said Mira.

Junka's face twisted into a fresh arrangement of confused folds.

"What?"

"In Whinnia, we never build outside the walls. Anything out there would be a sitting duck for raiders."

"Did you get attacked by raiders often in Whinnia?" asked Nerishma, who moved with the self-conscious shuffle of someone more used to slipping along a wall in the darkness. She kept twisting as though she was about to move sideways.

"I mean... It didn't *not* happen." Mira walked in silence after that, considering the raids that she could remember. Once, a group of men in spiky armour had ridden up to the gates, raised axes above their heads and yelled a lot, before riding away. Another time, a group of goblins had tried to come in and trade mushrooms and deep cave isopods, only for the merchants in town to throw stones at them until they left. But she couldn't remember a single time that a group of angry people had burned and looted any part of any of the towns she knew. At least, not any group that the town didn't already know about. Surely there must have been a proper raid sometime in all her years in Whinnia?

"I can see what you mean, it would help to have walls around the other buildings too. But you'll be pleased to know that Lord Cornucervin announced that a new set of walls is being considered. In the meantime, he has also warned people that if danger arises then it's entirely possible that the buildings outside the walls could be razed." Junka pulled her shawl closer around her shoulders. Mira didn't know why she wore it. The sun was building a layer of sweat in her hair and under her blouse.

"He wasn't expecting so many people to come is the problem," added Nerishma. "When Lord Cornucervin built Senoonheim he was trying to take advantage of the sudden interest in the Unlit Hills. There were so many adventurers heading out this way, or returning with their treasure, and he was just tapping into a lucrative market. So he had some walls built and sold the land inside to various businesses. It was all a way to get the city started so they could take advantage of the adventurers."

"But there was plenty of other entrepreneurial types who were keen to get in on it all, not to mention a neverending stream of adventurers!" chuckled Junka. "So the city grew too big!"

"And in all this time, there have been no raids on the outer buildings?"

"Who would raid?" shrugged Junka. "There's rumours of an undead lord somewhere in the hills but whoever is hidden away up there seems happy enough to stay hidden. There're a few wandering hordes on the plains, but adventurers kept them pretty well occupied. Any other concerns are petty bandit gangs, holding up caravans and travellers, not nearly enough to actually threaten a city!"

The trio turned a corner, following the road between two buildings, then were suddenly walking between green fields. Thick blades of grass waved in the air. The city ended all at once behind them, like a cliff at the edge of the sea.

Mira could see the dark green trees of Gloombark Forest in the distance, along the road that led away from Senoonheim and back towards the more populated lands in the North. It took them nearly an hour to walk close enough to cut west towards the trees.

Walking through the Gloombark Forest when they reached it was not a pleasant experience. This is of course not very surprising. The forest was not named the Friendly Mossy Glade Woods which travellers had to assume was intentional. The inclusion of the word "gloom" right up there at the front of the name set up exactly the right expectations. This was not a forest for picnicking soft toys, though it was certainly the sort of place where monsters set traps to steal honey.

The trunks surrounding the witches were thick and speckled and pale. Low bushes spread between them, making it impossible to see far into the gloom beneath their boughs. Branches and leaves spread overhead so densely that they appeared black from beneath. Only a rare spear of sunlight made it through tiny gaps in the canopy to the dead leaves and mud under their feet. Unsurprisingly, mushrooms were everywhere.

Junka and Nerishma walked through gaps between the trees that Mira didn't even realise were paths and reached down to pluck the soft, brown lumps from the ground, dusting them off and dropping them into canvas sacks that hung from their sides. Nerishma smiled at Mira.

"Go ahead, grab as many as you can. I know a great soup recipe."

Mira stared at the bulbous things bubbling up from every surface around her. She reached out for one cluster near the bottom of a tree trunk.

"No, not those ones!" yelped Nerishma. She crunched through a pile of decaying branches to grab Mira's hand. "Those are nasty!"

"Poisonous?" gasped Mira, flinching away.

"No, they just taste like sick," Nerishma spat, as though even having the words in her mouth made her want to vomit. Mira groaned.

From then on, she only picked up mushrooms the others pointed out to her first.

Junka had just pulled a massive, ball-like mushroom off the ground and was trying to fit it through the small opening of her sack, when Mira heard crunching noises deeper in the forest. The women froze. Their eyes were huge and round. Nerishma clenched her hands into fists.

"Is that not normal here?" Mira whispered roughly.

"Shhhh," hissed Nerishma.

Junka rolled her large eyes towards the source of the sound.

"Animals?" she suggested.

"You said that it wasn't dangerous out here," said Mira as quietly as she could. "You said that it didn't matter that the city walls were inside the city."

"I said that there weren't really any armies who might try to attack," snapped Junka. "But I also said there were bandits out here!"

The three stayed still for a few moments more. With an unspoken agreement they decided to take the time-honoured course of hoping that the scary thing went away by itself. When that didn't happen, the woman began to creep backwards through the trees the way they had come.

Chapter Thirty-Eight

The crunching grew louder and laughing voices began to ring in the darkness beneath the trees. Unexpected laughter is well-known to be one of the most terrifying noises ever conceived, and the cold grip of fear clutched at Mira's spine.

A group of small, red creatures burst through the trees, swinging through the branches on long arms, dropping to spin and dance on their equally long legs. Their hands left black handprints on the wood and smoke hissed up from the leaves that crunched beneath their feet. One of the red figures saw the women and began to shriek and point at them. Its fellows raced to surround the witches.

The creatures had all sorts of faces, from long and thin ones that pointed into a beak, or flat and broad with a pudgy nose, but all of them had eyes that burned a brilliant yellow. Orange, mottled fur burst like collars around their necks. The tallest of them only came up to Mira's shoulder at best, but their presence was threatening. Waves of heat rolled from them as they surrounded the women. There were six in total, giggling in high-pitched voices, pointing and leering.

"Do something," hissed Nerishma out of the corner of her mouth. She patted at the sides of her clothes as though looking for something in a pocket that had been left somewhere else by mistake. This is a typical thing to do in an emergency. Even people on sinking ships will pat their pockets as the waves roll over the deck, though only twice has anyone ever discovered a lifeboat that they had forgotten they had tucked inside.

"Who?" asked Mira at exactly the same time as Junka yelped "Me?" The two women looked at each other, both flinching away from the panic and confusion mirrored in the other's eyes.

"Either of you!" snapped Nerishma. She jammed a hand into the pocket on the side of her waistcoat and a triumphant smile lit up her face. She withdrew her hand quickly, stabbing it towards the nearest of the imps. Their eyes widened and they flung their arms up in front of their face, but when nothing happened they lowered their arms again and took a closer look at the object.

Everyone in the forest clearing looked at the toothbrush in Nerishma's hand.

"Is my breath that bad?" hooted the imp, and all of the creatures doubled over in laughter, loud and thundering laughter that was far too deep to come from their small bodies.

"Mira, do a spell," urged Junka. "Come on dearie, it's time to put those witch skills to good use."

"Witch skills? What about you both, don't you have any witch skills?" Mira spluttered, trying not to let the desperation flooding her body leak out into her expressions.

Junka spread her hands and shrugged.

"Nerishma said she'd teach me a lovely recipe for good mushroom soup, but she doesn't know any more than I do about using mystical forces to drive away one's enemies. Go on, do a fireball or summon a swarm of mystical darts."

Mira's skin crawled as fear and panic fought a shivering war for control of her reaction.

"I-I don't know many rituals at all, I'm much better at following recipes," she said. "And there's nothing shiny here, no reflections for me to work with." She felt as though the entire forest was watching her now, the trees themselves looking down on her from their great height with their knotty eyes and ancient thoughts. "I'm not really much of a witch," she said, and the admission robbed her of the energy that held her upright. She sagged towards the ground.

"You're more of a witch than me," objected Junka.

Before either Mira or Junka could say anything else, the imps' patience wore out and they began calling to each other as they spun around the witches.

"Look at this one, I think she wants to play!"

"But what sort of game should we play?"

"I think this one is too old for games! She's probably too old for anything!"

"Maybe we should play pass the head!"

One of the imps pulled off their leg as though it had been tied on, like an extra prop on a travelling actor's stage. Mira hoped to see strings that had been undone, but then the foot wiggled its toes and she felt her stomach rise.

"Give us a head!" yelled the leg-holding imp. One of the others put both hands to the sides of their own jaw and then grunted and pushed. Their head popped off like a child's doll, and then laughed and rolled its eyes.

"Give me a go!" The head yelled, and one of the other imps spun past, grabbed the head, and dropped it at the foot of the one holding their own leg. The leg-holder lifted the leg backwards, yelled, "Heads up!" and swung.

The imp's head screamed joyfully as it launched away into the trees, interspersed by yells and thuds as it bounced off branches before landing somewhere in the distant bushes. The headless body stuck out both arms and began tottering away in the direction the head had gone. The imp's voice carried softly through the forest.

"Warmer. Warmer. No, colder. You idiot, you're going to walk into a–Yeah, into that tree."

"Who's next?" said the imp nearest Mira. They reached out their hands towards her. "Your head looks ready to go for a ride," they said, red lips pulling back from jagged teeth.

"Maybe her head can journey with your backside when I kick it, you rascal!" called a new voice from behind Mira. She spun around to see who had called out and saw an old woman dressed in a heavy dress walking slowly forward out of the underbrush. The woman leaned on a thick, whorled stick as she hobbled closer, and her eyelids were so swollen and black that for a moment Mira thought that the woman had just come from a fight. A huge wart popped off the end of her nose, and her pale hair hung limply down the sides of her face.

"I think these women have had enough of your games," she said. "You lot need to clear off." As she spoke, a large, black bird flapped down out of the trees to land on her shoulder. Something was wrong with its head, but Mira was still in shock and didn't get a good look.

"Oh yeah?" One of the imps stepped forward. They stood in front of the woman with arms crossed and smoke curling up from where their feet pressed into the forest floor. "Says who?"

"Says the only woman in this clearing who knows she is a witch." The woman leaned forward and smiled. It was the sort of simple expression that should have turned any troublemaker's blood to ice. A smile like that is only smiled by two creatures in the world: a shark that has just spotted a swimmer in deep water who is quite alone apart from the tuba player, and someone with no confidence in their ability to deal with a situation, the sort of person who doesn't need to have confidence in themselves because they actually have already dealt with everything, and now it's just a matter of the rest of the universe catching up and realising it.

But perhaps the internal heat of the imps made it harder for them to feel a chill of premonition, because the arms-crossed imp just said, "There's nothing a witch could do to stop me now!"

"Is that so?" asked the witch. Her eyebrow raised slightly. "Allow me to show you exactly how to banish a minor horde of imps," she said to the other women.

She pulled her arms wide, and her black dress hung from her limbs like the encompassing wings of a giant bat. She still clutched her walking stick in one hand, and wind rose behind her, sending leaves tumbling across the ground towards the imps and whipping the edges of her dress like a tempest. She opened her mouth as the insubstantial light of Gloombark Forest dimmed further. Mira held her breath.

"Would whoever owns these children come and sort them out please!" bellowed the woman, without breaking eye contact with the folded-arms imp.

Chapter Thirty-Nine

I mmediately, the imps scattered. Some climbed up the trunks of the nearest trees, others tripped over each other as they raced towards the bushes. The folded-arm imp uncrossed their arms and slumped like a snowman in the sun. One of the other imps curled into a ball at their feet and clutched the first imp's ankles like a lifeline.

"Awwww, naaooooo, that's so unfaaaiirr," whined the imp standing in front of the woman. "What did ya hafta go 'n' do that fooooorrrrr." Their voice vanished up their throat and emerged in a piercing hum from their nose, a siren wailing at the injustice being meted out upon the imps by an uncaring world. Mira had heard the exact same irritating tone from children who had been refused chocolate-covered treats from her shelves.

"What have they been up to now?" growled a voice from the forest. Everyone turned to look at the figure that stalked out from behind the trees, twigs stuck in the fuzzy collar that sprouted from his neck. The imp man who joined them was a little taller than Mira, and had a dark beard around his lips and chin, trimmed short.

"Good afternoon ladies," he said politely. His gaze travelled around the group and took in the scarpering imps in the trees. His brow furrowed. "What have these miscreants been doing now?"

The old woman bobbed her head to acknowledge his arrival.

"Hello sir. My name is Fina, and I live around these parts–"

Mira blinked and snorted. The woman lived near here? The idea seemed bizarre. Where could she live when there was barely enough room for a bird to fly between the trees and the paths spiralled endlessly in on themselves?

"–sorry to say that these children were making threats to these ladies here."

"Really." The word wasn't a question. He wasn't saying it to doubt what Fina had told him. The man said the word in that parental tone that carried a wide variety of consequences along with it, and the imp children still in sight all cowered at his utterance. "What sort of threats?"

"I believe that one there said they should take off her head so they could whack it away into the trees."

"I was just kidding," protested the imp who had made the threat. They were busily trying to jam their leg back on at the hip. "We know that their heads don't actually come off." The imp was trying to smile, as though a display of happiness might convince the man that it was all in good fun.

"I don't care if you thought it was a joke, I've told you before not to make threats to take apart other people," snapped the man. He strode over and took the imp by one long pointed ear, which popped off. The taller imp sighed and put a hand on the small imp's shoulder and began tugging them along in his wake. "All of you, follow me. We're going home now, and you know how your mother will feel about having to cut our trip short."

"Oh noooo," chorused the imp children in a long, dying moan. "Don't tell muuuummmm!"

The man turned at the edge of the clearing.

"My name is Virgil. I must offer the biggest and sincerest apology to you all on behalf of my family. I've been trying to teach them some manners, but you know how teenagers can be."

"I do indeed," agreed Fina. "We'll be seeing you."

The imp pursed his lips and then pushed his children in front of him between the trees. The echoes of him berating them wafted back to the witches for a long time.

Mira turned to see Fina leaning on her stick with both hands. She watched the other women with a slight smile on her lips.

"And that's how it's done," she said happily.

"Thank you," said Mira.

"Are you a witch, then?" asked Nerishma.

"Look at me," replied the woman. She lifted her arms and did a little turn on the spot and then leaned on her stick again. "Old lady, black clothes, lives deep in the shadowy Gloombark Forest. What else would I be?"

"But a witch knows magic," said Junka. "And you didn't do any magic. All you did was call their dad. I'm an old woman in dark clothes in the forest myself, and I'm not a witch yet."

"*Yet* is a very important word though. So many things are not what they should be 'yet'. So much danger and trouble in the world and 'yet'." Fina smiled at them again. "And you are not a witch 'yet'. I think it's very good to hear that word on your lips."

"No, seriously," said Nerishma. "Why didn't you drive them off with magic?"

"It turned out that they were only children," said Mira, touching Nerishma's arm. "Are you saying we should be turning children into frogs?"

Nerishma blushed and pulled her hood further over her face.

"Exactly," agreed Fina. "What makes a witch a witch is that she uses her brain to solve her problems. She considers the relationships that may come in handy, and the tools at her disposal. And I, I have met many different people in this forest, which means that I can recognise a bunch of hyperactive imp children when I see them." The woman stepped closer and put a hand on Neirshma's shoulder. "It's no shame to you if you haven't met imp children before and didn't recognise them. But now you know." She paused and looked into Nerishma's face for a moment. She was studying the younger woman closely, in the way some witches stare into a mug to examine tea leaves.

Mira had always wondered how the swirling of dried leaves in hot water reflected the future. The world could be a confusing place to live in though, so maybe the leaves were as good a way to look into the future as anything else.

Fina nodded sharply, clearly approving of whatever she found in the skinny woman's face before continuing. "Come along ladies! I'd like to hear more about these new witches that have turned up in my neck of the woods."

Fina hobbled away through the trees on her walking stick and didn't even look around to see if the others were following her. Mira glanced at Junka and

Nerishma as though she was going to wait on their decision, but it was for show really. There was no way she wasn't finding out more about this woman.

Trees spread apart like gates opening as Fina hobbled forward. When Mira looked further ahead the tree trunks still seemed to be packed edge to edge along the path, just as they had been in the rest of Gloombark Forest. Yet there was plenty of space for every step they took as they followed Fina. Mira wondered if the old woman had cast some sort of spell on the forest, perhaps as a way to keep out interlopers.

"Is it just me, or is it much easier to walk through here?" she asked.

Nerishma snorted as she awkwardly stepped around large, curling roots that flowed over the ground, and ducked away from a cobwebby branch jutting out from the tree next to her.

"Yeah. It's easier than before, but travelling through this place still sucks. Give me a nice alleyway to walk through, that's much better than any of this."

"Alleys are full of animal dung, stagnant puddles, barrels and broken glass," Mira said.

"There's dung out here too," said Nerishma.

"But no barrels blocking the way."

Nerishma glared at the trees around them.

"The alley is still better."

Junka was moving at a start-stop pace similar to the way Fina hobbled ahead of them. She smiled at the other two women.

"It's always easier to do things that have been done before. Earlier, we were just trying to make our way, and we didn't know which path to take. We butted up against every obstacle in this forest. But Fina knows the path, so she leads us along it. Not only that, but we are watching an older woman succeed at strolling through these trees. If she can do it, our minds must tell us, then so can we! That's why it's so useful to share our experiences with each other."

Mira doubted that it was as simple as that.

Before long, they reached a clearing at the end of the path. The trees stopped, and the thick underbrush that stretched out beneath the canopy, seeking any scrap of sunlight that got through, vanished. A short field of wild grass, dotted with pastel flowers, spread out from the edge of the forest into a space big enough to hold Mira's bakery, the Sprog and Sparrow, and half a dozen other buildings from the streets of Senoonheim all at once. In the middle of the clearing sat one of the strangest buildings Mira had ever seen.

It was a gingerbread house.

"Are you kidding me?" she yelped as soon as she stepped out from under the trees.

The house sat there, completely unaffected by her disbelief. Grass grew tall next to its dark, textured walls. Swirls of something white lined the eaves and the windows. Mira had to believe the decoration had been carved from wood and then painted. The alternative, that someone had made buckets and buckets of icing and then treated it somehow so that it might last while exposed to the sun and rain and wind and wildlife, twisted her mind. The idea was so hard to get her head around that she completely forgot how to walk until Junka stepped over and tucked an arm through her elbow.

"Come along dearie, let's see what this is all about then."

They followed Fina along a path of small stones and in through the front door.

Chapter Forty

M ira sat between the cushions embroidered into bumpy riots of colour that covered every piece of furniture. The furniture itself, from chairs to tables to cabinets full of little porcelain figures, was carved into whirling swirls of decorative wood. Papery lace doilies covered the table and the chair arms. It was like sitting in a blue butter cookie tin.

Fina told them to relax while she got a kettle of water boiling in her kitchen.

Mira sat carefully, certain that she was about to be stabbed by forgotten needles in the embroidered surfaces. She and her coven-sisters sat silently, waiting. They nodded at each other and tapped their knees.

Something strange happens to people while they are in a waiting room. Even if they know each other well, they are overcome by the need to keep the room quiet. If they must talk, then they will whisper.

"Do you guys come mushroom picking often?" asked Mira softly.

Nerishma shook her head.

"I've come out here a couple of times and Nerishma said she loves a mushroom," Junka said.

"Fried on a breakfast plate," muttered the skinny woman.

Mira nodded and the silent waiting returned. Thankfully, so did Fina, carrying a tray bearing four delicate teacups. The black bird was sitting on her shoulder again. Mira took a closer look at its pale head and regretted it immediately. There were no feathers, and the skin was so taut that the bird's head looked like it was just a skull.

Fina set down the tray of drinks and fetched a teapot. She poured tea for them all, dropped four sugar cubes into her cup, and then offered the bowl to the others.

"Why gingerbread?" asked Mira, after she had sipped from her cup.

"What's wrong with gingerbread?" asked Fina mildly, her eyes on Mira over the edge of her own cup.

"You can't actually make a whole building out of it for starters!" replied Mira. "It's impossible! The structure wouldn't be sound! Gingerbread isn't wood for goodness' sake!"

Fina smiled.

"I like it. I have a bit of a sweet tooth."

"Seems a shame to cover it all up though," Nerishma contributed. "It must have taken a lot of work to create it in the first place."

"What do you mean?" asked Fina.

"You've put up wallpaper in all these rooms, and laid down rugs across wooden floors. Why didn't you leave all of that gingerbread exposed?"

"It's too sticky." Fina frowned, as though she hated to be reminded of this flaw in her current living conditions.

"Why doesn't it get all eaten by ants?" Junka asked. Mira nodded emphatically and pointed to Junka in support, glad that the others were noticing how implausible this house was.

"Ants know better than to get on the bad side of a witch. Come now, have you no respect for ants?"

This response confused Junka, but Mira wasn't going to be mollified.

"The only stories I know of witches in gingerbread houses are ones where they are luring in children and eating them." She leaned back on her chair with her arms crossed and the smug confidence of a lawyer who has finished laying out some pretty damning evidence.

"Is that what this is?" Her eyes slowly widened as she considered the implications of what she had said. "Have you poisoned the tea?" she gasped. She grabbed her throat with one hand.

Junka was in the middle of taking a huge gulp from her own cup and she spat it all back into the cup noisily. She peered down into the brown liquid, drips covering her nose.

"Poison? Really?" she asked the room.

"I wouldn't put it past her," grumbled Mira.

"There's no poison," said Nerishma as she added another sugar cube to her tea and gave it a tinkling stir.

"And how do you know?" asked Mira. "I thought you didn't know enough magic to do your own yet."

"Trade secrets," said Nerishma before sipping at her cup.

"Ladies, I quite understand your suspicion," chuckled Fina. "A gingerbread house is a strange choice, but I built it long ago, when these mountains were empty and few others came by. I have a sweet tooth and I wasn't the only one trying out some unusual materials. I ended up with this house and I had to make the best of it. Sometimes making the best of things means hammering in floorboards so your socks don't stick to the floor in the summer."

She finished her tea and leaned forward on her chair, resting both hands on the top of her walking stick.

"But I want to know more about you! In the forest, I overheard you talking about becoming witches?"

"Yes, that's right," said Junka. "Mira started a coven and we're all helping each other get going. But it is difficult when some of us don't know much."

"And just how much do you know, Mira?" The old woman's eyes were not as old and rheumy as they had looked before. There was a sparkle in them now, a glint of old intelligence. It was the light of someone who could smell lies as easily as most people could smell the piles of ox-dung left behind after a merchant's cart trundles down the street. Fina was looking past the surface Mira displayed, deeper inside than she might even know herself.

"I only know a little bit about being a witch," Mira admitted warily. "I was still quite new to my coven in Whinnia when I left. I had learned a little, but I haven't been able to keep in touch with any of those witches."

Mira had written to Bovo when she first arrived in Senoonheim, but there had been no reply yet. She lived in hope that Bovo's letter in return was just taking a long time to reach her, or that Loam had interfered with their letters out of spite. But she was worried that she knew the real reason that she hadn't heard from her friend.

"Hmmm." The old woman turned her head a little, looking at Mira in the same manner that a bird would look at something on the ground from a tree, studying it to see whether it was shiny and therefore worth stealing or moving and therefore worth eating. "A coven is a good thing. There's nothing better than sharing one's troubles and one's successes. How many of you are there?"

"About ten of us, I think?"

"And, with me included, that is a wonderful number! You should be proud of yourself!"

Mira resisted the urge to puff up her chest.

"But it is difficult to grow when you are all novices teaching one another. I think we should hold some lessons here."

Chapter Forty-One

M ira didn't know what to say. She didn't want to trust this woman. Although she had to admit that Fina's help when they were being taunted by the imps had been amazing. And she was clearly an experienced witch when they needed someone who could actually teach them how to be a witch properly. But anyone who lived in such a bizarre house as this must be someone who couldn't be relied upon!

"Why would you help us?" she asked suspiciously."I need all the help I can get up here," sighed Fina. "I've been the only witch in the Gloombark Forest for years now." She stood and walked to the window, pushing open the shutters. Crumbs crackled off the edges, and Fina absentmindedly brushed them off the window sill. She leaned on it and looked dramatically out and up. It was an inspiring pose.

Mira shifted on her chair so that she could peek around Fina and out the window as well. Trees filled every space outside the window, poking their leafy branches towards the house. Fina could probably only see about a foot beyond the wall.

"I have been here a long time. I am older than I look," said the old woman cryptically.

"How long are we talking?" whispered Nerishma to Junka. Fina ignored her.

"For an age, this forest and these hills were the isolated home to all manner of strange and ill-known creatures. That is why I created my home here; I knew I would be judged for my love of sugar in the cities of the North. The Gloombark Forest was filled with the sounds of jabberwocks and bandersnatch, and the mountains were the nesting places of dragons and more."

Fina continued looking out the window as she reminisced, as though her vision wasn't blocked by walls of trees and she was looking at the vistas around the Unlit Hills instead. She sighed and bowed her head.

"Then the adventurers started coming. Treating our home like it was a puzzle box full of treats. They believed that if they only solved the puzzle properly, they could strip out everything from these lands. And if they couldn't think their way through the puzzle, why, then they had big swords and plenty of spells with which they could break it open."

Fina turned back to the women sitting in her room. Though her shoulders were stooped and her skin old and wrinkled, the passion in her eyes was strong and bright.

"A few more witches to help protect the Unlit Hills is just what I need."

"Us? Protect this whole land against adventurers? Surely that's something you should get Lord Cornucervin involved in," said Junka.

"The High Lord of Senoonheim is part of the problem," said Mira, understanding what Fina was getting at. The old woman nodded.

"Not the worst part, by far. He is trying to strike a balance between leaving a space for adventurers and draining them of the treasures they have found, but he certainly encourages them to steal as much as they can from the land. If you let me train you, and help me keep the adventurers from delving deep into the hills, then I think we can save these lands for the creatures that have dwelled here from the depths of time."

The women sat in silence and contemplated this proposition. Mira could feel her opposition to Fina softening, though she still wanted to be careful. She looked at Junka and Nerishma, trying to work out what they were feeling, and was surprised to discover that they were both watching her. Finally, she drew a deep breath and spoke.

"This is a lot of pressure to put on women who aren't even witches yet. I can see why you would want to protect the land around you though, and we could certainly use someone who could teach us. I also don't know that any of us will be useful in your personal vendetta, but I think most of us would be happy to help where we can." She glanced at the other two women to see if they agreed. Nerishma and Junka both nodded.

Fina smiled.

"Wonderful. I'll send Plak to let you know when I'm ready to teach some of you." The skull-headed bird made an awful, throat-rattling croak from its perch next to Fina's chair and Mira shuddered. "In the meantime, don't let a bunch of imp children stop you in future!"

***

The witches walked back to Senoonheim, each wrapped in the insulation of their own thoughts. Fina's offer gave them a chance to really build their coven properly, but what she had said about adventurers draining the land was disturbing. As they walked out from under Gloombark Forest's claustrophobic boughs, she examined the distant landscape.

Senoonheim spread like stony moss across the lower hills ahead of them. Buildings rose in layers over the fields, built of stone and dark timber and roofed with tiles of slate and wood. Threads of smoke curled from chimneys, coiling up into the otherwise clear sky overhead. White puffs of cloud drew together over the city, mixing with the smoke and turning the dreary and mentally numbing off-white of an office ceiling.

Lord Cornucervin's castle squatted amongst the smaller buildings. It was a twisted thing, with turrets that curled out and up from its walls on every side, like a bouquet of cone-tipped flowers. It stood out from the wood and stone of the city, appearing to be constructed from black chitin, with jagged edges and bulbous outgrowths covering it. It was the sort of castle that belonged directly beneath a conjunction of triple suns, with a great purple crystal glowing ominously inside its central hall. Even from where she and the others were trudging back along the road from Gloombark, Mira could see the outer wall of the castle and its huge drawbridge.

Behind the city rose the Unlit Hills. The peaks rose higher and higher, like rising waves. At the limits of her sight, some crests wore a light dusting of snow.

Mira had seen them when she first came to Senoonheim, but they had been a backdrop to what had been more important to her at the time: a new home, a place that she might re-establish herself. Now she began to truly take in the hills.

They were so much more than hills, she realised. They stretched to the horizon, blocking one another from view, some peeking over from further away like eager children posing for a portrait. A few of the Unlit Hills bore peaks tall enough that they should really be called mountains, she was sure, though she didn't know whether students of geology would agree with her.

(In fact she needn't have worried about being corrected, as those students often engaged in heated debates about this very topic and would correct each other anyway. Many of the older and more serious scholars had suggested adopting a definition based on whether or not someone could enjoy a day's hike up and down the peak, but younger and more vigorous students opposed the idea on the basis that it would turn every elevation above one or two stories into a mountain if measured by the older group. In any case, tradition named the slopes and peaks around Senoonheim as the Unlit Hills and so they would remain, for the time being).

Mira's brow wrinkled. Where did all the stone for this city come from? There were very few signs of digging in the hills near the city from where she was looking. She had spoken to miners in her shop, but could see no pockmarked mines or gaping quarries tearing into the land. And an awful lot of rocks would have had to be broken down to build that castle. She would have understood if Fina had complained about the city ripping up the land in the hills, but that wasn't the issue. It was the adventurers that frustrated her.

As Mira wondered about the way Senoonheim affected the land around it, her thoughts wandered back to Whinnia.

Chapter Forty-Two

There was a large square next to the Great Hall of the First Seat of Whinnia. It was one of the few level surfaces in Wallis. Mira was far from the only person whose morbid curiosity had compelled her to come to the square, battered by the wind that had travelled far across the plains.

The wind didn't begin in Whinnia. The First Seat often claimed that there were no edges to Whinnia, only lands that would benefit hugely from realising that they should be part of Whinnia. But the wind did begin somewhere.

The wind swirled through the loose shawls and hoods of the crowd who were standing around the edges of the square. It passed over the cobblestones, marking a space that the crowd would not step on. They shifted on their feet in the cold dirt outside the stones.

There was a small knot of finanseers with their heads together on the far side of the square, close to the Great Hall. Before Mira could consider what they were discussing, the economic-augurs scattered apart, like sparrows disturbed by a barking dog. The First Seat strode through them as though they weren't there, leaning perilously forward like a yacht about to capsize. One poor man was bowled aside by the First Seat, but the leader of Whinnia didn't even slow down.

Tonal Bower stopped next to the waist-high stone altar in the middle of the courtyard. It had a broad base but narrowed at the top where a shallow wooden bowl sat. Carved jagged lightning bolts criss-crossed the front of the altar, with arrowheads at the right hand side of both, one bolt pointing up and another pointing down.

The finanseers hurried to stand alongside First Seat Bower in a semi-circle facing the altar. One of them wore cleaner robes than the others, and he stepped forward to place his hands on the bowl. Then some of the First Seat's court stepped up, forming a line behind Bower.

A few of these important men were Bower's trusted generals. Loam Ratsweat was there, of course, while others were members of his family. A few tied red cloth around their left biceps. Last time he was in Wallis, Malcomb had spoken of red-armed bandits attacking all across the plains of Whinnia, making their lives much more dangerous, and driving prices higher. Mira frowned. She hoped he came back to Wallis soon.

"Welcome to this wonderful sacrifice," said Bower. "It's going to be the best sacrifice, and we're all really glad that you're here to see it." He nodded at the head of the finanseers standing by the bowl. The economic-augur flinched and waved for someone to bring something forward.

An augur wearing a hoodless robe rushed up, carrying a chicken. She handed it to the man by the bowl, trying to look as serious as a person can while carrying around a chicken, then bowed very slightly and darted away. The man drew a sickly-sharp knife from his belt and Mira looked away briefly. There was a thick chopping noise, and a thump as the chicken's body was placed into the bowl. Mira looked back.

The finanseer had sliced open the chicken and was pulling bits from inside it, looking close at them as though they held important information. Which, of course, was what the finanseers believed. They were convinced that looking closely at the entrails of birds during ritual sacrifices was the most accurate way to predict whether Whinnia would see times of plenty in the future, or if poverty and famine were soon to strike the people.

Mira thought that it might be more useful for the economic-augurs to drop in at a tavern from time to time. Perhaps if they spoke to the merchants and traders that travelled through Whinnia, maybe find out what they were buying and selling from across the Misplaced Kingdoms, they'd be more successful in their predictions. Or if they talked to the shepherds and farmers to see how the seasons and bandits were affecting them, then they could reach accurate conclusions. But that was probably why she wasn't in charge of Whinnia and its economic policy. She didn't have the right understanding of the big picture.

A brown and slimy length of gristle was currently dangling from the chief finanseer's fingers. He frowned and dropped it back into the bowl.

Then he stepped around the altar and raised his arms. The muttering of the crowd faded away.

"Fellow people of Whinnia!" he said with a voice much louder and clearer than Mira had expected from his slight frame. "I have seen what the future holds for us!"

No one responded to this, which seemed to annoy him. The crowd had grown used to pompous but empty pronouncements during the rule of First Seat Bower, and had developed the habit of waiting to see if anything concrete actually came out of such a speech before they panicked or cheered. Mira saw the finanseer grimace, but then he shook his shoulders and continued.

"There are bad tidings! The planet Septos has been moving into the sign of the Bear all quarter, leaving behind the Bull. And now this chicken tells us that times will be difficult for a year to come. But hold firm, because great wealth will then flow through the lands!"

Grumbling broke out in the crowd, but his declaration wasn't actually very surprising. The winter had gone on longer than usual, and Mira imagined that crop yields would be low and lost livestock high. The poor weather and bandits had meant there was less trade coming from outside Whinnia as well.

The men of the First Seat's court were frowning too. One of the red-armed men stepped over and whispered into the First Seat's ear.

First Seat Bower nodded and touched the man's arm, sending him back to his place in the line, and then placed himself in front of the chief finanseer, pushing the robed man backwards.

"This is completely unacceptable," Bower said. "I don't know who got this bird, but it's a bad bird. It's the worst bird, I've always said that. We want a new bird, the best bird. Someone find us a real bird that knows that Whinnia is the greatest."

"Sir?" asked the chief finanseer from behind him. Bower turned and glared, and the man shrank back. He nodded. "At once, sir!"

It only took a moment before the tableau had been set up again. Bower had reluctantly been led behind the altar and a new chicken had been brought forward.

This time the chief finanseer only picked up a couple of slimy entrails before glancing over his shoulder at the First Seat and then coming forward to proclaim "The signs are clear! There will be plenty and good tidings throughout Whinnia, for as far as we can see!"

Bower nodded with his arms crossed.

The crowd waited to see if anything else would happen, and when nothing did, began to disperse. This was life under Tonal Bower. Any attempt to talk about the problems in Whinnia was ignored. Anytime the truth found its way to his presence, he found a way to squash it down.

Chapter Forty-Three

A breeze cut through the blanket of Mira's thoughts and brought her back to where she was, walking alongside her new friends back to Senoonheim.

"What are you thinking about?" she asked Junka, looking for a distraction from the unwelcome memories of First Seat Bower.

The older woman pulled her shawl closer around her shoulders, producing a scarf to wrap around her neck against the chill from somewhere inside the shawl. The layers of cloth around her neck somehow became thicker than they had been before, making her look like a snail peeking out of its shell.

"I was just wondering whether you have anyone special in your life at the moment, dearie, anyone who might whisk you away to a masked dance," said Junka from within the piled cloth.

"What?" Moria nearly tripped.

"You've been here in the city for so long, I just wondered if you had anyone to talk to." The older woman turned a large eye to Mira. The skin at the corner of her eye crinkled as she smiled. "What? You have something more important on your mind?"

"I was thinking about this land, and how Fina wants us to protect it," said Mira. She told herself she had been thinking about that before her memories overtook her, and so she wasn't really lying. "I was wondering how this city is affecting the place."

"Very high-minded of you," said Nerishma. "But I agree with Junka. Life is complicated and we could all use someone who makes us feel good at the end of the day."

The woman walked together in silence for a moment.

"If you must know, there was a dwarf who took me to the arena a couple of days ago," admitted Mira.

"The arena! Ooo, I haven't seen a good match in months," said Junka. "A bit of blood in the sand gets my heart racing, it does." The woman's eyes unfocused as she got lost in her own memories. "Especially when they're all oiled up, glistening in the torchlight."

Nerishma giggled.

"Have you spent much time with him?" she asked Mira.

"Not really, not yet."

"Do you think you'll see more of him then?"

Mira thought about this.

"I was going to," she said. "But he seems really into gladiator fights, and I'm not sure that I am."

"People can have different interests," said Nerishma.

"They can," agreed Mira. "But I didn't feel right while I was with him. I'm a bit worried he thinks that I am someone that I'm not."

What she realised but didn't say was that the way he paid attention to her made her feel just as she had with Loam. He didn't really listen to her, and she hadn't felt like herself. Mira fell into silence, contemplating her feelings about Master d'Earthy.

Buildings appeared in the fields around the city like mushrooms, gathering in clusters until eventually the women were walking through a city again. Nerishma visibly relaxed as they were surrounded by walls and stone.

Soon they could see the city wall ahead, guarded pointlessly by a small group of the High Lord's soldiers. As the trio came closer, one of the soldiers walked away from the rest and headed toward them. Mira recognised the huge shoulders of Troo, though her face was partially hidden by a helmet. It had been made for human soldiers and she had forced it down onto her head as best she could, but that had torn the helmet into vertical strips. She looked like she had wrapped tinfoil around the upper half of her face.

"Hey, ladies!" boomed Troo as she approached. A horse on the street behind her reared up and threw its rider to the ground. "I'm glad to run into you!"

"Hello Troo." Mira smiled. "What's going on?"

"Nothing much. You might be surprised by this, but gate duty rarely requires us to see off invading hordes."

"I'm glad for you, though," said Mira.

"I don't know," said Troo, rolling her shoulders and stretching. Her joints crackled like a thunderstorm. "Sometimes I think I could use the exercise."

The members of the coven reached the city gates and walked through the tunnel created by the thick stone walls. Troo bid them farewell and returned to the knot of soldiers standing by the portcullis, guarding the middle of the city from intruders. As Troo walked away, another soldier came out of a door in the middle of the tunnel.

It was a solid door, and there were heavy iron brackets on the inside of it, where a beam could be braced to lock it. But, beyond it, Mira caught a glimpse of the inside of the walls. Angled arms of wooden scaffolding propped up a timber skeleton that supported the external facade of the walls, wooden planks and cloth painted as stone. The soldier kicked the door shut behind himself, and Mira pretended that she hadn't noticed.

Mira said goodbye to the other women after they left the passageway. Nerishma said she had certain errands to run as the daylight faded and Junka said that her old feet were tired, though she did walk off in the direction of the Shrine of Melody which made Mira suspicious.

The Shrine of Melody was a well known temple to various gods of music from throughout the Misplaced Kingdoms. It held nightly communions that involved lots of multicoloured magical lights and thumping rhythms played by whole teams of drummers. If Junka was heading that way, she was likely to be dancing until dawn.

Despite being by herself, Mira enjoyed her evening stroll through the streets of Senoonheim. Some stalls were still propped up against the buildings, staffed by increasingly desperate traders, trying to offload the last of their wares so they wouldn't have to carry anything home again.

"Can I interest you in a trout, dear lady?" said one man as Mira passed. His blonde hair was tied back in a slick ponytail, and his stomach bulged roundly in front of him.

"Not really," she answered, but then she paused. She looked at the man's table closely. Low sided wooden crates lay along the table in a pungent cloud. Damp straw filled most of the crates beneath a few long silver fish. Mira looked back up at the man.

"Where did these fish come from?"

"What do you mean?" The man's eyes narrowed in suspicion. "It's a fish. It came from the sea."

Mira had just spent half a day outside of Senoonheim. She had seen the Hills that stretched away to the south. She had followed the road through tilled fields and little orchards that led to the broad and dark expanse of the Gloombark Forest. There was something important that she had not seen at all during her day.

"We are a long way from the sea here," she said.

The man shrugged.

"What can I tell you? Do you want it or not?"

Mira laughed. She didn't know where the fish came from, and she wasn't about to buy one and find out. She kept walking. At the end of the street, she turned the corner and bounced off a wall that she wasn't expecting to be there.

Chapter Forty-Four

M ira put a hand on her forehead and squeezed, trying to slow the spinning sensation that rolled around and around her skull. As her eyes slowly uncrossed she was able to focus on the wall that was standing in the street in front of her.

"Mira? I am so sorry. Are you alright?"

"Prevos?"

What were the odds that, of all the hundreds of people who were moving around the streets of Senoonheim as dusk fell, it was Prevos who Mira walked into.

The paladin extended a hand and Mira gratefully reached up. Prevos lifted her into the air as easily as a pillow, hoisting her so quickly that she grabbed onto his hand with her other hand in shock. He held her dangling from his hand and she extended one cautious foot, then the other, and found her footing on the street.

"Thank you."

"You are most welcome my lady, and I must offer my deepest and most inadequate apologies for this unfortunate manner of meeting." His golden eyes blinked and looked away. "I do say, it is very pleasant to see you, though unexpectedly."

"That's kind of you to say."

Prevos looked around the streets with a frown.

"And it doesn't appear that you have anyone following you yet again this evening."

"Of course not," Mira began but then she paused. "Yet again? How many times have people been following me, according to you?"

"I was talking of that business with the mugger the other night."

"Do you mean the skinny woman, Nerishma? The one who said she followed the Mosquito Queen?"

"No, there was someone last night as well."

"So it was you who scared them off!" Mira's eyes widened. "I thought you were there! But I didn't see any sign of you in the shadows. What were you doing?"

"I wasn't trying to hide," he protested, his muzzle frowning. "I was going to intercede on your behalf, but that skinny woman who tried to steal from you before was there as well and she made a sound and then the mugger left."

Mira was confused. Nerishma, from the coven? Why would she have been following her last night? And what was the sound she made? All of that aside, Prevos had admitted something important.

"Am I to understand that you really were following me late at night?"

It was hard to know when the catfolk were embarrassed. Blushes don't show clearly through the layer of fur that covers them. However, from the way his ears turned back and his whiskers drooped, Mira assumed that he was feeling exposed and vulnerable, which is pretty much the same thing.

"Uh..." The man made a long, low noise with no resolution, clearly hoping that something would happen to interrupt it. He shrank down a little as his nervous groan faded away.

"I suppose I was," Prevos finally admitted. His golden eyes flicked from side to side as he searched for a way to escape from Mira's watchful gaze.

"And? What do you have to say about that?" asked Mira.

"Sorry." Prevos's shoulders drooped and his nose twitched.

"Why were you there in the first place?"

Every part of Prevos looked as though he wanted to melt into the gaps between the cobbles and sluice away through the streets.

"I was just making sure you were okay," he mumbled. Even a quiet nervous muttering from the large man came out as a dull growl.

"I've had men follow me around and insert themselves into my life before," said Mira. "It's not appreciated. I like to know who's around me and what their intentions are."

Prevos nodded.

"I understand! Uh..." He licked his muzzle and took a deep breath. "So, you probably want to know that I came by and saw that bread fanatic you had to kick out this morning too."

"Oh for goodness sake," groaned Mira. She pinched the bridge of her nose. "Don't sneak around!"

Prevos nodded furiously, setting his mane undulating. Mira shook her head.

"I suppose you have owned up to it now. How many other times have you been checking on me when I didn't know about it?"

He shook his head. "None, I swear by Trankwill!"

"Fine. Just don't do that anymore!"

"Okay." Prevos rubbed his hands together nervously, which filled the street with the sound of grinding metal. "I'm afraid that I do have an appointment this evening, or I would offer to escort you back to your home." His face filled with regret, and his ears turned backwards.

"That's fine, I can get myself home." Mira watched him closely. "And if you see me again then I had better know about it!"

***

Mira was just about to climb the stairs to her apartment when there was a knock at the door. It had none of the business-like rhythm that a customer would knock with. It was a casual knock, the sort that suggested the knocker already knew someone was waiting for them. It fell around rhythm in the same way an intoxicated jazz drummer might.

"Mira?" called a sonorous voice from outside.

Mira walked back to the door, unlocked it and pulled it open to reveal Ulvilhelm d'Earthy standing on the road outside. He smiled up at her through his freshly-braided beard.

"Ah, it does me good to see you again," he said, and he leaned closer, his lips puckering.

In somewhat of a panic, Mira accepted his kiss on her lips as a peck, keeping the contact as brief as eyelids blinking. It seemed to satisfy him, though.

"Hello," she said. "Should I have been expecting you?"

"Only in the sense that you should always expect me to chase you down, my lovely!" D'Earthy grinned and motioned past her. "Will you welcome me inside?"

"Um. Yes, I suppose so." Mira stepped aside and the dwarf strode into her shop as though he spent all his time in her bakery. He looked around the space.

"Do you have nowhere to sit?"

"Not really, people don't generally stay here. They buy some bread and then they leave."

D'Earthy dismissed her comments with a quick shake of his head.

"It doesn't matter. Are you closed up for the day?"

"Yes, I had a long night last night so I decided not to open at all actually."

"Unusual, but it suits me, so that's good." D'Earthy turned his eyes, as bright as a midsummer's sky, onto Mira. She felt herself soften at the edges, as though she had been soaking in a warm bath. "I've come to take you out again!"

"What did you have in mind?" asked Mira as she walked towards the kitchen, hoping a fresh cup of tea might fortify her.

"You had such a great time at the games! I thought you should come and watch the monster trucks with me tonight!"

Mira grimaced. Her pulse had raced while she had watched the gladiatorial combat at the amphitheatre, but there was something unpleasant about sitting with a group of people who were cheering blood being spilled. She hadn't felt as though it was something she wanted to do again soon.

"What are the monster trucks?"

D'Earthy explained that trucks were wheeled carriages used to shift massive blackpowder weapons called cannons. However, contrivancers had developed ways of binding various beasts and monsters to the carriages in place of the large iron weapons and now they battled with each other in improvised arenas for the entertainment of excited crowds.

"So it's a lot like the gladiators then, is it?" asked Mira.

"Not at all! There's no personalities involved, no story. The monster truck fights are more about which contrivancers develop a good way to destroy their opponents truck. It's about being clever!" explained the dwarf.

"Give me an example of this cleverness," said Mira, crossing her arms.

"Last month there was one truck which had a crocodile demon bound to the front, so it had these giant jaws." He held out both hands to act out the chomping of jaws for her. "But there was some sort of giant spider contained in the body, and its legs gave Chomper the manoeuvrability to really bring that destructive power to bear! It smashed its opponent to bits!"

Mira looked at the excitement that shone from d'Earthy's eyes and thought of how she had felt while she was out with her witches today. She had spent time with d'Earthy before she had met them, and now she didn't feel as excited by his company. Although he burst with happiness at the idea of spending time with her, she had felt more secure and happy while wandering through the forest with the witches than she had felt while sitting in the arena. They didn't make her feel as though she had to meet their expectations, not the way d'Earthy was making her feel now. She sighed.

"I don't think I can do it," she said.

"Oh? Was last night really so tough on you?" D'Earthy looked at her with sympathy, taking one of her hands and patting it softly.

"No, it's not that," she said, pulling her hand back. "Its just that... I think that sounds quite awful. I don't want to watch creatures fighting each other, not if I have any other choice."

"What?" D'Earthy blinked. His forehead wrinkled. "But you had such a good time before. I thought you loved this sort of thing."

"I got caught up in it," agreed Mira. "I can admit that. But it's not something that I want to turn into a habit."

D'Earthy shook his head.

"You can't mean that. I saw your face, you loved it."

"I'm sorry to disappoint you."

"You have," he said in a voice of stone. His face was hard. "You've led me along. I thought I'd met a woman who had a distinguished palate for entertainment and excitement, but you're..." he frowned and looked down her to her feet. He looked up again. "You're just a fake, lying to an interested man because you need the attention."

Mira's jaw dropped open.

"I simply said that I didn't want to go to one event with you because it didn't sound like the sort of thing I would enjoy. And this is how you react? I think you should leave," she said. Her stomach trembled as she wondered for a moment whether he would. Would she have to treat him like the elven adventurer? Would she have to leave, as she had when Loam had used his position against her?

"I will." D'Earthy stomped out of the bakery in a huff. Mira followed him to the door and locked it behind him. Thankfully, he strode away along the street without looking back once.

Chapter Forty-Five

The nervous queasiness that d'Earthy left in her stomach lingered. Mira leaned over the counter in her bakery and wondered if he had a point. Was she just lying to everyone, seeking attention from them all?

By the time the feeling had faded enough for her to press a hand to her stomach and stand up, the street outside was dark. Mira considered heading to bed. Her head was still tender enough to appreciate it. But a rebellious part of her brain waved a flag for attention, and suggested heading back to the Sprog and Sparrow in the hopes that she would see some more of her coven. She gulped down her tea and tried to ignore the thought.

A bulbous and distorted reflection of her face looked out from the surface of the metal teapot at her.

"You just had someone try to undermine who you are," her face said to herself. "You could use some time with people who won't judge you. And it would be a good way to defy that silly court wizard."

Mira had to admit that it sounded like a good idea. But another part of her mind whispered that the coven might judge her if she told them the whole truth. Despite the traitorous thought, she took a deep breath to calm her stomach, then headed out.

Delorous and Leena were sitting in a booth to the side of the common room of the Sprog and Sparrow. They made a fascinating pair. Delorous embraced the stem of her wine glass with delicate fingers as she sipped, and Leena's slim, chitinous pincers clinked against her own glass. Delorous allowed a very small smile to flash across her tear-streaked face as Leena's mandibles chattered to her. Then her frown returned as she stroked the fur of the rat lying calmly across the back of her neck, rubbing its cheeks across her shoulder. Leena's reptile had grown large enough to stretch across her shoulders as well.

"I have to ask," said Mira after greeting the others, "why do you have that rat on your shoulders?"

Delorous raised an eyebrow.

"This is Charles. He keeps me happy."

Mira studied the tear streaks that cut down either side of Delorous's face.

"He's doing a very good job," she said.

"Yes," said Delorous, her lips twitching slightly towards what Mira assumed was a smile. "He's my little rat of sunshine."

"And what about your lizard?" Mira said to Leena. "He seems to be growing well."

"I've been feeding him mice!"

The booth the witches occupied was semi-circular, a bench-like seat curving around a table bolted to the floor. The booth was a perfect trap, and once Mira made herself comfortable there was no way for Leena to get out unless she rolled under the table or clambered up and onto the wall. These traps were the natural outcome of furniture design in a certain sort of business, anywhere that made more money the longer their patrons stayed. After all, after squeezing and pushing for twenty minutes to try and escape from where they were wedged between their friends, most people would just lean back and accept that they weren't going anywhere soon so they may as well order another drink.

"I'm sorry," Delorous said. "You're going to have to stay with us now, and I know that you probably just want to go back to bed."

"I chose to come out," protested Mira.

"Probably felt guilty," muttered Delorous. "You felt as though you had to come and see who might be here, a sense of responsibility for us all." Delorous sighed, both of her hands touching the sides of her glass. "But we're not worth your time."

"That's not it at all!" said Mira brightly.

"We may as well get started now though," chittered Leena. She reached up to pat her lizard on the head, and leaned away from its mouth as it burped a small cloud of dark smoke. "What can you tell us about witchcraft?" she asked Mira, pulling a pencil and a sheet of rough paper out of a satchel by her side.

As it turned out, neither of the women knew anything at all about witchcraft, other than what they had picked up from stories passed around in the community. All the usual stereotypes abounded: that witches were evil and were out to steal everyone's children, often for the purposes of eating them. Some other stories had cropped up from time to time; for example, Delorous had heard that witches were closely tied to nature and the moon.

"Is that why we find ourselves laying awake in bed all night at the new moon, unable to will ourselves to do anything at all?" she asked, leaning forward with uncharacteristic eagerness.

Mira wrinkled her nose.

"Sorry, no. Are you saying that you can't do anything during a new moon?" Delorous shook her head.

"That's right, not a thing."

"No, I don't know anyone else who has that problem," said Mira.

"But it is why you said we would meet after every full moon, right?" asked the younger woman.

Mira shook her head.

"I chose that because everyone pays attention to the full moon so it's an easy way to remind everyone that we are going to meet."

"Oh." The poor girl looked disappointed which, to be fair, may have just been her natural expression.

"You can imagine that we are meeting because it's when the moon is at its strongest if you like," suggested Mira. "Maybe the moon really does lend us power at that time, who knows! You could use that as your reason for attending."

Delorous sat up straighter. Black eye makeup ran down her cheeks.

"And that way we can draw on the moon's strength for our spells!" she exclaimed.

"It's not really like that though," Mira said. "For most people, magic is a form of ritual, a recipe. To achieve a certain effect only requires that a person knows the right forms, the right words, the right gestures." To demonstrate her point, Mira held her fingers just so and murmured some particular words below her breath. A small ball of light grew and detached itself from the gleaming surface of Delorous's glass and then lifted itself to hover over the table.

"Most of the time, there is no 'energy' required, in the same way that dropping an egg out a window would break it with no effort required by the person dropping it," she continued. "Creating that light didn't make me tired or hungry, or anything of the sort. And I didn't need to draw on the moon's power to do it."

"If it's that easy, then why isn't everyone doing it?" asked Leena. Her insect face was hard to read, but the way she had looked down made Mira think she was doubtful. The pale light hovering over the table reflected a rainbow from Leena's multifaceted eyes.

"It's a reasonable question," admitted Mira. "The recipes for most spells are tricky. This light was easy to conjure. It just requires certain hand forms and certain words, in a space where the conditions are right for it to arise."

Delorous was drinking in every word. Leena didn't seem to be quite as thirsty as the other woman, but was willing to at least try a sip.

"Other spells are more complex. They might require a specific part of a plant that has been gathered under very certain conditions. The caster may only be able to follow through on the spell on just the right day, or in just the right place. That can make it seem like a spell only works because you need to wait until the moon is at its most powerful." Moria spoke directly to Delorous now, and was pleased to see the girl was nodding.

"How do you learn these rituals? Where do you start?"

"The witch who taught me learned from her bravura honda, and she passed on a lot of those spells to me."

Mira remembered having almost this exact same conversation with Bovo. She had been just as excited as Delorous was when Bovo told her all of this, just as ready to take it all on for herself.

"Was she the witch who taught you how to make that light?" asked Leena.

Mira coughed.

"There's a lot of ways that people learn magic. Bovo told me that wizards do a lot of experimenting."

"And Satonak would be doing that." Leena wasn't asking a question, she was stating a fact.

"Yes, I imagine so. He is a wizard after all."

"Do you think that's got something to do with why he was so set against the coven?" the antfolk woman asked.

"I don't know," Mira said. "I haven't really thought about it."

"Lord Cornucervin used to be pretty hands off with the city, but now that Satonak is responsible for keeping Senoonheim running, there's more drones, and more rules being announced."

"Yes, it sounds like he is taking over as leader of the city piece by piece," agreed Mira.

"I thought that he was jealous," said Delorous. She lifted a pretzel stick up to the rat on her shoulder.

"Really?" asked Mira. "Jealous of what? None of us had even met him before, and he came charging in telling us not to gather, that it was forbidden. What could he have wanted from us?"

"No, that's envy," said Delorous. When the two other witches didn't say anything, she shifted in her seat and leaned in to explain. "Jealousy is what you feel when you have something that you don't want anyone else to have. You jealously guard your treasure, or you are jealous that someone might take it from you. But it's envy that you feel when you want something that is not yours. You are envious of the beautiful necklace that your friend is wearing."

"Okay," clicked Leena slowly.

"So, like I said, I thought Satonak was jealous," repeated Delorous, leaning back against the seat behind her.

Chapter Forty-Six

"I hadn't considered that the wizard could be jealous," said Leena. "I've been wondering all day why he got his beard all twisted like that, and I never once thought that he was worried we would be taking something off him. Do you think he worries that we will magically defeat him somehow?" She sat a little straighter at the idea, and her mandibles spread in what Mira would have sworn was an antfolk smirk. "Do you think that he could be right?"

"I don't know that we are going to be competing in any way with a court wizard," said Mira, She wanted to head this discussion off right away, before anyone got it into their head to go charging up to Lord Cornucervin's castle and challenge Satonak to a magical duel. Of all the things in the world that wizards were most prepared to deal with, of all the widely unlikely moments in life that a person could think up and take the time to get ready for, it was impromptu magical fights. There was a reason they all learned how to make fireballs so quickly.

"Before we could even dream of doing anything like that, we need to develop your magical skills. Now, the first thing a witch has to do is to find a bravura honda."

Mira explained that a bravura was a being that a witch developed a relationship with. A bravura should become a friend who could help a witch remember certain spells or recipes for magical elixirs. They might guide her to new knowledge to use, or give her advice when she called upon them. It was like living next to a good neighbour. You could chat over the fence about the ethereal weather and borrow some mystical sugar when you were low. But it was common for a witch's bravura to ask for something in return. Metaphorically speaking, they might ask you to help them paint the occult fence sometimes.

When she said this, both Delorous and Leena leaned back in their seats. Delorous pulled a broad white handkerchief from her bodice and dabbed at her forehead, pulling thin streaks up from the blackness around her eyes. Both women were clearly unsure about the implications of this.

"It's nothing sordid," Mira explained. "I mean, unless you are looking for a bravura who seeks such attachments, but you'd know that going in." Bovo had always implied that some witches did.

"It makes sense," said Leena slowly. "If you seek that closeness in such a magical relationship, that full awareness of each other, sometimes lines may get crossed. That probably leads to delicious disasters." The young woman gave her wine a swirl, looking at Mira carefully. "Would you tell us who your bravura is, Mira?"

Mira sipped from her glass slowly. When she put it down she asked: "Do you have any thoughts about who your bravura could be? Have you felt any connections to any gods before?"

"You won't be surprised to hear that I've often wondered if I could be friends with the moon," said Delorous. "I've always found it difficult to meet a man who can handle my schedule. I spent so much time learning about myself while I was younger that I didn't have time for them. But the moon, now, I think I can make a promise to see the moon every night and keep it."

Mira smiled.

"The moon is popular, but you never know what she might ask of you. I heard of one woman who was told to offer her daughter as sacrifice, only for her daughter to be turned into a white deer which ran off into the forest."

Delorous's face paled beneath her smeared black makeup.

"I didn't expect that the moon would ask something so cruel."

"You thought the moon was kind," said Mira with a wry smile. "A common mistake. But the moon watches down on the world even when the worst is happening. The moon can be cold."

"Maybe I won't seek her friendship then," said a subdued Delorous.

"How about you, Leena?" asked Mira, turning in her seat to look at the antfolk woman.

"I've never really thought much about this sort of thing," she admitted, twitching her antennae in a movement that Mira assumed was a blush.

"Alright, how about I set you both a task. When you go home after this I want you to go about your days with your mind open to meeting someone."

"Who?" asked Delorous. "I spend most of my time at my mother's house. No one ever comes looking for me."

"She's going to send us an expert," Leena assured the wispy young woman.

"No!" laughed Mira. "I'm not meaning that you will meet an expert! The sorts of beings that might be a witch's bravura are the sorts of beings who will be able to hear your heart as it seeks companionship."

Delorous blinked.

"Seeking companionship? Are you sure this isn't about seducing some un-named fae gentlemen with red hair, or entrancing a tall man with puffy white hair and red eyes?"

"No!"

"But it could be?" asked Delorous.

"If you are open to meeting a bravura, then a bravura will be able to contact you," Mira continued, ignoring the young woman's protestations as a boulder rolling down a hill ignores the flowers on the hillside. "They might visit you in your dreams. You may find yourself drawn to a particular place, or to create a certain recipe that might allow them to communicate more freely. This is good! This is what you want."

"Is that how you met your bravura, Mira?" asked Delorous again.

Oh my goodness, the girl is worse than a dog with a fresh piece of meat. She smiled at Delorous, a smile as short-lived and fragile as a snowflake.

"Sort of. I already had someone in mind, but circumstances changed."

"I've known men like that," sympathised Leena. "They promise the world, but then they just lay around in their filthy undies and socks."

Mira closed her eyes and counted to ten. When she opened them again, the two women were still sitting in the booth, watching her. They meant well, she knew that. And they were just curious about the whole idea of witchcraft. They hadn't learnt about it before, so she shouldn't be surprised that they wanted to ask so many questions. And what would it harm them to tell them the real answer, the full answer? But her heart quailed at the idea, so she didn't.

"Do you think that you'll be able to give that a try? You can let me know if you've had any success at the next coven night?"

"After the full moon? Agreed," said Delorous.

"Aye, I'll give it a shot." Leena's mandibles shifted wider. Mira assumed it was the antfolk version of a grin.

Mira wanted to keep talking to the others, but the last remnants of the hangover squeezing her skull forced her to make her farewells. Leena patted her hand while Delorous made sorrowful noises in sympathy.

Mira stepped out into the street and glanced around without knowing what she was looking for until she didn't find it. There was no tall figure wearing shining plate armour hidden amongst the thinning crowd.

When she got home, Mira caught the eye of her own reflection in the dresser.

"What were you looking for him for?" she asked.

"I suppose I thought he'd ignore my instructions, that's all."

Her reflection pursed its lips and nodded. She got herself ready for bed and crawled under the blankets. Tomorrow would be better. For one thing, she would no longer be hungover.

Chapter Forty-Seven

M ira dreamt of the first time she saw Bovo. The halfling witch had clambered up the walls of a house in Wallis and then tip-toed out onto the
roof in order to retrieve a kite lodged in the thatching. Each footstep was placed
as carefully as someone walking across a frozen lake as the thaw approached.
Mira and a dozen others paused in the street to see if the halfling would fall
through.

"You there!" Bovo called down to her audience. Mira looked around and then
pointed at herself, which was a gesture that was intended to convey the question
"Did you mean me?" but did a wonderful job of volunteering her instead.

"Yes, you!" called out Bovo. "This isn't exactly very solid, could you spot me?"
The halfling stamped her foot on the thatch, sending a rain of material sliding
down the steeply sloped roof and tumbling off to fall into the street. A couple
of older men clapped and nodded to each other.

"Why are you breaking it then?" yelped Mira, rushing to the edge of the
building in case she needed to catch the woman. Bovo poked her head out over
the edge to look straight down at Mira.

"I'll be fine. You're just there as a precaution. Stomikaek will protect me."
And with that opaque statement still floating unintelligibly in the air, the
halfling ducked back out of Mira's sight.

Dust and twigs fell in a gentle rain onto Mira, who wondered if this was in fact
a job she really wanted. Every time she looked up, checking whether the halfling
woman was about to tumble off the roof, she caught a face full of grime instead,
specks of dust blinding her and twigs slipping into her mouth and choking her.
Mira considered walking away. After all, the halfling seemed very confident. But

then she imagined what would happen if the woman did plummet off the roof. Mira grimaced and stayed where she was, resigning herself to brushing off dust and spitting out tiny clumps of mud.

"Psst," came a voice from overhead. Mira winced and then, when nothing struck her from above, slowly raised her eyes to the roof. A bird's nest smacked her directly in the face. The halfling had returned. Some of the onlookers laughed dutifully.

"Yes?" Mira groaned.

"Here, you do it." Bovo's face smiled as it peered over the edge of the roof.

"Do what?" But the halfling's face had been replaced by the kite and it was dropping towards her.

Mira caught the thing awkwardly and then looked around the street. A group of children were staring at her nearby. She was amazed. The eyes of each child were so huge that she couldn't believe that each orb could possibly fit simultaneously inside their heads.

"Uh. Does this belong to one of you?" she asked slowly, holding the kite out towards them.

The children rushed her like a swarm of rats, arms outstretched, and Mira pressed back against the wall. The kite was snatched from her grip and there was a rush of wind as the children piled around her and then vanished down the street. The last thing she heard before they sluiced around a corner was a distant, squealed "'nks."

"What just happened?" she asked herself.

"You were the beneficiary of the gratitude of those small urchins," answered Bovo from overhead. "You looked so lonely down there on the street by yourself, I thought I'd let you be the one who gave it back to them. I figured you could benefit from some positive interaction."

"That was a positive interaction?"

"Well, it was an interaction for sure, and sometimes that's close enough. Alright, arms out."

"What?" asked Mira again. Over time she would discover that being friends with Bovo was similar to owning a falcon as a pet. While they were entertaining and always popular with others when you took them out and about, you had to be careful as their actions were difficult to predict and someone might end up with bitten fingers.

The halfling launched herself off the edge of the roof without further explanation and Mira swore as she leapt forward. She got under the halfling in time, but the pair of them immediately collapsed onto the ground in a twisted pile of limbs.

"Are you alright?" Mira gasped as she disentangled herself and tried to stand up, rubbing her leg to make sure that she hadn't twisted it.

"Fresh as a daisy!" Bovo smiled up from where she lay on the muddy street, twigs stuck in her hair and dust smeared across her skirts and hands. "Thanks for that! Much quicker than clambering down the windowsills on the side of the house. I'm sure the people in there didn't want me kicking my way around on their roof any longer than I absolutely had to. My name's Bovo."

Her smile was infectious. She wore her personality like a sign around her neck, declaring to everyone that she would engage with them whether or not they were actually interested. Mira found herself grinning back.

"I'm Mira. How can you throw yourself off a roof like that? Do you have no fear?"

"Not much. I walk with Stomikaek, and he's pretty good to me."

"Yes, you used that word before. What is Stomikaek?"

Bovo's smile grew even wider.

"Would you like to come and have a drink and I'll explain?"

Chapter Forty-Eight

B ovo's drink was bright orange and it fizzed. Mira stared as it bubbled up over the edges of the halfling's glass. Bovo saw Mira looking at the drink and misunderstood. She pushed the glass over.

"Wanna sip?"

"No, thank you…" replied Mira cautiously. She didn't want to cause offence, but the liquid in Bovo's glass looked like the most terrifying of alchemists' concoctions. She would sooner swallow a scorpion than risk a drop of that. Instead, she had ordered herself a small glass of red wine and took a sip to forestall any further questions. The wine was thick and syrupy and spicy and Mira loved it. "You were going to tell me about Stomikaek?"

"Yes. So, to cut a long story short, I'm a witch and Stomikaek is my bravura honda."

"I'm sorry, what?"

Mira had never met a witch before. Bovo had tight, thick, curly auburn hair that clung around her head like a helmet, and she wore a flowing floral skirt that accentuated the curves of her figure.

"I thought witches were skinny, and always dressed in black," said Mira.

Bovo laughed and drank a mouthful of her bizarre drink. It left a foamy orange moustache on the halfling's upper lip.

"That's what most people think! But there's so many different ways to be a witch. You don't have to be all dour about it." She took another sip of her drink and then paused. "Unless, of course, you want to," she added.

"But you don't want to."

"Not at all! Can you imagine me trying to be grumpy and cursing people all the time?"

Bovo grinned and wiggled her fingers towards Mira. Mira chuckled. The idea of this halfling laying evil spells on anyone was as ludicrous as suggesting that a fluffy little puppy would maul an intruder.

"Exactly! No, I heard about Stomikaek from an older woman in my home village and decided that I was interested in the benefits that he might offer. So I looked up the rituals that contact him and, one night, I went and had a chat with him."

"You needed a ritual to contact him?" Mira frowned a little. "What exactly is Stomikaek?"

"He's a local god, or a spirit, or an ancient ancestor of my people. It's not really very clear. But basically I do some things for him and he grants me a little of his magic."

"Really?" Mira was fascinated. "What sort of magic?"

The only magic she had been familiar with was the stupid trick her uncle always did where he pulled a coin from behind her head. It was impressive for children but it wasn't real magic. She knew that there were wizards and sorcerers and magi and all sorts of people out in the Misplaced Kingdoms that really could perform feats of magic, and she had grown up wondering what it actually looked like. Some of the stories told in the market were utterly outlandish and couldn't be believed, like people who could make huge balls of fire simply appear out of nowhere in their hands and then throw them across entire fields into a group of soldiers. That couldn't be real. So when Bovo said she could do magic, Mira was entranced.

Bovo raised her hands to forestall too much excitement, the same way a parent slowed down their child who might be expecting sweets but actually had to finish sweeping the house first.

"It's fairly limited magic, I have to admit. Stomikaek isn't one of your multi-kingdom deities, with mighty temples built atop each hill. He's much more local, but that's part of our deal. I carry him with me to new places, and he allows me to draw on his fortitude from time to time."

"Fortitude?"

"Yes, the most reliable thing he does for me is strengthen my stomach so that I can eat pretty much anything. It makes it easy for me to travel, and gives me confidence to try more of the potions and recipes that I have collected than I would otherwise. And he's been able to warn me of danger before it strikes, and lend me some strength when I've needed to keep going, things like that. All in all, he's been a very satisfactory companion."

Mira was amazed.

"It's like a deal."

"Absolutely it's a deal! He's my bravura honda!"

"You said that before," said Mira. "What does that mean?"

"The words are ancient but so far as I can tell, basically they mean an expert in wisdom. So your bravura honda is like an expert who you can call on to help you learn more magic."

"But you said it was a deal, so he helps you as long as you help him?"

"Pretty much. It's more like a relationship, so we grow to know each other and appreciate each other. And Stomikaek doesn't ask much, so it's been an easy deal! I have heard of witches who struck deals that were much less advantageous, with beings who can be much more capricious." Bovo took another big drink of her fizzing drink.

Mira narrowed her eyes and pointed at the orange foam.

"So, is that…"

"Knock most people on their backside potent, yes," replied Bovo happily. "I think the barkeep here uses it for cleaning mostly." She turned to look at the broad man standing further down the bar, wiping it down with a sodden cloth.

He glanced up and nodded.

"A drop o' that in my pans leaves 'em scoured fresher than a daisy!"

"See," smiled Bovo, before taking another mouthful of the angry liquid.

Chapter Forty-Nine

Mira woke up in Senoonheim feeling much better. The hangover had gone, and she was revitalised after talking about bravura honda with Delorous and Leena the night before. She hurried through her morning routine, feeling more enthusiastic about life in the city than she had in months.

Downstairs she prepared the ovens, baked bread and put it on display. The preparations felt easy and natural today. She felt as though she was getting into a good routine, she knew what she was doing, everything was falling into place. She hummed happily. Life was rising to a place where she could be content.

After her encounter with the addicted elf, Mira dug out her recipes for elven bread, dwarven bread, and goblin bread. *I wonder if he's the start of a new trend,* she asked herself as she looked down the lists of ingredients. He might have just been a random outlier. But if anyone else shows up looking, it would be good to have the relevant supplies.

She copied out a list of the things she was missing, and resolved to go down to the market after lunch.

Not long after the morning rush of workers heading out to farms and mines and patrols, she had to deal with someone more unusual than the regular patrons.

The man who came in was short, not much taller than her, and he had a broad chin. He squinted as he looked around the shop like a butterfly hunter in a forest clearing. His eyes said it was the perfect place to find his prey and now he just needed evidence the fluttering creatures were nearby. However, instead of choosing some loaves for himself, the man scurried to where Mira was standing behind the counter. He ignored the jam rolls on display next to her and leaned a little closer.

"Have you seen any rat-consuls in here?"

"What? No!" Mira was surprised and offended. "I run a clean shop! There are no rats in here at all!"

"Not rats!" the man scoffed. He looked amused at the idea. "No, I'm asking about rat-consuls." He pulled a stack of small cards out of his pocket and began riffling through them. Soon he found what he was looking for and turned it around for Mira to see.

He was holding a piece of cardboard with a drawing on it. It was the sort of drawing that a small child would show a favoured aunt during a family dinner, the aunt carefully asking, "Why don't you tell me all about what it is?" while holding the drawing upside-down. Mira could see a curved shape that might be a rat on the left of the card, and then a very similar shape on the right. The two were connected by a thin pencil line that swirled in a spiral between them.

"You see?" he asked with a smile.

"Two rats?" she replied, wondering if that was meant to be better.

"No, rat-consuls, see?" The man pointed to the top of the card which, Mira had to admit, did have the words "Rat-Consuls" inscribed along it. "They are a base level monster and I've been tracking them through this neighbourhood. I think there may be a few higher level rat-oligarchs here as well from the spoor I've found, but I don't think there's a single rat-king." The man sounded disappointed.

"I'm sorry, rat-kings now?" Mira was lost.

"Here." The man pulled out another pair of cards, these ones labelled "Rat-Oligarch" and "Rat-King." Mira looked at them while he explained.

"Everyone's heard of rat-kings, they show up all over the place. They look like a bunch of rats all connected by the tail. They can be a real problem, as they enslave nearby pests to bring them food. Then you end up with swarms of mice in the grain, or birds devouring your orchard, just to bring tribute to the rat-king."

"This is a problem that real people have?" Mira had never experienced anything of the sort in Whinnia. "In the real, actual world?"

"Yes!"

"Why do the animals do that? It must be really hard for a bunch of rats to survive when they are all trapped with each other like that."

"A rat-king isn't a bunch of rats. It's one creature. That's why I have to find the rat-consuls for the garlic farmers. You see, the only way to tell that one of these creatures isn't a normal rat is when it develops its second body, as a consul. Eventually it grows a few more, becoming a rat-oligarch, and finally, when it reaches at least five bodies, it can truly be called a rat-king."

"One animal?"

"Yes!"

"That sounds horrifying." Mira imagined a group of rats operating with one mind, launching itself at her from beneath a crate while she was shifting supplies.

"Its not really that different from a pack of wolves," said the man with a shrug. "Or bees in a hive. Ooo, or people!"

"People? Are you trying to suggest that we grow multiple heads?" She looked at the man as if he had grown an extra one right then and there.

"No, but by ourselves we aren't actually very strong! As we join together with others, we gain more influence on the world around us. Look at adventurers."

"Ugh, I'd rather not," groaned Mira.

"Yes, but even though they have mighty weapons and phenomenal cosmic powers, they form adventuring bands all the time, to multiply their strength and allow them to achieve great things."

"What about Lord Cornucervin?" asked Mira, grasping for a local example of an individual who wielded power alone.

"He is supported by the various people who have found success in his town, and his wizard, and his soldiers. Everyone gains from it, just as the rat-king gains from its multiplied bodies. Although, recently it looks like Satonak might want to be the head instead of a strong arm." The man grinned, with his fingers interlaced over the rounded protuberance of his belly. Mira found the satisfied expression on his face very irritating and wished she could slap it away.

"Alright, fine. And just why are you looking for these amazing things here in my bakery?"

"Notice that it says they are a rodent type," he continued, tapping a line of writing below the drawing, "which means they are more likely to live in places with steady food supplies and dark corners to hide in." With this statement the man gestured around the room.

"Hey! I do have food, but I don't give any rats a place to hide! I'll sort them out, don't you worry!"

"That's okay," said the man. "They are very cowardly and so I've had trouble finding any. It's probably because they have so few ways to defend themselves beyond a slash attack. The rat-oligarchs at least have a chance to confuse those who hunt them."

"You're beginning to lose me now," admitted Mira. She frowned. "Do you have to be in my shop for all this? What are you trying to do here?"

"The garlic merchant offered me fifty gold pieces if I could bring him back twenty rat-consul pelts. I'm beginning to think it may not be worth it."

The man turned to look around the bakery some more. Mira felt a comment rising from her belly, like a particularly troublesome bit of gas. She tried to clamp her lips shut in case the man was ready to leave, but the thought was too strong and it broke out of her mouth.

"Why not just catch some normal rats and tie their pelts together?"

The man looked at her, his focus slightly behind her head, looking beyond her as he considered this idea.

"That wouldn't be a real rat-consul."

"I know," replied Mira. "And, of course, you'd know as well. But who else would know?"

The man considered this statement in addition to the previous one.

"I'd know."

"Yes, but would the garlic merchant? How many rat-consuls has he seen before? I know I wouldn't be able to tell the difference between two rats tied together and a rat-consul."

Mira watched the man in fascination. Clearly he had a finely tuned sense of morality.

Eventually, he smiled.

"I don't think the garlic merchant would know that it wasn't a rat-consul either," he agreed cheerfully.

"There you are then!" said Mira. "Best you go find a bunch of regular rats, far away from here! I suggest you try over by the merchant warehouses, they'll be able to help you catch as many rats as you need."

"Yes, I think that will work," the man said happily, and he finally made his way out of Mira's bakery.

She caught the eye of her reflection in the window.

"I thought we'd never get rid of him," she said.

Her reflection winked at her.

Chapter Fifty

T he door tinkled and Mira looked up from where she was covering racks of dough, leaving them to rise until the next morning. Troo was squeezing sideways through the door and waved when Mira noticed her.

"Hey lady, how are you doing!"

"Much better now that I've got a friend here," laughed Mira. "Come in and..." She looked around the bakery. She had been about to ask Troo to sit down, but there was nothing in the shop to sit on. "Oh. Maybe there's somewhere out the back where we can put our feet up?"

She led Troo through to the kitchen but soon saw that the same problem held true there as well. Large ovens filled the small space like blackened, soot-covered physical representations of the feeling you get when you forget someone's name. The long worktop was covered in a layer of white dusty flour, which Mira would prefer not to sully by using it as a seat, and so she led the way out the back door. Troo followed her into the narrow, damp space between the buildings on Siltrap Street and the next street over. Dark puddles spattered the muddy ground and the scruffiest cat Mira had ever seen stared at them both from a doorway nearby, with the coiled muscles and stance of a sprinter waiting for the starter's call.

Crates and old barrels filled the alley and Mira motioned for Troo to sit on one. The soldier did and they both winced as loud creaking echoed through the alley.

"I'm not sure that this is going to last long," said Troo, patting the side of her ad-hoc seat. It groaned like an ancient door closing.

"We'll sit as long as we can. It's just nice to have a real visitor instead of running around after annoying customers." Mira lifted a hand, ready to ask if

Troo would like a drink and then lowered it again, her cheeks flushing, as she realised that she had nothing to offer.

Troo smiled sympathetically and then glanced up at the building they sat behind. Heavy black wooden beams drew the structure of the building around panels of flat white clay daub.

"Do you not have your own home above the shop? Would it be more comfortable to sit there?"

Mira thought about her living space. It was just up a simple flight of stairs off the kitchen. A single room with her bed and dressing table, and a wardrobe that must have been built in the room from lumber carried up the stairs, because it was monstrously huge and heavy and there was no way anyone could have brought it into the room through the narrow flight of stairs. Mira sometimes wondered if the wardrobe had existed before Senoonheim, and the buildings had grown up around it.

In any case, there were no chairs in there either. Although she was grateful to have begun making friends in this city, she didn't feel as though she and Troo were close enough to sit together on her bed.

"It's not more comfortable than this, I'm afraid."

Troo looked around the cool moist shadows of the alley and snorted.

"If you're not living somewhere more comfortable than this then I need to stop complaining about the barracks. Joodi snores like a bear, but at least there's less mud," she laughed. "Anyway, I wanted to come and show you this."

She pulled a tightly woven assemblage of thin bone and string out of her pocket. It was folded up into a thin bar of material, but as she held it out it fell open. Strands of thread and thin sticks of bone flicked into position. The structure looked like a spider's web, if that spider had been lucky enough to catch and eat a few small birds.

"Is that the charm you mentioned the other day?" asked Mira.

"Yup," declared Troo proudly. She beamed with delight as she held it higher. It spun gently in the breeze. "I wove that hair of Satonak's into it, and if I got all the steps right then he should find himself much more concerned with the weakness of his bladder than with the meetings of a bunch of women. Until the hair snaps, anyway."

"That sounds good," chuckled Mira. "Is there any way we can be sure it's working on him?"

"Do you really want to know more details about that old coot's bladder?" Troo raised her eyebrow.

"Ew, no! But it would be satisfying to know we'd annoyed him as much as he annoyed me the other night."

"Other than watching him run to relieve himself multiple times a day, not really," sighed Troo. "I think it should work better the closer I get it to him, so I'm going to take it with me next time I patrol Lord Cornucervin's castle. I'll leave it dangling somewhere near the court."

"And hope nobody finds it and pulls it down?"

"I'm sure I can have a chat with one of the maids."

Mira leaned back on her barrel against the wall of the alley, and then lurched forward away from the dampness on her shoulders. Like all right thinking people, she had a natural preference not to feel like she had just rested against slime.

"Maybe that could be one of the first spells we teach the others," she suggested, motioning to the charm.

"This one's pretty complicated," frowned Troo. "Not so good for beginners. And they'd each need one of the old idiot's beard hairs." She rolled up her charm and tucked it away again into her pocket. "But I think I know a good protective charm that they could hang over their front doors. To try to keep their homes safe."

"That sounds promising! What does it involve?"

"A simple sigil shaped out of twigs and grass. It turns away ill intent. Of course, it's only a weak charm. The more determined someone is to get inside, the more ease they have breaking past it." She shrugged. "Like I said, good for beginners."

"Does it work on annoying people who might not have ill intent exactly?" asked Mira. She considered the types of customers that she had been encountering recently. Would the charm protect against their ill intent as she saw it, or would it do nothing as they considered themselves to have good intentions? Perhaps it would be a good way to keep any idiot men like d'Earthy away as well.

Troo blinked and her forehead wrinkled as she began thinking her way through Mira's question. Mira waved her hands.

"No, forget it, that's silly. Alright, let's grab some materials and head over to the tavern. It's time to teach some witches some magic!"

On the way to the Sprog and Sparrow, Troo and Mira walked past some flower sellers and gathered up the materials they would need to make the charms. They found thin, knobbly twigs that would bend easily into loops, plenty of long, thin leaves and grasses that could be used for string, and even some actual string. They put them all into a wicker basket.

The two women walked through the streets, joking about the sorts of people that the charm would turn away: door-to-door salespeople, or con-artists claiming they had found a huge sum of gold that they would gladly share but first you had to pay for their adventuring equipment to retrieve it (they would see you repaid within a season, they swear), or family members who just 'had a quick question' or who just 'needed a little help'.

Mira and Troo cackled to each other, turned the final corner to the tavern, and froze.

Chapter Fifty-One

A small knot of Lord Cornucervin's soldiers were shoving their way out of the Sprog and Sparrow, wearing the same uniform and dark cloak as Troo, and pushing two women from the coven ahead of them.

Othniel stumbled and fell to the ground. She spun over and pushed up both middle fingers at the soldiers instead of climbing to her feet. Her face glowed with anger, almost as brightly as the short, fiery hair that spiked up from her head. She opened her mouth and yelled "Why don't the four of you go and–"

"Hey what's going on here," interrupted Troo as she strode up to the group blocking the door, making sure to flash her deer's head badge as she approached. One of the soldiers grimaced when he saw her and ducked his head.

"Hey Troo," he hissed, turning as if he could hide behind one of the other soldiers.

"Rinald?" Troo was standing over Othniel now, and leaned around the soldiers to get a good look at the one who had tried to hide. Mira could see thick, yellow threadwork around the upper arm of his jerkin, which she supposed must be a symbol of his rank.

"Yeah," he admitted in a slow whine.

"What are you doing here? What's going on with all this?" Troo asked. She held out a thick arm to Othniel, who slapped a hand around the larger woman's wrist and hauled herself to her feet. Othniel made an intimidating figure when she was angry. The white paint on her face glowed and the muscles across her broad shoulders tensed. The soldiers were now faced with two angry women who were clearly quite capable of pushing back. Mira did think Othniel undercut the effect by her choice to wear gossamer gowns, clothes that drifted around her like black and white spider webs, but there was no accounting for personal taste.

Mira caught up with the crowd and put an arm around Ti.

"Are you alright?" she whispered.

Ti sniffed and tugged at the green shawl around her shoulders, pulling it back up and into place.

"I will be, no thanks to these scoundrels," she muttered with a frown. Her gaze didn't leave the soldiers. The two closest to her, at the front of the small group standing in the tavern doorway, had the decency to blush and lower their eyes.

"It's all a misunderstanding, Troo," said Rinald, stepping out with hands outstretched and palms up. "Honestly, there's no need for any violence."

"I hadn't considered that there was," said Troo, folding her arms across her chest. It was like watching a bridge being built, massive structures rising and locking into place with deliberation and controlled effort. She shifted her shoulders and sniffed. "But now I am."

The other soldiers all shrank back, like puppies who had been told off for chewing at the curtains.

"Look, we were sent down here and told to break up the coven," Rinald said with a shrug. "And I tried to tell them that it was a stupid idea, and that you wouldn't be pleased with it all, but you know how they get. It's all 'As part of this family, you need to uphold the expectations of the citizenry' and 'These rules were made for a reason, they support the team's core values' and once anyone starts talking about guiding principles like that, there's no way they'll listen to reason."

"They do like their silly values up at the castle," Troo agreed. "But even if you were going to "break up" the coven, what's the idea with shoving my friends around? Surely you could have told them to leave the pub and they could have told you to stuff off and you could have gone back to the boss and told them you tried. You wouldn't even be lying about it!"

"We didn't shove anyone!" protested Rinald.

"You absolutely did, you lying sack of–" Othniel began.

"No really," interrupted another one of the soldiers. "You tripped on the sword rack." He stepped back and pointed at the door to the tavern behind them. It was still jammed open, caught on a pile of swords spilled on the floor next to it.

Another woman stood in the doorway. She wore the rosy cheeks of someone who had found a lot more spare time than she expected, and spent it all in the fine company of a golden ale. She blinked when she saw the crowd outside.

"Oh, excuse me," she said as edged her way around the soldiers and squeezed through the witches.

Behind her, Mira could see the rack that normally sat beside the door, loaded with swords in their scabbards. The rack had been kicked away from its spot against the wall. Everyone looked at the swords silently. Together, the coven and soldiers turned their eyes to Othniel.

"That might be what happened," admitted Othniel grudgingly.

"But they forced us out of our seats! And they marched us out onto these streets!" said Ti, stabbing a finger at the soldiers, who flinched as though the finger was a sword.

"Sort of," said Rinald, holding a hand out palm down and twisting it like a set of scales. "We told you we had instructions to split you up and you stood up. It is our job to take you out, so we stood close enough and encouraged you to leave. No one touched you, right?"

Ti pursed her lips and narrowed her eyes.

"See! No harm done, no violence needed at all." His eyes watched Troo closely. After a moment of silence he even smiled a little. "Right?"

Mira reached up and up and up and put a hand on Troo's shoulder.

"I think they've done the job they were sent down here to do and they should probably leave now," she said. "And then the rest of us can go inside and have a drink."

"What right do you have to hold up these women?" boomed a loud voice from behind her. The witches turned to see who had spoken, except Mira who simply closed her eyes and hung her head.

"Who's the loud ponce in the shiny armour?" asked Troo.

"Prevos," replied Mira without opening her eyes.

"Oh ho, friend of yours then?"

"I guess so. He keeps turning up." With a sigh, Mira turned to see what Prevos was doing.

The armoured man was marching down the street, his shining metal boots splodging into the mud as he went, spattering the polished armour of his greaves with dark speckles. He swung his arms back and forth as he strode right through the witches, grabbed Rinald's collar, and hoisted the man a good foot off the street. Prevos's stance gave every indication that he was about to use a bad foot to bring the man down.

"By what right do you mean to detain these fine women?" he snarled through the thick metal faceplate of his helmet. The bland expression moulded onto the faceplate seemed all the more horrifying with his angry voice ringing from inside it.

"Hey whoa, hands off, big man!" snapped Rinald, his eyes flashing with anger. The soldiers around him all reached for the swords at their sides, but one woman looked up at the armoured catfolk paladin and paled. "You are threatening a sergeant of the High Lord's soldiers, on business of the court wizard!" His voice rose as he spoke, and people on the street slowed down to watch. Mira heard a few "ooooh" appreciatively.

"You are representatives of the local authority?" Prevos's voice was still loud, but Mira could hear a note of confusion in it now, souring the tone like an untuned violin in an orchestra. He lowered Rinald to the ground.

"Prevos," she said, moving between him and the soldiers, breaking his grip on the sergeant. "What are you doing?"

The shining faceplate of the helmet turned to her. Prevos reached up to lift it off his head and place it against his hip. His golden eyes were confused and little wrinkles in his fur lined his forehead.

"I was coming to help," he stammered. "You appeared to be in distress, and I must always come to the aid of a damsel in distress."

Troo whooped from somewhere behind Mira.

"And her friends also," finished Prevos, motioning to the other witches with his eyebrows.

"That's very kind of you," said Othniel. She had her hands clasped in front of her.

Mira rolled her eyes and sighed.

"It's a very generous impulse," she admitted. "But we're okay. We've had a discussion with Rinald here, and I think we all understand each other now."

"We do?" Rinald said in surprise.

"Yes. You've told us about your orders, and now we are all going back inside the pub while you go back to Satonak and tell him that you tried." Mira raised an eyebrow at the sergeant. "Isn't that right?"

Rinald's eyes flicked around the group, taking in Prevos's tall figure in its gleaming armour, Troo's crossed arms like tree trunks, and the glares of the smaller witches. He drew in a long breath.

"Come on guys," he said. "We've done what we were told to do. Let's go back and get some dinner."

Chapter Fifty-Two

T he soldiers trailed after Rinald like a line of ducklings, scuffing their feet and poking their beaks into doorways as they went. Before they vanished around a corner, a massive bee crested a roof nearby and swooped after them.

Troo grinned at Mira.

"Nicely done Mira, you handled that like a champion."

"Thank you. Sorry you were treated so awfully, ladies," Mira said to the other witches who were dusting themselves off.

Ti was shaking out the tension from her shoulders.

"We're going to have to think of ways to make sure they leave us alone," she considered out loud. "Especially seeing as Satonak has one of his drones watching over the situation."

"You do seem to have attracted a lot of attention," said Prevos.

"Sorry? What do you all mean?" asked Mira. "The drone wasn't watching us."

"It will have seen what happened with the soldiers," muttered Othniel.

"I suppose," said Prevos. "But I was speaking of the way Mira stands out in a crowd."

There was a moment of silence as everyone took this in. Mira saw each of the other women peering around from behind Prevos's shoulders. Othniel was giving a thumbs up, and Troo's eyes were as wide and gleeful as a clown's. Ti's smile was so suggestive that it made Mira blush.

Mira coughed.

"Would you like to come in and have a drink with us?" asked Ti from behind Prevos's back. Mira's eyes widened and she tried to glare at the other woman as Prevos turned around.

"I should not," he said. "I took a vow to avoid temptation."

"Taking vows is nice, but locking yourself into one path can leave you in trouble," said Othniel. She pressed a hand onto her lower ribs. "Sometimes there aren't any pleasant ways out."

"Taverns are places that ruin people, like bakeries and their sugary treats," explained Mira.

Prevos frowned. He shook his head briefly, sending his golden mane shimmering, and then looked back at Mira. "It is a kind invitation, but I find that I get into trouble when I allow myself to come too close to temptation."

"Really?" Mira was surprised that the paladin sounded as though he was considering the idea. "I didn't think you were someone who would get into fights or have too much to drink!"

"What?" The fur covering Prevos' face puffed on end in shock. "Absolutely not! Trankwill would abhor anyone who might disturb the peace in such a way!"

"Oh, sorry." The small flicker of appreciation that had sparked in Mira guttered and died. "So why do you get into trouble?"

Prevos bared his teeth in frustration.

"It is not my intent, it is just that..." He frowned as he looked around for inspiration, seeking the right words. "Sometimes my presence is... disliked." The fur on top of his nose wrinkled up in his discomfort.

Troo smiled and reached forward to put a hand on his shoulder.

"You're welcome to join us. If you find that trouble is following you, you can just leave."

Prevos smiled tightly. He lifted his helmet and slid it over his head. Just before it covered his mouth he said, almost too quietly for Mira to hear, "I'll leave if I notice it coming."

As is entirely normal for most people, the patrons in the Sprog and Sparrow were not concerned with the clattering of swords outside the warm space they occupied. So long as whatever was going on didn't affect them then they were going to have a wonderful afternoon. Prevos followed the witches halfway across the common room and then saw a pair of men playing darts. He paused to watch them throw the darts in their turns.

"He's very pretty," murmured Ti, smoothly stepping up alongside Mira at the bar. Her dark lips hovered near a smile.

"Maybe, but he's a pretty idiot," said Mira. She was busy ordering a drink and missed the smirk that Ti exchanged with Troo.

A group of farmers was throwing dice out of cups onto a table and roaring with pleasure and frustration as the results sent piles of coins from one person to another. A pair of dwarves in the corner had their arms over each other's shoulders and were loudly singing a song about friendship and clanging their axes together in accompaniment.

It is hard to remain sombre when surrounded by such good feelings. This is a survival trait most people develop to avoid being driven out of the village by annoyed neighbours, sick of someone who always "harshes the vibe". This trait is, self-evidently, not always a good thing. Ignoring the commotion outside the doors often allows the commotion to come inside the doors as well. But for now, Jacqui's bar felt like a good place to be.

Troo demonstrated how to put together her protective charm, and the other women tried to twist grass and twigs into matching shapes. Sticks suddenly straightened themselves, sending snapped off ends of wood flying across the room, and the women twanged each other with string.

"Mind those bloody reflections! You blind me during my throw and you'll need more armour than that! Who'd wear armour that bloody shiny anyway!" snapped a voice somewhere behind them.

Ti's charm kept ending up looking like a spider's web, which Troo had to explain meant that it wouldn't work as intended. Ti shrugged and said that it would decorate the walls of her home better that way.

"I'll tell you what I'm talking about Mr Bloody Bright-sides!" snarled someone across the room.

A spider's web portrayed in twigs bent into a circle barely was practically normal compared to Othniel's proudly presented charm that looked exactly like the skull painted over her face, eye sockets shaded in strings of varying densities.

"That's not quite it either," said Troo, her eyebrows bunched together. Othniel pursed her lips, unpicked the skull at great effort, and tried again.

Something clanged in the tavern behind them, sounding exactly like a sharp spike of metal that had been thrown into a flat piece of metal and gone ricocheting away. Someone shrieked in just the manner that would be expected of someone who had been unexpectedly stabbed by a small flying spike.

After holding up three more skull-shaped charms, including one that Troo had woven all but the final knot of herself before she handed it to Othniel, Troo threw up her hands and declared that it would have to be good enough.

There was an explosion of rhythmic thudding noises behind Mira, interrupted by an occasional bong and the choked exhalations of someone losing their breath.

"Maybe we should put up a bunch of these at the door to the tavern," grumbled Ti. "Then perhaps those bloody soldiers would leave us alone."

Mira laughed in agreement and turned to see what Prevos was up to. On the other side of the common room, he was holding each of the darts players up off their feet by their throats, their legs running in place furiously. He nodded to her and dropped them. As soon as their feet hit the floor ,they sprinted forward and slammed into the wall.

Prevos walked over to her and bowed slightly.

"I think that I should leave now," he murmured. "Thank you for inviting me in. It wasn't as bad as I expected."

The others all made farewell noises while Mira smiled awkwardly.

"Until next time, I suppose," she said. "I'm sorry we didn't talk much."

Prevos nodded.

"Until next time," he agreed.

Troo caught Ti's eye after the paladin left and shook her head.

"Unfortunately these charms wouldn't have stopped those soldiers. It's really not a strong enough charm. They were following orders, and they specifically wanted to find some of our coven, so they would be able to push past any feelings of unease that it raised in them."

Ti snorted.

"I dreamed of the Cockerel Prince last night, maybe I can make a deal with him to chastise anyone who comes seeking us."

"Maybe you should!" laughed Troo. Mira wasn't so sure. She had heard a little of the Cockerel Prince before and from what she knew, he was a difficult bravura honda for a witch to rely on.

The Cockerel Prince was a minor deity of the dead, and notoriously demanding in what he asked of witches who sought his favour. He was also equally stingy in the gifts that he handed out. For some reason, this sort of selfish behaviour, combined with his admittedly stylish manner of dressing and the swaggering self-confidence that was only found in demi-gods, made him incredibly attractive to a lot of young witches. If she was honest with herself, Mira recognised that he inspired something similar in non-witches as well.

Still, there was a fire in Ti's eyes, and iron strength in her arms, and Mira was pretty sure that if anyone could give the self-assured Cockerel Prince a run for his money, it would be her.

With bellies full of wine and arms full of scratch-built charms, the witches bid their farewells and strolled out of the Sprog and Sparrow, heading back through the night-shrouded streets of Senoonheim to their homes.

Chapter Fifty-Three

Mira reflected on all the sudden changes to her life as she walked home. Only a week earlier, she had been lonely. She had felt as though she was waking up and completing the same endless, thankless tasks every day for no purpose. But now, after she had taken action and decided to seek out others who shared her interests, she was spending more time out and laughing. She had been out courting. Although he had the wrong impression of who she was, at least she had gone out! She had found more happiness and energy in the last week than if she had piled all of those feelings from the year before into one moment.

Of course, it wasn't all sunshine and sweet treats. She was out in the uncertain streets after dark where she had nearly been robbed twice that she knew of. One time, the thief had been someone she might become friends with, which was a little confusing, and the other time that same person had intervened. She didn't know how she felt about any of that, but at least she was okay so far.

She had also been targeted by one of the most important and powerful men in the city, who had publicly and loudly declared that she had to stop what she was doing to find friends. That was a problem that was only going to grow, she was sure of it. They had managed to convince Rinald and his soldiers to leave them alone today, but the very fact that soldiers were showing up to interfere with them was a clear sign that they should expect more harassment from Satonak. Clearly, he wanted to impress his will on the city, and his ambition might lead him to try something worse than sending easily cowed soldiers.

And lastly, somehow, she had picked up a... She wasn't really sure what to call Prevos. He was certainly hanging around like a bad smell, always just on the edge of her senses so that she couldn't forget about him, but indistinct enough that she didn't focus on him much. She was concerned that he might turn out to be as much trouble as every other man seemed to, but something in the way he spoke with her felt different. He accepted the things she said to him. He didn't seem to see her as something else. He had even come into the tavern with her.

Mira reached her shop and admired the display in the window facing the street. Large loaves, with golden crusts and elaborate twisted decoration filled the edges of the window, and a few long, stale cakes that she would no longer sell still provided a sweet-looking centrepiece. It was a good display, and she knew that it enticed passersby inside.

Her smile faded when she saw a small envelope resting against the door. She picked it up and studied it as she unlocked the door and stepped through, closing and locking the door once she was inside. Her name was written on the envelope, but there was no other way to tell who might have sent it.

Mira climbed the stairs to her rooms and tore a strip off the top of the envelope and then reached inside. There were two pieces of paper in the envelope, one folded in half so that it fit and one smaller. She read through the small piece first.

Mira,

I enjoyed joining you and your friends this evening and I am sorry I had to leave early.

I see you have been trying other cultural bread recipes, and you must have been very successful in your endeavours, giving the devotion to elven bread that I witnessed the other day.

I thought you may be interested in this recipe that has been handed down my family for generations. It is a personal favourite.

The letter was signed with a large P.

Prevos. Mira reread the letter, looking for veiled insults or unrecognised arrogance. There was nothing. Signing the letter let her know he had come by instead of his previous sneaking around, which was certainly an improvement.

Mira got changed and tucked herself into her covers. She took a look at the recipe that Prevos had included.

She was surprised to see that the recipe called for more cake-like ingredients. Prevos had made it clear that one of his many personal vows was to abstain from sweet treats, but this recipe included sugar and eggs. As she kept reading, her eyebrows rose further. The recipe also called for a large serving of chopped, fresh fish. The method said to bake the bread into small, thin pieces, and, if Mira was any sort of expert, she knew that it would result in brittle and crunchy pieces of 'bread'.

She put the recipe onto her bedside table and blew out the candle. She couldn't imagine making this catfolk bread recipe any time soon. The thought of the smell of baking fish flooding her bakery made her shudder before she went to sleep.

***

Mira felt woollen-headed as she bumbled her way through preparing fresh loaves in the morning. She wasn't getting enough sleep any more. Instead she was spending too much time out with her new friends in the coven. But she wasn't sure what to do about it. She needed to see people. She couldn't do another year by herself. On the other hand, what was she going to do about the shop if she was too exhausted to run it?

She was worried that she was losing control. She rebuked herself for her sloppiness as she accidentally dropped bits of dough to the floor and tried to bring her focus back to the work. She was worried that there was too much going on, and not just in her kitchen.

She dutifully smiled and spoke with the people who came through her bakery. They bought rolls for their lunches, small cakes for their children, loaves to take home with them, but none of their faces registered in her mind. Mira operated purely on habit as her mind tried desperately to wake itself up until she found herself looking at an empty space on the other side of her counter, occupied by a small hand holding up a large coin.

Mira blinked and followed the hand down to an arm and then she followed the arm down until she found a large green hat, and contained within the hat was the big face and wide eyes of Shara. Poking up above the edge of the desk next to his mistress's face was the head of the duck Widgeon. The duck quacked sternly when Mira met his eyes.

"Hello, can we please have another loaf of bread please?" said the small girl.

"Of course," said Mira. "Which one would you like?"

"Oh, I don't really mind," smiled Shara. "Widgeon thought that your last one was so delicious that we had to get some more. But they all look so good! I'm sure anything would be lovely."

"Alright." Mira looked around her shelves. "Why not try a rye knot?" She pointed out the twisted loaf behind the girl. "It's quite flavorful, but simple so the duck should be happy with it."

The duck quacked angrily.

"Yes, he might like that. But his name is Widgeon."

"Oh yes," said Mira.

Shara and her duck watched her expectantly.

"Sorry Widgeon," Mira said.

The duck quacked again, in a tone that expressed his satisfaction with the apology.

Shara fetched the loaf, paid Mira, and then looked around the room.

"Do you have somewhere I can sit down?" she asked.

"People don't usually sit in the shop."

"Really? Then where do they eat their bread?" Shara's eyes were shockingly large as she started up at Mira. Mira found herself wondering if Shara was some other type of folk that she hadn't encountered in Senoonheim before. It was hard to believe that eyeballs so monumentally orb-esque were possible in a head that belonged to a human. Perhaps she had some birdfolk background and had inherited owl eyes from her parents.

"I don't know. At their homes or workplaces, I suppose?"

Shara stared at her with those massive eyes and then smiled.

"I suppose they must. Come on, Widgeon!"

Together the young girl and her duck left. Mira watched as Shara stepped out of the bakery door and squinted into a direct beam of bright midday sunlight.

She looked up with a bright smile and said, "Good afternoon Mr Sun. Thank you for being nice and warm." As they walked out the door, the duck turned to look over its shoulder back at Mira. She could have sworn it was glaring at her, and then in a moment, the pair had gone.

Mira leaned down on the counter. That little girl was intense. And her duck was genuinely frightening.

Chapter Fifty-Four

At the end of the day, Mira stepped out of her bakery and was immediately confronted by a tall man in dark leathers. He wore a hooded cloak that shrouded his face. Black stubble sprouted fetchingly from his jaw. A leather vambrace was strapped to his forearm and a sword hung low on his belt. Even on the city street in the middle of the afternoon, he brooded.

None of this was immediately obvious to Mira, as he was holding up a two foot long fish and pointing its face directly at her. She went cross-eyed trying to focus on the silvery fish mouth gaping at her before she stepped backwards, wiping her own mouth out of instinct.

"What on earth are you doing?" she snapped.

"Do you like it?" asked the man. Thankfully, he lowered the fish as he spoke.

"Do I like what? A random fish being shoved in my face?"

"I saw that you like fish," said the man. He sounded affronted, as though she was the one behaving rudely by suggesting that a fish-to-the-face was not a good first impression. "This is a really good one." He held it up higher, perhaps thinking she must not have inspected it properly before. Maybe she just needed a moment to truly acknowledge how good a fish it was.

Mira shook her head, clearing her thoughts.

"Sorry, are you suggesting that I should be grateful that you have brought me a fish and jammed it in my face?"

"It's a good fish," he grumbled sourly.

"Who cares? Who are you and what are you doing lurking outside my door with your piscine product?"

"People call me Treader." The man had his face down now, and was speaking in the same tones as a sullen teenage boy who's been told to go out and get some fresh air.

"Look, Treader, what exactly were you hoping would be the outcome of this fishy ambush?"

He looked up again.

"I saw you buying fish the other day. You looked pretty. I thought we could go out for dinner sometime."

Mira bit her lips to stop from laughing in the man's face.

"Might I suggest that posing with fish isn't the ideal way to entice a woman?"

"But I caught it and it's a good fish!" he protested.

"Okay, I'm willing to admit that it's impressive that you caught a fish anywhere near here," began Mira. Treader's back straightened a little and she waved a finger at him.

"Oh no you don't!" she snapped. "Even if I was a fan of fish, I hardly need to have a dead one thrust at me without warning. If you are interested in someone, you need to get to know them. Find out their name for one thing. You still don't know mine!"

He blinked.

"Is it Isla?"

"Why would you think my name is Isla?"

The man shrugged, which caused the fish's tail to flick salty drops of water onto Mira's face. Her back stiffened and she wiped her face again.

"Okay, Treader. It's time to go now."

The man harumphed then sulked away into the crowd on the street, taking his fish with him.

Mira glanced at the reflection of herself in the bakery window.

"Honestly, what gets into the heads of these men?" she asked herself.

Her reflection shrugged then she straightened her skirts and tucked her dark hair back behind her ears. But before Mira headed off along the street herself, she noticed the reflection of a bird sitting on the roof opposite her. It was bigger than most of the other city birds, and its head was pale. It was staring down at her.

It was easy to recognise Plak, the bird Fina had said she would send. Although unusually large and covered in midnight plumage, it was the skull-white featherless head of the bird that really caught one's attention. Plak shuffled on the gutters like any other bird, hopping from one scraggly claw to another as ready to leave but waiting while someone checked for any new messages yet again.

Mira wasn't sure whether a pale layer of skin wrapped the bird's head or if it really was a skull. Perhaps Fina had summoned an undead construct as a companion. Light glittered from the black sockets on either side of Plak's skull. It was hard to tell if the sparkle was a reflection from eyes deep inside the sockets or whether magic was leaking out of the creature.

In any case, Plak was clearly waiting for her, as it flapped noisily into the air and swooped to another building further down the street.

"Alright," Mira said out loud. "I'm coming, I'm coming."

Plak led the way through Senoonheim towards Lord Cornucervin's castle. As she followed, Mira wondered why Fina was in the city. The older witch was certainly no fan of Lord Cornucervin, so why hold a meeting right under his nose? Was it a way to insult him?

Eventually, the bird led her to a beautiful park, deep inside the city but surrounded by a high brick wall. The walls were covered with moss and lichen. Mira picked at them as she walked towards the iron scrollwork gate. The lichen crumbled away under her fingernails, revealing large grey bricks in good condition. She picked off a little more lichen and examined it closer, crumbling it between her fingers.

She looked up at Plak, sitting on the gate, watching her.

"It's cornflakes and paint," she laughed. "To make the wall look old."

The bird opened its beak to crawk at her, but she didn't know if that meant it understood what she had said, or was hurrying her along. Maybe it was just how these birds sounded and didn't mean anything at all.

Beyond the gate, Mira was entranced by the park that grew inside, hidden from the rest of the city. A gravel path curled through groves of trees, between thick underbrush. Vines wound up tree trunks, and colourful flowers bloomed at every height, some poking out the tops of trees she hadn't been able to see from outside the walls.

Deeper in the park was a broad pond, with water that was thick and green. Rushes stabbed up from the water's surface, like dozens of green and glorious swords being presented to establish a legitimate monarchy that would not be contested by any mandate from the masses.

Beside the pond, on a blanket, sat a small gathering of her coven. Fina had brought a little stool with her and was comfortably perched on it, while Junka had hung a small black kettle over a fire. The strange young girl Shara was with them, and her huge duck was splashing happily in the pond. Kirka was cutting a caramel slice into portions, using one of her large and glistening knives to do so. She leaned just a little bit too close, and her eyes were just a little bit too wide as the blade bit through the smooth surface of the confection.

Chapter Fifty-Five

"Hello Mira!" Fina smiled. The expression looked odd on her. She looked as though she was pleased someone had bitten into her poison apple. "I thought you might like to come and join us. We were going to have some tea and talk about how magic works."

"Yes, that sounds good, thank you."

Mira settled herself on the blanket that was spread on the grass and watched steam spill from the kettle as it boiled. Junka poured the hot water into a teapot and then produced one mismatched teacup after another from the bunched recesses of her clothing. She placed them in a line on the ground beside her and began to pour the tea. Once poured, she handed one to each woman present.

Mira examined the dark, malty liquid. Then she glanced around the blanket. Then she looked at the thick, green water of the pond beside them. The bulbous twin eyes of quite a large frog emerged from the surface of the pond and winked at her, first one eye then the other.

"Did you bring some water with you for the kettle?" she asked as nonchalantly as she could.

"No, I just scooped some out of the pond here," replied Junka cheerfully.

Mira smiled back and pretended to sip at her tea.

"Alright ladies, I know some of you were feeling a bit out of sorts because you haven't found your bravura honda yet," began Fina once a certain half of the tea and slices had been consumed and the women had leaned back to relax. "But I wanted to reassure you that your bravura is only one half of witchcraft."

"Are you even a witch if you don't have one yet?" asked Kirka.

"Some might say that you aren't," allowed Fina. "But I think that it is not so important. After all, there are people in the world who love men, and people who love women, and some who love both. But whether they currently have a partner or not, they know what sort of person they are. So it is with witches. Though you may not have a partner yet, you know what sort of person you are, and that is that you are witches."

Kirka's frown suggested that she wasn't convinced. Mira wasn't sure either.

"Is it really important that we are witches? Wizards exist and seem to be able to do magic even without bravura. Or is that some sort of trick?" Kirka asked with wide, innocent eyes, sliding a cloth along the flat of her knife to clean away any crumbs sticking to it.

"That's true, wizards have access to magic," Fina said.

"Then why do we even need to be witches? What's the difference?" repeated Kirka. Mira listened closely.

"It's a matter of personality," explained Fina, leaning forward with both hands resting on her walking stick. On the ground next to her, Plak hopped forward and pecked up a chunk of caramel slice. "Wizards think of the world as a problem to be solved, if only they can work out where all the pieces fit. And, in a way, it is. If they find all the edges and corners and can match each pattern to the piece next to it, they could eventually put together the puzzle that is the full understanding of the universe." She chuckled softly.

"But does the world around you look like something that will hold still long enough for someone to write down where each piece belongs?" She gestured up to where clouds were gusting through the sky, unpeeling like fruits and wisping away into nothingness. Fina laughed. "Every time a wizard thinks he has made a breakthrough, the world shifts again, and they have to find out what has changed."

Fina pushed off her boots and stretched her toes out on grass beneath her feet. She breathed in and out slowly and smiled. Then she raised her eyebrows and lifted her face to look at the other witches again.

"But the wizards do have some of it right. The world is a logical place."

Kirka snorted.

Fina smiled again and continued.

"No really. People complain that it doesn't seem to be that way, and I can see why. The world is so full of cruelty and madness. Natural disasters crushing villages in faraway valleys for one example! But these things are just the consequences of actions made in the past. One change in the world leads to another, until the mind of a good person is overwhelmed and they snap, or one more pebble added to the pile is nudged by the wind and so a landslide begins. There is a logic, if only we understood every single cause, and so the wizards have the right of things there."

"But magic isn't logical," protested Junka. "With magic, I could conjure a ball of fire that I can hold on the palm of my hand and then throw to the top of a mountain, where it will explode. There's no logic to that!"

"So the common people would say." Fina smiled. "But if you understood the deep workings of the world, you would discover that there are words that can command fire. You would know that certain gestures will protect your skin. Certain ingredients might persuade the winds to carry your fire to where you want it to go. As I said, the wizards know this much. And so magic is just a matter of knowing which of those words and gestures are needed."

"But, if that is true, then it's possible that common people might do magic by mistake," said Mira.

"And so they do, all the time." Fina watched Mira closely. "Everyone makes the world change all the time. We bind the future to our desires by our every action. Some of us do this deliberately, seeking to achieve some end of our own. Others pay it no heed and allow the consequences of their actions to unfold around them as they may. But even the utterance of a single word changes the world. After all Mira, didn't you find your world upended by a few words spoken by a man with no magic in his soul at all?"

Mira blushed but nodded. Loam had said that he would punish her and anyone who supported her, and immediately her business had fallen apart, and her friends had gone. A few words from the wrong person meant she had to flee Whinnia and start her whole life again.

"I find that my magic word is 'please'," said Shara from where she sat cross-legged on the blanket, chewing on a mouthful of bread. Widgeon swam in small circles on the pond behind her.

"That is a renowned magic word indeed!" laughed Fina. "Would you show Mira what you mean?"

"Okay," said the small girl. She looked at one of the trees overhanging the small coven and said, "Excuse me Mr Plum Tree, but could you please let a little more sun down here to warm me up?"

The tree shivered, as though a breeze ran through its leaves, then the branches bent softly aside, allowing through enough light that Shara squinted her massive eyes.

"Thank you very much," she said. She returned to her bread roll.

"So you see! It's all a matter of knowing what to say and how and when," Fina finished.

Chapter Fifty-Six

"That's very inspiring," said Kirka. "So then why should we be witches and not wizards, studying these things?"

"Because witches know that we can't understand everything ourselves. It's only through sharing that knowledge that we can hope to know enough to do what we need to do. Have you ever wondered why so many wizards shut themselves away in towers?"

The other witches nodded.

"They get jealous of their knowledge. They work so hard to find it out, and then they panic that someone else will discover it without working as hard as them, and they hate that idea."

"Don't they study from books? Don't they write books about magic?" asked Mira.

"Yes, but they write down spells in the same manner a butterfly hunter pins her discoveries into boxes. They feel that they have trapped the knowledge in one place, where they can use it when they wish."

"If they are worried that someone would learn something too easily, why do they use books at all?" Mira continued, trying to sort all this out in her head.

"Because they wish to gain this knowledge as easily as they can. They will take it from others if they get the chance, while defending what they have found from everyone else. While many of them undertake research of their own, there are some wizards who focus only on the studies of others. They collect books and scrolls that explain how to perform spells and they try to find out how to reduce that spell to only the most essential elements. They experiment and cast the spells over and over, each time differently, noting what happens if some aspect wasn't correct." She grinned. "And they are terrified that others might do the same."

"Isn't that hugely hypocritical?" asked Mira.

"Of course!" declared Fina dismissively. She made a sour face. "P'shaw. Wizards!"

"So, being a witch rather than a wizard means sharing that knowledge," said Kirka.

"Exactly. That is what a coven is all about. That is why we seek a relationship with a bravura honda, so that we can have the assistance of beings whose understanding of our world is higher than our own."

Mira nodded. When she listened to Fina talk, it all made sense. Bovo had never explained it as fully as this.

"Satonak is a wizard, and he's been trying to control everything going on in Senoonheim recently, watching everyone with his drones. Do you think it's the same?" she asked the others.

Kirka grunted. Fina nodded.

"Wizards don't trust other people. I imagine he must find it very difficult to allow others to control their own lives. Anyway, let's discuss something happier than wizards! Kirka, what do you say we try to introduce you to a bravura this afternoon?" said Fina.

"Yes," said the woman, exposing her teeth in a grin. Her eyes flicked over to Shara and then back to Fina. "Please," she added.

"I thought meeting your bravura honda was a slow process," said Mira. Her forehead wrinkled in confusion. "I thought it was a special connection that should not be rushed?"

Fina waved a hand around, dismissing the idea.

"Yes, that's all well and good, but we can also be a bit more active in our efforts," she said.

Mira's shoulders slumped. Had she been wasting time, waiting for the world to come to her? Bovo had told her to be patient. Should she have been getting out and involved in the world instead? She had to admit it wasn't until she had taken charge of her life in Senoonheim that she had met these women, and now she felt more alive than she had in months. Even in Whinnia she had been letting the world happen to her, rather than taking control of it.

"How does it work?" asked Kirka, leaning closer to the older witch. Her eyes, always disturbingly alert and bright, opened wider and glistened like the edge on the knives hanging from her belt.

"I've got just the thing. Copy my hand movements and repeat after me."

Fina held up her hands and made slow winding gestures, extending one or the other finger into the air, as though gathering floating strings. At the same time she spoke unusual syllables in a soft but carrying voice. Kirka followed her directions exactly, and Shara waved a hand around in roughly the same way, giggling as she did. Mira watched closely, but a blush warmed her cheeks and held her back from copying Fina's directions. She was supposed to know all of this already, but Bovo had never made it clear for her. She felt like a fraud, someone the others would see through any moment.

Suddenly, the air in front of the other women shimmered and golden light coalesced into geometric shapes. A large rectangle hung in the air like a picture frame attached to nothing, the gilt whorls of its frame shifting in the slow loops of distant summer clouds.

A reptilean face filled the frame, with a strong brow and two sharp horns stabbing up from the sides of its head. A broad mouth grinned, revealing lines of thin, sharp teeth.

"What is this?" breathed Kirka. She reached one hand out towards the image.

"This is a spell that can be used to find local bravura. If you touch the picture he will speak with us, and then you can push the image away if he seems uninspiring."

Kirka nodded and reached out. Mira sat up straighter, keen to see what would happen next.

"Dread greetings to you," hissed the image as soon as Kirka's fingers brushed the curling frame. "Cower before the might and glory of Kreetash!" His thin tongue slid over his tiny lips.

Kirka turned her attention to Fina.

"Alright, so he sounds evil. That don't impress me much."

Fina chuckled.

"Chat with him a little."

"I'm looking for a bravura honda," said the small witch to the reptilian image. She raised an eyebrow. "Why should I build a connection with you?"

"Those who worship me suffer the greatest earthly pains and delights that can be known! To submit to my force is to know that your life is bound in service to one who deserves all obeisance! I reward those who live in my service well! Simply look at my many top ranked reviews!"

As he spoke, the scaly being gestured below his image. Silvery words appeared, written on the air and wobbling slightly, like reflections on a pond.

Mira could read some from where she sat.

"Kreetash refuses my every need in a personal and creative way. No one gets to know those they consume like Kreetash!" she murmured as she read the first one.

"If you are tired of life getting you down, why not let Kreetash take control of it instead? Then you can truly be sure your depression is not your fault. It's his!" read Kirka. She snorted.

"I take it you don't want a bravura who is going to dictate your life to you?" asked Fina, with a twinkle in her dark eyes.

Kirka smiled with thin lips.

"I'm not very interested in doing what other people want."

Fina nodded.

"Most witches agree with you, but there are some expectations! Alright, shove him aside and let's see who else might be around."

"Bye bye Mr Scales," said Shara from her end of the picnic blanket. Widgeon quacked.

Kirka reached forward and pushed the image to one side. It faded like morning mist and a new image wound itself out of the air to replace it.

Kirka shoved aside uninspiring possibilities for a long time that afternoon. Mira couldn't blame her. The pickings were not impressive. Why should it be so hard to create a connection with a being that was good for both entities involved? Mira found herself thinking of Master d'Earthy and Prevos.

D'Earthy had good qualities, but he had not paid attention to who Mira was, being far more focused on what he enjoyed. So long as he thought she liked the arena as well, he had admired her. When she made it clear that she didn't enjoy watching violence for entertainment as much as he did, the dwarf reacted as though she had tricked him. What sort of person was so self centred?

And Prevos. He had said some very judgemental things about her baking, and about lots of people in Senoonheim, without realising that she might be the sort of person that he was judging. At the same time, at least he didn't seem to hold any unrealistic ideas about who she was. He had spoken well of her, and wanted to join her doing the things that she was interested in. He asked about her life. And he even come into the tavern with the coven! Maybe he could change a little?

Chapter Fifty-Seven

Mira breezed through the next morning as though she was half asleep. She moved through habit. Her head overflowed with concern that Fina's lessons would uncover her secret. She had been so pleased to start the coven, and then so determined to ignore Satonak's attempts to stop them meeting. They made her feel like she could value herself. They saw who she was and liked it. It had given her enough confidence to tell a good-looking dwarf she didn't want to court him! But they didn't see her completely, and that hidden remainder made Mira nauseous.

She caught a glimpse of her reflection in the window. Her face looked worried and pale.

"It's going to be alright," she told herself in a whisper, then she breathed in and smiled at herself. "You just need to pay attention to the lessons too. It'll all be fine."

"What was that?" asked the round, halfling woman peering over the bakery counter. The woman squinted suspiciously up at Mira.

"Sorry, madam," said Mira. "I was just talking to myself. What can I get for you?"

Mira tried to focus on her customers for the rest of the day, but her mind kept wandering. More than one left with a sour glance over their shoulder.

"Excuse me?" snapped a voice from the other side of the counter, lisping slightly.

"I'm so sorry," Mira said as she blinked and refocused on where she was. "My mind was somewhere else."

"Yes, I could tell," grumbled the customer. He was tall and thin, and his skin was peeling off, which made sense because he was a zombie.

"I'm sorry," Mira apologised, averting her eyes from the curl of skin coming off his cheek. "Could I ask you to repeat what it was you were looking for?"

"I just need some muffins to take to a baby shower," said the zombie. Only a small part of his lower lip remained, and his teeth shone whitely even when he had his mouth closed. Mira assumed that was the cause of his lisp. One of his eyes dangled from its socket onto his chest, as though he was worried about the stains on his ragged clothes and was making a close inspection.

"Might I suggest these?" Mira gestured towards a selection of savoury cheese muffins on a shelf to her right. "Just the right amount of paprika, and a little bacon."

"That does sound good." The man lifted the eye from where it lay on his chest and pointed it closely at the muffins. He sniffed through the gaping hole where his nose should have been. "Yes, they seem perfect!"

"Hang on a minute!" interrupted another voice. It sounded exactly the same as the zombie, but had no lisp. There was a distant quality to the new voice, as though it came from the far end of a small tunnel, giving it a faint echo.

Mira looked for the new speaker. In the middle of the bakery was a shimmer like the air above boiling hot cobbles in the middle of summer. Then the air turned sideways, the light refracted, and the outline of a figure stood in the middle of the bakery. The transparent figure looked just like the zombie standing at the counter. His nose was straight and very becoming.

"Oh, what do you want?" the zombie asked the ghost in a voice that dripped with exasperation.

"It's a baby shower! I should be bringing something sweet!" said the ghost. He crossed his arms, which looked very strange. Mira could still see the door to the bakery through his arms and body.

"I should bring whatever I want," declared the zombie, emphasising each "I" as he spoke. He turned and smiled at Mira, a horrifying sight that pulled his cheeks completely away from the skull beneath, and said, "I'll take eight please. Do you have anything to pack that into?"

"Yes, I can get you a small basket if you like," she said.

"Wonderful."

The ghost drifted closer, changing his position without moving his feet, which hovered an inch off the floor.

"You think you're so clever, just because you can carry money around and I can't," complained the ghost. "But we all know that you're just a rude mechanical version of who I used to be. One day I'll get the reins back in my hands, just you wait."

"We all know that you're not even real!" growled the zombie without turning around. "You're just a particularly intrusive figment of somebody's imagination!"

"Then how come she can see me? Huh? Go on, explain that Mr Braaaainssss!"

The zombie staggered as though he had been struck in the stomach. His mouth dropped open as if he had been slapped.

"I can't believe you said that!"

The ghost had the grace to look away, embarrassed.

"Okay, I apologise. I shouldn't have said that. But I still want to know why she can see me." He pointed towards Mira who busied herself packing the muffins into the basket and tried not to get involved.

"I don't know whose imagination is coming up with you," said the zombie. "But I hope they stop soon." He paid for the muffins, picked up the basket and began to shuffle slowly towards the door, taking a step with one foot and then dragging his other up to the first.

The ghost shoved at the zombie with both hands, which passed through him completely.

"Hah!" laughed the zombie snidely. He nodded to Mira. "Thank you miss, and I apologise for the rude behaviour of this imposter."

"You're the imposter!" wailed the ghost as the door tinkled behind them.

Mira shook her head and fetched her broom from the kitchen so she could sweep the shop. She would be able to close soon. But before she even began, the door tinkled again behind her. Mira sighed. Then she set her shoulders and her smile, and turned to welcome these new customers.

"Good afternoon, what can I–Oh, ladies, it's you!" Her smile softened out of the rictus pose that all retail workers wear to appear polite towards people who might pay them.

Troo was the first through the door, reaching out with both hands and grabbing Mira by the shoulders in a sort of distant hug. Mira's body compressed between the woman's hands and then she felt the relief of release. After Troo came Nerishma, who gave a stern nod to Mira. Mira nodded back.

"Hello Hattie," Mira said, addressing the tiny woman standing on Nerishma's shoulder with one hand on the thief's head, steadying herself.

Hattie's face was twisted into a scowl, but that was nothing unusual. She huffed and nodded at Mira, which was practically the same greeting as gathering her into a hug and spinning her around from anyone else.

"So, Nerishma," said Mira. "Prevos seemed to think that you helped me out the other night, but I don't remember seeing you. What was he talking about?"

The skinny woman's face flooded with embarrassment and she twisted her fingers together in front of her stomach.

Chapter Fifty-Eight

"Uh. Well. There was someone from the Guild, and they were following you the other night, and I told them to leave you alone, that's all."

"Prevos? That big catfolk man in the shiny armour?" said Troo. "You've been talking more with him have you?" The huge orc woman grinned.

"You're a member of the Guild are you? I didn't realise that." Mira ignored Troo's interruption and kept her arms crossed. She wanted to clarify what Nerishma was up to. If talking about something else meant she could ignore the blush creeping up her neck, then that was just a pleasant coincidence.

Nerishma's eyes bulged and she grimaced. But all she did was lower her gaze to the floor, and mumble in a voice that clearly wanted to explain but at the same certainly didn't want anyone to hear her.

"'es" she whispered in the exact manner of a five year old who had been caught stealing bikkies.

"I haven't heard much of the Guild here in Senoonheim. Troo told me that it's actually quite a new city, not nearly as ancient as it seems. I suppose the Guild haven't had as much time to get themselves established."

Nerishma snorted and then clapped a hand over her mouth.

"My mistake," said Mira with a raised eyebrow. "They have got started in Senoonheim then?"

Nerishma nodded. She lowered the hand from her face.

"When Lord Cornucervin decided to build the first facades on Pseudoprime Road, the Guild was already settling into their den here."

Mira nodded.

"Okay, the Guild is here. But still, I didn't know you were part of the Guild."

"Of course I am. If you try to make a living doing what I do, and the Guild finds out that you're not contributing a share to them, then they make life very awkward for you."

"How awkward are we talking?" Mira was familiar with guild rules. As a member of the Reverential Ensemble of Bakers, she could have her shop taken over by the guild if she didn't hold to their standards. In the manner of petty bureaucracy everywhere, they were very quick to levy fines for anything they perceived as an indiscretion as well. "Does it get very expensive?"

"I'd say it's expensive. It can cost you your life," Nerishma said.

"Ah. Very awkward," said Mira. She nodded. "Well, in that case, thank you for helping me out!"

Nerishma pressed her lips together.

"You're welcome."

"And what brings you all out to my bakery today?" asked Mira.

"I wanted to come and tell you that Satonak is furious, that's what!" Troo grinned, a sight made all the more impressive by her tusks. "He's been ranting at all the soldiers in the castle, trying to gather a fresh group to come and detain you guys. Apparently he wasn't pleased with Rinald leaving everyone alone."

"I don't see that Rinald did anything wrong. He explained the situation to us and we told him we were going to ignore him." Mira smirked up at Troo. "What's Satonak's problem with that?"

"Apparently he should have grabbed you all and thrown you into the cells, according to Satonak."

"I don't think any of us would have enjoyed that." Mira shook her head. "I don't think Rinald would have enjoyed the experience of trying to make us do that either."

"You're right, he wouldn't have. I've been reminding a lot of the soldiers in the castle that I'm one of them, but that I'm also part of the coven." Troo rolled her shoulders, loosening the muscles like an ox being hitched to a wagon. "I think they are listening to me so far."

"I bet they are!" agreed Mira. "You can be very direct in your thoughts!"

"You can as well," replied Troo.

"No–" Mira began to argue, but Nerishma nodded furiously, nearly shaking Hattie off her shoulder. The tiny witch scowled down at her human steed.

"You are definitely a direct person as well," said the skinny thief.

Mira's mouth was hanging open. She forced it closed and thought about what these women were telling her. They thought that she was direct? She felt as though she hid so much from everyone. Was d'Earthy right? Was she presenting a fake person to her friends?

"We are going to need to do something about Satonak before long," Troo continued. "We aren't his soldiers and I haven't heard Lord Antlers complain about the coven once! Unless he reins in that wizard soon, he might lose some of his authority."

"Hopefully he'll decide that the wizard is causing too much trouble." Mira shuddered. Satonak had clamped onto the coven like a hungry dog and now he was going to hang on until he was satisfied. But Mira really didn't understand why the wizard had decided to make such an example of them.

"What's his problem with us anyway?"

"I couldn't tell from the gossip in the castle, sorry," said Troo. "But everyone agreed that he is really angry. I heard he's been throwing things around in his library."

Nerishma gasped. Mira turned to her.

"Does that mean something to you?" she asked.

"Not specifically," said Nerishma with a pale face. "But I know wizards are obsessed with their books and scrolls. I've encountered a few people who are precious about their possessions." She glanced up at Troo. "And you're telling me that he's damaging his own belongings? That sounds like some level beyond angry to me!" She shook her head. "I'll ask around. Some of the people I know can uncover very well hidden information."

"Of course they can," said Mira. The Guild was very good at discovering exactly the sorts of secrets that no one wanted revealed. There was good money to be made in blackmail.

Hattie scowled and snorted and huffed from her position on Nerishma's shoulder.

"That's right," agreed Troo. "We didn't come here to talk about that. We're going to the Trivial Lampshade. Would you like to come with us?"

"What's happening at the Lampshade?" asked Mira.

"Ti told us to join her. I think there might be some good musicians."

"Isn't the Lampshade an adventurer's tavern?" groaned Mira, her shoulders falling.

"Yes, but that's why the music is so good!" said Troo, her eyes lighting up. "Come on, come with us!"

"Alright," Mira finally agreed. "I just hope the music is as good as you say."

Hattie made a pleased growl.

***

"How well do you know that catfolk paladin?" asked Nerishma as they stepped along the dusty road, skipping across the cartwheel ruts that lined it.

"Me?" Mira felt as though the other woman had reached over and pushed her in the chest. "Prevos? What do you mean?"

Nerishma's eyes narrowed and the corner of her lips slipped into a smirk. "I'm just curious. He showed up outside your place that night, and you've been talking to him more."

"He came thundering in to say something to Rinald and those soldiers too," offered Troo.

Neirshma's smile widened until it looked as though the top of her head was about to fall off.

"I don't know him very well really," protested Mira. "If anything, he's been a nuisance."

"Really?" asked Troo. "What has he done that's so annoying?"

"He implied that I allowed some goblin thieves to get away."

"How awful. You have been mortally wounded by such dire accusations. It must be terribly insulting to think that some thieves escaped due to your actions," said Nerishma drily.

Troo ignored her.

"Did he claim you owed him money for that?" she asked. "Is he trying to make you pay for what they took?"

"No." Mira pursed her lips.

"Then how did he treat you after blaming you for that?"

"He asked if he could come with me to the artisan's quarter."

"Where he insulted you, and made it impossible for you to do what you needed to do, right?" said Troo. Nerishma watched her expectantly.

"No, he just chatted about himself with me." The other two exchanged a look. Troo's tusks shivered as she tried not to mirror Nerishma's grin.

"What?" Mira asked. The witches walking alongside her didn't answer. Nerishma covered her mouth with her hand.

"Are you suggesting..." Mira began. She could feel the colour draining away from her face. "No, don't even think about it!"

Nerishma shrugged.

"I'm just thinking here, I didn't say anything!" But that smile was as wide and self-pleased as a cat chewing on a mouse.

Chapter Fifty-Nine

The Trivial Lampshade was the one of the biggest taverns in Senoonheim. This, combined with its location by the eastern gates that led directly to the rest of the Misplaced Kingdoms, meant it was the first port of call for every adventurer seeking their fortune in the Unlit Hills. As the witches walked up to the three-storey building, Mira saw crowds of adventurers pressing through the doors while irregular flashes of light and bursts of colour belched from the windows.

"Are you sure about this?" she asked Troo.

"Ti said it would be great!"

The tables inside were stuffed with huddled adventuring parties, each glowering out the corners of their eyes at the others. Drunken warriors stumbled around the room yelling incoherently with their arms over each other's shoulders or shoving one another until they could start fighting.

"Really?" Mira asked the world in general.

"Excuse me, mighty travellers." A small elf girl had stepped in front of them. She wore a puffy dress and her hair was bound in a braid. "I come from a small village in the north and we are being tormented by raiders. If only a group such as yours–"

Nerishma put a finger on the girl's lips to shush her.

"We aren't adventurers, kid," said the skinny woman.

The elf pressed her lips together and shrugged. When she spoke again, her voice was suddenly much less vulnerable.

"Thanks for not wasting my time. Have a good one, ladies." The elf strode over to a nearby table and began the same speech. Troo crashed a hand down on Mira's shoulder.

"Ti's over there! Come on!"

Ti sat at a table on the far side of the room, wearing an emerald-coloured top that clung to her figure, and transparent green silks that trailed from her waist down over her leggings. Next to her sat Leena, the antfolk woman. Curled up on the floor next to Leena's chair was her lizard Tiny. Leena absent-mindedly scratched Tiny between the shoulders as the lizard breathed in and out. It looked as though Tiny was asleep. A wisp of smoke curled into the air above his head.

Ti stood up to welcome Mira, leaning in to kiss the air next to her cheeks.

"Hello darling, how are you? I'm so glad that you decided to come out. The musicians playing this week have been delightful."

There was a crash from behind them. Mira glanced back and saw an adventurer had landed on another party's table, breaking it into splinters. The party at the table had all snatched their drinks out of the way then rolled their eyes and walked away.

"I hope you're right," said Mira. "I've not heard anything good about the Lampshade."

"You just wait," said Ti with a wink.

Mira and the others took a seat. Before they drew breath to shout to each other over the din, the roiling hubbub stilled, a quiet blue sky in the middle of a storm. One of the High Lord's soldiers in their blue cloak had just walked in. The bearfolk soldier paused by the doorway and passed a severe gaze around the room. Adventurers stared back at him in silence. Mira wondered whether a brawl was about to erupt and if so whether the witches should try to leave first. She caught Troo's eye but the orc didn't seem concerned.

The soldier turned and walked over to a part of the wall covered in bits of parchment. He pulled a small scroll from a pouch at his side and unrolled it. The adventurers all sat straighter, eyes sharpening in the manner of seagulls hearing the rustle of fish and chips wrapped in old paper. The soldier put the scroll on the wall and stabbed a small knife into the top, holding it there, before stalking out of the tavern.

Instantly a swarm of adventurers launched themselves out of their seats and scrambled to the wall. Mira watched as a dwarf in cleric's robes ran up the back of a lizardfolk soldier and stomped on the soldier's face to launch himself through the air towards the scroll, only to slam into a wall of golden energy thrown up by a sorcerer wearing a skin-tight, black, skull cap. A pair of kobolds, one wearing a heavy axe over her back and the other wielding two short daggers, swirled through the legs of the other adventurers and made good ground until someone tripped an ogre in a mercenary uniform who fell on top of them.

Ti rolled her eyes.

"May the Cockerel Prince keep the adventurers away from me," she chuckled.

The other laughed too.

"So has the Prince been treating you well?" asked Mira.

"What do you mean?" asked Ti. She raised one exquisitely lined eyebrow.

"I've heard that the Prince is quite selfish," said Mira. "Meaning you have to do a lot for him and that he doesn't give back very much. I hope you're happy with the relationship you are creating with him."

Ti smiled the lazy smile of a snake who has just eaten a cow and is ready to lie in the shade digesting it for the next three weeks.

"I think that we understand each other, the Prince and I. I myself am very sure of what I want and what I'm willing to share with who. A better question might be whether the Prince is working hard enough to keep me."

Hattie shrieked with laughter from the tabletop where she had already procured a glass of beer as big as herself. She hefted it up off the table and spun it towards Ti, who obliged by clinking her wine glass against it.

"The thing about the Cockerel Prince," said Ti, once she had sipped her wine, "Is that he does not suffer fools. Most people act like fools more often than they would like to admit."

"Speak for yourself," clicked Leena.

"No, really! When you doubt yourself, when you second guess your choices, when you fear that you won't be good enough, that's when you can look like a fool. Nervous and uncertain and always apologising. The trick is to be truly sure of yourself. Figure out who you are and what you want." She gestured along herself. "I know who I am. I won't suffer any more fools than the Prince will. And so we are a good match."

"That's why people think he's so charismatic," nodded Nerishma. "That confidence in himself."

"Exactly."

"But it's easy for a fool to look confident," continued Nerishma. "There's plenty of soft touches who mark themselves out for the Guild through their confidence."

Ti frowned and nodded.

"Yes, that's true. I would argue that such people are demonstrating their hubris, not confidence. They think that they have everything under control when actually they have less power than they realise. They cover their foolishness with bravado. They don't actually have a true understanding of their deepest self. It's that understanding that comes first."

Mira's stomach churned as she listened to the others discuss Ti's bravura honda and the lessons she was already learning. Mira desperately wanted to own up, to let them know who she was at her deepest self. But she couldn't bring herself to do it.

The melee by the papers on the wall burned itself out and now a pile of groaning adventurers covered the floor while the few final victors stood wheezing and staring at the scroll. It looked like it was a wanted poster with a birdfolk's head sketched on it.

There was another shift in the noise and Ti brightened up.

"Here we go! Come on everyone, get up. Let's dance!"

A group of musicians had gathered at one end of the common room, to the cheers of the assembled adventurers whose ribs weren't cracked. A gnome waved to the crowd and slung a large drum between his legs, settling down and giving it a few exploratory taps. The sound shushed more of the crowd in the tavern.

A snakefolk woman slithered up next to him and started tuning her mandolin. Mira was surprised to see a clay construct holding a set of pipes join them. The construct looked like a child's figure made of clay, but its eyes glowed red and the pipes looked tiny and fragile in its sturdy fingers. Then a young elf woman stepped forward and introduced the first song, a lively traditional song about a new wife in the springtime.

Mira and the witches spun across the floor together, holding each other's hands in a circle of joy, laughing and singing along when they knew the words. Mira felt her worries flying away as she whirled, her hair reaching out and her skirts lifting briefly from the floor. With the other witches holding on to her, she felt as though she could fly.

Mira staggered out of the tavern before midnight, still dizzy and smiling from the dancing. Troo walked her to the door, with the miniscule figure of Hattie swaying on her shoulder.

"Are you sure you'll get home alright?"

"Positive," declared Mira with the confidence of someone who had drunk two wines more than they should have. "Nerishma set everything up with the Guild!"

Troo looked doubtful, but she nodded.

"Alright then. Take care, Mira." She was stepping forward to hug Mira, who braced herself for the impact, but then the orc woman stopped and stared over Mira's shoulder.

"What, what is it?" she said, turning to see what had stopped Troo.

Prevos was standing behind her.

Chapter Sixty

"Oh," said Mira, the sound pushing itself out of her mouth without conscious interference from her mind.

Hattie gave a low chuckle from her perch on Troo's shoulder. She raised an eyebrow and pointed conspiratorially at Mira as an evil smile spread across the tiny witch's face.

Prevos was talking earnestly to a dwarf who must have left the tavern earlier. The dwarf was nodding, desperately hoping that agreeing with the paladin would stop the torrent of words flooding over him. Every now and then the dwarf wobbled on his feet. He had drawn his slim rapier and was using it as a leaning post. The sword buckled dangerously, point down on the street.

"Mira?" said Prevos when he saw her at the doorway. The dwarf's eyes widened, and he bolted off into the darkness. Prevos turned and called after him.

"Sir? Wait! I didn't have time to give you a pamphlet about Trankwill! Sir?"

He watched the dwarf vanish into the night and then turned back. His shoulders drooped.

"Good evening, Mira. I hope that you are well?"

"What were you doing there, Prevos?" Mira asked him.

"I just wanted to spread the peace of Trankwill to the adventurers at this tavern," Prevos explained. "They are often so chaotic and spread much discord through the city. I thought I might be able to calm them at the source." He drew a deep breath and sighed slowly. "But it hasn't worked very well yet."

"I'm sorry to hear that," she said. Mira looked at Prevos and a flush of determination washed through her body, tingling her fingertips. She remembered what Fina had said by the pond. Magic happened every day, with the things people said and did. A witch took control of those things and made their life happen instead of waiting for it to happen to them. Just like Ti had said about the Cockerel Prince and confidence. She needed to be sure of herself.

At least, she hoped what she was feeling was determination. There *had* been a lot of wine.

"Actually, it's good to see you. I have something that I want to ask you."

"I would be pleased to be of assistance," Prevos said, his ears pricking up.

"Good." Mira's nerves trembled as she got closer to saying the actual words. It was strange. She hadn't felt this fear before, even while she was confronting the First Seat of Whinnia and risking the loss of everything she had built in her life there. She faced down the sensation and ran hard towards it, embraced it, and said the words.

"I was wondering if you would like to take a walk with me."

Prevos stared at her in silence. It was quite a thing to be on the receiving end of a catfolk stare. The dark, vertical lines of his pupils had spread so wide they nearly filled his golden eyes.

"I'm just going to leave you to it," said Troo, resting a hand on Mira's shoulder. "But I won't be far away if you need anything."

"Don't do anything I wouldn't do," came the strangely high-pitched voice of Hattie as they left.

"What wouldn't you do?" asked Mira, shocked to hear Hattie's voice. Mostly, the tiny witch communicated through grunts, snorts, and growls. She was similar to a wild pig that way, and contained roughly the same amount of undirected fury in a much more compact package.

"I wouldn't hold back," whooped the tiny woman from her perch on the other witch. "Just ask my husband!"

Mira shooed the others away, relieved to hear Troo's stomping feet recede, but kept her eyes on Prevos. He bobbed his head lower, never looking away from her eyes.

"It would be an honour. When can I expect this pleasure?"

Mira felt as though she was standing on loose stone, crumbling down the side of a hill. Her stomach shifted as she tried to catch her balance, and her head felt light. She hadn't known how he would respond to the suggestion, but his sincerity was certainly much more than she might have expected.

"Good. Yes," she said, filling time with short meaningless syllables while her mind tried to catch up to the rest of the conversation. "Um. Tomorrow?"

Prevos nodded. His muzzle twitched closer to a smile and his golden eyes sparkled.

"I hardly imagined you would like to promenade at this time of night."

"Yes, right, obviously!" Mira emphasised each word with wide eyes and exaggerated gestures. "Tomorrow then." Her confidence grew as she used more words. "After I close the bakery."

"I will be ready to meet you." And Prevos smiled, fully and completely. Mira wondered if she had ever seen the large man smile before. He always seemed to take life so seriously, considering the will of the gods and how he might affect the world. But his face softened when he smiled, his lips pulling back and exposing thin, sharp teeth, his muzzle wrinkling sweetly. His eyes sparkled like molten pools of fire.

"That's great!" said Mira. She felt brittle, like a glass sculpture, and she was worried that if she said anything else she might crack. "Wonderful. I, uh, I guess I'll see you tomorrow then."

"I will escort you home first, if you do not mind," the paladin said.

Mira nodded. Prevos walked over to her and offered her his elbow. She put her hand through it, and they set off through the streets.

Time felt like it had stopped as they walked. Mira couldn't think of a single thing to say, and before she knew it, they stood at the door to her bakery. She stepped away from Prevos, her stomach fluttering.

"Thank you. Good night," she said awkwardly.

Prevos reached out and took Mira's hand, lifting it to his lips and kissing the back of it.

"Until tomorrow, then."

With that, he smiled again and walked down the street. Mira turned and watched him leave.

She had thought Prevos was another man who was showing up and getting in the way. Another man who had his own preconceived idea of who she was and judged her for his own thoughts about her. A silly paladin who complained about cakes.

However, the way he had taken her so seriously so quickly took her breath away. She had met men who wanted to woo her before. They tried to impress her with their stories, although why she would think that their chummy relationship with the boorish leader of Whinnia was impressive she had no idea. So far as she was concerned, that was a huge obstacle to impressing her.

Prevos wasn't trying to impress her. He was just existing as he really was and, although some of that was a bit uptight and a little pompous, it meant that he was serious when he kissed her hand. He wasn't trying to act in a way that might convince her of his value, he just thought it was an appropriate way to bid her farewell.

The back of her hand still tingled. She clutched it with the other hand, turned around, and went inside. She hadn't anticipated how happy she would be that he had said yes.

***

Mira prepared bread the next morning in a daze. She carried the same load out into the bakery and then back into the kitchen three times before noticing that she never put it down. She had to keep reminding herself that she had made this decision on purpose, that she was stepping with confidence into her life.

"Then why can't you stay still?" her reflection whispered from the window. "Calm down," it told her.

She took a breath and smiled back at herself.

"I'm okay. I'm ready."

Mira tried to focus on her customers but her thoughts kept imagining what might come in the afternoon. She was curious where she and the big, dopey paladin she had asked out might walk and what they might see. Would they have anything to talk about? Prevos seemed so devoted to his goddess. Would that be all he wanted to talk about? Was this as good an idea as she had thought?

Alongside these concerns elbowing their way into her mind, Mira's shoulders tensed when she wondered if he would put his arm around her. They did look like such strong arms. What would it be like to be held in muscles like that?

Chapter Sixty-One

There was a tinkle from the bakery door and Prevos stepped inside, ducking under the door frame. Mira stared at him. He looked out of place with his gleaming armour next to her shelves dusted with crumbs.

"Is it that time already?" Mira said without thinking.

"What time?" asked the old man standing in front of her counter. He paused his counting of coins from his money pouch.

"I said I would meet you in the afternoon," said Prevos. There was a small crease in the fur of his forehead. His eyes flicked to the old man at the counter and then back to Mira, and his whiskers shivered. "Have I arrived too early?"

The old man turned his attention back to Mira. She was horrified to see his mouth widen into a smile and he winked at her. Her cheeks began to grow hot.

"No no, not really. It's just that I haven't quite closed up yet. I just need to do that first."

His pointed ears flattened on the sides of his head.

"I was wrong to be here now."

"No, it wasn't wrong at all, young man!" declared the old man. He threw the final coins onto the counter and scooped his bread up into his arms. "I'm all done here! She's all yours!" He waggled his eyebrows at Mira like a pair of hyperactive caterpillars.

"Are you sure?" Prevos' ears looked happier again, but his tail flicked spasmodically. "I wouldn't want any resentment to form over my taking her away from her business." He looked up at Mira. "Truly, if you need me to come back later...?"

"No, I've been looking forward to this!"

The old man stepped around Prevos and gave Mira two thumbs up at the door. Then he remained in that spot, watching expectantly instead of leaving. Mira wanted to throttle him.

She stood behind the counter, unsure what to say. From the way Prevos kept clenching his hands into fists and releasing them, he felt similarly nervous.

"You know what, I just need to clean up a little," she said. "Why don't you step outside and I'll be there in just a second."

Prevos nodded, spinning his helmet in his hands. He and the old man left one after the other, and Mira immediately set to work. She swept, covered the leftover loaves, and even managed to tidy herself up a little, dusting flour off her skirts and cleaning her hands and face.

Then she stepped out to meet Prevos on the street, locking the door behind her. Finally, they were alone together.

To be more precise, they were each the only person that the other knew on the street, but the street itself was quite full of passersby, whether cityfolk moving from one errand to another or traders trying to separate those cityfolk from their money. One of Satonak's fat, fuzzy drones hummed overhead, bobbing up and down in the semi-bouyant manner regular bees displayed as they bumped their way through a garden of flowers. A pair of the High Lord's soldiers walked by, presumably to keep the peace. From the way half the traders scooped their wares into bundles and disappeared, Mira assumed that peace was bad for business.

But none of those people paid any attention to either Mira or Prevos, and so, in a practical sense, they were alone together.

"Thank you for coming to meet me," she said awkwardly. She had no idea what sort of conversation they might have. After suggesting this walk she had barely said more than a few words to the man. They had spoken to each other the whole time when they were walking to the contrivancers' quarter, hadn't they? What on earth had they talked about? She racked her memories. Somehow she was more nervous about what to say to him now.

"I was honoured that you asked," said Prevos. He offered her his elbow and she tucked an arm through it. He put his hand on top of hers and lifted his face to the street around them. After a moment, he coughed.

"Uh. Where would you like to go?"

Mira was prepared for this.

"Actually, I was wondering if you would show me what you do most of the time. You've seen where I work, and you have met some of the women I'm making friends with. But I know so little about you."

"That sounds wonderful."

Walking with Prevos through Sernoonheim was like being given a personal tour by the sort of keen museum owner who loved filling in labels for the displays but didn't care about visitors. Prevos knew nothing of the people who lived and worked in the streets they were walking through, but he did know a lot about the buildings. He pointed out what he said were deliberate design choices in the buildings they passed, from hollow columns that made important buildings look even more important, to stone walls he claimed were little more than painted canvas with a layer of plaster for texture. According to Prevos, all these facades were intended to create a certain ambience in the city, to compel the right sort of people to come and spend their money in all the ways the city could devise.

"But why didn't Lord Cornucervin simply build a normal city? Why go to the trouble of all these facades?" Mira pointed at the Merchant's Exchange nearby. From the street, it was a tall building made of fine stone, including a frieze that depicted the birth of Nazdak, the god of merchants, over the entrance. It looked like the sort of place that was sturdy and profitable and would certainly be able to convert reputable notes of credit into cash and vice versa.

But Prevos explained that the building visible from the street was little more than a mask, and behind it the rest of the Merchant's Exchange was simply a rectangular wooden box, divided into as many rooms as the merchants needed.

"Speed," answered Prevos. "Lord Cornucorvin realised that, if he waited, the adventurers in the Unlit Hills might go with no one there to help them spend their money. All of that money would just be lost."

"I think that the adventurers would probably not consider their money lost if it was still in their pouches," argued Mira.

"Don't let Lord Cornucervin hear you say that!" Prevos grinned down at her, revealing huge sharp white teeth in his rounded muzzle. She smiled in response. "Gold kept safely in a pile is effectively the same as a gold vein remaining undiscovered in the ground, according to Stanley Cornucervin."

"It's like the city walls," mused Mira. "Everything in Senoonheim was put up so quickly that it's not real."

"Whether or not things are real depends a great deal on the people who are interacting with them." Prevos's voice was deep as he began to explain his thoughts. It would have been easy for his words to sound patronising, as though he were lecturing Mira. Instead, he sounded as though he couldn't hold the words in his head any longer. They tumbled out of him in a great rush, like a child trying to explain everything that they had done in one day all at the same time. Mira couldn't help but smile at his excitement.

Chapter Sixty-Two

"For example, take the way you act towards your customers. Are you showing them who you really are?" Prevos began. "I know that many people treat strangers at a distance, because they don't really know them. I have seen the smiles people wear when they are politely talking to someone they don't know. Strange things that rarely touch their eyes. But, at the same time, no one can know who you are behind that smile, so that is the reality that you are giving them. As far as your customers know, you really are the person you act like when they buy their bread from you."

Mira blinked. She wasn't sure if she liked the idea that so many citizens of the city might think the Mira they met in her bakery was the extent of who she was.

"I feel like you don't do that," Mira said. She looked up at the amber fur that covered Prevos's face. She tried to squeeze his arm where her hand rested on it, but the armour plating didn't shift at all. "Even from the first time I saw you, charging down the street in pursuit of those goblins. You didn't put up a different version of yourself for the people around you to see. I like that. Even if it did mean that you blamed me for something that wasn't my fault!" She grinned so he would know she wasn't really angry.

"Trankwill doesn't ask us to be something that we are not, so why would I behave in such a way?" His eyes twinkled. Then his whiskers drooped. "But I fear that is why some people find me annoying, which I do not enjoy."

Mira thought of his mission to Varivixes, the Mosquito Queen, in search of a solution to his difficulties with others. She didn't know what to say to that.

He sniffed and straightened his shoulders.

"But it does demonstrate my point. This city is as real as it needs to be. It is real enough for the adventurers who pass through. It is real enough for the many people who have come to make their lives under the watchful eye of Lord Cornucervin."

"And it is real enough to mess with the creatures of the hills and forests," murmured Mira, thinking of Fina's complaints to the coven.

"I don't know why you would mention that example specifically, but it does fit the schema, yes."

"And now that he has his city, he is going to make these things more solid and permanent, isn't he?" Mira said out loud, speaking more to herself than to Prevos. She was giving shape to the thoughts running through her mind, turning her focus inwards. So she was surprised when her companion responded.

"Why do you think he will do that?"

"Because that's what the other ladies told me." Mira stopped and turned to face Prevos. "They said that Lord Cornucervin collects taxes and says that it will pay for the building of new city walls and buildings."

"They already seem real enough to many people just as they are," said Prevos. "Perhaps you are right and he is going to build these things." He didn't sound convinced. "Perhaps he only says he will build them. Perhaps it gives him a good reason to collect taxes from the businesses within his city." He shrugged, setting off a cacophony of dinging as his armour resettled over his broad shoulders.

They continued their walk and Prevos returned to his descriptions of the buildings around them. He led them on a path that followed streets sloping gently higher, moving around the dark and ominous castle that squatted in the centre of the city and then past the smaller and more livable homes on the hillside. Eventually, they reached the southern end of the city without passing through any city walls as they walked, whether real or not. Evidentially, Lord Cornucervin didn't think that there was anything dangerous to the south. Or maybe he didn't think the people in this part of town needed his protection at all, even if it would only be the flimsy protection of fake walls.

"Do you spend most of your time up here?" she asked when they paused at a crossroad. Prevos seemed in no hurry to choose a direction, and she took the time to turn and look back down into the city. From this vantage point, the city spread out before her like a blanket, patched in greys and browns and whites. She could even see beyond the end of the city to the farms and fields and forests that stretched away to the horizon.

Prevos nodded as he answered her.

"There is a Trankwill temple near here, where I spend much time in meditation. The rest of the time I try to bring peace to the city on behalf of the goddess."

"Which is how I first met you."

"Exactly. I had been hired to guard a merchant's caravan in that instance, but the goblins were cunning. They struck before I got there. Luckily, I arrived at the caravan early enough to see them running away with their ill-gotten gains, so I gave chase."

Mira nodded.

"Are you taking me to see this temple?"

"Yes."

Mira expected the temple to be all facade, like the other buildings in Sennoonheim, but it wasn't. Nor was it very big.

She ran her hands along the thick wooden planks on both sides of the entrance, enjoying the rough shape of the carvings that covered them. They stood like rectangular guards on either side of the doorway, with the figure of a heron on each.

Inside, the roof of the temple rose from the floor in angular slopes that met at the sharp apex a dozen feet overhead. Every surface was covered in carved woodwork: pews, vines in relief along the beams that held up the roof, around the edge of the circular wooden pool at the far end of the room. Lily pads floated in the pool broad and green, with small white flowers growing from their centres.

The temple was stuffed with ceramic pots, from little pots overflowing with bright flowers to strong pots holding small trees that stretched up to cover the walls behind them.

Sitting on the edge of the pool was an old human man with long, white hair gathered behind his head by a strap of leather. His serene face looked up when they entered and he began to say something. Then a grimace flashed across his face and he spluttered to a stop, blinked, and hazarded a smile.

"Prevos?" he said, just a little too brightly. "You have come back?" The smile was hard, his cheeks pulled taut. "Again?"

"Well met, Retis," said Prevos as he led Mira into the temple.

"You brought a friend this time?" The old man stood and walked towards them, his white robe swirling around his legs as he walked.

"Yes. This is my friend Mira."

The man held out a hand as he reached the new arrivals and Mira met it with her own. He shook Mira's hand enthusiastically. As he spoke he kept a hold of her hand, gripping it tightly as his smile relaxed.

"I can't tell you how happy I am to see Prevos has found someone else to spend time with, it truly takes a weight off my shoulders. Oh, this is happy news! But, why are you here?" He finally let go of her hand and stepped back, looking between them. "Why are you here?"

"I wanted to see where he spent his time, seeing as most of our conversations have been in places from my life. I thought it might help me learn something about him."

The man shivered slightly and the muscles in his cheeks spasmed in the corner of his smile, but then he nodded.

"Yes, Prevos spends a lot of time here, that is indeed the truth of it."

Chapter Sixty-Three

R etis led Mira and Prevos to the front of the temple and motioned them into the pews near the pool of water. Mira wriggled on the thin cushions in the pews, trying to get comfortable. They were the sort of cushion that outlined the discomfort of a seat, rather than reducing it. Mira would just as happily have thrown them aside for all the good they did.

"What do you do here?" Mira asked Retis. "I mean, this is a temple, obviously. So I assume you lead rites or ceremonies? Do you sacrifice to Trankwill?"

The man laughed.

"Nothing so grand. This is a small temple and all Trankwill asks is that we keep it clean and calm so that anyone in need of her peace can come and shelter in it for a while before they return to the unrest of the city. Some of her larger temples in other realms do hold all sorts of ceremonies, but that isn't required of us here."

"Why do you come here so often then?" Mira asked Prevos, shifting her attention.

The old man nodded firmly. "An excellent question! That really is such a good question!" He turned wide eyes to the armoured paladin and tucked his hands together between his knees, leaning forward eagerly.

Prevos sat in his pew with his back straight, hands clenched into fists that rested palm down on each of his thighs.

"I come to make sure the temple is in good condition. Of course, I do not mean to judge Retis–"

The old man sighed behind Mira.

"–but there is much to do, and he is no longer a young man."

Another sigh.

"So you clean?" Mira asked.

"I clean, I polish the wood, I prune the plants, I sweep. I have attempted to repair some of the cushions for the pews as well, though I must admit that this is not an area I have a particular faculty for."

"He helps," said Retis. The old man walked to the far side of the pool and pulled a long cylindrical cushion from behind it. Big black Xs were sewn along its length and a tear in the fabric was still visible. Threads dangled loosely from each X. Mira covered her mouth and tried not to giggle.

"I have been suggesting that he spends more time out in the city," said Retis after he put the cushion back and rejoined them. "Senoonheim is so big. Many people live at odds with one another. Surely his talents would be better suited to calming the city, wouldn't you agree?" His eyes looked deeply into Mira's with the desperation of a drowning man.

"Oh, the city seems safe enough to me," replied Mira with a cheeky smile. "Are you sure you don't need another hand in the temple? What about the spiderwebs up in the corners?" She bobbed her head towards one under the nearest beam.

Retis shuddered and he whipped a finger up to his mouth, shushing her.

"Are there spiderwebs?" said Prevos, turning to peer about him. "I apologise Retis, I have been negligent in my attention here. I will redouble my efforts."

Retis's shoulders drooped.

Mira decided to take pity on him. "No, I think you're right. Prevos, your desire to help does you credit, but I think you should spend more time in the city."

"I would be happy to spend more time in the city." The big man always looked so serious. "But it is full of temptations that could sully my soul."

"Like my cakes," Mira suggested.

"Yes, like your cakes. And the strong drinks you and your coven enjoy when you meet at the tavern."

Mira narrowed her eyes and watched his face but he looked back at her with pure innocence. Perhaps he really wasn't judging them for having an ale. It was still an annoying thing to say.

"Not to mention the lies and politics of the lord's court, and the brigands who take advantage of the community. It is an unrestful place outside the temple," he added.

Mira watched this huge man, covered in shining armour, wrestle with his fears of the world outside the quiet place that he felt comfortable in. She found it hard to understand how he could appear so powerful and yet not feel as though he was safe to leave the spaces that he knew. She reached over and placed a hand on the back of his.

"That's why it might be good for you to be out in it," she said. "You are being yourself: calm and honest. You might be the tranquility that spreads from a forest glade, soothing the breeze. Maybe just you being out in the streets will settle some of the things going on out there."

She hadn't believed Prevos could sit any straighter, but somehow he managed it. His back looked like a plumbob string. Then his shoulders shifted down slightly and his whiskers shivered.

"But what if it sullies me? What if I am made worse by my experiences in the world?"

Mira thought about the way he refused to try her sweet slices, and how he had stopped himself at the door to the Sprog and Sparrow. *Perhaps you could do with a little sullying*, she thought to herself. Aloud, she said, "I am sure Trankwill appreciates everyone who tries to spread peace, even if they find it hard or get it wrong sometimes. Isn't that right, Retis?" She turned and looked at the old man.

"Oh yes, absolutely," he rushed to agree, his head bobbing up and down like a child's yo-yo. "I can be very sure that Trankwill will appreciate you spending much much more time out there in the city on her behalf!"

"Perhaps I will try." Prevos looked contemplative, turning his gaze down to the still water in the pool. "It was pleasant to join you and your friends in the tavern Mira. But do not worry Retis, I will be sure to return often and check that Trankwill is still happy with me."

Retis grimaced and his eyes pleaded silently with Mira, who shrugged at him. Retis hung his head.

"Yes. Okay Prevos. That sounds good," he said.

The sun set while Mira and Prevos walked back down into the main districts of Senoonheim. Mira felt as though she was sinking into a dirty pond, every step taking her lower into a mire that sucked at her limbs, pulling her into the grime. The natural landscape beyond the city vanished behind the buildings that rose around them.

When they eventually turned a corner and Mira saw her bakery, she stopped.

"Are you alright?" asked Prevos.

"Yes." She moved her fingers slightly on the smooth metal of his armour. She wondered what the fur on his arm felt like. How thick and warm was it? "I just... I've had a nice time and I wasn't ready to go in yet."

"I'm pleased to hear that you have had a good time. Hopefully we can spend some more time together soon."

"I think I'd like that," Mira replied. She was somewhat surprised to realise that it was true.

Prevos leaned down towards her slowly, watching her expression as he grew closer. She leaned in and he kissed her cheek gently. The fuzz of his muzzle tickled a little, and then he drew back.

"Until next time," he said.

Mira walked away from him, trying not to lift a hand to her check. When she reached the door, she turned and saw Prevos still standing at the corner, watching her, waiting for her to go inside. She lifted a hand to wave, and he waved back. Then she was inside, and the door tinkled closed between them.

Chapter Sixty-Four

Mira whistled happily as she baked through the morning. She twisted her loaves and scored the tops, sprinkling sliced nuts on a few. A shelf of sweet rolls took moments to coat in a soft drizzle of icing and Mira licked a loose drop from her finger gleefully before cleaning her hands. She was really beginning to get her hands dirty, and life was looking more delightful because of it.

She even decided to make some of Prevos's catfolk crispbread recipe, despite having to race down to the nearest market for some fish to put in it. The round man with the blonde ponytail spoke to her in a voice almost as oily as his fish when she made her order. He smiled triumphantly and wrapped her purchase in coarse cloth. He even threw in a couple of boiled cockles, *out of goodwill,* according to him. *Just to rub salt in the wound,* Mira thought.

There was a small bowl of live cockles next to the basket of boiled ones, and Mira found them odd to look at. A tiny slip of the animal's soft body poked out from between the halves of the shell before taking fright and slipping back inside.

Back in the bakery, the crispbread was quick to make and bake, and then Mira tipped the small treats into a thick, woven flax bag with a coat of purple dye over the top. On a whim, she took a piece of charcoal and sketched a cat face on the bag, with broad whiskers. She smiled as she thought of the way Prevos's whiskers signalled his emotions so clearly. She imagined he found it nearly impossible to hide his feelings.

The shop door tinkled and she walked out of the kitchen to greet her customers, wiping floury dust onto her apron.

"Good morning, how can I help–" she began as she came into the shop, and then froze.

By the doorway were three of the High Lord's soldiers. Their helmets were jammed tightly over their heads, and they squinted out through tiny rectangles of metal. They looked just like shellfish hiding inside metal shells.

Mira crossed her arms. Some people did behave like the shellfish she had made a snack of earlier. Something soft and vulnerable hid inside, but they could only get through the world by making sure they were covered in a protective shell. Unfortunately these soldiers had a particularly aggressive shell, made from tearing others' down.

Prevos was like that too, she realised. He spoke and acted as sincerely as anyone could hope, but in return he had to physically encase himself in armour and seek sanctuary so that he could cope with temptation and the way others perceived him. But he didn't hold that vulnerability against anyone else, as though it was the world's fault that he was scared of being hurt.

The three, sour-faced soldiers in her shop right now certainly looked as though they blamed the world for their problems.

She supposed she hid softness inside too. Prevos noticed that about her and had told her that others wouldn't get to know her if the shell was all that anyone got to see.

"You that witch baker that Master Satonak told not to be a witch?" asked the soldier nearest her. He was quite tall, and somehow, despite the fact that he was wearing the same blue cloak and leather armour as all the other soldiers she had met, he looked dirty. Some people exude the uncleanness of who they are, regardless of their actual presentation. Their foul personality leaks through their pores, even when they're freshly scrubbed and dressed by the finest fashion merchants in the kingdoms. The soldier had a scar down his cheek and gave the impression that thick stubble covered his chin, though he was clean shaven.

"Which baker?" asked Mira.

"Yeah, that's right!"

Mira paused and frowned.

"Sorry, what?"

"What?" The soldier shuffled anxiously, one hand on the pommel of the sword at his side.

"What did you mean? You asked me about which baker?" Mira stuck her hands on her hips, although it made flour puff around her like some kitchen fairy and she regretted it immediately.

"Yes." The soldier swallowed extravagantly. "You are the witch baker, right?"

"That all depends. Who's asking?"

This amount of conversation was clearly pushing the soldier to the absolute limits of his mental capacity. His forehead wrinkled, as though his brain was rolling up its sleeves to really get to business.

"I'm asking," he said, although he sounded unsure about it.

"Okay. And who are you?"

"Serven," he answered. By this stage he was looking much less aggressive and he stepped back towards the other soldiers.

"And why have you come into my bakery, Serven?" said Mira, stepping around the counter to share the shop floor with him and his companions.

"We are here because Master Satonak heard you weren't going to stop meeting your coven," declared the next soldier, a short woman behind Serven. She stepped forward and pushed Serven behind her, though her head barely covered his stomach.

"Yeah, you tell her Cringvil," muttered the taller man as he stepped back. He started counting on his fingers, clearly trying to sort through what had gone wrong with his attempt to intimidate Mira.

Cringvil glared up at Mira.

"Whether I am the witch you asked about or not," said Mira, "I hardly see why it's any of Satonak's business, let alone yours."

The short woman glowered. It was like being threatened by a pot belly stove. Heat washed off her, and the woman's forehead was beginning to glow a dull red. Mira had to fight the urge to fetch a kettle to put on top of her.

"You listen here, miss witch! Master Satonak is a very important man, and he won't be trifled with!" Cringvil pointed a finger up at Mira, narrowly missing jamming the thing up Mira's nose.

Mira laughed without smiling.

"What's so funny?" fumed the shorter woman.

"Trifled. In a bakery with desserts in it." Mira gestured at the shelves. "You were making a joke, right?"

"Crager!" snapped the woman, calling in the support of the last soldier.

"Alright sweetheart, that's enough," he said to Mira with a smile. He was thin and wore the sort of sharp facial hair that should immediately put people on their guard. This was the manicured face of someone who knew how to sound polite while they slipped a dagger into your back.

"I'm not your sweetheart," Mira snapped, and immediately realised she shouldn't have. By letting his snide comments get to her, she revealed that he had found his mark.

He knew it too. His smile broadened, like a cat over a mousehole.

"Oh dear, perhaps I've been overly familiar? Look, Master Satonak gave out some orders, and he doesn't like it when people don't follow his orders. So we're here to let you know that he has ordered you to come before him at Lord Cornucervin's court."

Mira crossed her arms. Cringvil filled the space in front of her, and this third soldier was closing in. She was trapped. She glanced over the soldiers at the broad window that filled the front of her shop. Dawn light was beginning to glow in the streets outside, but it was still quite dark. Dark enough that she might still be able to find a way out of this mess.

"You can go right back to him and explain that I don't take orders from him," she said.

The third man's lips stopped smiling but his eyes were still crooked with amusement.

"Oh love," he purred. "He thought you might say something like that. So he told us that we were to do this."

He drew his sword. Cringvil reached out for Mira at the same time, her fingers clawed like talons. Serven, still caught up in his mental replay of their earlier conversation, simply stared at the others gape-jawed.

Mira spoke quickly and quietly, reciting her words as best she could remember them. She spread her hand and lifted it to her face, palm out, covering her view of the soldiers' reflection in her window.

With a *bloop* like a stone falling into a spring pool, the soldiers froze in place.

Chapter Sixty-Five

Mira sagged onto the counter, breathing out heavily. Her heart was pounding. She squeezed her forehead with one hand, then bent over and tried to catch her breath. She hadn't expected the soldiers to get so threatening so quickly. She had been sure she could talk them into leaving.

When she had run from Wallis, she had known that there was no way that she would be able to talk her way past First Seat Bower's soldiers. He only recruited the most square-headed thugs for his personal enforcers, giving them the ludicrous title of "Security Nurturers Of Wallis". Such obvious flattery worked for the simple minded, and they came in droves to join him. As First Seat, Bower was supposed to be able to rely on the Houses for support. They were the ones he had to convince and who would enforce his decisions. But Bower had proven unwilling to convince the Heads of the Houses, finding it much easier to create his personally loyal S.N.O.W. instead. It hadn't taken long for the House Heads to fall into line.

Mira knew there was no point explaining herself to soldiers. When she escaped Tonal Bower's troops, she got out with a few belongings in a cloth bag slung over her shoulder, bundled onto a wagon with Dulamo. Her merchant friend Malcomb said Dulamo was reliable, and then he tried to slow down the soldiers. She hadn't seen him again.

Her shocked mind retreated into the memory.

It felt as though everyone in Wallis was staring at Dulamo's wagon as it trundled through the streets at an achingly slow pace. Mira tried to stay low, so that no one would see her as Dulamo steered her way down the hill towards the gates. This meant she didn't see the short, round figure step out into the road in front of them. She tumbled forward as the wagon slowed and stopped.

"What's going on?" hissed Mira as she scrambled towards the driver's seat. "We need to keep going." She looked over the edge of the wagon to see why they had stopped.

The placid face and small black eyes of Amella looked back at her. The witch nodded to acknowledge Mira, and then leaned forward onto her long knobbly walking stick, resting both hands on top of the glass orb at the top.

"Amella, what are you doing here?" said Mira. She slipped over the edge of the wagon and sat next to Dulamo on the driver's seat.

"I wanted to hear what it is you plan to do next, my little entree," nodded Amella. "Where are you going all in such a rush that you pay no attention to who is in the street?"

Mira's throat seized.

"You knew I was in the wagon?" she asked.

Amella nodded.

"I'm sure the whole neighbourhood knows that you were huddled in the back there."

Mira looked back along the street and saw half a dozen eyes turned towards her, watching the conversation. Her cheeks grew hot as she realised her attempts to stay unnoticed had back-fired.

"Oh dear, I'm sorry," she repeated.

"You waste so much time apologising," said Amella. "I've always thought that. It's as though you have no control over anything going on in your life." She emphasised her point by lifting the walking stick and banging it onto the ground. "You are the one taking your actions and making decisions about your life. Start being responsible for what you do. Choose how you move through this world with purpose."

"I will, thank you for the advice Amella," said Mira. She hefted the bundle on her shoulder and looked past Amella. "Um, and with that in mind, I just need to—"

"Where are you going?" asked Amella again, still with no expression on her plain circular face.

"Bower is angry with me. I told him that he was a terrible leader, and now his soldiers are after me. I tried to go to your house before, for help, but you weren't there." A nagging thought raised a hand for attention in the back of her mind. "You *weren't* there, were you?"

"I told you that defying Loam would be dangerous," was all Amella replied. "This is what happens when you don't consider the consequences of your actions. And all of your foolish behaviour will reflect badly on me." Her eyes were two small pieces of coal, dark and light consuming.

"Would you at least send them the wrong way?" Mira stammered.

"Why should I make myself a target? You had no qualms about making me into one."

Mira was shocked. She had never imagined that the witches that she had become close with could possibly react like this when she was in need.

There was shouting somewhere in the street behind them.

"We're going," declared Dulamo and she whipped the reins, setting her horses into motion. Amella simply watched the wagon as they rolled around her and continued out of Wallis. Mira stared into the sky over Whinnia and wondered what the stars would look like wherever she ended up.

Chapter Sixty-Six

In her bakery in Senoonheim, Mira reined her nerves back under control. She leaned forward against the counter and drew three long, slow breaths. On the floor in front of her stood the three soldiers, like statues caught lurching towards her. Well, except for Serven. He was frozen in place, scratching his head.

Mira needed a plan. She couldn't leave them there forever. Someone would notice.

To emphasise that point, the shop door tinkled again and a slim ratfolk woman came in. She scurried around the soldiers like a deer skipping between tree trunks in the forest, scooped up half a dozen bread rolls and a cheesy loaf and then hurried over to the counter and dumped her armfuls down.

Mira ducked below the counter to grab some cloth to wrap the bread and stood back up.

"Good morning miss," she said. She gathered the bread onto her cloth. Then she looked at the small woman, standing under Cringvil's outstretched clawing frozen hand. "Uh. Do you have any questions?"

"Questions?" The woman's long snout wrinkled in confusion. "No, I don't think so. I just need something to keep the kids' mouths full today so they stay quiet."

"Of course," said Mira. Her eyes flicked past the woman again. "But, the soldiers?"

"What about them?" The woman turned and glanced over the statues filling the room with their positions of half-violence. "A bunch of idiots trying to use their fists and swords to cause who knows what trouble, yeah? That looks like the High Lord's soldiers to me."

She sighed.

"They've been throwing their weight around a lot more since Satonak's been watching over the city."

"You've noticed that too?" asked Mira. "And all the drones?"

"It's always the same with advisors, they can't help but think they should be the ones in charge. As if Senoonheim hasn't done perfectly well under Lord Cornucervin until now!" The ratfolk woman shook her head at Cringvil.

"You don't wonder why they are frozen in place?" asked Mira.

"Doesn't bother me, so long as the bread's good. Now come on," urged the woman, her long dark nose snuffling. "I left the kids outside, and they'll be screaming any moment now."

Mira glanced out the window. In the brightening light, she saw a little wooden cart sitting outside the bakery. It was a few feet long, and a couple of feet wide, with a cloth canopy stretched over the top. A long wooden handle was attached to the front and leaned back against the canopy. Inside the cart were six or seven ratfolk children. Mira found it hard to count exactly how many were crammed in there, because the children wouldn't stop rolling over each other, swirling like a whirlpool of fur and pink tails. As Mira watched the swarm, one of the children slowly opened their jaw wide, like a drawbridge ratcheting itself slowly into the air, until, finally, their teeth crashed down around the tail of one of the others. A wail erupted into the air with the force of familial betrayal behind it.

An older woman was passing by, hobbling along on her cane, and she immediately turned and glared into the shop.

"Oh nooo," moaned the mother. "There's nothing more judgemental than an old woman who doesn't have to deal with the pressures of modern living anymore."

Mira shoved the bread into the woman's waiting hands and didn't even check if she had paid.

"There you are! Go, go!"

The ratfolk woman wove back around the soldiers as she raced to the door.

"Thank you, and good luck with sorting these numbskulls out!" she called over her shoulder.

Before the door closed on her tail, two more people came bustling into the shop.

Kirka was first. The woman was still wearing her butcher's apron, fresh blood spattered across the front, though her face was clean and soft. Delorous followed after her, with her rat Charles on her shoulder.

"Hello," Delorous began, but then she paused and examined the soldiers. Delorous never quite stopped moving completely. She looked like laundry drying in a soft breeze, even if the only movement came from her fingertips drifting towards the things she looked at. "I see you didn't think to teach us whatever magic you used here. That's okay. We probably aren't good enough to do it anyway."

"Satonak sent them to threaten me for running the coven again," Mira tried to explain.

Delorous's eyes widened and she touched her fingers to her lips.

"Oh no. A disaster." The young woman's mouth threatened a smile.

Kirka's eyes narrowed. Her fingers touched her hips, slipping when they didn't find whatever she was looking for hanging at her waist.

Mira waved aside the other woman's concern.

"It's okay, I was able to hold them."

"So Delorous is right, you actually did this?" asked Kirka. She stepped up to Serven and leaned in to examine him closely. "That's very impressive."

"Yes, it's a very useful spell. But I have to recite a very specific set of words, and the slightest mistake means it doesn't work, so it's tough to use in emergencies like this. I'm relieved that I managed to pull it off!"

"But easy to use in other circumstances, such as if you had more time to check your wording, correct? Particularly easy if someone was constrained first?" Kirka's voice was light.

"Someone?" asked Delorous.

"Something," replied the other witch flippantly. She turned to Mira. "What shall we do with them?"

"They got more aggressive than I thought they would. I think Satonak is genuinely furious about the coven."

"So we need to get rid of Satonak," nodded Kirka.

"Not quite," said Mira slowly. "But I think that it is time for me to–" Mira stopped herself and swallowed the words she had been about to say. She cleared her throat.

"Yes?" encouraged Delorous, her dark hair falling like a curtain across one side of her face. "Are you choking?" she added, with that faint smile peeking out again.

Mira had been about to say that it was time for her to go and try to clear the air with the court wizard. She thought that there might be a chance that she could calm him down, if only she was able to understand what it was that was making him so angry towards the coven in the first place. But the idea of telling these women that she was going to confront one of the most powerful men in Senoonheim made her blood run cold. She was certain that they would react just the way her last coven did. They would try to tell her not to do it, and then abandon her if things went wrong.

Any confidence she had scrounged up recently drained away when she considered facing Satonak down.

"I was just saying, I think I'll need to close up for today." Mira forced herself to laugh, a cracked and hollow effort. "It'll be hard to sell much with these guys in here anyway."

Kirka shrugged.

"If you say so. Do you want me to get rid of them?"

"No!" She didn't know a lot about Kirka, but one thing she was sure of was that letting Kirka get rid of something would inevitably involve a lot of pieces that needed to be buried. That wasn't what Mira wanted for these soldiers, even if they had been aggressive with her. "No, that's alright. I'll be able to release them as soon as I've," Mira pursed her lips, "closed shop."

"That won't work, they'll just want to rough you up anyway," said Delorous. She reached up to stroke Charles's back. "It's the same old story everytime. People can't help but cause problems."

"Look, I have some errands to run," said Mira, hoping she could convince the other witches to leave without doing anything irreversible to the soldiers. "I may as well do them now, seeing as I'm going to close up the shop, and I'll make a plan for these soldiers before I come back."

Kirka's big eyes looked deeply into Mira's. Mira had the unpleasant feeling that the small, smiling woman could see into her thoughts. Kirka watched and then drew a deep breath.

"If that's what you want Mira. Come on Delorous. I need to pick up some fresh meat." Together, the two witches headed for the door. Kirka stopped halfway out the door and looked back at Mira.

"Make sure that it is what you want," she said. "And just let us know. We're here to support you." And then they left.

Mira followed them to the door and locked it before anyone else could come in.

They say they're here for me. But that's only because they don't know the reality of what I'm going to do. If they knew I was going to go and have it out with Satonak, then they'd try to talk me out of it, or run before I came back. Just like the others did. Memories of feeling alone beneath the eyes of an entire hall made the hair on her arms and neck prickle uncomfortably. The memory of running home and finding no one waiting for her made her breath catch.

Was she risking all of that again? Was she going to get herself banished from Senoonheim and lose her bakery, her new friends, whatever it was that she had started with Prevos? Was it going to be even worse than that? Would Satonak imprison her?

Mira breathed in slowly through her nose and out through her mouth. She looked around the bakery, seeking her reflection, but the rising sun had made the street outside too bright now and there was no sign of her reflection in the window.

"You've done this before," she said out loud, trying to convince herself. "It didn't go great then, but that's okay. You know that you can do it."

Mira looked at the backs of the soldiers stuck in her bakery. She would only be able to release them once she had sorted things out with Satonak. And after that, hopefully the coven would still be her friends.

Chapter Sixty-Seven

Mira hurried towards Lord Cornucervin's castle. If she was going to have any chance to speak with the court wizard, she needed to get in quickly, while he still thought his soldiers were capturing her. This was a good reason to hurry, but she also didn't want anyone else in the coven to see her either, in case they thought she was a fool just like Amella had. She wasn't sure she had the strength to push herself on if they didn't support her.

The castle reared over the buildings of Senoonheim, filling her vision with its black and twisted turrets. Not for the first time, Mira wondered why Lord Cornucervin had decided to create a castle that clearly shouted out to the world that this was the lair of an evil villain. It was dark and covered in spikes, exactly the sort of castle that one might expect to be filled with giant beetle soldiers fulfilling the bidding of their wrinkled half-vulture overlords.

The road sloped gently up towards the castle gates. Only when she was inside the broad plaza beyond them did Mira slow down. Around the walls of the plaza small alcoves held doors leading further into the castle. Soldiers stood guard outside each, talking to those who tried to pass through and turning some away. People milled around like ants in a nest, moving from one place to another without making changes to anything around them. This is typical behaviour from most people who find themselves in a new place. It's how people try to subdue the uncomfortable feeling of not knowing where to sit or what is expected of you. Mira was no exception.

For a few minutes she walked around the outer edge of the space, trying to figure out where the different doors led. She had marched up to the castle with the intent of confronting Satonak about his ludicrous demands, but now she realised what she should have realised before. She wasn't the only person who had business in the castle and her personal concerns were probably not high on the priorities of anyone else here. How was she going to convince anyone to let her see one of the most powerful men in the city?

Mira stepped up to one of the guards. The woman under the helmet had a stern face and held her shoulders firm. Mira said "Excuse me?" three times before the soldier blinked and refocused her eyes in Mira's direction.

"What? Yes?" said the woman.

"Good morning," said Mira. "I was wondering if you could tell me where this door leads?"

"Absolutely not," the woman snapped in response, whipping her face back to face directly forward.

Mira was surprised.

"Oh, sorry. Why not?"

"Because she can only tell lies," chuckled another soldier passing by. "Whereas I can tell only the truth."

"Oh shut up, Ryder," the woman growled.

The other soldier walked on, still grinning to himself.

"Ignore him, he's just sour because I didn't want to go out for a second drink with him," explained the soldier.

"Sure," said Mira. "But then what's the actual reason?"

"The Lord's Secrets!" declared the woman, stamping the butt of the spear on the floor for emphasis. "We can't have spies and intruders figuring out the lay of the castle so easily! What would happen if anyone who said they wanted to come in was just allowed to do so!"

"There'd be greater trust between the people and the leaders of the city?"

The guard glared at Mira.

"Alright, sorry, I didn't mean to be annoying. I was hoping to get an audience with Master Satonak, but I can't see how to find him. Do I ask someone to send him a message or..." Mira left any further questions unsaid, hoping that the guard would fill in the empty air with a useful suggestion.

"That's easy," said the woman. She smiled now. "You need to go speak with an appointments clerk. Try the one in grey over there."

She lowered the point of her spear to indicate a woman sitting at a small table in one of the alcoves across the open space of the plaza.

"Thank you," said Mira.

She moved across the hall in the awkward dance of someone navigating a crowd. Every step sent her directly into the path of someone walking crosswise and so it was a long zig-zagging journey before she finally reached the table she sought.

Behind the table sat the woman in grey. She had faint wrinkles across her face and her cheeks hung a little loose, the signs of someone who had recently crested the peak of their years and was now facing the downward slope of life, wondering what the momentum of all their past actions was going to lead to. From the faded clothing and skin of this woman, Mira doubted that she had built up the sort of speed that would propel her into exciting turns ahead. Her clothes were snug and she was reading a sheaf of papers while a scowl deepened the furrow on her forehead.

"Excuse me," Moria began, but she stopped when the woman held up a single finger without looking away from the paper.

Mira stood by the table, expecting the woman to finish whatever she was reading and then respond, but the woman placed the papers back on the table, lifted the top one off and set it to one side, and then picked up the whole stack again. She did not remove her finger from the air.

The air in the plaza was surprisingly stale, despite the large gates that led into it and the movement of so many people around her. Mira's skin began to feel clammy, and a single bead of moisture detached itself from the hair at the back of her neck and snuck under her collar.

"Hello, I just wanted to–" she began again, wondering if the woman had somehow forgotten that she was waiting.

The woman coughed a series of annoyed harrumphs and waggled her finger around until Mira shut her mouth and rolled her eyes.

She was able to count to one hundred three times, and had reached forty-four for the fourth time, when the woman set the papers down, lowered her hand, and looked up at her.

"Yes?" she said.

"Thank goodness," enthused Mira, leaning forward on the table. "I've been told that you are the person I need to talk to. I am looking for an audience with Master Satonak. How does that work?"

"Do you have a prior reservation?" asked the woman.

"Sorry?" Mira was confused. "I just said that I would like an audience with the court wizard and asked how to arrange it. You heard me, right?"

"Yes," agreed the woman.

"So, logically, that must mean I don't have a reservation with him, right?" Mira was proud of herself. Although she was annoyed by the dim response from the grey woman, she had kept her tone light, as though she was just a little confused herself, rather than scathingly undermining the woman.

"Yes, I understand," nodded the woman. "But do you have a reservation with me?"

"Have I made a prior reservation with you, a woman in a job that I didn't previously know existed, and that I didn't know I needed to speak to? Have I booked this time to talk to you? That's the question that you are asking me now?" said Mira, fighting to keep her voice calm.

The woman in grey nodded.

"No?" ventured Mira.

"I'm afraid I can't always see walk-ups," sighed the woman, as if this was the most obvious response that she could give in response to Mira's request. "I have to give priority to those who have made proper reservations."

Mira looked around the room. No one was looking in their direction. There was not a single person hanging around near the table, or walking over from somewhere else. "And who are those people?"

"Clients, generally," said the woman. She sighed and pointed at a small box near Mira on the table. It was filled with a pile of neatly cut squares of paper. Mira could see that the one on the top had the number forty-two written on it. "If you take a number I will call you when I am available, but I must warn you that I may not become available today." The grey woman stretched her mouth wider as she pressed her lips closed. After a moment Mira realised that the woman was attempting to smile.

"Thank you, I suppose," mumbled Mira as she picked up the slip of paper. The woman didn't respond.

Chapter Sixty-Eight

H olding tightly to her numbered piece of paper, Mira retreated into the middle of the plaza. There were no seats, so she mimicked the numerous people who claimed space around the edges of the fountains bubbling happily in the middle of the plaza. Now that she knew what to look for, she realised she wasn't the only person with a numbered paper in hand. But neither was the grey woman the only one handing them out.

Almost a half of the alcoves in the walls were filled by tables, although about a third of those tables were empty. The remainder were staffed by people wearing similar grey clothing. Mira watched as they handed out more of the numbered squares, though sometimes they handed over larger sheets of paper. The puzzled and tired expressions of the people that flowed around the plaza in endless loops suddenly made more sense.

An antfolk man lay against the side of the fountain to her left, with one leg crossed over in front of the other. His head was propped up by the fountain, though turned to one side, and his mandibles shivered in a slow, regular buzz. His paper was clutched to his chest in one spiny hand.

An elf man walked quickly but cautiously up to the man, crouched down, and slid the paper out from his hand. The elf then pressed a different piece of paper in between the antfolk man's fingers, stood up, and began to walk away.

"Hey," hissed Mira as the elf passed her. He spun around, fists up ready to fight. The paper square crunched in between his fingers.

"What do you want, I didn't do it, you can't prove anything," he squawked.

"How did you do that?" Mira asked quietly.

"I already told you, I didn't do anything!" he protested, speaking in the same quiet hiss that she was.

"But how could you be sure he was asleep?" Mira pressed. Antfolk eyes were large and bulbous and made of hundreds of small facets. They didn't have eyelids to blink.

The elf snorted and grinned.

"He was snoring."

"But what if he was faking the snore?" Mira continued.

The elf's smile melted away and his skin paled. His eyes widened and he looked to his side. Mira followed his gaze, fully expecting to see the antfolk man climbing to his feet angrily. But the man was still lying down, seemingly just as asleep as he had been before.

The elf relaxed.

"Just worry about yourself, alright," he told Mira, and then walked off.

Mira watched him head towards one of the alcoves, waving his numbered square. She also noticed five other antfolk walking rather directly towards the same table. She turned back to the sleeping man.

He was propped up on one elbow now, antennae twitching over his head. The man lifted a hand to give her a small salute. Mira waved back. She would have to remember not to mess with the antfolk.

With nothing to occupy her time, Mira turned to examine the fountain she was sitting on. It was wide and shallow, lined with dark blue, ceramic tiles that made the water look clean and clear. She saw her face looking back up at her from the water's surface, stretching and wobbling from the gentle ripples that bounced back and forward across the surface of the pool, spreading out from the simple cone in the centre that pushed water up in a small spout.

"What am I doing," she muttered to herself.

"I need to make sure that this doesn't go any further," she replied to herself under her breath. "If Satonak is willing to send soldiers to get violent, then who knows what he could do to the others. And most of them haven't practiced much magic yet."

Her reflection nodded.

"It's scary," she admitted. "I don't know how I'm going to stop him. And the last time I tried to take on someone important like this, my friends abandoned me."

"But that's not going to happen this time," her reflection urged her.

"Hopefully."

"Mira! What are you doing here?" asked a warm voice behind her. She turned and tucked her hair back behind her ear. She felt as though she had been caught doing something she wasn't supposed to be doing, even though she had done nothing wrong.

Standing a few feet away was Elschefla, with her green, spotted frog perched on her shoulder, staring at Mira with its wide eyes.

"Have you been pulled in by one of the judges?"

Mira stared at Elschefla and shook her head. The other woman sat herself down on the edge of the fountain next to Mira. The frog dove off her shoulder and began awkwardly doggy paddling through the water.

"I wish Phranki wouldn't do that, he's no good at it," said the green-skinned witch.

Mira watched the frog as it struggled to the stone structure in the middle of the fountain.

"I came here because I want to see Master Satonak." She couldn't see much point in denying it now that she was here.

"Ugh. I don't see why anyone would want to do that." Elschefla's face puckered as though someone had tipped lemon juice into it.

"I have to try though," said Mira. Her face hardened as determination rose to the surface. "He's sent soldiers to bring me to him this morning."

"What?" Elschefla's soft, smiling face fell and Mira saw a glimpse of something hard as nails under the friendly exterior. Oh ho, she thought, Prevos had a point. Everyone really is hiding something else inside themselves where the world can't get to it, aren't they?

Elshefla looked around, her forehead wrinkling.

"Where are they? Did they just leave you in the plaza?"

"No, I dealt with them," admitted Mira. She felt a spark of pride flicker in her chest as Elschefla nodded admiringly. It quickly faded as she swallowed and then admitted her plan to the other woman. "But I decided I needed to confront him about it all." Mira licked her lips as she waited to see how Elschefla might react to her foolishness.

"But why would he do something so aggressive?" muttered Elschefla. "He's a grumpy old fool, but he's more obsessed with his books than anything else. Whenever adventurers or merchants arrive in town with scrolls and tomes, he is somehow the first one to find out about it. He'll be waiting on their doorstep, ordering them to let him examine them and make the first offer of purchase. I thought that's what all the drones and stuff were for."

Mira heard a spluttering, panting noise from beside her and looked down to see Phranki had pulled himself from the water and was sprawled on his back on the stone edge of the fountain, fighting for his breath.

"This needs sorting out. It will be difficult to get you to him. The old grump locks himself away in his library most of the time. I don't think he holds many audiences at all. Tell you what, I think I can get you through the doors and give you some directions. You'll have to take it from there."

Mira sat taller and opened her mouth to thank the other woman. Elschefla shushed her.

"I just want to know what he's up to. You be careful though."

"That would be incredible." Mira stood up and grabbed Elschefla's hand, shaking it vigorously. "And you aren't going to try and convince me not to find him?"

"Why would I do that?" Elschefla looked puzzled.

"Because he's a powerful man and if I annoy him I could be in danger? Because I might bring his anger down on the people I know?"

Elschefla laughed and scooped her exhausted frog off the side of the fountain.

"You already know all that, right?" she asked Mira.

"Yeah," answered Mira. And it was true, she did already know all that. The fear was what kept her from seeking her coven for support. It was why she had rushed to the castle.

"Then all I can do is wish you luck!" Elschefla tucked the frog into a pocket on her skirt. He stuck his head out of the pocket and looked gratefully up at her.

Elschefla took Mira's numbered paper and crumpled it before leading her across the plaza to a new alcove. A grey-clad woman sat at the table here, but she barely looked up before realising Elschefla was leading the way and then just waved them towards a nearby door. The soldier at the door saw them walk past the table and gave them a short nod as they opened the door and walked into the hallway beyond.

It was much quieter in the hallway. Mira hadn't realised how much noise was made by a crowd of people with nothing to do but wait. Suddenly the shuffling feet, the muttered complaints, the half-sung snatches of melody, were all blocked off by the slam of the door.

"Okay, if you follow this hallway that way," Elschefla said, pointing to a nearby intersection, "You'll start finding stairs. If you keep taking the stairs up then you should find the library tower quickly. All wizards like to have their towers at the very top of the castle. I think it does something for their egos, like cats sitting on fences to look over their gardens. Good luck!"

"Thank you," said Mira. "I don't know how to repay you for this!"

"Get him to back his interfering nose out of the coven and I'll be satisfied," grinned Elschefla.

Chapter Sixty-Nine

Embroidered tapestries displaying stories of daring and carnage lined the hallways beyond the plaza. It was surprising just how much carnage actually. To be frank, Mira hadn't seen so much red thread in one place since that time her grandmother spilled jam through her sewing basket.

She paused to take a closer look. This tapestry showed a group of people on horses riding towards dozens of people in conical helmets all clustered together and holding spears. They were depicted with simple circles and rectangles, eyes stitched in roughly the right places, arms and legs poking out like children's stick-figure drawings. The second half of the tapestry showed the aftermath of the two groups meeting, and with a lot more care than the first half. The pieces spread out over the tapestry had been sewn with what Mira could only describe as loving detail. Every looping entrail was shaded and shaped just so. Mira was learning something about the people who made the tapestries in this castle.

Servants bustled past, carrying platters of goblets and covered plates, or scrolls sealed with dollops of wax, or armfuls of folded laundry, or staggering under baskets full of dirty clothes, and more. They all moved around Mira as if she was an ambulatory part of the decorations, no more meeting her eyes than they would say hello to a chest of drawers when they entered the room.

She found the stairs that Elschefla had mentioned and followed them up to another floor. Here, torches were set into scones along the walls, and tall windows allowed thin beams of natural light to brighten her passage. The activity on this floor was much the same as the one below, a hive of activity. Mira was reminded of the ant nests she had played with on the plains as a child, cuffing the dirt from the top and then watching as the small black insects scurried in aimless circles, racing as fast as they could to do nothing that she understood.

She followed the hallway down a passage on her left to a flight of stairs, and climbed them. The next flight of stairs continued from the top of those, and then she began exploring a new set of hallways for a long time, unable to find any more.

She wondered if that meant that the wizard's library was somewhere on the same floor, so she tried to catch the attention of a passing servant to ask.

Mira stepped into the path of the first man she saw, hoping that he would stop when he saw her. He did not. In fact, he leaned like grass in a strong wind to avoid her. Mira was sure he was going to fall over. Instead, he wound around her like an eel and continued on his way.

When she saw the next servant approaching, Mira lifted a hand, as though waving to the woman. The woman showed no sign that she saw Mira's hand until she slid under it legs first, bending backwards and barely missing Mira's hand with her upturned chin.

Finally, Mira spread herself across the hallway, arms upraised towards the corners of the ceiling, legs spread further than her shoulders, blocking the corridor as completely as she could. The next servant in the hall avoided eye contact by moving his head in an owl-like loop, for all the world as though his neck had come unattached.

In desperation, Mira called out, "Hey! You!"

The man spun on his heel, and immediately marched away from her, back the way he had come.

"Stop!" cried Mira, and she launched herself after him. "Wait! I just need you to answer a question for me! Where is the wizard's library?" The man was well groomed, with his hair slicked down and a tidy suit buttoned securely around him. He stepped lively, but could not be described as running. And yet Mira was unable to make ground on him. She kept calling out, but he ducked around corners, slipping past other servants who paid no attention to Mira and yet still danced unerringly into her path.

The annoying dance pedestrians perform when one is about to walk into another and both switch sides of the path at the same time is a well-known occurrence throughout the universe. Mira could understand that frustration happening once or twice as she chased the well-groomed servant through the halls. But when a seventh woman carrying sheets stepped sideways into her way, Mira reached forward, grabbed the woman by the shoulders and moved her, gently but firmly, off to the side of the hall and then raced after the man who had just disappeared around a corner.

Mira darted around the bend and found the man waiting for her. He stood next to a large set of wooden double doors. One hand rested on the heavy circular metal handle.

"Is that," began Mira as she walked up next to him, but then she had to stop and bend over to catch her breath. "Is it the…" She panted and put her hands on her knees. The man in the tight suit wasn't remotely bothered by the exertions they had both endured.

He finally met her eye. He closed his eyes and slowly nodded, once. Then he opened his eyes again.

"It is?" she wheezed. He nodded once more. "Thank goodness." She stepped forward and the man pulled the door open for her. Mira lifted a hand to gesture some token of acknowledgement to him, too out of breath for any sort of spoken gratitude, and then entered the room beyond. She wasn't looking at him, and so she didn't notice his eyes narrow and the corners of his lips creep upwards. The door thudded shut behind her as she looked around.

This was not the library.

Traditionally, libraries are known for the number of books they contain. That was the first thing that caught Mira's eye as she looked around. The walls were conspicuously lacking shelves, and those non-existent shelves certainly held no books of any sort. Mira had heard of newer, fancier libraries that enticed visitors through the use of modern techniques, such as audiobooks. One woman buying bread from her had praised the system. She said it involved taking home a small artificial servant made of metal and springs, and contrivancer enchantments got it to recite the contents of any book that was desired. Her voice had gone all wistful at that point, and so Mira wasn't entirely certain what made borrowing a mechanical servant that spoke stories so enticing. However, this room did not appear to be a place that lent out mechanical people.

Instead, Mira found herself staring at two groups of the High Lord's soldiers, half-armoured and buckling on swordbelts and capes. They stood at either side of the long narrow room, gathering their belongings from chests and lockers and wooden pegs on the walls.

"Can I help you miss?" said a snakefolk soldier, not unkindly. She slithered a little closer.

"Uh, I was told that this was Master Satonak's library?" stammered Mira.

"Oh it's you!" called a voice from behind the snakefolk woman. The voice was oily and smirking and Mira found it familiar but couldn't quite place it. Then Rinald stepped out from the crowd. He spread his arms and grinned.

"You've made my duties for today much easier." He paused and the smile faltered for a moment. "It's just you here, right?"

For a second Mira considered bluffing. Maybe she could convince Rinald that the other witches were somewhere nearby, ready to support her as she had supported them last time he tried to interfere with the coven. But her nerve failed as the soldiers drew close.

Chapter Seventy

The soldiers escorted Mira to the dungeon cells below Lord Cornucervin's castle. This concerned her at first. However, she fully expected that, once the soldiers left her there, she would discover the cells were only as real as the rest of the city. She should be able to poke holes in the walls like moths eating their way through dresses in a wardrobe until she could push herself through and escape.

Unfortunately it turned out that Lord Cornucervin had not wanted to save time when it came to his dungeons. He had clearly asked the builders to take their time with real stone, and Mira sprained a finger trying to pry them loose.

Which meant she was stuck in the small, damp room, with nothing to look at outside the bars but an empty hallway, for the remainder of the day and then overnight. If it wasn't for the bards singing a four part harmony in the next cell, she might not have slept. Thankfully their lullabies were the most soothing that Mira had ever heard. Mira spent the next day with her forehead resting on the thick iron bars of the cell, wishing she had a plan.

"What misfortune has befallen you, madam?"

The voice was deep and resonated through the real stones in the cells. Mira blinked and lifted her head, looking down the hall to another cell which held two men.

The first was seven feet tall and round as a ball. He wore his red hair in a long braid behind his head, and his shockingly tight clothing was pale blue. He nodded when Mira's eyes met his, as cold and clear as a glacier.

"You do not seem the type who would normally be abandoned in this low place," he added. "So I wonder how it is that you are our lone companion."

The second man twitched and shivered like a small hairless dog at the larger man's side, his eyelids spasming. The larger man rested a hand comfortably on his shoulder. He had a thick yellow moustache and massive hands, which gripped the cell bars, or smoothed his clothes, or lifted a green flask to his lips so he could sip from it, but never stayed still.

"Master Satonak tried to have me brought in," Mira began.

The tall man's eyebrow raised slightly.

"It would seem that he succeeded in his endeavour."

Mira snorted.

"Actually, I managed to deal with the soldiers he sent, but then I thought I could come here to sort things out in person and ended up walking into a barracks."

"From the frying pan and into another bigger frying pan then."

"Exactly."

"I must say, Satonak does seem to be extending himself further than he has before." The rotund man frowned. "The court wizard must have uncovered some new design that he feels gives him leverage over the Lord of the Porcelain Throne."

"What do you mean?"

"Satonak has been issuing more commands than usual in recent weeks. I presume that it is only a matter of time before he is confronted by Lord Cornucervin." The man leaned forward and smiled, more cruelly than he had before. "It will be entertaining to discover which man has the authority that he thinks and which will be disenchanted of his false notion."

Mira frowned. Being caught between the wizard and the city's lord as they lashed out to establish control was going to make things much harder for her.

The smaller man leaned forward to the bars, shivering wildly.

"How about you two? Why are you in here?" she asked, to change the subject.

The taller man smiled and placed a hand on the shorter man's head. The little man jerked as if shocked but then took another pull from his small green flask, tucked it to his side and leaned forward. He turned his head sideways and set his teeth around the bars. Mira's stomach turned as the sound of grinding filled the hallway.

"As it transpires, Lord Cornucervin has a distaste for those who would spread their prosperity amongst the down-trodden of this sprawling urban aggregation." The tall man smiled again. "My name is Interrobang and this overly energised homunculus is Manicule. Might I ask your own?"

"I'm Mira. It's a pleasure to meet you both. What is it that you were giving away?"

Interrobang laughed and just the sound of his pleasure made Mira smile as well.

"My dear, we would never give anything away! The prosperity we spread was no gift, but dispensed via mutually beneficial transactions!" He reached into his clothes and pulled out another of the small green flasks his friend carried. "This is the magic potion that brought our alchemist friend Hedera the renown that he so deserves. A more potent brew you will not find within this city's walls."

"Not that the walls surround the whole city," chuckled Mira.

Interrobang echoed her laughter and put the flask away again.

"Indeed."

There was a bang as the bars Manicule had been chewing fell with a clatter to the flagstones.

"Ah, I see our efforts are not in vain. How delightful." Interrobang gently guided Manicule away from the gap in the bars and then pushed his own large arm through to undo the latches holding the door shut. The severed bars bent where Interrobang's arm pressed them. The man was a lot stronger than Mira realised.

Once the cell door was open the two men walked out. Manicule scurried across the hall and pressed his face against Mira's door to leer at her, his yellow mustache puffing around the edges of the bars.

"Are you a pepper?" he asked. He squeezed a huge hand through the bars. A green flask was clutched in his thick fingers and he offered it to Mira.

"Uh…"

"Don't mind him. He gets unstable when he's drunk too much of Hedera's potion." Interrobang put a hand on Manicule's shoulder and pulled him away from the door. Manicule snuck a sip from the flask as he stepped away.

"I wouldn't recommend that you have any either. It can become overwhelmingly compelling," said Interrobang, then he stepped closer to her door. His huge frame filled Mira's vision and she stepped away.

"Now, I do apologise for this Mira, but I'm afraid that we are going to have to leave you here."

"What? Why?" Mira had hoped that the men would break her lock as well, though she had to admit, after watching Manicule, she was relieved they were staying on the other side of the door.

"Because we don't know you well enough to predict whether you would be cumbersome to us or not; whether you might attract attention that we would prefer remained focused elsewhere." The massive man lifted his small round helmet from his head and leaned it towards her. "But I wish you well in your attempts to play one fool against another. Good bye!"

Without another word he strode down the hallway and out of sight. Manicule scurried after him, bouncing off the walls on his gigantic hands and snuffling. The sound of his frantic breath echoed long after the two men could no longer be seen.

Mira waited in her cell. At first she listened to a distant drip as a way to count the time, but it stopped and started so often that she quickly lost track of where she was up to. She tried humming a few tunes, but the bards from the other cell the night before weren't singing now.

By the time a trio of the High Lord's soldiers came marching into the hall and stopped outside her door, Mira practically cheered. The bearfolk man at the back turned to look at the broken cell door Interrobang and Manicule had left behind them. He stared at it for quite a while.

The other soldiers were more focused on Mira than the evidence of escape behind them. They opened her door and prodded her through the halls and up multiple flights of stairs.

"Where are you taking me?" Mira asked.

"To see Lord Cornucervin," said the young dwarf behind her left soldier, just as the construct soldier behind her right creaked "You do not need to know."

There was a scraping as the construct turned their head to look at the dwarf.

"Why would you tell her that?"

"I didn't think it was a big deal," protested the dwarf. "She asked a question and I answered it."

"But you did not have to answer it. She is our prisoner, and she does not have any authority over us."

The small group trudged in silence along the corridor.

Finally Mira heard the dwarf sullenly mutter, "I can answer someone if I want to answer them." Before the construct could reply, they turned a corner and Mira stood before a huge set of double doors. The construct stepped in front of her and motioned for the bearfolk man to open the doors. The doors moved as slowly as fog, and revealed a hall beyond that was big enough to contain entire buildings from Mira's street.

Chapter Seventy-One

A raised dais occupied the far end of the room beyond lines of columns stretching forward from the double doors. Tapestries dangled down the walls on either side, coats of arms and sigils and carefully embroidered words covering them. This was a Great Hall, just like the court of the First Seat's. Oh, the court in Whinnia had been made of wood where this space was built from stone, and the First Seat had a bonfire in the middle of his hall that made the whole place hard to see and breathe in, but it was the same. Lord Cornucervin's Great Hall.

Heart pounding, Mira walked along the carpet that led to the dais.

When she had gone to speak with the First Seat, the hall had been full of his loyal followers, the heads of various houses of Whinnia. This hall was currently almost empty. A couple of servants were occupied on one side of the room. Mira squinted to see what they were doing. They were carrying in seats from somewhere else and installing them in lines along the floor. A few glanced over their shoulders at her and, though they looked confused or annoyed, they did not stop her. The soldiers who had brought her to the hall stopped at the edge of the carpet, watching her walk forward.

The Porcelain Throne was atop the dais. Mira was impressed. The Porcelain Throne was not simply a white chair made of an exotic material, as she had imagined when she first heard about it, but an elaborately designed piece of art. The solid base of the throne was covered in relief sculpture, figures barely larger than her thumb in all sorts of poses and situations. The layers and levels of these figures were carved to suggest they held one another up, rising to the seat and then continuing up the sides of the arms. At the top, where the occupant would rest their arms, the statues bunched together to create a functional surface. It was composed of tiny shapes and was not a single smooth surface though. Larger forms filled the back of the throne, an outline of a mountain with figures ascending on either side. The mountain made a smooth surface to lean back against. Above this scene the throne spread out like water from a fountain with a final vision of clouds in an open sky.

Looking up at someone in the throne would be like looking at someone sitting upon an entire world in the clouds, lifted by crowds of people. Mira was very very tempted to step up onto the dais and try it out. The seat looked more inviting than she would have thought, the hard material smoothed over time by the wriggling of whoever sat upon it. Mira imagined it would be remarkably comfortable for such an unyielding substance.

A door creaked open and thumped shut again somewhere behind her. The tone of the air changed. Before she would have said the room was silent, with that brushing over of the truth that ignored the rustle of clothing, the footsteps, the quiet murmurs of servants discussing where exactly to put the next chair, harshly whispered threats such as, "Colin, if you don't sort out the rest of the chairs without asking me to hold your bloody hand, I swear that I'll show you precisely where you can put them."

But, after the door closed, it really did become silent. There was a sudden emptiness in the air, and Mira could tell that all the servants had paused and were now watching someone. She turned around.

Lord Cornucervin was walking towards her up the long carpet between the columns.

She knew it was Lord Cornucervin because of the way every servant froze until he had walked past them and then performed a sort of half bow, half awkward shuffle, and fled as subtly as they could.

The Lord was younger than Mira expected. His head was shaved smooth and a narrow line of beard ran from his lower lip to his chin. He wore dark breeches and a dark shirt, and had a long black cloak pulled tight over his shoulders. He smiled at Mira as he walked past her, stepped up the dais, and approached the porcelain throne.

He stood in front of it and turned around without sitting down. He looked at Mira again, and his forehead wrinkled.

"You're not one of the servants, are you?" he asked.

"No sir, I am not one of the servants," stammered Mira. If she mimicked their half bow shuffle manoeuvre now, would it be enough to get her out of the hall?

"I could tell," said Lord Cornucervin. Now he swished his cloak aside and sat on the throne, letting the dark fabric settle over an armrest. "You don't look like a servant." He nodded, as though he had made a particularly insightful comment. Mira resisted the urge to point out how obvious this was, when she was wearing the same clothes she wore in her bakery, with floury marks on her skirts, while his servants wore the livery that he himself must have ordered them to wear.

"That's right sir," she agreed out loud instead.

"And you didn't bow. Oh! Of course, I should have thought. Are you that witch from the dungeons?"

Mira opened her mouth and found no sound would come out. She tried a second time and made a choked whistling noise in the back of her throat.

Lord Cornucervin raised an eyebrow and leaned forward, his eyes glowing with the same shine as an owl watching a mousehole.

"Yes," said Mira finally. The tightness in her throat had loosened enough for her to speak, though her voice still came out exceptionally high pitched. She hated it, and coughed to try and loosen the muscles.

"Are you sick?" asked the Lord. He frowned. "Can you talk normally or do we need to send you back down to the cells until you get yourself in order?"

Mira shook her head frantically.

"Good. What were you doing down there?"

"I– What?" Mira stumbled over her reply. "I came to speak to Satonak about his declaration that we were not to create a coven and then his soldiers captured me and took me–"

"Satonak's soldiers?" interrupted the Lord. He sat back on the throne and clenched his hands. "They took you down there?"

"Yes sir."

Another servant arrived and walked to stand beside the throne, a cylindri-cal-looking man with a sharp nose and sad eyes.

Before either of them could say anything else, there was another bang from somewhere behind Mira. She turned around to see what had happened. Master Satonak was striding into the hall.

The court wizard did stride impressively. He wore the typical long robes that people would expect of a wizard, and they swirled around him dramatically. His long, white beard shifted with each of his steps, and though the effect could have been comical, in practice it made him look like a warship under sail.

He barely glanced at Mira until he had almost passed her, but then his head spun sideways and his eyes bulged. He pointed a long knobbly finger at her and cried, "You! What are you doing up here?"

"I asked her to come and talk to me about life in the streets of my city," drawled Cornucervin from the throne. "It's been very enlightening already, I must say."

The oddly geometric servant standing next to the Porcelain Throne opened his mouth and spoke in a carrying voice.

"Ironic Detachment!"

Mira felt blood rise to her cheeks.

"My lord, this is no everyday commoner who you might interrogate for information about Senoonheim! This is the leader of that witches' coven that I told you about!" Satonak looked furious. The hairs of his beard stood on end, quivering. It was as though a cold dog was clinging to his chin.

"Cruel Delights!" called out the servant next to the throne. Lord Cor-nucervin took no notice of him at all.

"Really! How wonderful!" Cornucervin leaned forward, his eyes lighting up and a grin spreading across his face. He sat with his elbows on his knees as he turned his attention back to Mira. "The court wizard tells me that you were in charge of a group of witches that he specifically ordered you not to form, and you did it anyway? I would love to hear more about this."

Chapter Seventy-Two

M ira's heart pounded so loud that her whole body thumped with each pulse. Even the floor shifted in time with her panic. Or at least, that was how it felt to her, but then other sounds snuck past the reverberations and into her ears. The hubbub of dozens of conversations were echoing through the hall. It wasn't just her heart moving the floor, it was the crowd that had been allowed into the hall.

"Conversational Clamour!"

"Yes yes Federstein, I'm trying to listen to this woman and her desperate explanations."

"I just don't understand why we aren't allowed to form our coven," Mira blurted. "What did we do wrong to cause him to give us that instruction? And why is he sending his soldiers to threaten us when we do meet?

"His soldiers, you used that word again," smiled Lord Cornucervin, turning his head slightly and wrinkling his nose. He waved beyond Mira, motioning someone she couldn't see to step forward. Mira turned and saw a crowd of well-dressed merchants and nobles standing between the seats in a gaggle of befuddled faces. At Stanley Cornucervin's gesture they came closer and settled into the seats.

"It is very interesting that she keeps using that phrase, don't you think Master Satonak?" he continued.

"Whispers of Intrigued Amusement!"

The murmuring behind Mira shifted in tone. Notes of amusement appeared now, and there was definite tittering in the crowd, alongside concerned discussions. She assumed they were all debating who the woman talking to the city's lord was and what she had done. The eyes of these onlookers pressed on her shoulders, weakening her legs and her resolve. She wanted to curl up on the floor, pressed down by their weight.

"My lord, she is just a silly commoner, with no appreciation for the hierarchy of command," said Satonak in a voice like oil. "Of course all the soldiers in the city are your soldiers. I admit that I did give instructions to a few, just to rein in this woman and her coven."

Lord Cornucervin's eyes turned back to where Mira was cowering.

"Why didn't you just follow this very reasonable instruction from the Court Wizard?" he said, emphasising the word "reasonable" with a widened eyes. "A man who has been tasked with keeping me informed of what is going on in my city?"

Mira didn't know what to say. She had come to find the wizard and convince him to let go of his vendetta against her coven. She hadn't planned to be standing before the lord of the city and the important people that clustered around him like moths around a fire. Her throat was shrinking so she couldn't speak. She looked around, hoping to find her reflection in some surface, but there was nothing. She couldn't catch her own eye.

"You go ahead and explain Mira," called a voice from behind her.

"Expressions of Shock!" called Federstein, and the crowd burst into a chattering cacophony, like nesting birds.

Mira spun to search the crowd for who had called to her. It didn't take long. Standing at the end of a row to her right was the small hill of Troo, still wearing the uniform of the High Lord's soldiers. Troo nodded at Mira.

"You know why you're here, go ahead and tell him about it," repeated Troo. She darted her eyes sideways and Mira saw a tiny, charm hidden by the tapestry in that direction. *How is Satonak's bladder holding up?* she wondered.

Mira smiled as relief soothed her shoulders. Plenty of the High Lord's soldiers were standing on duty around the hall, but she was pleased to discover Troo was one of them. Then she realised the rest of the coven were sitting and standing on Troo's lower slopes as well.

Delorous with her rat on her shoulder, her diaphanous dress swaying liquidly in a non-existent breeze.

Kirka next to her, with a calm face but eyes that burned like an inferno. Her hands patted at the space on her sides where her knives would normally be. The holders were empty. The blades must have been confiscated before she was allowed into the hall.

Junka had nabbed herself a seat, and the original occupant was none too pleased about it. He stood next to the chair and kept edging back towards it, as if he could convince Junka to return it by appealing to her sense of propriety and personal space. Junka responded by patting him on the thigh and producing a paper bag from somewhere in the folds of her clothing. She pulled a black and white candy from it and offered the bag to the man. Ti's silver jewellery flashed and jumped about while she chuckled at Junka and the man.

There was a crash as a window high in the hall smashed open and a large, yellow bee buzzed through it. The crowd gasped as it swooped low over their heads and Mira saw Hattie riding on its back. She couldn't quite see what Hattie was doing, but from the way the tiny witch bounced and vibrated, Mira had a good idea of which hand gestures were involved.

"That miniature witch has abducted one of my drones!" yelled Satonak, pointing a furious finger at her as she wound the huge insect lower and lower in a spiral.

"Oh yes, the drones that you were supposed to give me weekly reports from," said the High Lord. "The drones you began sending out after I asked you to watch over the city." Again, his eyes widened as he said the word "watch". He leaned on one elbow with a finger over his mouth as he watched the action in the hall. "Remind me, when did you last give me one of those reports?"

Satonak began coughing. Mira smiled and looked at the rest of the coven.

Nerishma appeared to be trying to hide behind Troo. She had pulled her black hood down to cover most of her face and was scrubbing at the charcoal streaks on her cheeks that she wore to help her hide in shadows. She grinned nervously as the hall's attention was directed towards the coven and lifted a hand slightly to wave at Mira.

Othniel simply stood in her black corset, her torn skirt, with fishnet stockings pulled over her arms and her legs. She wasn't doing anything inherently aggressive, but between the skull face paint she wore and the way her crossed arms made the muscles in her shoulders shift, the crowd in the seats nearby were leaning away from her.

Leena clicked her mandibles next to Elschefla who waved at Mira. Her lizard Tiny was nowhere to be seen.

"I told the others!" Elschefla called, with her hands cupped around her mouth. "We knew we had to come and support you. This needs to be sorted out once and for all!"

Mira felt as though her body was filled with air. She was as light as a feather, so light that she might rise off the floor and drift up into the rafters in the ceiling. The sight of her new friends, her coven, who had all come into the castle to support her, reinvigorated her and gave her a renewed sense of bravery. She hadn't realised just how alone she had felt as she tried to find her way through this castle until she felt the strength of the connections with her friends.

Trying to face down someone with power, and alone, was a daunting thing. She told herself she could do it, but it's hard to believe in yourself while you are in the middle of such a situation. With her friends here, telling her that they believed in her, she was beginning to believe herself.

"Why is that ill woman yelling at you?" asked Lord Cornucervin.

"She's not ill, she just looks that way," murmured Mira. She turned to look into his eyes. "I came here to talk to him," she jerked a thumb at Satonak who was still standing next to her on the carpet. "So that's what I'm going to do."

"Gasps of Indignation!"

Lord Cornucervin rolled his eyes.

"Federstein, it's not that big a deal."

It had come down to this. Mira had the source of all that harassment standing here, right in front of her. Finally, she had a chance to sort things out.

"What is your problem with us having a coven?"

Mira felt as though the air had been pulled out of the room after she questioned Satonak. Sounds fell away and the edges of her vision grew darker. All that was left was Satonak's face.

He looked shocked that Mira had even spoken to him, his mouth falling open behind the beard, his eyes wide. Those eyes darted around the room, like a terrified rodent in a house looking for an escape, but found nothing. Mira stood, waiting to hear what he had to say.

"Well?" asked Lord Cornucervin. The bald man was leaning forward on the throne and watching his wizard closely.

Satonak deflated slowly, like a sad birthday balloon left in the corner of a room for weeks after the party was over. He looked away from Mira, unable to face her fully.

His lips barely moved as he muttered something almost inaudible, even to Mira who was standing right beside him.

"... buy it all up..."

"What?" she asked, leaning forward and cupping a hand behind her ear.

"You'll all buy everything up," Satonak muttered a little more clearly, still looking down. He accompanied the whisper with a shrug.

"Did you hear that, my lord?" Mira called over her shoulder to Lord Cornucervin, but kept her eyes on Satonak. With his head lowered this way she couldn't help but notice a patch of thinning hair on his crown that made his head look like a freshly hatched bird, all pink and covered in stringy white fluff.

"I'm afraid not," called the lord from his dais cheerily. "Go on Satonak, speak up!"

Satonak straightened his shoulders and looked up at the man on the Porcelain Throne. Sometimes when someone says their thoughts out loud, it gives them a certain renewed confidence in themselves. This certainly seemed to be the case with Satonak. Unfortunately, this effect happens even if the thoughts the person is giving voice to are awful and should not have been spoken.

Chapter Seventy-Three

"I banned them from forming a coven because they will buy up all the magical ingredients in the city, making it impossible for me to work my own magic," explained Satonak to Lord Cornucervin.

"Stunned Silent Shock."

"Federstein, it can't be silent shock if you're calling it out, can it?"

"Expression of Dismayed Regret."

"No, just say sorry if you're sorry! Look, just be quiet for a minute would you?"

Lord Cornucervin turned back to the pair standing below his dais.

"You banned this group out of professional jealousy?"

"My lord, as the Court Wizard, there are many things that I have to do, many spells that I am called on to perform for the safety and improvement of Senoonheim," protested Satonak.

"Really?" exclaimed the High Lord, wearing an expression that exploded with innocence. "Someone has put all those expectations on you? It must be so hard for you to do all that magic and to order my soldiers to threaten the people in my city."

Satonak's face turned crimson.

"My lord, I can't be expected to do all the things you ask of me if I am waiting on a delivery of mandrake root because these witches have bought it all up for their own dark purposes!"

The hall remained silent after Satonak's declaration. On his throne, Lord Cornucervin lowered his head and pinched the bridge of his nose.

"Satonak…" he said in a low voice. It was the exact same tone a father uses when they walk back into the house to discover the children are making small castles in the drifts of flour they have poured on the living room floor.

"Sir, please, you have to understand, the needs of a wizard can be volatile," wheedled Satonak. He sounded so needy that Mira leaned away from him. His thick-knuckled hands were clasped together and he faced the dais directly. "It is so hard to know when I might discover some new and valuable spell in the tomes, or if some distilled selkie pelt will be consumed faster than expected. I can't spend all my time chasing down reagents for my elixirs before these witches use them all up in love charms."

Mira frowned and leaned forward, with her arms crossed below her chest.

"Have you ever met any witches before?" she asked incredulously. "What is it that you think we do? Honestly, love charms?"

"He has a point though. The Court Wizard is asked to perform all sorts of spells on behalf of Senoonheim, and I won't have him limited due to the interference of your coven." Lord Cornucervin leaned back with his eyebrows raised. "I am inclined to support him on this ban."

Mira felt desperation claw at her stomach. When Satonak had given his pathetic little reason for banning them, she was thrilled. It was so petty that she was sure that Lord Cornucervin would laugh at him and declare that they could have their coven. Hearing him take the wizard seriously was devastating.

Despite the love and support of the coven lifting her exactly when she needed it, Mira was reminded that she had walked into the Lord's Castle, and come to the Wizard's Court, demanding that he stop doing something that he was actually quite entitled to do. Had she just made things much worse? Were the coven even going to be allowed to leave this hall? Mira became very conscious of how many of the High Lord's soldiers were standing around the outside of the crowd, with spears in their hands.

Mira paused and took a deep breath. She closed her eyes, trying to imagine what she might tell herself if she could see her reflection. An idea tickled the back of her brain and her eyes snapped open. What if it could be that easy?

"Sir," she began slowly, taking a step towards the dais. "What if we share?"

"What do you mean?" asked Lord Cornucervin.

The wizard spluttered behind her, but she spoke urgently, so he couldn't interrupt her thoughts.

"What if we promise that we will contribute any reagents we have to the city when called on?"

Lord Cornucervin scratched his cheek. He leaned back on the throne and looked up into the ceiling.

"You would share with the city if called upon, eh?"

"My lord!" squealed Satonak. It was a delight to hear an old, dignified man like the wizard reduced to scrambling for words. "Surely you can't expect me to share with these witches!"

"She's not asking you to share with them though Satonak. She's telling you that she will share with you, when the city asks her to." He smiled slowly, a cat laying in the sun as the sparrows hop closer and closer, sure that the predator is sleeping. "All you would have to do is let me know that you need something, and I will send word to this fine woman and her coven. Isn't that right, miss?" Even from this distance, Mira could see the glee that sparkled in the Lord's eyes.

"That's exactly right," she confirmed. She turned to look into Satonak's eyes. "Once we hear from Lord Cornucervin that there is a need, we will gladly provide any reagents we have to meet that need. After all, you have explained the hierarchy of Senoonheim to me now, so that I understand who is in charge." She struggled not to grin as the wizard's face darkened. Eyebrows were raising on the faces of the crowd behind him.

"Do you agree to those terms, ladies?" she called out to the rest of the coven.

"You bet!" yelled Troo and the rest of the ladies cheered in affirmation.

Mira watched as the angry colour drained out of Satonak's face. He looked like he had lain to bleach in the sun for years.

"My lord, I–" he stammered, but Cornucervin sliced his hand horizontally in front of him and the wizard froze.

"Surely you can't have a problem with that, Satonak?" said the city's lord as he stood up. "After all, as you just said, you have so much to do for the city. It wouldn't matter if you had to come to me and let me know what you were doing if there was something that you needed, would it? After all, it's all in service of my city, isn't it?" His voice was cheerful, and he was smiling, but that sparkle of glee in the lord's eyes had become hard and cold. It had shifted from the colourful sparkle of a diamond to the sharp gleam of the edge of a blade. "You wouldn't need to cause trouble for these women or anyone else just for your own experiments and personal magics, would you?"

Clearly there had been conflict between Satonak and Lord Cornucervin over what was going on in the city. But whatever problems the two of them had, Mira was relieved that she had found a way to get what she wanted and keep on the Lord's side without Satonak managing to countermand it. At least not here, not now, not yet. She would need to keep an eye out for him continuing his plots to be the authority in the city, but the coven would be able to continue.

Satonak's face had fallen so far that Mira wondered if it was about to slip right off the front of his head and flop onto the floor between them. She reached over and put a hand on his shoulder.

"I'm so glad I came to the castle to talk this out with you. Thank you so much for your time."

"I agree, it's been very edifying to have you visit," said Lord Cornucervin. "And I hope it has clarified a few things." His gaze jumped up to take in the crowd in the seats. "For everyone." There was a rustling noise as the crowd nodded furiously. "But I have many people to speak with today, so I would ask that you and your coven please take your leave. And Satonak," he said, a hint of iron exposing itself again in his light-hearted tone, "we can talk more about these onerous responsibilities of yours later."

"Thank you, sir," said Mira and she walked as quickly as she dared down the carpet. Troo stepped forward to meet her a few paces before the others and wrapped her in a hug that would have defeated most bears.

"You did so well," Troo whispered into her ear, before guiding her to the others with a massive arm weighing across her shoulders.

"Come on," said Elschefla. "Let's get out of here before anyone changes their mind!"

The voice of the cylindrical servant standing beside the throne rang out behind them.

"The first submission for the consideration of Lord Cornucervin!"

Mira saw a familiar man stand up from the chairs nearby. His hair was shoulder length and curled in toward his face in a bob, and he wore a sharp little moustache and tidy beard on the tip of his chin. As he raised a hand to gain the attention of the city's lord, she realised that he was the scribe who she had gone to to make her posters.

"My lord, you have to help me! All my apes are gone!"

"Confused Hubbub!"

Chapter Seventy-Four

M ira stepped past where Nerishma was huddled over a heavy kettle of hot water. She had started helping in the bakery most days, making hot drinks for the customers in the afternoons. She kept kettles of water boiling on the ovens in the back, and had created a variety of concoctions to serve. Thick, creamy chocolate drinks, strong coffees, a variety of dark or fruity teas. They were immensely popular, and customers filled the chairs that Mira had gathered and filled her shop with. Each chair was different from the next, an eclectic collection of whatever Mira had been able to find and carry back to the shop herself.

With all Nerishma's equipment on it, as well as Mira's scones and iced rolls, the counter was no longer big enough to contain everything. Mira was thinking about expanding it, or whether she might even be able to move the whole bakery somewhere bigger.

Mira still needed to fill the shelves with her breads, patterns sliced into the crackly crusts, or tied in delicious-smelling knots. But now she was making more cupcakes and muffins, more biscuits and slices, and people would sit to eat their treats in the bakery instead of dashing away.

She picked up a platter of Nerishma's hot drinks and stepped between the smiling and chatting customers in the bakery until she reached the door.

On the street outside, Mira had set up half a dozen small tables scrounged from markets and alleys around the city, and they were currently filled with her whole coven. She wove between them all and placed their drinks on the tables.

"Thank you dearie." Junka grinned a gummy smile. She picked up a delicate teacup with her thick fingers and slurped happily. "Fantastic! Maybe a little more sugar though, just to give me a little pep." She pulled a ceramic container the size of a fist from somewhere in the region of her waist, opened the lid, and tipped it into the teacup, raising the level of the liquid inside dangerously close to overflowing. She made a noise like an old cat licking at a plate of cream as she tried the new drink. "Perfect!" she declared.

Elschefla sat with Othniel and Shara on the next table. Shara's duck Widgeon was also sitting in a chair, his beak resting on the edge of the table. A passerby grabbed Mira by the elbow as she approached their table and pointed at Elschefla.

"Miss, what have you been serving that poor woman, she looks nauseous!"

"Oh she's fine, I promise."

"I doubt it. Just look at that colour!"

Before Mira could explain any more, the pedestrian humphed, lifted her nose as high as possible, and stalked off down the street.

Mira shook her head and turned back to the witches at the table.

"—means that I can fill in any number of forms while other lawyers are still waking up," Elschefla was explaining to Othniel. Othniel nodded seriously; there are few things that emphasise a serious expression as strongly as the thick black-and-white skull makeup Othniel wore over her face.

Mira placed a bowl of hot chocolate in front of Shara, who smiled up at her. The small girl squinted into the sun behind Mira's head. She was holding a single slice of bread that she had taken a large bite out of.

"Thank you so much Mira. Please Mr Cloud, could you help me out?"

A thin shadow spread across the street and shaded Shara's huge eyes. She opened them fully and sighed happily.

"That's much better. Thank you!"

Widgeon quacked angrily. Mira sighed and put a slice of bread on the table in front of the bird. Widgeon squawked and started flapping his wings wildly as he attacked the bread, sending crumbs flying everywhere.

Mira handed a raspberry tea to Delorous, and a coffee so dark that it looked as though the night had been decanted into a mug to Kirka. Then she put the empty platter on the table and flumped into an unoccupied chair.

"Going alright Mira?" Delorous asked. Her rat Charles was coiled across her shoulders like a short but very thick and furry scarf.

"Yes, it just gets so busy now," said Mira. "I'm grateful for a moment when I get to stop and catch my breath, even for a second."

"You deserve it," said Delorous with a rare smile. She didn't give them often, and the muscles in her face didn't quite know how to do it properly. A group of passing kobolds jumped in shock and crossed the street to keep away from her.

"You worked so hard to get the coven going," continued Delorous. "It's only right that you get to enjoy the coven properly now!"

"That's right," agreed Kirka. Her smooth, pale face smiled and Mira shuddered. The small woman let a hand drop under the table, and Mira knew she was fondling the handle of one of her knives. "We witches need to stick together so that no one can cause any trouble for us. Never, ever again." Her voice was light, despite the clearly communicated threat. Delorous reached over and laid a hand on Kirka's arm.

"It's alright Kirka, we've gathered up pretty much every witch in Senoonheim or nearby. We don't need to worry about that silly wizard any more, in my opinion."

Mira looked down and pursed her lips.

"Actually, there is something I think I need to let you know about," she said. She was nervous, but thinking about sharing this secret with her friends in the coven no longer made her feel like an old cloth that was being scrunched up. After the coven turned up in Cornucervin's court, she had felt stronger about herself, more confident that there were people she could count on. But she was worried that she was about to let them down.

"What is it, young lady?" asked a familiar voice from over Mira's shoulder.

She turned in her chair to see Fina stomping her walking stick along the street nearby. The older witch clomped over to one of Mira's customers sitting at another table and glared at him. The man gulped down the last mouthful of his drink, gathered up his belongings, and then leapt away into the crowd moving along the street. Fina nodded and then turned to settle herself onto the chair like a broody mother hen fussing her way onto her eggs. Her creepy, skull-headed bird Plak flew down and sat on her shoulder. It looked around with its empty eye sockets and cawed before it started preening its black wings with its long pale beak.

Fina raised her walking stick and waved it at Mira.

"Go on then, what is it that you need to tell us? We're all listening."

Mira looked around and realised that it was true. All her friends at the tables nearby had stopped their conversations and turned to see what was going on. Shara munched on her slice of bread. Ti was lounging back in her chair as though it was a couch at some decadent banquet.

"Um," she began. She could fishing heat rising to her cheeks, but she reminded herself that these women had showed up for her, they had supported her going into harm's way, even when her actions might have come back and caused problems for them. They had believed in her.

"Okay, here it is." Mira took a deep breath. "I am not a witch." She closed her eyes.

There. It was out in the world now. She had said it, and so now she would have to deal with the consequences, whatever they may be.

When nothing seemed to happen, Mira opened her eyes again.

Chapter Seventy-Five

T he coven still sat exactly where they had moments before.

"Did you hear me?" asked Mira. She was confused. Surely her friends were shocked by her confession?

"Yes, love, we heard you," said Junka.

"I think it's just that we don't understand what you mean," clicked Leena.

"I know what she thinks she means," said Fina. "But let's hear it from her to be sure. Explain what you mean Mira."

"I mean, I'm not a witch." She shifted to sit taller in her chair. "I want to be, and I'll work to be, and I hope it doesn't make any of you feel differently about me, but I never was. I'm sorry for fooling you all."

"And why don't you think that you're a witch?" asked Fina.

"Because I have never found my bravura honda," Mira said. "Learning spells is all well and good, but even that narrow-minded miser in the castle learns spells. When I was first learning about witchcraft in Whinnia, Bovo really emphasised that a witch was defined by her relationship with her bravura. Even you have been teaching us that it's our relationships with the world that make us witches."

Fina nodded.

"Aye. I want you all to build that relationship with this land, this place, and help me protect it as much as we can."

"I don't have a bravura yet either," protested Hattie in her tiny voice.

"That's alright, you've just joined a coven, and you're learning," explained Mira. "That's normal. Just like any relationship, you have to build your understanding of yourself in order to find a bravura that is strong and true. You have to know who you are by yourself before you can find a relationship with someone else that is strong. It's not a bad thing, but you all keep saying I'm a witch, and I haven't made that relationship yet. I just don't want a lie to come between us all."

"Mira," said Fina in an eternally patient voice. "In times of trouble, who do you look for?"

Mira blinked. It was her turn to be confused by what someone had said.

"What do you mean?"

"Just as I said, if times are tough, who do you look for? I've seen you glancing into corners, whispering to someone. Who is it?"

"That? That's myself, I suppose." Her blush was returning. "I look for my reflection, so I can give myself advice, or sort out my thoughts by explaining them to myself."

"Does your reflection ever say something back to you?"

Mira paused.

"Yes, of course. But that's not unusual, everyone talks to themselves, and seeing your reflection just makes that easier." Mira looked at her coven, all of whom were staring at her with slightly wider eyes. As she looked around, she caught a glimpse of her reflection in the huge window at the front of her bakery, leaning forward in a reflection of a chair. Her reflection smiled and shook her head.

"Don't they?" finished Mira, turning back to meet Fina's eyes.

"Oh my innocent, wee duckling," said Fina kindly. "No. We don't."

"Then what–" Mira's face crinkled in confusion.

"I think you discovered yourself, exactly as your previous coven told you to," said Fina. Her weathered old hands took Mira's. Mira felt as though her hand was being held inside a large dog's ear: soft and warm and strange but not unpleasant. "You got to know yourself, and opened yourself to the possibilities of the universe, and you have been rewarded with your bravura honda. Your reflection." Fina gestured towards the bakery window where Mira's reflection sat in a reflected chair amongst the reflections of the coven. The other witches' reflections were simple mirror images, copying their every action, but Mira's raised a hand and waved to her. Mira waved back. She felt somewhat lightheaded.

"I thought a bravura was meant to share all sorts of knowledge and gifts with you."

"Yes, that is often how they behave with their witches."

"But how can my reflection do that? I mean, doesn't my reflection only know what I know?"

"I rather think that is something that you will have to find out. For now, she certainly seems to have given you many talents that the rest of us do not share."

Mira stared into the eyes of her reflection. She tried to consider the implications of Fina's words, but it was all so overwhelming.

"Mira!" called a voice from inside the bakery.

"Oh no, Nerishma!" Mira yelped as she jumped to her feet and raced inside.

In front of the counter, a queue was grumbling. Nerishma had a string of mugs lined up and was tipping boiling water into them one after the other. The woman at the front of the queue tapped her foot impatiently.

"I'm so sorry," said Mira as she rushed over. "Have you been waiting long?" she asked the woman with the mobile foot.

"I'll say I have!" said the woman. "I ordered a mint tea from this girl nearly a minute ago, but none of these are what I ordered!"

Mira looked at the liquid still sloshing from side to side in the mugs.

"None of these drinks that were literally just made now are what you ordered?"

"That's exactly my point!"

"Perhaps she's going to make your drink next?" Mira offered.

"Are you suggesting that I am expecting too much?" gasped the woman.

"Never my intention," answered Mira, turning to Nerishma. "Nerishma, I want you to put this woman at the top of the list, do you hear me?"

"What?" Nerishma's eyes flickered from side to side, confused inside her smudged dark face makeup. She held up the mint tea container in one hand and a mug in the other. "I was literally going to make–"

Mira held up a single finger and pressed it onto Nerishma's lips to shush her.

"I don't care what you were about to do," she said slowly, meeting Nerishma's eyes in the conspiratorial communion of retail workers everywhere. "You stop everything else until this woman is served with her mint tea as a priority!"

Nerishma's eyes rolled as she caught up with what Mira meant.

"Yes, of course! I'll put everything on hold and do that right away." She continued doing exactly what she had been doing and the woman made a satisfied harumph from behind Mira somewhere.

"I'll take these," said Mira, gathering up the platter of drinks that Nerishma had just finished making. "Which tables?"

"The other end of the room," said Nerishma, pointing at a long narrow table that had been set up deeper inside the bakery. A group of women with shaved heads and deep red robes sat there.

"Thanks," said Mira, and she swooped away. It still shocked her how many people wanted to stick around at her bakery instead of just buying their loaves and rolls and cakes and leaving. She still saw those sorts of customers, granted, but every afternoon more of this new type of customer began showing up. The red-robed women were now daily regulars!

This, of course, made it very easy to distribute coffees and teas to the correct women. Mira saved the head of the group for last. She leaned in as she handed over the mug with its red-tinged chocolate drink. "Thank you so much for coming here every day," she said. "It really means a lot to know I have the support of devoted people such as yourselves."

The leader, who wore layers and layers of thick black makeup around her eyes, smiled at Mira, revealing twin rows of sharpened teeth.

"We are grateful to have someone who serves xocolot the old way." She picked up her mug and sipped, her eyes rolling backwards in ecstasy as she tasted her drink.

Mira nodded and smiled and made her way back to Nerishma at the counter.

Chapter Seventy-Six

"Nerishma?" Mira asked as the other woman put a selection of scones onto a piece of cloth and then folded the cloth over the food and tied it shut.

"Yes?" she said after she passed the package to an elderly elf.

"What makes your hot chocolate count as 'xocolot the old way'?"

"Oh, for the red ladies?" Nerishma glanced at the end of the room. When Mira nodded she continued. "They just wanted it much thicker. I put in extra servings of chocolate and less water. And they wanted me to add some of this spice as well." She dug around under the counter and produced a small, ceramic, skull-shaped jar. The teeth and jaws carved on it were strange and blocky, a rectangular pattern that covered its surface. The inside was filled with small, red flakes. "They said they were cold flakes that made the drink hot."

Mira lifted some to her nose on the small wooden spoon resting in the jar. It smelled like a blacksmith's forge, heavy and metallic.

"Cold flakes?" she asked.

Nerishma shrugged. "Something like that."

"Okay. I was worried for a moment that they weren't getting what they thought and they might complain, but you're totally on top of it I see."

"Mira!" called a voice from outside.

"What now?" she moaned. She shrugged an apology to Nerishma and rushed back outside to see what was happening.

Prevos was standing next to Ti and Hattie's table. Ti sat traditionally at the table, by means of a chair alongside, whereas Hattie was sitting cross-legged on top of it. Ti smiled broadly up at Prevos, a snake watching a bird on a branch not far enough overhead to keep it safe.

Prevos stood with his helmet in his hands and his ears flattened back over his thick reddish-brown mane.

"Prevos?" said Mira. She was surprised to see him.

Prevos smiled at the sight of her and stepped over quickly. He reached out with one hand to touch her side as he leaned in to kiss her softly on the cheek. Mira smiled and touched his hand as he straightened.

"Why are you here? I thought we were going to meet for a walk this evening?" Mira asked. She tried to ignore the rising whoop from Hattie only a few feet from her.

"Yes, that was what we had arranged," agreed Prevos. She could see from the way his whiskers drooped slightly that he was unsure if he had done the right thing by coming to see her early. "However, I saw that a travelling bard has recently arrived in Senoonheim from Whinnia, and he has taken up residence at The Trivial Lampshade."

"I know that it is not your favourite venue," admitted Prevos, still turning the helmet clutched in his hands in a nervous circle. "And as you know, I myself prefer to avoid such places. But there are fewer patrons during the afternoon, and I know that he is planning to sing soon. It could be an easy place for me to try spreading peace that I have not gone before, as you suggested." His deep voice rumbled to a pause. "I wondered if you might like to accompany me to hear some songs that might remind you of your home?"

Tears prickled the corners of Mira's eyes.

"That is so sweet Prevos, thank you. Unfortunately, it's very busy at the moment. I don't think that I can–"

Othniel stepped up next to Mira and dropped a plate of biscuits covered in thick chocolate icing onto the table.

"She'd love to," grinned the woman through her painted-on skull, double rows of teeth shining. "We'll all help Nerishma finish up the afternoon, right ladies?"

Delorous and Elschefla both nodded. Hattie jumped to her feet, clenched both hands into fists, leaned backwards, and whooped into the sky.

"I don't know if that's a good idea," began Mira, watching the small witch in her green overalls. The tiny witch was jogging on the spot now. Frankly, Mira was concerned about just what it was that Hattie thought happened at the bakery.

"We'll be fine," insisted Othniel. She clapped a calloused hand onto Mira's shoulder. "It's just serving now right? I'm not going to burn anything because I forgot to check the ovens, am I?"

Mira shook her head.

"Then go have a good time!" Othniel smiled again, and the coven smiled with her. Mira felt the love and support that they offered her, buoying her as she turned back to Prevos.

"It looks like I'm all yours!" she said, slipping an arm through his and holding his elbow.

"I am honoured by your company," he replied in his warm deep purr. "But you are not mine. You are yours."

He reached down to the plate of biscuits beside her and picked one up to give to Mira. Then he picked up another and lifted it to his mouth, crunching into it with relish.

"Mmmm," he growled with a delighted sparkle in his eye. "That's good!"

"Who would have thought that you would succumb to the lure of a sugary confection?" Mira laughed. He leaned in closer, bumping her affectionately with his armoured shoulder.

"You are rubbing off on me," he said. "And I think it is for the better."

"I agree, I am good for you," she said with a laugh.

Happiness bloomed in Mira's chest. It had taken her a while to find her place in the noise of Senoonheim, filled with shouting adventurers and false facades. The bakery was only growing from strength to strength. She had moulded her coven and it had baked into something strong, warming, and rich. Each of the witches she called her friends lifted her higher. And she had discovered something in Prevos that she had not expected, something that made her heart glow. Now, she was excited to make her new home in the city, to really explore what it meant to be a witch, and to discover who Prevos was underneath the shining armour.

She and the paladin walked into the streets of Senoonheim, together.

THE END

Find more from this author online through
https://linktr.ee/aarondickauthor

Acknowledgements

I first had the idea for "A Baker's Coven" when the title came to mind around February of 2025. I loved the pun and it sparked a whole bunch of ideas about the witches that would be a part of the coven alongside the baker that starts it. Somehow I managed to write the whole book during the rest of 2025, around a full-time job and my very patient family. Finally, I scrambled to get it published during December.

To achieve something like that can only happen due to the outstanding support of a lot of people I am lucky to have in my life!

First of all I want to thank my editor Kat for all her support over years of writing. She has helped me get better and better at polishing my books, and I hope you are seeing the benefit of that. Its all of that effort that I wanted to acknowledge by dedicating this book to her!

Secondly, I have to thank my wonderful author friend A Jane Dove. She was the one who pushed me to go to my first author event, setting up a table to sell books. While we were there we spoke about our next book ideas and she convinced me that, as both of our books were quite cosy and witch based, we should release them together! She kept me on track through the year and gave me the oomph to get everything wrapped up in time for our release, which I probably would have missed if it wasn't for her. If you enjoyed this book, go and check out her book "The Witchness Protection Programme"! Her website is:

https://www.ajanedove.com/

I also had support from some other early readers, who helped me spot inconsistencies and errors, and tightened up the story. Thank you Lexi, Claire and Sue.

Thanks to Jono for making some outstanding cover art. I think he captured the spirit of the Misplaced Kingdoms well, and I'm thrilled that his image is the first thing many readers will see as they pick up A Baker's Coven.

I've been lucky to have a group of friends and family around me who were always keen to jump fully into the geeky games and hobbies that helped inspire the world of the Misplaced Kingdoms. Thank you to my mum and sisters and sibling who all loved Red Dwarf and Discworld and Monty Python and all the other things that made us cackle. I hope you laugh at this! Thank you to all of the bogans, but particularly Josh, Tony, Stephen and Allen, who delved into the spider's mines, wandered through fairy tale dreams, and embraced the murder hobo lifestyle with a little too much glee. Thanks to my best mate Julian for knowing all the good Simpsons lines.

I always want to acknowledge the inspiration and support of my friend Steffanie Holmes. She has been incredibly generous and encouraging of my writing efforts, and I really do have to thank her for me getting as far as I have. She writes spicy cosy bookish murder mysteries which you should probably go check out!

https://www.steffanieholmes.com/

Speaking of other authors, this year I've been connecting more with indie New Zealand authors and their creativity and perseverance is an inspiration. There's too many of you to name, but you are all killing it, don't stop!

And of course, I can't thank the people in my life who have helped me get this book out into the world without mentioning my wife Andy. A Baker's Coven took up a lot of my mental energy while I was drafting and editing and preparing it, and she has supported our family incredibly while I did. I love you babe.

I hope you enjoyed this first foray into the Misplaced Kindgoms and would like to read more, because I have already got some plans for the other witches in the Baker's Coven. The more you tell me about how much you enjoyed visiting Senoonheim, the faster I'll get the next book out!

About The Author

Aaron Dick is a teacher living north of Auckland in New Zealand with his wife, their two daughters, and a small menagerie of household animals. They all love when his eldest daughter visits too.

He grew up as a voracious reader of science-fiction and fantasy, often to the annoyance of his unheeded family. Becoming an author was a childhood dream, alongside being a palaeontologist, or a rock star.

His stories have featured in a collection of New Zealand short stories inspired by Grimms' Fairy Tales, the gothic art and lifestyle magazine Nocturne and the online literary journal Headland.

Find him online through
https://linktr.ee/aarondickauthor

www.ingramcontent.com/pod-product-compliance
Lightning Source LLC
Chambersburg PA
CBHW020249120726
47904CB00001B/141